Books by Wilder Penfield

~~~~~~

NO OTHER GODS

SPEECH AND BRAIN-MECHANISMS

THE TORCH

The Torch

THE TORCH

by
Wilder Penfield

McClelland and Stewart Limited
Toronto / Montreal

The Canadian Publishers
McClelland and Stewart Limited
25 Hollinger Road, Toronto, 16

Printed and bound in Canada

To
H. K. P.

*wise critic and good
companion*

THE
AEGEAN AREA

CALYMNOS

PSERIMOS

COS
MEROPIS

Timon's
villa

Temple
Apollo's
grove

COS

HIGH ROAD

Pelea

(ANCIENT)
ASTYPALAEA

HIGH ROAD

Halasarna

A E G E A N   S E A

NISYROS

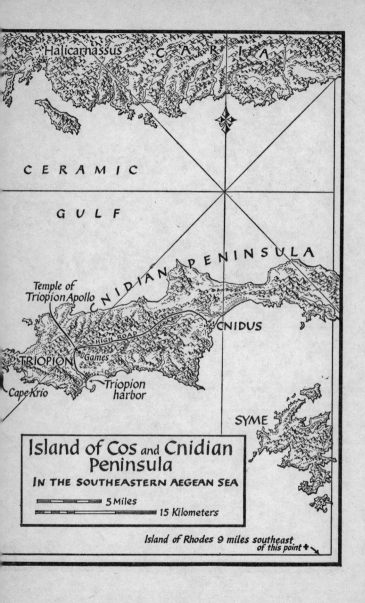

Halicarnassus   C A R I A

C E R A M I C

G U L F

C N I D I A N   P E N I N S U L A

Temple of
Triopion Apollo

CNIDUS

HIGH ROAD

TRIOPION   Games

Cape Krio

Triopion
harbor

SYME

Island of Cos and Cnidian Peninsula
IN THE SOUTHEASTERN AEGEAN SEA

5 Miles

15 Kilometers

Island of Rhodes 9 miles southeast
of this point

Contents

~~~~~~

The Torch

Prologue

~~~~~~

THIS IS A STORY from the life of Hippocrates the physician — a story of what may have happened one spring twenty-four hundred years ago. Many things have not changed since Hippocrates was young and Daphne came to the island of Cos. The sky and the wind and the bird songs, and the sound of the sea, are just as they were. Man's brain was as swift then as it is now, and physicians found problems in the practice of medicine not unlike those of today.

Hippocrates lived in the golden age of ancient Greece. When he began to study the secrets of nature critically, it was as though he had lighted a torch in the darkness, holding it high so that those who were trying to help the sick could see at last, and examine cause and effect.

The first clear statement of the scientific method — the method that has created modern medicine and natural science — is to be found in the Hippocratic writings. Copied and recopied century after century, they served the world for more than two thousand years as a textbook of medicine. Today men call him the father of modern medicine, and the Hippocratic oath is still the practicing physician's highest moral code.

But in spite of all this, history provides scanty reference to the man himself — and how it was that the torch was lit has been forgotten. Instead of true detail a scandal clings to his name, a strange and unbelievable story that has lingered on like an evil spirit. Truth alone can lay the ghost of falsehoods.

Now, since history says so little and since our recent research has brought us new and relevant facts, it may be hoped that the picture painted here in this historical novel is clear and true. If so — the man so nearly lost in the darkening mists of time will live again and we shall see and understand, at last, the lighting of the torch.

CHAPTER ONE

Consultation

~~~~~~

OLYMPIAS, wife of Timon, the First Citizen of Cos, regarded her reflection in the tall bronze mirror. She ran her comb caressingly through one long black curl after another and talked to herself, smiling, until she heard the soft shuffle of bare feet crossing the open court behind her. The sound stopped before the door screen.

"Hippocrates has come."

Olympias made a gesture of impatience and scowled at her reflection. The serving maid repeated the message, and when there was still no answer, stepped cautiously around the door screen and entered the room.

Olympias watched her in the mirror.

"Why do you disturb me?"

"You told me to let you know if Hippocrates should come. The other physicians are here as well."

When her mistress said nothing, the blonde slave laughed uneasily and continued: "We were only just in time to keep Penelope from taking a bath. You remember old Aeneas forbade the bath because of the falling sickness."

Olympias turned from her mirror abruptly. "My daughter Penelope is cursed. No one can help her." Her voice was low and resonant, with the husky quality of a flute. "I wish my husband would leave it at that. Why should he bring Hippocrates out here for consultation today just because Euryphon is here? Today of all days!"

"But," the slave objected hesitantly, "you know Aeneas has failed to cure Penelope, and I heard Timon say that Hippocrates of Cos and Euryphon of Cnidus are the two most famous physicians in all Greece."

"Perhaps they are, but they can't change a god's curse. And even if they could, Euryphon did not come to Cos today to treat Penelope. He came to bring his own daughter here to meet our son. He came to talk dowries and to make the marriage contract."

Olympias took a metal curling rod from the brazier of hot coals. "Penelope has been nothing but a hateful nuisance ever since she was born."

The servant crossed the room and held the rod by its wooden handle while Olympias wound a long ribbon of hair about the hot metal.

Suddenly Olympias stopped and asked, "Have the physicians gone to Penelope's room?"

"Euryphon and Pindar are there. Hippocrates said he would follow after he had talked with old Aeneas outside on the terrace."

"Put the curling rod down," Olympias said, suddenly decisive. "Take my chiton off — be careful not to touch the curls. Get my saffron tunic and put it on me."

When this was done, Olympias returned quickly to her mirror. "Did you show Euryphon's daughter to her room on the gallery?"

"Yes. I did all the things you told me to do."

"Is she as beautiful as my son says she is?"

"She is lovely — But look! There she is now, coming along the gallery."

Above the door screen they could see the gallery on the opposite side of the court. Olympias slipped quickly to the screen and shifted it so they could watch without being seen.

The young woman in a simple white chiton started down the gallery stairway, but, startled by a sudden whirring of wings, stopped halfway down the stair. A turtledove had dropped to the floor of the sunlit court. The bird was followed in a moment by another dove, which strutted round and round, making the mating sound of springtime: "Vroove, vroove, vroove." The young woman leaned on the rail and looked up at the cloudless blue above her.

Now Olympias saw a man enter from the outside door. He strode across the court, his long blue cloak swinging open behind him, and started up the stair. He was tall, broad-shouldered and young, with a square black beard. He was evidently lost in thought, for his eyes were on the ground as he walked, and he looked down at the steps as he climbed until two delicate sandaled feet came into his field of vision. Then he stopped and looked up in surprise. The owner of the feet laughed and moved aside to let him pass. As she moved, a blue scarf dropped from her hand and fluttered to the pavement of the court. He ran down the stairs to pick it up, and she followed him.

As the man returned the scarf he smiled at her. "You must be Euryphon's daughter, I suppose."

"Yes," she replied and thanked him. Nothing more was said. He climbed the stair and passed along the gallery, still obviously preoccupied.

Olympias looked at the serving maid. "Who was that man?"

"Hippocrates."

Olympias nodded. "I thought so — and that is Daphne, the woman Cleomedes wants, the woman he says he must have. Well, if my son wants her he shall have her. Cleomedes cannot be denied. He must not be."

She pulled the screen back into place and turned to the servant. Her eyes were cold, calculating now. "Daphne dropped that scarf on purpose. I don't like it. I don't like her meeting Hippocrates here in this house before Cleomedes comes to woo her. That is a bad omen. A bad omen," Olympias repeated, talking to herself and turning away. "And what can I do to balance that? I know these physicians well enough. If Hippocrates is like his father, he would be bound by oath not to look at the wife of a man who is sick. It should be the same with a promised bride. I need help with Cleomedes. Perhaps he could —"

The slave had been moving the brazier of coals to its proper place. As she glanced furtively at her mistress and reached for the curling rod, she burned herself. The rod dropped to the floor with a clatter. Olympias cried out and struck the woman.

"Why do you frighten me?" Then she struck her again and again in mounting rage, until the slave escaped through the door in terror. When she was gone Olympias stood in the middle of the room, muttering. But the anger subsided quickly and she stood in thought. At last she laughed aloud.

"That's it! With that device I'll turn this physician's eyes from Daphne. And what is more, I'll use Hippocrates to regain control over my son. And after all, who can tell? This famous young asclepiad may know a cure for madness, even when it is in a family. He may cure my son and his trainer and me — he may cure us all, all three!"

She moved quickly out of the door and stood within the peristyle, whose pillars ran around the inner courtyard and supported a gallery that gave entrance to all the rooms of the second floor. The paving stones of the open court were dazzling in the sun of early spring, but the air was cool and bracing. Olympias looked about, listening. Her fingers moved restlessly along her ropelike curls. Below the sleeveless saffron chiton only her ankles showed, and the painted toenails.

Suddenly she moved across the court and up the stairs to the gallery. Her soft sandals made no sound as she passed along to the door of the spinning room where Hippocrates had disappeared. She peered into the room and then stepped inside.

Penelope's bedroom opened into this room by a doorway on the far side. It was heavily curtained now. The floor of the spinning room was clear, for Olympias herself had ordered the looms pushed back against the walls until the guests from Cnidus should be gone. There was no sound except, from the courtyard outside, the cooing, cajoling croon of the turtledoves, which seemed to intensify the silence. If the physicians were in her daughter's room, they must be keeping very quiet.

Now she heard a sound. She watched the curtains. When they did not stir she stole, quiet as a cat, across the room and listened. There was a long, sobbing groan and the sound of a body falling on the floor, and following that, loud slow breathing.

Olympias raised her fists. Penelope! She was at it again! Hateful child!

She put her eye to a cleverly placed hole in the curtain — a hole she had obviously used before. Inside Penelope's room she could see a frightened maidservant standing against the wall. Three physicans watched in silence while Penelope lay writhing on the floor. Her face was dusky, eyes closed and hair disheveled. Her body arched forward while her head went back; her legs were extended, elbows pulled back and fists clenched. She gave a second shuddering groan, then rolled slowly over on her side.

The servant exclaimed and stepped forward, but one of the physicians held up his hand to stop her. Penelope's eyelids fluttered spasmodically. Suddenly she relaxed and lay quiet. She seemed unconscious, but as her eyelids stopped twitching, she raised them ever so slightly. Her eyeballs were not turned upward like those of a person in sleep.

Pindar, the youngest of the three physicians, towered above the others. He stooped and pulled her chiton down to cover her body and legs. She was breathing deeply, freely, now and her face was turning pink against the tumbled disarray of her black curls.

Hippocrates had watched it all from a little distance, but Euryphon came close and squatted beside the patient.

"Well, Euryphon," Hippocrates said, "the attack seems to be over. Have you seen enough to establish your diagnosis?"

"I have a test that I would like to make," Euryphon replied without looking up. He placed one thumb just above Penelope's eye and pressed strongly on the rim of the orbit. The young woman winced with pain and shook her head. Euryphon rose to his feet easily and quickly.

He was a thin, bald, angular man of about fifty, with a long impassive face and a neatly cropped beard. He stood very straight and drew his cloak over his shoulders deliberately, with the dignity to be expected of a famous physician. He nodded.

"Yes, I am ready with diagnosis and with prognosis as well. The treatment I shall leave to you."

He glanced down at Penelope, lying in a crumpled heap on the floor. "Perhaps," he said, "we may talk more freely outside."

Hippocrates helped the servant lift Penelope, and put her on the couch. He placed the palm of his hand on her forehead; then he led the way out of the room. Olympias was nowhere to be seen when they passed out of the sewing room and along the gallery. But Hippocrates thought he caught sight of a saffron tunic disappearing into a doorway.

The three physicians turned from the gallery into a short corridor which led to an outside balcony overlooking a wide expanse of forest and farmland and the sea beyond. They stood talking there, while their cloaks flapped in the wind that blew from the sea.

Hippocrates turned to Euryphon. "The Archon called me to see his daughter a few days ago, for the first time. It was then that I learned that you and your daughter Daphne were coming to Cos. Consequently I asked to have your opinion before I should give the Archon my own diagnosis. There are many learned physicians in Hellas, but the greatest teachers of medicine are among the asclepiad physicians of Cnidus, and you are their leader now. I am delighted to have your help."

Euryphon scratched his short beard with his thumb. His face was expressionless, but his eyes smiled. "Surely, Hippocrates, you flatter us recklessly. You are an asclepiad too, decended from Asclepius the same as I, and there is a rumor that comes to our ears on the mainland in Cnidus from time to time, a rumor that the asclepiads on this famous little island speak with contempt of our methods of treatment. We, the rumor runs, treat symptoms, while you Coans treat the whole disease."

Hippocrates was about to interrupt, but Euryphon held up his hand.

"Wait. Let me see if I can deserve your good opinion now. I shall give you a name for this disease. I shall state its cause and suggest its treatment.

"You saw me press my thumb on the tender spot above Penelope's eye. She winced with pain, and so I concluded that the attack was not an epilepsy, not a convulsion of the divine disease. If it had been, she would have felt no pain so soon after the movements of the fit had ceased."

Hippocrates nodded, and Euryphon continued.

"No. She suffers from a disease which we have called hysteria. We give it that name because it is produced by movements of the womb, the *hystera*, within the body. I have observed that the disease occurs most frequently in virgins, especially those that are ready and anxious for marriage.

"Cnidus is so close to Persia that many Persians come over the mountains of Caria to seek our medical advice. We have found that the disease is more frequent among Persian women than it is among Greeks. You have heard how Amyntas was called to their court to cure the daughter of the Persian king. The child was certainly suffering from hysteria.

"The womb moves back and forth more actively in virgins, and most actively at certain stages in the waxing and waning of each moon." Euryphon was speaking now with the assurance of a teacher whose word had been rarely questioned, too rarely perhaps. "I have discussed the matter at length in a papyrus which I have written and brought with me from Cnidus. Let me say no more about it for the present."

He rubbed his hands together as though he were sure that he had pronounced the final word for all time regarding this malady. Then he added:

"I might state, further, that the best treatment for the condition is marriage and pregnancy." He paused. "Her father may think of Penelope as still a child. But Aphrodite has taken a hand here and is bringing about in her young body all the exciting changes that men find so mysterious, so irresistible. Surely the fathers of a great many young men must have made plans to call upon Timon. The dowry will be large — very large in fact! Her mother Olympias was rich, and the Archon has multiplied it all as a successful shipowner."

Pindar had been listening as any apprentice should. Euryphon glanced at him roguishly and turned back to Hippocrates with exaggerated gravity.

"After careful consideration of this case, I suggest that the treatment be entrusted to Pindar."

The young man flushed, and Hippocrates intervened good-naturedly.

"I agree, Euryphon, with much that you have said. Marriage might well be good for Penelope. But I do not believe the benefit would be the direct result of her entering the marital state, nor would it be due to the eventual filling of the womb, although that might be calculated to put an end to the monthly movements you have described to us.

"Marriage would change her environment, would free her, perhaps, from —" Hippocrates stopped and glanced deliberately behind him. Then he spoke in a low tone. "Someone in a saffron tunic is watching us from the roof above." With a half-smile he continued, raising his voice:

"With her mother's help Penelope will soon be well. The child has been shut up in the house too long. She must be out of doors and have a course in gymnastic exercises. I agree with you that her trouble is not epilepsy. There is no curse upon her."

The physicians sauntered to the end of the balcony, where there was no danger of eavesdropping, and Hippocrates went on. "From what Aeneas tells me, I conclude that Olympias is a peculiar woman. I suspect that she loves her son Cleomedes too much and her daughter Penelope too little."

"I am astonished!" Euryphon exclaimed. "Olympias seems to me a most charming woman, intriguing in fact. The long spiral curls, I know, are very old-fashioned, but I like them. She has handsome dark eyes, and she dresses superbly. Oh well! Perhaps this is evidence of a late spring in Olympias, late spring in both of us!"

Euryphon's eyes twinkled, and Hippocrates realized suddenly that he liked this thin sardonic man in spite of his self-assurance.

"I should have explained," Hippocrates said, "that the problem of treating Penelope is complicated by the fact that she is already being treated by a much respected asclepiad. He is, no doubt, still waiting for us below — a good man, very pious, prays to the gods for his patients and uses purifications. His name is Aeneas."

Euryphon nodded. "Yes, I know the old man. He has been my guest in Cnidus."

Hippocrates smiled faintly. "I hesitate to suggest that he was taught in Syrna the treatment he has used. Syrna is not far from Cnidus, and you Cnidian physicians all stem from there."

"Syrna!" Euryphon exploded. "The asclepiads of Syrna are proud, hopelessly old-fashioned, stupid!"

Hippocrates laughed. "Aeneas does much good," he said, "though he did make the wrong diagnosis here. We may all do that. But he also gave her a silly regimen — he forbade her to bathe and warned her that she must not come near a goat or even goatskins, that she must not eat fishes or birds, especially the pigeon, the cock and the bustard, that she must avoid mint, leeks and onions, since they are pungent, that she must not put one foot upon the other or one hand upon the other because of evil spirits — and much more nonsense of that sort. She is half starved now."

"I know," Euryphon answered. "If the poor girl were to starve to death on such a regimen, everyone would say, 'Alas! The work of the gods!' And the fees would be his whatever the outcome. Sometimes I think men pay more willingly for a physician's folly, provided of course that he serves it up with a suitable sauce of piety, than they do for honest counsel.

"Pindar!" he said to the young man. "Learn a lesson! The way to wealth is to be pious and plausible. And if you make a mistake as a physician, just bury the result as quickly as you can."

"I did not mean," Hippocrates broke in, "that Aeneas is not honest. In character he is all the things that a good physician should hope to be — all the things that you are, Euryphon, however much you may like to jest."

Euryphon made a quick movement, as though he were handing something back. "I have given you my opinion, Hippocrates, and I shall leave you now. The problem is yours. I admit that I am more interested in the disorders of women's organs than I am in their states of mind.

"Asclepius had two sons. I must be descended from Machaon the surgeon. Perhaps you come from Podalirius the physician. You can have the diets, the herbs and the persuasion. Let me have surgery and the things I can see and feel."

"But," Hippocrates replied, "Homer tells us that Machaon really cured Menelaus with herbs and medicaments. No, we must use all means to help the sick. Diet and regimen are not the least of these."

Euryphon shrugged and turned to leave the balcony, but he paused again, his eyes twinkling.

"My final conclusion, then, is this: we would be well advised to leave the problem in Pindar's hands. When he is better acquainted with the — ah — the situation, he is sure to agree with me. Fill the *hystera* and you will cure the hysteria!" He laughed and disappeared.

Hippocrates stroked his square black beard, hiding a smile behind his hand. He could see that the shy Pindar was distressed and perhaps a little confused.

"You see, Pindar, we have come to the same conclusion, Euryphon and I. The important issue here lies in the diagnosis. That attack was indeed not an epilepsy, not a symptom of the divine disease. When you have seen more such cases you will recognize the difference at once, without pressing upon the sensitive spot above the eye.

"Euryphon would have us call this condition hysteria. Use the name if you wish, but do not be misled into the belief that the womb is the cause. You will find that hysteria occurs in men also, although I admit that it is much less frequent. He is right when he says that it is especially prevalent among the Persians, and he might have added Phoenicians and Israelites.

"Penelope's trouble, in my opinion, is a trouble of the mind rather than of the body. That does not mean, however, that a god or a devil has entered into her body, as so many seem to think. I suspect that when she was a small girl, she would sometimes fall upon the floor and kick and scream. Perhaps she found it the surest method of getting what she wanted in a hostile household. A very little whipping, together with the understanding and love of a mother, might have prevented all this, but now the treatment is not so simple."

"Yes, Master," Pindar said. "I understand."

To himself, he marveled how understandable Hippocrates seemed to make the most complicated conditions. Pindar was something more than a disciple of medicine. He came from an aristocratic family in Thebes and for a time had studied to be a sculptor. Finally he had decided to change to medicine and to study with an asclepiad, so his father had paid the tuition to Hippocrates' father Heracleides, who had since died.

They walked back along the balcony and Pindar watched his master, wondering how any sculptor, after chiseling out the handsome head, tipped at times in critical consideration, could give to marble the expression of excitement and understanding he saw so often about the eyes, how capture the ready smile.

Entering the house, they walked through it and stood on the gallery, looking down into the court. Hippocrates ran down the stairs and strode around the altar of Zeus. It was his air of confidence, Pindar thought, that impressed people. But it was confidence born of knowledge, honesty, simplicity.

A stocky little man, Timon the Archon, was waiting for them in the shadow of the peristyle. His hair was graying at the temples, his beard pointed, his manner grave. He led them along the peristyle to his reception room, where a lively old man, the ancient asclepiad Aeneas, was waiting impatiently. Aeneas wagged his gray beard and stamped his staff on the tiled floor as they entered.

"Hippocrates, you must have made a most careful examination, most careful and painstaking indeed. But why so long about it? Well, what do you think of my little patient? Is it not too bad that the Archon's only daughter should be the one to suffer from the sacred disease? But there it is. I've done everything, everything that can be done for the condition."

Hippocrates smiled at the old man and turned to the Archon. "Yes, Aeneas has done a great deal for your daughter. And now that you have asked me to take charge of her, please leave us alone for a little time so that I may learn all that Aeneas can teach me about her."

When Timon and Pindar returned some time later, they could hear as they crossed the court the tremulous voice of the old man:

"You may be right, Hippocrates, but if the evil spirits do not do it, why does she fall and groan and shake? Why? Why?"

As they entered the room, Aeneas fell suddenly silent. Then he straightened himself as much as he was able and spoke with dignity to Timon. "We have had a good discussion. But I shall leave you now. Our ewe lamb needs only one shepherd, and — well, I believe this young man may be right. In any case, my old friend Heracleides had a good son, and now that he has returned here, our island has gained an asclepiad who is kind as well as wise. I wish I had such a son myself!" And he hurried from the room.

In simple words, Hippocrates explained the situation to the Archon, giving him a good prognosis for the young woman, but urging that she be freed from her mother's undisputed rule. Timon nodded emphatic approval with the greatest relief and pleasure — it was clear that his daughter had been of great concern to him. The three went back to Penelope's room, where they found her lying on the couch, pale, languid, sad.

Timon put his arm about his daughter. "You are going to be well again, my little lamb." But his voice broke, and he turned away to look up at the sky through the high window.

After a moment he left them, saying to Hippocrates, "I shall talk with her mother before she goes to the harbor to meet our son Cleomedes."

When Timon had gone, Hippocrates stooped and took Penelope's hand.

"Why do you lie here on your bed?"

"Because," she stammered — "because — well, there is nothing else for me to do — because I have the sacred disease" — she sobbed a little — "and my mother says —"

"Never mind," he interrupted. "Just tell me what makes you think you have the sacred disease."

"We have a slave who has it," she answered. "I've seen him. He falls down —"

Hippocrates gave Pindar a delighted and meaningful glance and then looked back at Penelope.

"And so, my child, you thought you had it too?"

She nodded and sobbed again.

He stood up. "Come with me, Penelope. Never mind your sandals."

Hand in hand, they walked through the house to the outside balcony.

"Penelope," he said to her, "I'm sure you haven't that disease. It was all a mistake. You must work hard now to build new strength. You may bathe now, and eat — Pindar is going to plan a diet for you. Three days a week you will walk all the way to the city yonder, you and your handmaid, and back again. Your donkey may go along to rest your legs for the first seven visits, no more."

He pointed out toward the city. "There, above the housetops, you can just see the line of columns that crown the island on the far side of the harbor. Follow those columns with your eye to the right, to the temple. Just below the temple, hidden in the trees, on this side of the harbor entrance, is the *iatreion* where I see patients, and the *palaestra* is there too, where my brother Sosander will be waiting to teach you gymnastics."

"Oh, yes!" she cried. "I know it well." Then, glancing down at her torn chiton and folding her thin arms over it, she looked at Hippocrates eagerly.

"One more thing you must do," he said. "You see the water that is gushing up from the fountain below us there in the garden? It comes from the Vorina cave high up above us on the mountainside, doesn't it? On the days that you do not visit my brother Sosander, you must climb up to the cave and drink the water as it wells up out of the ground. No water in all the world is more health-giving than that, when you drink it fresh from the earth."

He took the long black braids of her hair in his hands and noted the hollows in her cheeks. But all he said was: "Your hair is lovely."

He coiled the braids on her head and nodded approval. Her dark eyes filled to overflowing, but she smiled. As she left, Hippocrates beckoned to Pindar, who had been listening at a distance.

"You see, don't you, Pindar? No evil spirit has entered into her. There is no real disease, but there is a cause, and the cause is not in the womb, not in the body at all.

"Penelope saw the slave having a true attack of epilepsia, and his falling and shaking and groaning terrified her. She was probably unhappy, baffled by something, someone — possibly her mother.

"Then she thought — What if I had the sacred disease, would people be more kind to me then? So she imitated it, and then her terror was greater than ever, for she thought she had really come to have it.

She found she could summon attacks at useful times. She did so before us this morning. A sufferer from the sacred disease cannot do
that, however hard he tries."

Pindar nodded. "Yes, I understand."

"And for treatment," Hippocrates continued, "we can only help her
to understand, build her up, keep her busy, free her from something
menacing, the nature of which we must consider further."

He looked at the young man. "You might go back to your work
now, but return this afternoon. You know the diet and the regimen as
I have outlined them. Be firm in your directions."

CHAPTER TWO

The Mantle of Heracleides

〰〰〰〰〰〰〰〰〰〰〰〰〰〰〰〰〰〰〰〰〰〰〰〰

Oυτ on the terrace, Hippocrates found Timon waiting for him. Now that the consultation was over and he was reassured about his daughter, Timon's manner had changed. The anxious father had been replaced by the pompous little leader of the affairs and politics of Cos. He laid his hand on Hippocrates' arm.

"I have not yet told you of my sorrow at the death of your father. I knew Heracleides very well. We were in the Navy together as *epheboi*, being trained to fight for Cos — there was grave danger then that the Persians would attack us. After that Heracleides became the good physician, and I a humble owner of ships. You must know how the citizens of Cos mourn his loss. And we are all rejoiced that you should return from the court of the King of Macedonia. Will you remain with us now and take up the teaching of pupils in your father's place?"

"Yes, Cos is my home, and there is a long tradition of teaching and practice in my family."

Timon nodded. "You are yourself, men say, directly descended from Asclepius. Is it eighteen generations or twenty?"

Hippocrates shrugged his shoulders and said that no one seemed to know. Then he made a polite gesture of leavetaking, but the Archon, once he had started talking, was not to be interrupted easily.

"Cos needs you," he was saying, "even though we cannot pay you the princely salary that King Perdiccas must have given you during your year in Macedonia. The whole island of Cos only pays three tal-

ents a year to Athens for membership in the Delian League, and yet
men say you received an equal sum. Is that possible? But after all, the
king was dying, was he not? And now he is well."

"Yes, he is very well," Hippocrates replied. But he ignored the rest
of the question.

The Archon continued: "There are, of course, many responsibilities which I myself must shoulder as Chief Archon of Cos, and I
use my personal fortune for the good of the island, as Pericles does for
the city of Athens. This month I am busy organizing our part in the
Festival of Apollo at Triopion, less than a month from now."

To his relief, Hippocrates saw Euryphon coming along the terrace
to join them, accompanied by the young woman he had seen on the
stair.

"This is my daughter Daphne," Euryphon said. Salutations were
exchanged; then Timon returned to his monologue.

"Let me ask you now, Hippocrates. Will you act for us as a judge
in the Triopian games? Once, I remember, you won the victor's crown
in the boys' wrestling competition yourself. How long ago was that?"

"I was seventeen," Hippocrates replied, "so it must have been eleven
years ago." He looked about him, wondering how soon he could escape, and discovered that Daphne was watching him.

So this is Euryphon's daughter, he thought . . . Daphne — the
unwilling nymph who changed into a laurel tree when Apollo
pursued her. Is she like that? he wondered, noting that she was
dressed modestly in a simple white chiton belted about her slender
waist by a girdle of woven gold and supported over her bare brown
shoulders by little round balls of gold.

Hippocrates had a way of scrutinizing a person he had just met.
Perhaps this was due to his father's early teaching that he must study
his patients — must observe, record, remember. The habit was sometimes embarrassing to those who chanced to meet him.

He turned his attention to Daphne now. The glow of her skin, he
noted, indicates that she has been much in the sun. Her carriage and
the curve of neck and arm are good — she must be just past twenty.
The black hair would lead one to expect black eyes . . . but they
are not — that is curious. The pupils are large, very large, and the

iris brown — or is it blue? I must have her in a better light to decide. . . .

A sudden awareness shot through him that she, on her side, was looking into his eyes, perhaps examining him as he was her. She turned away suddenly with a toss of the head and a faint blush.

"I have promised Daphne," Euryphon was saying, "that I will make no marriage contract against her will. She is here to meet Cleomedes, who has fallen in love with her from afar. We expect that she and the Archon's son may be married after he has won the boxing crown in the games next month."

"Oh, my son may not win the crown," Timon exclaimed, "but he is a fine athlete, that I do admit!"

Hippocrates swung his cloak over his shoulder and fastened it in place with his cloak pin. Timon looked up at him.

"My wife Olympias could not wait to talk with you, but she hopes to see you at your *iatreion* before she returns to the villa."

"I shall be glad to talk with your wife," Hippocrates said. "But before I leave you, Archon Timon, let me speak to you again about your daughter Penelope."

The two men walked a little way off. "She will recover," Hippocrates said, "if she follows the regimen that we plan for her, and if those about her do their part. Her mother and the servants must understand that she is not cursed, and that these fits are not those that come to men and women who are said to have the sacred disease. She should take up some duties in the house, and she must leave the house each day for the exercises we have planned. Her diet will be greatly altered."

They rejoined the others, and Hippocrates made his farewells. To Daphne he added: "Will you do something for me, and for Penelope?" She looked at him in surprise. "Will you go for a walk this afternoon and take Penelope with you?"

Instead of answering, she walked with him toward the steps leading down to the gardens.

"Physicians are all alike," she said finally. "I've lived my life in Cnidus with asclepiads about me. They expect everyone to do their bidding. But I shall do what you ask — with pleasure."

"Thank you," he said abruptly, and started off; then he stopped and looked back at her, wondering. She was smiling. "Good-by — Daphne."

He ran lightly down the steps and, passing through the gardens below, turned to the right on the highroad toward the city of Cos Meropis. The road soon left the cypress grove and took him into the sunlight on the hills. The spring of that year — it was 432 B.C. — was particularly beautiful, but spring is almost always lovely in the Aegean islands.

Daphne's eyes and smile seemed to go along with Hippocrates as he came from Timon's villa. His cloak blew out behind him, for the wind was fresh from the sea, and he found himself strangely alive to the sounds and sights of spring. He smelled the sweetness of growing things on the banks of "Burina's rill," where "poplar and elm showed aisles of pleasant shadow, greenly roofed." The pebbles scattering underfoot made singing sounds, so it seemed to him, for his heart was suddenly gay. He hummed an air while his heavy sandals crunched on the crown of the road. Then, falling silent again, he turned his ear to the drone of the turtledoves, the bells of the distant flocks, and the chorus of bleating that came from the fields, now loud, now soft.

He watched the goats and sheep drift over the distant rolling hills. A shepherd boy on a rock nearby was piping softly an old refrain. He followed that with a tune of his own and laughed when Hippocrates waved. Overhead the falcons soared on silent wing, with an eye to the lizards warming themselves on the roadside stones. A plowman close at hand followed his oxen, watching the black earth turn and fall in the furrow. In passing, the two men hailed each other, country fashion, trading jest for jest.

Beyond a bridge some women knelt by the brook to wash their clothes and to laugh and talk in the sun. Hippocrates watched the paddles rise and fall — thump, thump, thump. The women smiled at him, and one young girl, rising swiftly, picked a daisy and brought it to him, blushing. He took it from her hand and looked at her.

"Your mother could use this flower for springtime tea. It is good for the stomach, *vruvis* tea, so the old wives say."

That was not what she had expected him to say, but nonetheless, she smiled and dimpled and turned her head.

The smile, he thought as he walked away, had little to do with *vruvis* tea and much to do with the call of spring. Aphrodite asked no help from manmade tea to summon a blush or speed the heart. The magic force, renewing life, lay deep in the nature of things. What creature that walked or crept or flew in the air could fail to feel the force of spring? The lizard yonder, lying so still on the stone — did he not sense there was something new?

Hippocrates shook his head. One thing was clear. The practice of medicine and the problems of teaching would leave him little time to respond to such a call.

The road ran out on level land and he looked back at Timon's villa high on the foothills of Mount Oremedon. The house shone white against the black cypress forest, and he could see the temple of Apollo with its marble pillars a little way off to the left. That forest had always been called Apollo's grove, and an old servant in the Archon's household had whispered to him that Penelope had the falling disease because her father had cut Apollo's trees. That was nonsense, he mused, but all the same, there was something strange about that household.

Now he was approaching the city, and he turned his thoughts to his own affairs. He had been a little boy when his father Heracleides had brought him, with his mother and brother, to this growing seaport city. Before that, they had lived in the town of Halasarna, on the south shore of the island.

He could just remember the move. But he had a clear picture in his memory of the kindly old man, the *pedagogos*, who used to take him to school. Those were happy days — learning to write on sheets of wax and at special times on papyrus, reading aloud, scribbling arithmetic, playing the lyre, memorizing Homer and Hesiod, wrestling, swimming, dancing, riding.

After that had come the hard training for sports; then the years of discipleship abroad — in rhetoric, philosophy, medicine. He had even traveled about the world, the Greek world and Egypt, making the circuit of the Inner Sea, visiting the seaport cities where men talked Greek. Democritus had come from Thrace to join him in his travels. How they had laughed and talked and argued as they went! Finally they had parted company, and he had begun, as a fully trained asclepiad, to practice medicine under his father.

Then one day the unexpected invitation of King Perdiccas had taken him away to Aegae, the mountain capital of faroff Macedonia. It had been exciting at first to be physician to a king, a king who was thought to be dying. But when the danger was past and the king was well again, it was lonely. So few people in Aegae understood a Greek, even if they spoke his language; so few thought as he did.

Only three short months ago, word had come that his father had died; his mother and brother had written begging him to return, to become master in his father's place. And so he had come back to Hellas — Hellas!, where men took time to discuss life and truth, where they were aware of beauty.

It had been good to go to Athens again on the return voyage while the ship stopped in Pyraeus, and to be welcomed by Socrates as a re-turning disciple; and it had been a great surprise to hear his Athenian friends talk of the reputation that had come to him because of his success in the Macedonian court.

After the Athenian visit he had taken passage on another ship and set sail again. Steady winds had blown them south and east from Pyraeus across the sparkling Aegean Sea, where a ship is never out of sight of some Greek island. At last they had come to the little is-land of Cos, with its bare brown mountains towering upward out of green valleys. How he had exulted as the sails were furled on the yardarms and the great ship swung around the harbor island, with all three banks of oars sweeping her toward the entrance, then coasted through into the quiet harbor!

From his place high on the afterdeck of the trireme, he could look into the walled enclosure, almost at the ship's side, that contained all his father had owned. It was now to be his — the home, the *iatreion*, the *palaestra*, the great plane tree under which he had so often listened to his father as he taught his disciples.

But the enclosure had been empty and he saw no one. A sudden fear had come over him. Then he saw his brother run out, and his

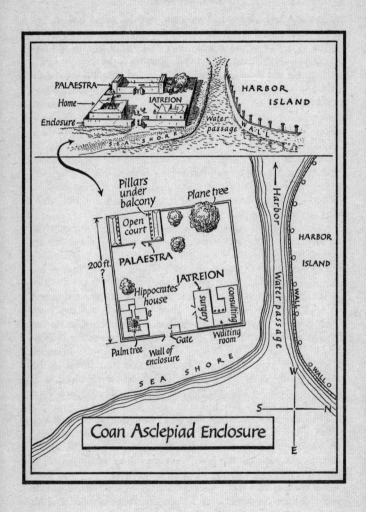

PALAESTRA
Home
IATREION
Enclosure
HARBOR ISLAND
Water passage
SEA SHORE
WALL

Pillars under balcony
Plane tree
Open court
PALAESTRA
200 ft. ?
Hippocrates house
IATREION
surgery
consulting
Palm tree
Wall of enclosure
Gate
Waiting room
SEA SHORE
Harbor
HARBOR ISLAND
Water passage
WALL
W
S
N
E
WALL

Coan Asclepiad Enclosure

mother. He had tried to call to them, but the sound had choked in his throat.

And now, almost two months after that return to Cos, he was happy, yes — but anxious. There was so much to be done, so much to learn. He had loved his father and he missed him. But the mantle of Heracleides had fallen on his shoulders now. He would do his best to wear it well.

CHAPTER THREE

Olympias

~~~~~~

Hippocrates made his way through the city of Cos, and came to the shore of the sea, and the walled enclosure that was home to him. He hammered on the great gate and Elaphus, the gatekeeper, swung it wide on its screeching hinges. Inside were three white buildings set pleasantly among the trees. The house, where he lived with his mother, was off at the left, and before him was the *palaestra*, which was used for gymnastics and physical medicine. On the right was the *iatreion*, with its large high-ceilinged room for surgery. The doors of the surgery stood open to let in the light, and he could see the familiar figure of Pindar bending over a patient, while a younger disciple watched.

The gateman's dog, a large ungainly beast, whined and capered with joy, wagging his head and his tail with equal vigor. Hippocrates laughed. "What's happened to him, Elaphus? Does Bobo know it's springtime too?"

"Yes, he knows all right. He got away yesterday and was out all night — came back this morning in a terrible state, dirty and with one ear torn."

"Perhaps he found friends," Hippocrates suggested. "There are times when dogs must gather like their masters to have their own symposia. But I hesitate to think what subjects of discussion the symposiarch may suggest. Seriously, Elaphus, that gate makes too much noise. I'd rather not be announced so loudly. Pour some water into the sockets of those hinges."

"I think your mother likes the sound. She hears it, and then she can look to see who's coming in."

Hippocrates smiled and glanced toward the house. His mother was in the doorway. He waved, but before he could call to her, he was confronted by the towering figure of Pindar, who had spied him from the surgery.

"Master," he said, "the wife of the Archon Timon is waiting for you in the *iatreion* with that enormous boxer, Buto. He has interesting scars on his face, a nose that must have been broken many times, and very large thick ears, the kind you see on old wrestlers rather than boxers."

Hippocrates nodded his approval of this evidence that Pindar was learning the art of observation, and Pindar continued.

"I told Olympias that I was afraid you might not have time to see her. But I think, Master, that it would help me to impose a satisfactory regimen upon her daughter Penelope if you would be good enough to see Olympias now."

Hippocrates nodded again and started toward the *iatreion*. "Tell my mother," he said over his shoulder, "that I shall be a little late for lunch. And Pindar!" He looked back, smiling at the young asclepiad. "You don't need to follow out Euryphon's plan in regard to Penelope. It won't really be necessary for you to marry the young woman." His eyes twinkled as he watched Pindar's embarrassment.

He passed around the *iatreion* to his consulting room at the back and sent for Olympias. She entered with a swishing of her ruby-colored cloak. Behind her, an enormous man came stepping softly. She introduced him as her son's boxing instructor. Hippocrates looked carefully at the boxer as he shuffled forward — a man of about forty, erect and very muscular. He had a scarred, puffy face, with small eyes and a very large mouth. That, with the flattened nose and receding forehead, gave him, Hippocrates thought, the appearance of an enormous upright fish.

"It is about my son Cleomedes," Olympias continued, "that I want to consult you."

"Your son?"

"Yes. I know you thought I came to hear you diagnose my daughter's case. No, I came to discuss my son. Buto is here with me because he knows a great deal about my son and because he insisted on coming. He can talk with you later."

She waved the boxer away, but he stood motionless, his beady eyes on Hippocrates. He grunted and, finally, spoke slowly in a rumbling voice.

"He's hard to handle, this boy Cleomedes — gets sad like, won't talk — mostly when he's thinking about that girl — never looks at boys or men."

Buto shook his head with an expression of anxious gloom.

"Cleomedes," he continued, "has a bad temper — might even murder somebody some day. He has the best muscles and the fastest footing I ever saw. If you can cure him of getting mad — make him forget that girl — I'll teach him to be the greatest boxer in all Hellas!"

Slowly, an enormous grin spread across Buto's face. Then, with surprising abruptness, he padded out the door and across the court, lithe and light of foot as a giant cat.

Hippocrates stood staring after the boxer. "That interests me very much." He looked at Olympias speculatively. "Was he always like that? Was he always so slow in his thinking?"

Olympias flushed and hesitated. "Do you mean — do you mean Buto?"

"Yes," Hippocrates nodded, "of course. Boxing seems to do that to the mind, you know, after a certain length of time. I've seen it before in boxing trainers and long-time competitors." He was silent for a moment. "Yes, it could be," he went on. "The brain is in the skull. It could be due to the years of head blows!"

He looked at Olympias with a delighted expression. "Did you know him by any chance when he was the age of Cleomedes?"

"What? No — no, of course not." She flushed, surprisingly. "We brought Buto here from Sparta. He is well known there — he once trained an Olympic winner."

Hippocrates motioned her to a seat placed so that the light from the open door would fall full on her. This was his habit during all interviews. Why, he wondered, did she seem suddenly ill at ease? She adjusted and readjusted her mantle. He noted that her fingernails were colored to match the mantle and that her hands were shaking. She looked at him with her large dark eyes but did not speak. Her eyes reminded him of her daughter Penelope.

"Your daughter looks like her mother," he said. "She will be a handsome woman too, and that very soon."

Olympias bowed her head slightly. "My husband told me the result of your consultation this morning, and he tried to spare my feelings. But he can hide nothing — like all men."

She laughed as though with relief. "I discover that he thinks I am the real cause of Penelope's illness — I have been cruel to her — I have not given her the love a mother should give. Now he imagines that I have asked to see you in order to protest my innocence."

She paused, but he said nothing, so she continued: "No, I shall not protest, not to you. You may as well know that I have sudden fits of hate and love. My love, perhaps, has always been more for men." She passed her long fingers downward from breast to thigh, smoothing again the shining surface of her robe, and shot a quick glance at him.

"With you, Hippocrates, only the truth will serve my purpose. You, of course, can penetrate all pretense." She laughed again, a little sardonically. "Most men are so simple, so easy for a woman to control — unless they are mad. . . . Unless they are mad." She repeated this softly.

Hippocrates waited, tipping his short black beard upward while he passed a finger and thumb over it. It was no simple problem, he surmised, that weighed on this woman's mind. He busied himself with his shoulder pin and let the robe slip down from his broad shoulders. The heat of the day was beginning to be felt.

Finally Olympias said, "Let me come to the real purpose of this interview. I know that you keep secrets, like your father Heracleides."

She looked out through the open door and watched the drifting clouds while he took note of the little lines in the smooth skin of her throat, lines that keep a physician's record of the passing years. Then she looked at him squarely.

"Before I was married I did not live on the island of Cos, but near it on the little island of Astypalaea. I had a cousin there whose name was Cleomedes. He was a few years older than I and he became a great boxer, the islanders said he was the best boxer of all time. He was the only Olympic champion who ever came from our tiny island.

"But when he returned from Olympia, instead of being a hero, he was in disgrace and people said he was mad. After he had beaten his opponent in the Olympic final, he killed him before anyone could stop him." She was squeezing her hands nervously. "The judges denied him the crown of wild olive. They dishonored him and fined him two talents, a sum my grandfather could pay, since he was the rich shipowner of the island.

"When Cleomedes came back to his home he would not talk. He stayed indoors. He said he could hear the people talking about him even there. But one day he went to the school where he had gone as a boy. He had never done well at school. He sat down with the scholars there, and when the teacher asked him to leave, he grew suddenly furious and tore down one of the roof supports with his mighty arms. The roof fell. Somehow he escaped unhurt but some of the boys were killed.

"He ran away to the temple of Apollo, and the people said they saw him hide himself in the great chest in the portico of the temple. So, men gathered round with weapons to kill him. But when they opened the chest he was not there. In time they began to say that a god had carried him away. On the island today they call him the son of Heracles."

"Yes," Hippocrates said. "I have heard the story many times, of course. Now, I am told, the people are planning to build a shrine to Heracles over the chest!"

She nodded. "But what you do not know," she continued, "is that he escaped from the chest and my mother hid him in our house. A magnificent young athlete he was, handsome, a little slow in his thinking, but gentle and kind unless you denied him something. I was sorry for him. I did not think he was mad. But I know now that there were other cousins who did go mad."

She was sitting erect, her lips tight as though she were on the verge of tears.

"I think I've seen the beginning of this madness now in my son Cleomedes. He defies me, or he looks at me and mutters. I've never denied him anything. I was always afraid this would come out in him. Buto suggested when he first came that you might cure the boy. Can you?"

"Tell me about Buto," Hippocrates said.

"Oh, Buto is just a trainer from Sparta. My son heard of him and wanted him to come, so at the beginning of the training season the Archon sent for him.

"Last year Cleomedes saw Daphne, Euryphon's daughter, in Cnidus, and again this year. Now he seems to think of nothing else. Buto says that if they are married, Cleomedes will settle down and forget the girl. Then he may become a great boxer."

"What does Cleomedes say?" Hippocrates asked.

"He says nothing; he won't talk to me. I am afraid of what he may do if he doesn't get her. It's the beginning of madness, I fear. People are beginning to talk."

"Who?" Hippocrates asked.

"I don't know." She looked about her almost furtively.

"When did this mad cousin, the boxer, hide in your home? How long before you married Timon?"

"A month or two," she said, speaking almost in a whisper, with eyes downcast. "I was already engaged to Timon — I know what you are thinking. I hoped you would guess it. It is easier that way — Yes, Cleomedes may be the son of a boxer or he may be the son of an Archon. Who can tell?"

She shrugged and looked out through the open door. "My son is beautiful. You should see him naked! I had a beautiful body, too, when I was his age." Her throaty voice was suddenly strong and resonant. "Some said I was very beautiful. Men said so. Some say I am still beautiful."

She looked at Hippocrates, but he neither spoke nor altered his level gaze.

"Can you cure men who are going mad — men who have gone mad — men who have madness in the family?"

"I need more information," he replied, and stood up. "I will keep your secret," he said. "Send Cleomedes to talk with me."

"No," she replied, and remained seated. "He would not go to you if his mother were to ask him. We expected him on the boat this morning but he could not leave Triopion. Buto says he will come in early tomorrow. Tomorrow you will be invited to the ceremony of his wedding contract. You must come and watch him at the villa."

"Perhaps I shall not accept the invitation," he said.

"Please come."

Hippocrates shook his head. "Cleomedes is a man, not a child. I shall not consider him as a patient until I make a positive diagnosis. Even then, a physician can do little for a true madman — except perhaps change his surroundings. I suspect, Olympias, that all is not well with you. Perhaps you may be the patient."

She shrugged again. "If you will not come to the Archon's villa tomorrow to watch Cleomedes, then come and watch me."

Hippocrates sat down. "You are afraid," he said. She nodded and put her face in her hands. "Fear," he continued, "must be examined before it can be conquered. The cause must be studied, in all honesty. Fear comes from threats that are not faced, and unhappiness comes with it. Fear can drive you to unwise and unworthy acts. There is something you have not told me."

He waited, but she did not speak.

"Are you afraid that the Olympic boxer may come back from the dead and that the world may discover your secret?"

She gave no answer.

"Is Buto — what shall I say? — Is he the Olympic boxer, a little older perhaps?"

Olympias sat as though turned to stone, her cheeks suddenly pale.

"I see," he said with a half-smile, "you had not intended me to ask that question — But perhaps you are disturbed for no reason. Perhaps you have some other cause to be unhappy. Do you sleep well?"

"No, not very well." She raised her head and smiled with relief.

"Is your life with your husband what you would like it to be?"

She shrugged. "Yes and no. He is proud of me, and when his friends are with us he is pleased to hear their admiration. But except at such times, he is not often at home. I want no more children."

She hesitated. "As for me, I take my pleasure in various ways, and my servingmaid is always with me."

"Are you happy?" Hippocrates asked.

"Happy?" she questioned. "What is happiness? Cleomedes is my happiness. And he is my sorrow, my fear. No, I am not happy. And I'm afraid, always afraid."

Hippocrates stood up again. "Go, now. I may come tomorrow, if there is time and if I am invited by the Archon."

She rose and obeyed, as though she were a child. But at the door she turned back toward him. "My secret is safe with you? You will not forget your oath of secrecy?" A glow came to her cheeks and a faint smile to her lips. She came close to him, turning her face upward. "You may kiss me — the physician's fee, you know."

But he put his hands on her shoulders and turned her around gently.

"Good-by," he said.

At the door she turned once more. "Please take Cleomedes as your patient. I need your help very much."

CHAPTER FOUR

Aphrodite and Artemis

~~~~~~

WHEN DAPHNE returned across the terrace, after watching Hippocrates leave Timon's villa, she found her father waiting for her alone. They walked back and forth together. Cuckoos called from the wood. A magpie sailed gaily up from the gardens below, showing the shawl of white on his back and legs. He perched on a nearby cypress and cried defiance to the world: *"Chak-chak, chak-chak."*

"I love the spring," Daphne exclaimed suddenly, "and the birds and the growing things. I love life. But somehow —" she faltered — "somehow I don't . . ."

Euryphon completed the sentence for her: "But somehow you are afraid you will not love the man I've selected for you to marry."

She nodded.

"Daphne, this is the way marriages have always been arranged. How could a maid judge the man she would marry? She knows so few men and she might be so easily misled. Many young women have felt just as you do at their first meeting, only to change their opinion later. Love comes to the man and the maid whom chance or plan holds together, unless one of them has learned to love someone else before that time. Love is like a fever. When one of the pair has it, the other can hardly escape after they are shut away from the world in house and room and bed. Wait until you know Cleomedes and have slept with him and borne him children. Aphrodite is strong. When the soil is ready she plants her seed and life goes on, life with its endless rhythm of love, birth, growth and love again. Passion gives us our best hope, our only hope, of immortality here on earth."

She made a gesture of dissent, but her father continued.

"There are other things that grow out of the union of man and woman. How shall I say it? — happiness, satisfaction, common hopes and aims. If your mother were only alive, she could explain these things to you so much better than I can. Cleomedes is healthy and handsome, and in time he will be very rich. Those things make it easier."

Daphne looked at her father thoughtfully. "I suppose it is my duty to marry and have children. But must these duties be disagreeable? Shouldn't I be charmed at the sight of the man I am to marry? I've only seen Cleomedes once. When you brought him to our home, I was afraid at first — but I was pleased, too, and excited. I wanted to talk with him and be friends. I wanted to like him. But he seemed to think of nothing like that. He only wanted to touch me, kiss me. Somehow I couldn't. I had to run away. I couldn't help it."

Her father looked baffled, and she continued with flushed face. "Am I so different from other women? I want something more than the marriage bed."

"*Chak-chak,*" laughed the magpie from the cypress. "*Chak-chak, chak-chak.*"

"Look at that bird," she said. "I suppose when he first met an un- attached female magpie, he was drawn to her and she to him, and the match was made. But I'm a woman, not a bird, nor a cow, nor a sheep. Perhaps you let me stay at home too long, looking after you. I was happy to do it. But I grew up. A father should marry off his daughter when she is just old enough to feel but not to think."

She stopped, but her father was still silent.

"I have been bursting to say this to you before, but — I was shy, and you were busy." She looked away into the distance, and con- tinued: "A girl has her dreams while growing into womanhood. Aph- rodite comes to her, naked and fresh from the foam of the sea. She whispers the thrilling fantasies of a wife's love and a mother's joy. There is no thought at first of the pain and the purpose of life."

Euryphon started to speak, but she put her hand on his arm.

"Let me finish now I've started. When a girl grows up in a happy home, as I have done, where Aphrodite cannot have her way too soon — then Artemis, the virgin sister of Apollo, visits her.

" 'Fly in terror from all men,' she warns. 'Keep that something of the body and the mind that can be yielded once and only once. It is the treasure that will get you happiness as well as pleasure, when your time has come.' "

Daphne paused and smiled at her father. Then she added, "Don't misunderstand me. I have longed to be overtaken, longed for that complete surrender. But if there is no such man that I can love with all my heart, then let me join the maidens in the train of Artemis and hunt some other quarry."

Euryphon shook his head.

"Daphne, I have never talked with you about these things — do you know all about love?" He wished more than ever that his wife could be here to help him find the right words. "Have you ever felt yourself drawn to a man in that way I mean?"

"Yes, Father, I have."

Euryphon looked at her in surprise. "You have?"

"Yes. Do you recall the young asclepiad who came from the hill country of Aeolia to study medicine with you — Pyramus? He died of the fever, you remember."

Euryphon nodded soberly. "I remember him very well. He talked about you a great deal in his delirium, before he died — You wanted to go to him in the sickroom, and I would not let you. But he had no money, no family. I was afraid . . ."

She nodded sadly. "Pyramus fascinated me at our first meeting. I think I should have loved him, had the gods not taken him away. Who can tell? Since that time I have always compared other men to him.

"But Mother was on her deathbed with the fever when he fell ill, and they died — you well remember — the two of them on the same day. So I did not talk to you of Pyramus then because of Mother's death. You needed me so much."

Euryphon turned away from her abruptly and walked to the other end of the terrace. After a little time, she followed him.

"Father," she said. Then, when there was no answer: "Father — you've been good to me — I've been happy living with you. Couldn't I become an asclepiad instead of being married — even though I am a woman?"

Still he was silent.

"Let us talk about something else, then . . . Tell me about this Coan asclepiad Hippocrates. He interests me, like all asclepiads — perhaps because I wish so much that I could have been a physician myself. How is it that he has grown so great when he is still so young?"

Euryphon cleared his throat and turned back to his daughter with an air of elaborate composure. "Hippocrates has a remarkable mind. He was for a short time a favorite pupil of Socrates, I am told. But he is famous now because his patients talked about him. When the gods would smile on a physician, the right people get well. That's the way it was with Hippocrates. A wealthy Macedonian who thought Hippocrates cured him happened to tell King Perdiccas about it at the time when the king fell ill. So Hippocrates was called to care for Perdiccas and all the world has heard of his success there.

"But, Daphne, you will give Cleomedes a chance to woo you, won't you? You will learn to know him?"

"Yes, Father. I will do it because you ask it and because you have promised me that you will not force me to marry against my will."

She put her hands on the stone wall of the terrace and looked into the distance. Sails made points of white that moved slowly, steadily over the purple sea.

"The world is so beautiful, and yet I am sad. And you would be sad alone in our nest if I should leave you."

Later in the day Daphne asked a servant to take her to Penelope's room. They found the door heavily curtained. Daphne sent the servant away and called: "May I come in? This is Daphne, daughter of Euryphon." After a moment, she called again: "Penelope, may I come in? Hippocrates has sent me to walk with you."

She heard an exclamation then, and Penelope pulled back the

heavy curtain. The room was dark, for the window curtain had been closed as well.

"I wasn't asleep," Penelope explained with embarrassment. "You see, I am all dressed."

"Do you sit here in the dark?" Daphne asked in surprise.

Penelope nodded and opened the window curtains.

"When I close the curtains they leave me alone — the servants and my mother. Aeneas said I was to rest and to give up the bath. But now, since Hippocrates said I might, I have had a wonderful bath and I'm all dressed and ready. I thought Pindar might come."

She gave Daphne a wan smile and then looked in her mirror, pulling a cloak around her shoulders.

"What a lovely cloak," Daphne said. "That soft yellow sets off your dark eyes and hair wonderfully."

Penelope swung her long braids over her back and looked at Daphne with tremulous excitement.

"Do you know what I've done?" she said. "I put some color on my cheeks, just a little. I hope Pindar does come before it's time for dinner. He's going to plan my diet. I had barley broth as usual, but suddenly I wanted more. I haven't been hungry for a long time, but now I can't wait to eat. And I'm to have all I want!"

Then the vivacious expression faded from her thin face.

"I don't know what my mother will say. Since she saw me in one of my falling attacks, I've hardly been out of my room, not even to walk in the cypress grove. But Hippocrates said I wouldn't have the attacks any more. Do you think he knows?"

Daphne nodded. "I'm sure he does; and he told me that I was to go with you for a walk this afternoon."

"But my mother forbade it," Penelope objected.

"Never mind," Daphne said. "Your father knows we are going. He did not object."

When they reached the terrace it was quite deserted. Penelope looked back at the house. There was no one on the balcony, no one on the roof to spy on them. She faced out toward the rolling hills and the sea and said quietly: "It is spring. I had forgotten that." She raised her arms and took a little skipping step, unsteadily, like a young lamb.

Daphne watched her, not knowing what to expect. Having grown up in a physician's family, she had learned never to ask what was wrong with a patient. Penelope laughed, though at the start it sounded more like crying. Her pale face was strangely excited.

"I know what I'll do!" she cried. "I'll take you through the sacred grove all the way to the temple of Apollo. I'll show you my secret pathway. It is so long since I've seen it!"

As they passed through the towering trees into the forest, the two girls felt suddenly very small. Their feet made no sound on the needled floor. A curtain of shadow and silence closed behind them. The tree trunks stood like mighty pillars in some giant temple carrying the eye upward to the roof of branching green. Here and there a shaft of golden sunlight slanted downward through the haze of forest twilight.

"Did you know," Penelope asked, "that a curse falls on those who cut these trees? They are sacred to Apollo and there is a law against felling the trees unless the Council of Cos gives special permission. They do that sometimes when men want to build the longest ships, the greatest triremes."

Daphne looked up at the mighty tree trunks. "I remember when my father took me to Athens. It was the year that Pericles was finishing the building of Athena's temple, the Parthenon. We climbed the Acropolis in the dark and waited on the steps of the Parthenon for dawn to come. When the sun rose over the hills, level bars of golden light, like those up there in the trees, passed through the pillars of the Parthenon into the dark temple. And the face of the virgin goddess Athena was lit with sunlight, as though she had been standing there in the darkness, waiting through the night for the kiss of Apollo. I have a strange feeling now — as though you and I were waiting here for something."

Penelope looked at the lovely woman at her side with the wide-eyed surprise of a little girl.

"I'm waiting for Pindar," she said, "and for something to eat." She looked wistfully back toward the villa. "I suppose you are waiting for my brother Cleomedes. You have certainly cast a spell on him."

"No." Daphne shook her head. "No, eating and being loved are not enough. It's something more, much more — a beautiful dream, perhaps, and in it someone to share life's joys and sorrows and work."

They walked along together, following a path.

"When I was small," Penelope said, "I used to dance and hop along this path. As I went, I pretended that Aesop's animals would come out to meet me and play with me. I had no children to play with, you see, and so I talked with the little mouse and the lion, the fox and the hare and the frog. Each had his home along this path, and I would stop and visit with them.

"We are near where the lion lives, behind this enormous tree trunk. Wouldn't you like to see him? He's such a wise, kind old lion. There he is now! — just where the shaft of sunlight touches the great moss-covered stone. Here, on the other side of the path, you see, is the dog in his manger. The ox is there too, forever trying to get his head into the manger so he can eat the hay." Penelope tossed back her braids and laughed. "It was great fun."

Daphne laughed with her. They were two little girls now in an enchanted forest filled with the friends of childhood.

"You see," Penelope continued, with a sudden change of mood, "I used to come out here to be away from my mother. She is so clever with strangers, so loving to my father, and she adores my brother Cleomedes. But she doesn't like me. She never did and she is afraid of this lovely forest. She says she hears strange things when she is in it. So I had it all to myself. Out here I was free! At least I was until she stopped my visits here."

"Listen!" Daphne exclaimed. Above their heads and far away they heard a melody of pure, clear tones.

"The nightingales," Penelope said. "They begin about this time."

They walked along in silence for a while. The singing continued to echo through the wood, and Daphne said at last:

"Voices from another world! A muse might sing that way in spring — to please Apollo."

"Well, here we are," Penelope interrupted, "at Apollo's temple. Aeneas had a sacrifice offered for me here to cure me of the sacred disease. But Hippocrates said I never had it. I am so happy! I think we should turn back, in case Pindar has come. Isn't he wonderful? So tall and handsome! Perhaps you didn't see him —"

"Look," Daphne said. "Someone is coming."

A man in a long white robe was approaching along the path. His uncut hair fell to his shoulders, and on his head he wore a laurel wreath.

"It's the Priest of Apollo," Penelope said, and went on ahead to meet him. He welcomed the two girls and led them around to the front of the temple, which stood on a hill, like the Archon's villa.

"I hope you are well again," he said to Penelope. "I don't see you so often as I did when you were young."

Daphne climbed the steps and passed in between the marble pillars to gaze at the statue of the god. She stood aside while a man with his wife and sons, all wearing wreaths, came out carrying away their share of the flesh of a sheep they had offered as a sacrifice. A flute player they had brought along walked with them and played as they went.

When the family had gone, Daphne was aware that a woman who stood on the other side of the altar had been watching her with a kind, wistful expression. She had ruddy cheeks; her hair was turning gray. They smiled at each other. Then Daphne left the temple.

Outside, she found the priest still standing on the steps, a small, middle-aged man with delicate features.

"May I ask you a question?" Daphne asked.

"Certainly."

"Have men been cursed for cutting trees in this ancient grove?"

"What the gods may do," he replied, "and whom they curse is not for man to say. At the last cutting of the trees around the Archon's villa no sacrifices were made here to Apollo Cyparissius. I am told that the Council of Cos gave him consent."

The two girls said good-by and started back through the wood.

"Let's run," Penelope said. "Do you like to run?"

"Do you think you should?" Daphne asked.

Penelope laughed. "I am well again, and Hippocrates said I was to exercise."

"All right, we will race," said Daphne.

They slipped off their sandals and tied them to their girdles, tucking up their tunics to leave their legs bare, and winding their cloaks around one arm.

Then off they went, leaping along the pathway like two fawns, Daphne small, delicate and quick; Penelope longer-limbed, swift and surprisingly graceful. They called to each other and laughed as they went until suddenly, on rounding a bend in the path, they ran headlong into Pindar. Penelope's legs gave way then and she sprawled on the ground. Daphne helped her up.

"Well, well!" Pindar exclaimed. "I was coming out to find you. Is someone after you? Or are you the nymphs of Artemis, following that swift huntress? By Zeus, that must have been the goddess who fluttered past me. She was aiming her silver bow and I saw the arrow fly."

The two girls could only laugh, having no breath to speak.

"I saw a lion, too, with an arrow through and through his middle."

"Oh," panted Penelope, "you didn't really see my lion, did you?"

"Your lion? — Yes, yes, I saw him, quite distinctly. In fact, he asked me if I would please remove his arrow."

Pindar had spoken gravely, but now he smiled. "I told the lion I had a patient to see first. After that I would pull out his arrow."

When the girls had rearranged their dress and regained their breath, Pindar said: "I have come to plan your regimen, Penelope. You seem to have begun the course of exercises we had in mind for you quite well!"

They moved along the path toward the villa and Daphne loitered behind to leave them alone. Penelope looked up at Pindar.

"I like you," she said — "somehow I'm not afraid of you at all. It does me good to walk beside you because I have to look up at you. I'm too tall with other people. I even look down on my own father when I stand beside him and it makes me seem so awkward."

She giggled a little and took his hand in hers, but he drew it away as though afraid of fire; perhaps he merely remembered the precepts of asclepiad conduct. He turned to Penelope gravely.

"I shall outline for you a careful diet. Some people eat but one meal daily, but you are to have more than that. I urge you to eat much more than you have in the past."

She looked delighted, and he continued: "Your barley gruel is to be made thin for three days and, after that, it may be somewhat thickened. The bread, to be made of unwinnowed wheat, must be thoroughly kneaded and well baked. You may take barley cakes and honey sparingly at first. Fish on the other hand you are to take —"

Here Penelope interrupted: "Aeneas strictly prohibited fish and fowl and onions and leeks — and many, many other things!"

"From now on," Pindar said sternly, "you will accept a new regimen."

"But —"

"There must be no 'buts,'" he said, raising his voice. "I must be severe with you, Penelope. You must listen to me now, and I shall give full instructions to your servingmaid."

"But I was only going to say," she persisted, while she gazed at him with an expression little short of adoration, "that I will do everything you order, if you will only come to see me often. I'll even eat a he-goat if you tell me it is good for me. But I could start with barley gruel. I hope they make it thick — and soon." She put her hands on her stomach and laughed gaily.

They were approaching the house now, and they could see a woman at the entrance in a shining ruby-colored cloak.

"That is my mother," Penelope whispered. "She is putting garlands on the statue of Hermes. I'm afraid she will be angry."

At the entrance, Pindar saluted Olympias. "I am directing your daughter in a new regimen of life and diet," he said.

Olympias finished arranging the flowers, and then turned with a smile.

"What about the rules that Aeneas and I worked out to save this child from the sacred disease?" she asked in her soft contralto. "Are they all to be broken?"

Pindar bowed with great dignity. "Yes, Olympias."

Penelope saw anger blaze suddenly in her mother's eyes, but Pindar saw only its response, the fear in Penelope's face as she glanced back at him and hurried away into the villa.

"Ask your servant to come to me," Pindar called after her with quiet authority. Then he turned to Olympias. "I will outline the regimen to her in full detail."

"Certainly," Olympias replied, and smiled at him again. "Certainly — the orders of Hippocrates and of my husband must be obeyed on earth. The new regimen shall be carried out, whatever the gods on Mount Olympus may think and even if Zeus himself should thunder his disapproval."

She looked toward the villa. "My daughter's servant is waiting for your instructions there, just inside the court."

Olympias watched him go, then turned to greet Daphne, who was coming along the terrace.

"*Chaire,* greetings to you, Daphne. Welcome to our household. I am the mother of your future husband."

Daphne smiled shyly.

"My son," Olympias continued, "was not on the boat when I met it, but his boxing instructor arrived to tell me that he will be here in time for the betrothal tomorrow. He is allowed only two days' leave from Triopion."

Olympias turned toward the phallic pillar on which the chiseled head of Hermes was set, and Daphne saw the garlands of flowers.

"You see the bridegroom's decoration. It is for the bride too. You are a very fortunate young woman, Daphne. Cleomedes is as handsome as Apollo."

"Yes," Daphne replied, "I have seen him — once."

"And you ran away, I am told."

Something in the older woman's mellow voice made Daphne stiffen and flush.

But she answered, "Yes." Then she added demurely, "This time it will be different, I hope."

CHAPTER FIVE

The Sacred Disease

~~~~~~

LATE THAT AFTERNOON Hippocrates emerged from one of the city's narrow streets to walk home along the shore of the sea.

He sighed with relief as he stepped out on the beach. It had been a long afternoon seeing patients in their homes, long and tiring. Two disciples had followed him and he had tried to teach them as he went along. But there were so many suffering men and women and children — so many different diseases! He realized with exasperation that he had spent the whole time comforting the sick and directing their care — there had been no time to think. And to make matters worse, acute fever had made its dreaded appearance on the island again. How could he say no when sufferers called for help, even though he realized he was spending too little time with each one. He must find time also to study and compare, time to write his daily case notes, time for reflection and teaching.

Between the claims of compassion and his determination to study, he felt frustrated. And there was something else . . . perhaps he was lonely.

His father, he mused, must have faced all this before him. Perhaps that was why he had quoted the words of Solon so often: "Nothing in excess," all things in due proportion. But it was not so easy to apply that motto to the use of time in daily living.

He looked out across the water. There were fishing boats near at hand, and a trireme in the distance. The wind was cool and he breathed it in. How familiar were the salty smells and the sounds of the sea.

Wave after wave came rolling swiftly in. Each rose in turn to pound upon the beach and, hissing, make the pebbles click, and the clicking sound to race away along the shore. And so peace returned to his mind as he trudged along toward home.

"Hippocrates!"

The sound of his own name startled him. Looking up, he saw his mother Praxithea coming toward him. She laughed, and he was glad that she had come. Her laugh, he thought, was a mellow, musical sound, and she was a handsome woman with her graying hair and ruddy cheeks.

"I could see you walking along the shore," she called. "You nearly fell over one of the boats! Was your mind so far away?"

"Not far in place. But a good distance in time. The wind and waves have wings for me, you know."

They walked together to the entrance of the asclepiad enclosure. There they paused and he looked up at the temple that topped the wall on the far side of the water passage. The ship that had brought him home from Macedonia had come through that passage only two months ago. Men were walking now along the colonnade, their cloaks blowing out in the wind.

"Greeks," he said to his mother, "Greeks talking, arguing, talking. There you have the difference between Greek and Barbarian, between Hellas and Macedonia. Men don't do that in Macedonia. They only fight and toil — and eat, and love, and sleep. I doubt whether they even dream. They must be too tired for that!"

She smiled. "Your dinner is ready. Come to the house, son. Take off your sandals and wash at once. We have fish for dinner."

"Don't we always have fish? The food was different in Macedonia."

Her face fell. "Yes, but this is your favorite — a red mullet — a big fish, caught this morning."

Mother and son dined alone, he lying on the couch while she sat at his feet. When they had finished she moved about the room, glancing at him from time to time. But he seemed lost in thought.

She was wearing a light blue tunic with a purple sash which she adjusted now. She smoothed her hair.

"I'm wearing the sash you brought me from Macedonia. Do you like it?" He smiled and nodded.

"I forgot to tell you," she continued, "a Hebrew arrived here today. He has come straight from Jerusalem. His name is Nicodemus. He says he is suffering from the divine disease. I told him you would see him this evening when you meet the asclepiads under the plane tree. I hope that was right?"

"Yes."

After a further silence she asked: "Is there any news at the house of the Archon Timon?"

"The daughter of Euryphon," he replied, "is to marry Cleomedes, son of the Archon. Her name is Daphne. At least that is the plan if she likes the young man. He was to have come this morning so they could meet before the betrothal, but he failed to arrive."

"Well," she exclaimed, "that is news indeed! What is the young woman like?"

Hippocrates collected his thoughts: "Small, tanned, muscular, black hair, unusual face; the profile of forehead and nose is remarkably straight. She would do for a sculptor's model. They are always searching about for that profile. Eyes blue, I think, but I'd like to see them again. She is normally developed as to breasts and hips — in excellent health, I should say."

"Hippocrates!" his mother exclaimed. "Don't always be a physician! Daphne is a woman, not a patient or a horse." Praxithea shook her head and was silent for a time. Then she said:

"Hippocrates, I know how great are your responsibilities here as master in your father's place. You need help with it. Of course your brother Sosander is a wise gymnast, and your cousin Podalirius will always help you with details, as he did your father — fortunately, although they are so much older, they worship you. But neither of them could be master. It is the teaching and the diagnosis and the handling of men — only you are wise enough and decisive enough for that. The help you need is the help a wife could give you. Through her you would learn the other half of life. Without her you may live to be only half a man. Your father used to say, 'Nothing in excess.' Too much medicine, too much work, even too much kindly service may be excessive."

Hippocrates looked at her, startled. "That quotation of his was in my mind when I met you on the beach."

She nodded. "Living here as you do, and wearing his mantle, as you must, you may hear him speak to you often . . . I do — so often."

She turned her head away, then left the room abruptly. Hippocrates looked after her and understood the heartache. Presently she returned and, looking down at her son, continued as though there had been no interruption:

"No one knows you better than I do. Ordinarily you are gay, talkative, amusing. But when you are struggling with some unsolved problem you are different — you build a wall about yourself, as you have tonight. A wife, the right wife, might be with you inside the wall and help you. You must have someone to talk with. I am old, I suppose. You do not see me or listen to me. Many a time I told your father he should find you a wife, but he said you were not ready. You wanted to learn more — and more — and more!"

Hippocrates stood up suddenly and put his arms about his mother. Then he began to walk back and forth.

"Perhaps — if I could find a woman like you . . . I have seen women who were exciting, but when I found they could not share my thoughts, they bored me. I want sons sometime, but —" He smiled at her and did not finish the sentence.

Twilight came, the hour for him to lead the teaching and discussion of medicine. So they walked to the doorway of their house, mother and son. She stood and watched him pass on through the garden toward the gathering place. She had watched his father go to his teaching like this, so often. She moved quickly to a bench under the trees and sat down heavily. After a little time she spoke softly, as though someone unseen were standing beside her.

"How can a lonely widow find a woman to match that son? She must match him in spirit as well as in body. And how am I to find her?"

Hippocrates crossed the garden and paused to look out across the blue gulf. The sun had turned the mountains of Caria into rosy gold, and below the mountains he could see the harbor of Halicarnassus as it opened out toward Cos, and the temples on the hillsides, white and tiny in the level light of the setting sun. How often in the carefree days of his boyhood he had seen this beauty, just as it was tonight. Life was full of dreams then. All things were possible, it seemed — to gain the victor's crown in athletics, to excel in literature, philosophy, medicine.

Now he had set himself one task, one problem. His goal was to rid medicine of blind belief in the supposed wisdom of the past and to found a science in its place. Other men had done something like this in other fields than medicine. Pythagoras had made of numbers and lines a true science. Greeks were creating the arts, drama, poetry. In Athens he had watched Phidias discovering beauty in a block of marble — carving out the truth with chisel and mallet. He had listened to Socrates exposing the sham and dishonesty in the hearts of men and discovering something in the process — a spirit within the body. But no asclepiad had as yet done the thing he hoped to do.

And if he should take a woman into his life? Would she not interfere with his work? Or would she help, as his mother thought? For a moment he seemed to see Daphne's eyes looking into his, as though she were taking his measure. Yes, his mother was right about one thing, Daphne was a woman, not a patient . . . For a moment he remembered another woman, Thargelia in Macedonia. She had been beautiful and exciting too . . .

He stood still. The garden was quiet, quiet except for the song that poured down from the throat of a little *ramithas*. There it was in the oleander above him, with its long tail, red on the wing and greenish-brown breast. He looked at the neat white buildings about him within the walled enclosure — his house in the far corner where his mother was sitting, watching him, the *palaestra,* the clinic — all shut away from the world, opening only to the sea and to the sick who entered the gate. This was enough. He would use his own chisel and mallet here to discover truth.

He walked on toward the far corner of the garden. A small group of men stood there beneath the plane tree in animated discussion. Pindar was in heated argument with Podalirius, the senior asclepiad, who had been Heracleides' assistant for as long as Hippocrates could remember. Now he was Hippocrates' senior assistant — always the same, unbending, conscientious, tireless, humorless.

Sosander, a squat giant of a man, caught sight of Hippocrates and came to meet him. This elder brother had a large handsome head, with a high forehead, shaggy eyebrows and neat square beard. But the head was set low on a shortened, crooked body. His arms and legs were long and powerful, so that at first he might seem a tree with stunted trunk and lusty branches. But those who came to know him forgot the ugly back and were conscious only of his great intelligence, his kindly sensitive spirit, and his flashing wit and humor.

The two men embraced and Sosander placed an enormous hand on his brother's shoulder and peered up at him.

"We missed you today. I had many patients in the *palaestra*. There were as many taking their exercises here today as I used to see in Selymbria when Herodicus taught me gymnastics. Men come to Cos now because of your fame, and once you get them here I cure them for you with gymnastics!" He grinned at his brother and held up his arms — great hairy arms, like those of an enormous gorilla.

"When they leave us, they chant your praises and say nothing about me. Then they hurry off to sacrifice their savings in the temple of Asclepius without having paid us anything!"

Hippocrates laughed. "Yes, perhaps you are right. I do the talking and writing, you do the work, and the credit with the reward goes to our ancestor Asclepius! But there are problems your gymnastics won't solve. I studied one this morning. It had to do with two women. The symptoms appear in the daughter, but the cause of the disease is, I suspect, in the mother."

"Women!" grunted Sosander. "I advise you to give that problem up. You may hope to compete with Anaximander and Socrates in philosophy. You might become a greater mathematician than Pythagoras, a wiser physician than Alcmaeon — but no, you know nothing about women. There are some things men were never meant to understand. My wife told me that this morning."

The two sons of Heracleides laughed as they walked into the circle beneath the spreading branches of the plane tree. A sudden silence fell on the company.

"Greetings," Hippocrates said. "What is the subject of your discussion?"

Podalirius, a big man with a closely cut gray beard, who took the responsibility of his senior position seriously, answered. "Hippocrates, Pindar here has made statements about the sacred disease that I find it impossible to accept. Also, I should tell you, Master, that a young stranger is waiting in the surgery hoping you will see him tonight. He has come to you from Jerusalem to be cured of that very condition."

"Let us hear his history first," Hippocrates said, "and return to discussion later." He seated himself in his father's chair, with his back to the great tree trunk. Podalirius and Sosander took their places on either side, while the others sat on the stone benches arranged in a half-circle about them. When the stranger was brought before him, Hippocrates smiled and beckoned to him.

"Be good enough to come and stand here and tell us your story — what you complain of, how the trouble began. We will help you if we can."

As the young man came forward, the light of the sunset fell full on him. He bowed low, after the manner of the East, and his richly ornamented mantle swept the ground. His black beard was trimmed in the Persian manner and he had heavy, handsome features.

Podalirius stepped forward. "Take off your cloak and give it to me." When the stranger had obeyed, he said, "Now off with your chiton," and when the Hebrew hesitated, he added abruptly, "Barbarians are ashamed of nakedness, not Greeks . . . that is better. You may keep your loin cloth if you wish." Podalirius then nodded and almost smiled at the young man. "Now tell your story to the master."

The young man had flushed. He now spoke slowly and with dignity. "You Greeks call all men Barbarians who are not born to the Greek tongue. But we Hebrews had our prophets and our wise men before the days of Homer. I am not blind to the greatness of Hellas. But as I am a scholar, I am mindful also of the greatness of our past, mindful that we are a people chosen of Jehovah."

"Well spoken, young man," Hippocrates said. "But tell me now the story of your illness. Tell it simply."

"I am twenty-two years of age and my name is Nicodemus," the young stranger said, speaking Greek in a husky voice with the accent of the East. "I come from Jerusalem. We men of Judah are rebuilding its walls and the Temple of the Lord our God. You know, perhaps, that we have returned to our own land after one hundred and forty years of captivity.

"While I was still a boy, my father left the Persian court, following the great prophet Nehemiah back to Jerusalem. I went with him. It was a long and difficult journey, and while we were yet on the way I began to notice from time to time an evil odor that was apt to come to me suddenly. To my astonishment I found that others present could smell nothing. Sometimes the odor would be followed by a feeling of dread, and at the same time something seemed to press upon me here." He placed his hand on his abdomen and moved it slowly upward.

"Then, on the day we reached Jerusalem, my father told me that I lost consciousness and fell to the ground. I only remember that the mysterious evil smell came to me, and the fear. Then all was darkness. I had been very tired. We had no place to sleep. The men of the tribe of Judah, who were already in the city, did not welcome us as returning brothers.

"Since that day I have had many attacks. The Chief Priest tells me that an evil spirit enters into me. Sometimes I walk about, they say, and do strange things, but I do not know that I am doing them. Perhaps I have sinned against God. Perhaps this is my punishment. They tell me so. But I have prayed for deliverance, and no deliverance comes.

"My father has grown rich, for he entered into trade with Tyre after we reached Jerusalem. So I was able to travel from city to city but I could find no one to cure me. Finally a wise physician whom we consulted in Miletus, said: 'Get thee to Heracleides and his son, the great Hippocrates.'" He turned to Hippocrates. "Here I am. Help me! Men shun me, and women too, as though I were unclean or dangerous. I am an outcast, a man accursed."

The young man held out his arms as though in despair. Then he dropped on his knees and, seizing one of Hippocrates' hands, kissed it. Hippocrates looked down at him and shook his head, withdrawing his hand gently.

"There is no evil spirit in you. No incantation can cure you. You must expect no miracles here. Nevertheless, we will help you as much as we can. Get up now and go."

Nicodemus rose. "What must I do?" he asked.

Hippocrates smiled at him. "You must take wholesome diet, without wine. You must have sleep enough. You will remove your fine clothes and work hard at gymnastics under the direction of my brother Sosander. Your muscles are flabby. We will then consider carefully what further may be done for you. Go now." Turning to Podalirius, he said, "Call his servant." Then, to Nicodemus, he added, "Wait a moment before you go." He called the asclepiads to come and stand beside him.

"Observe this man," he said. "When he talks or smiles, the right side of his face moves less than the left side. The right arm is slightly smaller. Are you left-handed?" Nicodemus nodded in surprise. "Notice also that he has the scar of a severe burn on his leg . . . Did you fall into the fire?"

"Yes, Master. I sat in it, so they told me, during an attack. I felt no pain until afterward."

"One more question. What has your father told you about your birth or early childhood?"

"He said I was a weakling and was slow to move my right arm. But by the time I had reached one year of age, I was a strong child. No doubt if I had been a Greek, my father might have put me in a pot and set me out to die. I was fortunate to be born a Jew!" He glanced at Podalirius.

Hippocrates laughed. "Good! You have spirit, I see. Go now."

But Nicodemus did not move. A strange expression had come into his eyes. He stood staring at nothing, and his features were contorted as though with fear.

"Watch him," said Hippocrates, rising from his seat.

Nicodemus was now holding both hands over his abdomen. He smacked his lips repeatedly and made swallowing movements with his mouth. Then he fumbled stupidly with his loin cloth and pulled it partly off, while saliva ran out of his mouth. His legs seemed to give way under him and he sat down on the ground suddenly and was still. No one spoke.

After a time he looked about and tried awkwardly to get to his feet. Podalirius helped him up. He was mumbling to himself: "I'm all right, I'm all right, leave me alone." Then, after a period of silence, he seemed to look about him with dawning awareness. "Musht have had . . . musht have had . . . I must have had an attack. Did you see it?"

Podalirius said, "Poor fellow — yes, we saw it," and led him away. Hippocrates paced back and forth under the tree for a time, in silence. Then he stopped and looked at the little company.

"That is the 'divine disease' in one of its many forms. You have seen a small attack from beginning to end. I have seen this more than once. The young man was lost for a little time, while he smacked his lips and fumbled. He might well have sat in the fire during it. If he had, he would have felt no pain until later. But it would have burned him just the same, and left a scar such as you saw on his leg. Sometimes the attack, no doubt, becomes more severe at the end, and then he probably falls and shakes and froths at the mouth and wets himself.

"You who have never witnessed such an attack as this might well imagine, as ignorant men have done from old time, that an evil spirit had seized him. But it is not so. It is true that he seems to be seized by something, since he is so suddenly not himself. Call it then a seizure, an *epilepsia*. But when you use the word epilepsy, try to understand its true nature.

"This disease, in my opinion, is no more divine or sacred than other diseases. Like them, it arises from natural causes. Say if you will that the gods have a hand in all things for good or for evil, and

I will not deny that it may be so. In that sense all diseases are divine. But this malady is no more the work of the gods than any other illness.

"The men of our day who undertake the cure of this disease with purifications and incantations and superstitious regimens are no better than magicians, charlatans, quacks! They pretend falsely that they have greater piety and superior knowledge.

"This disease appears in many forms. So it is that ignorant physicians have blamed different gods for the trouble in different patients.

"If the patient imitates a goat, if he roars, or suffers convulsions in the right side, they say that the mother of the gods is to blame. If he utters a piercing and loud cry, they liken him to a horse and blame Poseidon . . . if he foams at the mouth and kicks, Ares has the blame!

"The sacred disease, and madness also, comes from the brain when it is not normal, due, no doubt, to stoppage of air and to the presence of an ill humor. These are factors that we will discuss at another time.

" 'Some people say that the heart is the organ with which we think, and that it feels pain and anxiety.' Empedocles would have us believe that consciousness is in the blood that flows, he says, around the heart. But I hold, following Alcmaeon, that this is not so. We think with the brain.

" 'To consciousness the brain is messenger. For when a man draws breath into himself, the air first reaches the brain, and so is dispersed through the rest of the body, though it leaves in the brain its quintessence and all that it has of intelligence and sense.' "

"And just where," a voice broke in, "is the brain?" It was Dexippus who had interrupted, the youngest member of the asclepiad disciples. Dexippus had been leaning forward, his handsome young face flushed with excitement.

Hippocrates put his hands about his own head. "The brain is here, from neck to forehead, hidden and protected from harm by the bony roof of the skull."

There followed a period of excited question and discussion which continued until the practical Podalirius asked:

"What is to be done with the young Hebrew? Anything more than you have already prescribed?"

"Yes," Hippocrates replied. "The disease comes from natural causes. Therefore it can be cured, sometimes at least, by regulation of the body and its environment. But success in the treatment of this malady is very difficult to achieve. It calls for much thought and greater understanding of the brain than we have at present."

Pindar had been listening in silence. He knew that this amazing conception of the uses of the brain was a summary of the conclusions which Hippocrates was gradually constructing. He knew that much of the evidence had been found in the wide variety of epileptic attacks that he had watched and recorded.

"Master," he said, "I will write out what you have said, and when you have approved it, I shall write a final copy on papyrus so that we may have it for future study."

Hippocrates did not answer, but his brother Sosander said, "Yes, Pindar, you must do that. You have the memory and the wit to summarize it accurately. I'll have it copied."

Hippocrates had stood with his lips parted in a half-smile, not hearing what they said.

" 'Men ought to know,' " he continued, " 'that from the brain, and from the brain only, arise our pleasures, joys, laughter and jests, as well as our sorrows, pain, griefs and tears. Through it, in particular, we think, see, hear, and distinguish the ugly from the beautiful, the bad from the good, the pleasant from the unpleasant . . .

" 'It is the same thing which makes us mad or delirious, inspires us with dread and fear, whether by night or by day, brings sleeplessness, inopportune mistakes, aimless anxieties, absent-mindedness, acts that are contrary to habit.

" 'These things that we suffer all come from the brain, when it is not healthy.' "

CHAPTER SIX

Reluctant Nymph

~~~~~~

I WANDERED through the whole world last night looking for a woman to suit my son." Praxithea followed Hippocrates to the door as he was leaving the house to go to his surgery. "Such dreams as I had!"

"You are too much concerned about me, Mother. I've gone along quite well without a wife. Please don't talk to me about it again. I have trouble enough as it is." He strode off.

"Come back, Hippocrates!"

The son returned with a half smile on his face and stood before his mother. She shook her finger at him.

"There are so many things physicians forget, or never learn, especially those who teach and those who write wise manuscripts. Their wives could leave some writings for posterity that would be worth reading!"

Hippocrates laughed. "I'll bring you my reed pens and ink and all the papyrus you can use."

She smiled knowingly and changed the subject. "I never ask about patients, but I wish I knew why Olympias came to see you yesterday. I never liked that woman. It seems to me she keeps strange company with that enormous boxer Buto."

Hippocrates shook his head and turned to go. At that moment the gates of the enclosure screeched as they swung wide to admit a messenger from the Archon Timon. He rode in on a mule and, dismounting, presented a small scroll to Hippocrates.

While he read it, Praxithea waited, smoothing the braids coiled like a gray crown about her head.

"Tell the Archon," Hippocrates said to the messenger, "that I will come when my surgery is finished."

Then he turned to Praxithea with a smile. "I am invited by the Archon Timon to come to his villa before midday today, and the physician Euryphon begs me, on his own behalf, to be present at the ceremony of betrothal between Daphne and Cleomedes. He calls me his asclepiad kinsman."

Praxithea nodded. "That's why Olympias came to see you yesterday. But did you not tell me that Daphne has asked to meet her future husband again before her father closes the marriage contract?"

"Yes. Her father seems to have promised her that, and further, that he will not force marriage on her."

"I don't think, Hippocrates, that the strange anatomical description you gave me of Daphne during dinner yesterday quite did her justice — 'muscular,' and 'normally developed' — dreadful description! You don't deserve ever to have a good wife. Nevertheless, it did make me realize that I had seen her in the afternoon."

"Where did you see her?"

"I walked out to the temple of Apollo the Physician. I prayed to the god that he would show me how to find a wife for my son. And while I waited there, a lovely young woman (I feel sure it was Daphne) came into the temple and stood looking up at the god. As she turned away she smiled at me. There are things in this world that men will never understand."

Hippocrates looked at his mother speculatively. "Do you think men ever have ideas that are not prompted by a woman?"

"Rarely," she replied with a smile.

When Hippocrates climbed the steps of Timon's terrace, he found the fathers of the intended bride and bridegroom engrossed in conversation. They welcomed him with great warmth. The stocky little Archon had been telling his guest the history of the villa; now he pointed away toward the cypress grove.

"You see where that pathway comes out of the forest? Originally it led from Apollo's temple to an old ruin on this terrace. I used to hunt here often as a young man and I knew it well. We used to water the horses here at this spring. Sometimes we tethered them and went on foot into the forest. In those days, there were wild boar here.

"After I was married I bought this site on the edge of the wood and cut enough of these trees to build the villa. It was an enormous task. Look at that wall of cypresses, the finest trees in the Doric East. It took me two years to cut and to build. But by the time Cleomedes was able to toddle about, we moved here. Then, after Penelope was born, we cut more trees to free the terrace and our view of the sea."

They stood for a moment admiring the view of the slopes below and the islands on the horizon; then Timon said, "But let us join my wife. She is waiting yonder."

Olympias and Penelope were standing on a grassy square at the end of the terrace. Olympias, haughty and handsome in an orange robe, stood almost as tall as her daughter, for she was wearing new sandals with cork soles that raised her more than a hand-breadth, after the latest Athenian style.

As the men started across the terrace, Euryphon turned to Hippocrates. His long thin face lit up in one of his rare smiles. "I'm glad you have come here today. When Daphne becomes a Coan, you and I will see each other more often, no doubt."

"Indeed, you will both be welcome here always," put in Timon, and Hippocrates smiled his response.

Olympias watched the three men approach along the terrace. Her husband had begun to talk with all the gestures of a public orator. Euryphon listened thoughtfully, his narrow shoulders stooped from his many years of study. Hippocrates walked along with head tipped to one side as though he were not listening at all, but watching her. What, she wondered, would he think of Cleomedes? Would she be able to control her boy after all, through his physician?

She stepped forward. "*Chairete*, rejoice." Her voice was sonorous and her bracelets tinkled as she addressed each in turn. "*Chaire*," each replied. None bowed. Bowing suggested the manners of the Persian monarchy, and these were the days of Greek democracy. Nor did they shake hands, since that was reserved for solemn farewells or the swearing of a formal oath.

Penelope came forward shyly and Hippocrates saw that she had coiled her long black braids about her head. He noted the deep hollows in her cheeks, but her face lit up when she smiled at him.

"My mother said I could wait to greet you. But now I must leave you and begin the treatments. I'm going to your *palaestra*." She laughed softly as she left them, a tall, gaunt, winsome child, dressed all in white, like a bud about to open.

"Daphne is not here yet," Olympias said. "Dress and hair and a hundred other things call for attention on a day like this. And Cleomedes is still working hard with his trainer. It is just as well. This is the time when, by old custom, we should tell of the bridegroom's strength and the bride's beauty."

"Let me finish," Timon said, "in just a word what I was saying to Euryphon and Hippocrates as we came along. This is a very important matter." He spoke with pompous emphasis. "The old city of Astypalaea, at the other end of our island, has a poor harbor. It was good enough in the days when Astypalaea sent her ships to the siege of Troy. But times have changed. Ships are bigger and more dangerous now. With the modern ram at the bow, a ship can no longer be beached. It must be anchored in a deep harbor. The Persians have learned at last how to go to sea. They will attack us again — I'm sure of that. And we must depend upon the ships of the cities of the Delian League to protect us — but we must have strong harbors. The best proof that we were right to build up the defenses of this harbor here on the eastern end of the island is the fact that Athens now prefers to deal with me here in Meropis rather than with Astypalaea. You have seen the Athenian tablet of Pentelic marble that they sent here? I had it set up in our Agora. It states the rules for the tribute that we must pay to the League of Delos. That payment is the tax for the whole of the island, except that there is a small tribute still levied directly on the mountain city of Pelea in the center of our island."

Euryphon nodded. "And Meropis is growing fast as the result."

"Exactly. It is just as I predicted when they made me First Archon. But I have other plans too." He pointed up the mountainside. "I plan to bring the sparkling waters of the great Vorina fountain all the way to the city."

The two men expressed surprise.

"Yes, yes," he continued. "It can be done, with hollow pipes of terra cotta."

"My husband," Olympias said, "has given his life for the good of the Island of Cos. His success has been astonishing. He never finds time to spend with his son, however, though he can always find time for his daughter."

"Don't flatter me, my dear. You see" — Timon turned to the men — "there is one way at least in which I resemble the Chief Citizen of Athens. Pericles and I have each of us discovered a charming woman. But I did better than he did. I found my Olympias when I was free and married her, but he came upon his Aspasia after he was married to another."

Euryphon smiled. "Many say that Aspasia discovered Pericles, that she was the hunter and he the quarry."

"Wait." The mellow voice of Olympias broke in. "Don't waste your breath on Aspasia — there are enough men in Athens to do that — nor on me, for Daphne has come to Cos and I feel the cold shadow of an eclipse. We are gathered here to hymn the virtues of the young woman our Cleomedes has chosen. And if any breath remains, let us breathe the praises of Cleomedes himself."

"There you are," said Timon. "She has said what I would say, and said it in the words of Homer. But I may tell you, Euryphon, that my son has let us know more than once that Daphne has no equal in all the world for beauty and grace."

He laughed. "And who should be a better judge of women than my son? He even says that when he stood outside your house, Euryphon, he recognized her voice chanting the hymns from Antigone."

Euryphon nodded. "That is quite possible. Perhaps this is the moment for me to boast of my daughter. She does love music and the dance, and she reads Aeschylus and Sophocles. She knows the poets, especially Sappho. We have in our family collection at Cnidus the scrolls of the Athenian Tragedies, and I purchase every year copies of the new plays, those that win the prizes and even those that do not.

At Daphne's request I have had copied all the poems of Sappho that we could find. She often reads to me of an evening, and sometimes plays the flute as well as the lyre. You see, after my wife died Daphne took her mother's place in the household. She did it well. I have come to lean on her and I shall be lonely without her.

"Other members of my family tell me I depend on her too much — too much for her own good, so I am ready and anxious that she should marry now. And what greater fortune could come to her than to marry the son of the First Archon of Cos? But knowing my daughter as I do, I know she cannot be forced. At least I hesitate to try it. You remember what happened to the first Daphne when Apollo pursued too hotly. She became a laurel tree, and not even Apollo could change that unresponsive tree back to the nymph of his desire."

"Have no fear," Olympias said. "I know what women are. If she will only look twice at my Cleomedes she will long to go to bed with him."

"*Our* Cleomedes," Timon objected. "I always say he is more like my side of the family than yours. He is like my grandfather, the one who threw the discus in the Olympic sports."

Olympias turned away and looked at Hippocrates with the faintest of smiles. Why, Hippocrates wondered, had this woman told him that Cleomedes might not be Timon's son? Was it only in support of her fear that the son might inherit madness? A strange woman indeed.

"Here is my daughter now," Euryphon said.

Daphne was coming swiftly toward them. She wore no cloak, and her thin chiton fluttered in the wind. When the company turned toward her, she was embarrassed and ran the rest of the way to her father's side, like a bird that glides from full flight to some chosen perch on the bough of a tree.

She wore a narrow crown of gold around her head, but it was almost lost beneath the tumbled pile of black curls. Except for that crown of gold and the golden balls that fastened the straps of the tunic over her graceful shoulders, she wore no ornament. The tunic was blue, light blue, and her eyes, Hippocrates thought, must really be blue too, or perhaps they were as changeable as the sea.

There was no paint on her nails or face, and her sandals were of the simple sort that dancers wore. Thinking of the contrast, Hippocrates glanced back at Olympias. The older woman caught the glance and guessed its meaning.

"Well, Daphne," Olympias said, "we have been waiting for you. Surely that toilet could not have taken you very long. I had such a time in your absence to keep the men from talking of Aspasia."

"That reminds me!" Timon cried. "I forgot to tell you the news. I learned from the barber this morning that Aspasia is now being tried for 'impiety' before the Council of Athens. Impiety!" He laughed. "Aspasia, the most notable of the great company of *hetairai*, the companions of men in mind and body. I have heard her called many things — a philosopher, a wit, a beauty, a courtesan — but no one to my knowledge has interested himself in whether or not she believes in the gods."

"Impiety," Hippocrates interjected, "is the most serious charge that can be brought against an Athenian, man or woman. It is reserved for those they wish to banish or destroy, regardless of what they have done! Pericles is a great orator, but he will need all his skill to save her. She is a very clever woman and must have helped him greatly. I have heard Socrates speak well of her wit."

Daphne had forgotten her embarrassment in the interest of this subject. "I think it is only because Aspasia is wittier and cleverer than most men, and because she fails to hide that superiority, that they want to be rid of her. It is not because she is unmarried. We heard her speak at a public meeting, my father and I, when we were in Athens. She was urging women to come out of their homes, to hear lectures and discussions and to talk as men do. We Dorian women in these cities in the East live a better life here, and in Miletus too, where Aspasia was born. Life for respectable women must be very dull in Athens."

"Daphne," Olympias said coldly. "You speak like Artemisia of Halicarnassus. She led the ships of Cos into battle, and she had as much wit and bravery as any man. But after all, she was a queen. Such sentiments come strangely from the lips of an inexperienced girl who is about to be married."

Daphne flushed and turned away.

Someone was running toward them along the colonnade and Olympias went on: "Here comes your future husband, Daphne. Is he not handsome? As handsome as Apollo himself? He'll keep you in the home."

Cleomedes stopped when he reached the company and raised his hand in greeting. In spite of a swollen nose and a puffy eye, he was handsome. He was bare to the waist and bronzed by the sun. His hair was cut short, as was the fashion among athletes.

"*Chairete!*" he exclaimed to all. But his eyes turned at once to Daphne, who drew close to her father and murmured to him. The young boxer looked around slowly after the manner of a little child. Then, since no one spoke, he laughed a little with embarrassment.

"What a workout old Buto and I had this morning — five matches as hard as we could go. He was more tired than I was."

He touched his swollen nose and smiled at his mother. "You should see Buto. I gave him worse than he gave me. He says my footing is better now. Here he comes, look at him."

Buto, the trainer of boxers, was shuffling swiftly toward them along the colonnade, an enormous grin on his misshapen and swollen face. Cleomedes began to leap from side to side in quick, lithe movements. He raised his powerful bare arms and hunched his shoulders, lunging at a phantom opponent. Then he stopped suddenly and turned toward Daphne.

She saw the silky black hair on his upper lip and chin, and his small beautiful black eyes — unthinking eyes, she thought, like those of a bull.

Timon interposed now, with easy speech: "Cleomedes, this is Hippocrates the asclepiad. Hippocrates was once a wrestler and won the crown in the boys' competition at Triopion. There was much talk about you, Hippocrates, at that time. The people of Cos wanted to send you to the Olympic games as a boy competitor. You had the strength and spirit, and the judges at Triopion thought you might even win the olive wreath of Olympia. But alas, your father chose instead to start you on your training as an asclepiad. Do you regret now that you could not go to Olympia?"

Cleomedes and Buto were listening with surprised attention.

"No," Hippocrates replied quietly. "I learned much about medicine in those early years, and life is all too short. My father was right. No slave can serve two masters, and Medicine is a very jealous master.

"But, sometimes" — he turned to look with admiration at Cleomedes' magnificent body — "sometimes I might envy you, Cleomedes, even now. There are things that you never quite forget. And when the wind blows over the sea, as it does today, or I smell the oil and the sand in the *palaestra*, I must confess that I long to wrestle and to run again."

He held up his arms in a quick gesture that recalled the posture of a wrestler about to engage. Then he laughed apologetically and said, "Nonsense, ancient nonsense! But memories go with you through life, and even Socrates said once that it is a disgrace 'to grow old without ever seeing the beauty and strength of which the body is capable.' "

"Oh, you might get into shape again," Cleomedes said. "But you wouldn't go very far at your age, even if you ever had a chance."

"I should tell you, Cleomedes," Timon interjected, "that Hippocrates wanted to try out for the Pentathlon at Olympia."

"What could you do more than to wrestle?" It was Buto's grating voice that asked the question.

"I threw the discus, and ran."

Buto nodded his head approvingly. "You've a good build for the Pentathlon — good neck, well-muscled, not too heavy anywhere. You should have tried it."

Euryphon cleared his throat and passed a hand over his bald head.

"Your conversation calls to mind," he said, "something I have long considered — how to define the greatest good in life. What is good to Buto is not necessarily good to all men. But nevertheless, I think that most Greeks who, as boy or man, could hope to win the victor's crown in the Olympic Games would say, 'Behold! This is the best that life can offer.' And most physicians who had the opportunity would choose a life of luxury in the courts of Macedonia or Persia rather than the humble role of an asclepiad in the Island of Cos. But Hippocrates, who might have had either of these things has turned away from both. It all depends on how you define the greatest good. That definition makes you what you are. It shapes the inner urge that drives you on through life."

Hippocrates had listened with a smile. "Socrates," he said, "could hardly have phrased that thought better."

"I have lived with asclepiads all my life," Daphne remarked quietly. "Pity, it seems to me, is the quality that most distinguishes physicians from other men. The choice that Hippocrates made seems natural enough if he is a true asclepiad. I love the lines from Aeschylus:

> 'Him who pitieth suffering man, Zeus pitieth,
> and his ways are sweet on earth.' "

Olympias turned to Euryphon. "Your daughter might have gone to school under Aspasia herself while she was in Athens. The *hetairai*, I understand, are taught to quote from the poets so that they may dazzle men. I am glad to see that Daphne has not dyed her hair yellow, not yet —"

"Daphne does not need to dye her hair." Cleomedes interrupted. "She could not look more beautiful."

"Well said, my son!" cried Timon.

Cleomedes was standing close to Daphne now. "Since I've been training in Triopion," he said to her shyly, "I've sometimes come to Cnidus in the evening to watch you come out of your house, and I've followed you."

She looked at him. "Yes, I know. But it is a long walk for you to come from Triopion to Cnidus."

"No," he said, "it doesn't seem long."

He came closer, but Daphne shrank away from him. Then, standing straight and strong before her, he said, "Come with me," and walked away resolutely into the shadows of the cypress grove.

Daphne did not move. She only pressed more closely against her father's side. But her father spoke to her in a low tone, and reluctantly she followed Cleomedes, her head held high. She disappeared from sight along the path that entered the cypress wood, her chiton fluttering, it seemed to Hippocrates, like the wings of a butterfly struggling to escape.

The company moved to the inner court to have dried fruits and wine. But after a time Hippocrates excused himself and, returning to the terrace, sauntered back along the portico lost in thought. As he reached the grassy square at the end of the terrace, Daphne came running to him. Hippocrates looked up in surprise.

"I came to ask you to wait here," she said. "My father will join you. He has something to give you. I hope you will like it." She looked up at him with a quizzical smile. "I have seen you in Triopion — no, not you, but the statue of you that the Coans placed there. It is with statues of the other athletes in the temple of Apollo. When I go to Triopion again I shall examine it more carefully to see how much you have changed."

Hippocrates smiled, and she continued: "I like boys so much better than men. How many years ago did you say it was when you won the boys' wrestling crown?"

"Eleven long years," Hippocrates replied. She turned her face away from him.

"Does it seem long?" Then, without waiting for a reply, she added: "I wish I could grow old quickly, very quickly."

"You will grow old quickly enough after you are married and have children. But where is Cleomedes? I thought you went for a walk with him."

"I did, but — I ran away again. Why should a woman be married when she would rather not?" Again she did not wait for his reply. "Are you ever going to be married?"

"Well, I don't know. I've never had much time to think about marriage."

"I have," she said, and fell silent.

Hippocrates looked away over the sea to the mountains of Caria while Daphne continued to examine him calmly, as though he were a new and interesting sort of man.

"Hippocrates." Euryphon was coming toward them, followed by

Timon. "I have something I want to give you." Euryphon held two large scrolls in his hands.

"I had planned to give you these later — to make this gift as master of the Cnidian school of medicine to the master of the Coan school in his own *iatreion*, but I have decided to do it here instead."

Olympias had joined them and stood listening. Euryphon turned to Timon and continued:

"Soon we will go before the altar of Zeus and make the marriage contract between you and me, between your family and mine."

He glanced at Daphne. She turned a little pale and did not look at her father.

"When my daughter marries your son I have little or nothing to give her as a dowry. You know that already. What money I have been able to save as a physician I have spent on medical writings. I have enlarged the great collection of manuscripts which my predecessors left in the teaching center of Cnidus. I have created a separate manuscript house in Cnidus and placed all the writings there so that they may be used by teachers and disciples alike. This is our Cnidian treasure.

"In the past, there have been differences of opinion and rivalries between the asclepiads in our ancient school and the asclepiads of Cos. But Daphne, my only child, is about to become a Coan herself. So I want to do something for Cos."

He turned to Hippocrates and spoke to him with obvious sincerity.

"You are my kinsman — distant, but my kinsman nonetheless. These scrolls that I bring you here are gifts from Cnidus to Cos, from the Cnidian asclepiads to the Coan asclepiads. This is also an expression of our pleasure at your return from Macedonia. You have made a great name for yourself, young as you are, and we pay you tribute."

He handed one of the scrolls to Hippocrates. "This one might be called the Cnidian Sentences. I have selected opinions and precepts from many of the older physicians and copied them. But I have summarized too, and expressed our general attitudes as seemed good to me. This second scroll contains my own previous writings and addresses on the diseases of women. You will find in it a description of the movements of the womb about which I spoke yesterday."

Hippocrates, surprised and deeply moved, accepted both scrolls. They represented, he knew, a great deal of work. It was quite without precedent that one scholar should make such a gift to another. He thanked Euryphon, and added: "During my travels throughout the world I heard the praises of the asclepiads of Cnidus sung everywhere. I realize that in these scrolls I shall discover treasures drawn from the minds of many men. We will guard these scrolls. We will copy them and they will add to your fame, Euryphon, as long as men remember the asclepiads of Greece."

"Speaking for the Island of Cos," Timon exclaimed, "I thank you too." He added some fine phrases about medicine and the approaching marriage. Then he said he would prepare the altar of Zeus and, when all was in readiness, would send a servant to call the marriage company together.

"Perhaps," Olympias said, "Daphne would like to walk with Cleomedes now."

"Not now," Daphne said emphatically.

"You are a stubborn child," Olympias exclaimed, her face flushing with sudden anger. "You will have to learn to mend your ways when you come to live in this house."

"Do you mean," Daphne asked with cold emphasis, "that I will be subject to your command as Penelope has been?"

Olympias was about to reply, but Timon silenced her with a gesture. "Not at all," he said. "Cleomedes will be your only master."

Olympias regained her self-control quickly. "Well, Daphne," she said, "come and walk with me. We may as well leave these physicians to talk of the things they love most — papyrus scrolls and fame and the patients who did not die."

"Please let me do that another time." Daphne said. "I must talk with my father now."

Father and daughter walked off together. After the marriage company had gathered in the court, where a fire was burning on the altar of Zeus, Timon sent a servant to summon them. As they approached, Hippocrates noted that Daphne seemed pale and her father looked stern. He held up his hand.

"Timon, I have something to say to you."

He spoke gravely and with dignity, while Daphne stood close to him: "It is my firm desire to see my daughter married to your son. But as you know, I have pledged myself not to force her in this matter. She has not set her fancy on any man as yet, but she begs for a longer time before the final step. Cleomedes will not be free to marry anyway until after the Festival of the Triopian Apollo. Daphne and I ask you, therefore, to postpone the making of this marriage contract, and to let us reconsider it after the Festival."

Olympias allowed an angry exclamation to escape her lips, and would have spoken, but Timon held up his hand for silence. An explosive curse came from Buto. Timon looked at him in astonishment, and the boxer walked off a little way to stand with his back turned. Cleomedes himself said nothing. He only looked at Daphne.

After a pause, Timon spoke quietly. "Let it be as you wish. Cleomedes will have an added prize to win in this boxing contest."

Then Cleomedes walked over to Euryphon and said steadily, "After the games, will you give my father the answer?"

"Yes," Euryphon replied. "After the games."

Buto grunted and turned around suddenly. "Now, Cleomedes, you can get down to work and forget her for a while."

"Stay out of this, will you?" Cleomedes exclaimed in sudden anger.

Hippocrates started to take his leave, but at that moment a messenger entered the court and spoke to Timon, and Timon called to Hippocrates to wait. Then he announced, with an air of excited importance, that a trireme from Macedonia had cast anchor in the harbor of Cos Meropis. Aboard the ship was Empedocles, who begged to know where he might visit Hippocrates!

"He comes to you as a patient! You have indeed brought fame to this island, Hippocrates. I shall send a messenger with fast-walking mules to bring him here immediately — Empedocles the Magnificent! I saw him once at the Olympic Games. He read his poetry there, standing at the top of the steps before the Temple of Zeus. Later, when he took his seat in the stadium, all the people applauded him. Not since Themistocles came to the games after his

victory at Salamis had anyone received so great an ovation." Timon
paused, and then asked, "Have I your permission to bring him here
at once?"

Hippocrates shook his head and smiled at Timon. "No, this is evidently a medical matter. I will return home and will see him in the
iatreion if he cares to come."

"You realize, don't you," Timon protested, "that he was an important political figure in the island of Sicily before he was banished
from his native city of Acragas? It is quite proper for him to visit
me in my villa, since after all I am the First Archon of Cos. He is
a statesman as well as a physician, a philosopher and a poet."

"Philosopher, yes," Hippocrates said, with a little show of impatience, "but medicine would be better off if he left it alone. I will
grant you that he expresses his philosophical thinking in the most
beautiful poetry. No. I will return home and see him there."

"Timon," Olympias broke in. "Please urge Hippocrates to stay
here long enough to talk with Cleomedes before he returns home.
Surely Empedocles can wait a little while."

Hippocrates looked at her for a moment. Then he turned to
Cleomedes.

"Perhaps you would like to walk along with me a little way? I
would be glad to talk with you about the Triopian games."

Cleomedes regarded him with slow surprise. But Olympias said
quickly, "Yes, Cleomedes, go with him."

Buto added, "Go ahead, Cleomedes."

Cleomedes shrugged his powerful shoulders and threw out his
hands. "Oh well, I'll walk with this old wrestler. I'll go as far as the
great wall, then I'll run back all the way. It's a good eight stadia
from here, eh, Buto?" He nudged his trainer and turned his beautiful bronzed body about for Daphne to see. But at that moment she
was smiling at Hippocrates.

CHAPTER SEVEN

Empedocles the Magnificent

~~~~~~

When Hippocrates reached the enclosure, it was the hour for the gymnastic class, and over the *palaestra* wall he heard the familiar piping of a flute and the singsong sound of his brother's voice:

"Up and down, over and back, up and down, over and back." Through the half-open door he could see naked bodies, sweating faces, swinging arms and legs glistening in the sun, row after row of men, old and young.

Sosander caught sight of him and came lumbering out, dressed only in a short kilt. He wiped the sweat from his forehead with the back of his hand and looked at his younger brother with affection.

"You know that you have a distinguished visitor?"

"Yes, I've been told so. Is he here already?"

"Yes. Podalirius is with him, but I fancy he finds it difficult to pacify the great man."

"Why has Empedocles come here?" Hippocrates asked.

"I don't know. He wouldn't talk to me. But I watched him, and I should say that he is suffering from backache, although he tried to move as though he were young and healthy. Even the greatest of men, unless they die young, must some day stoop to an aching back!"

In the courtyard outside his consulting room, Hippocrates found two handsome slaves, elegantly dressed. They were of equal height and had the yellow-gold hair of the people from the north. He looked at them with interest.

"Are you twins — identical twins?"

"Yes."

"Your master is inside?" They bowed together, an identical bow, with the pride of those who know they serve the great.

Hippocrates' consulting room was large, and was lighted by a high window as well as by the door. In his own chair, he found a man sitting rigidly erect. He had a large head with a high forehead. His hair and pointed beard were white but carefully trimmed, his face strong and handsome. He held up a hand in greeting, but he did not rise. He wore an enormous purple sapphire ring on his thumb; the cloak on his shoulders was of the same color.

Podalirius was standing beside him. "Empedocles has come to consult you," he said, with a note of irritation. "He does not wish to discuss his affairs with me. He has tried all the chairs and finds none to suit him, not even yours, in which he is sitting now."

Podalirius left the room abruptly. Empedocles waited until the heavy door curtains had closed before he spoke.

"Do you know who I am?"

"Yes," Hippocrates replied. "You are the son of Meton of the city of Acragas on the Island of Sicily, grandson of the Empedocles who won the chariot race in the Seventy-first Olympiad. Twice your native city has offered you the crown and would have made you king. Twice you refused the crown. What more would you have me know?"

Empedocles leaned forward, but as he did so, he stifled a groan. "Forgive me for not rising at your entrance. I am having a severe attack of pain and I did not care to make a confidant of your assistant. Oh, o-o-oh!" he exclaimed. "It is my back and my leg." His face was drawn with pain and he gripped his thigh.

"I have cured others," he panted, "but I cannot cure myself."

Sympathy showed in Hippocrates' eyes and he spoke quietly, "Do you want to consult a man as young as I?"

"Yes, though you are even younger than I expected. I must put my cure in your hands. I have no choice."

Hippocrates smiled faintly, and drawing up the bench, he sat across the table from Empedocles. "Tell me, then, what is your complaint?"

"There is a discord," Empedocles replied, "a strife between the elements within my body. You have but to bring these four basic elements that are in me, even as they are in all the universe, into harmony and you will cure me. Then I shall leave Cos singing your praises among the Greeks in every city of the civilized world." He stretched out his hand and the purple sapphire flashed. "Beyond that I shall tell the story in strange lands where men live who have never heard the name of Homer, nor listened to his harmonies, if men they may be called."

Hippocrates waited, knowing that an ailing physician is some-times the most difficult of all patients, and that the control of ques-tion and answer in any interview is an art in itself. Every experi-enced physician discovers that it is only the very young who come to him simply. Others bring their mistrusts and theories with them, and thus strive, unwittingly, to lead him away from what may be the simple truth.

Hippocrates leaned back and shook his head slowly. "Here in my *iatreion* you are not Empedocles the philosopher and poet. You are not a physician nor a god, not even a hero. You are a man in pain, asking for help."

He picked up a reed pen, opened the inkpot and pulled a small sheet of papyrus toward him. "I am not interested in your hypoth-eses, not now. Talk to me as a little child. If you will do that, I will try to help you. Not otherwise.

"Now! Let me ask the questions. Where does it hurt? When did it begin? What were you doing when you first felt it? What move-ment makes the pain worse?"

Empedocles heaved a sigh. "Very well, I am a boy again."

Hippocrates worked at his clinical problem with concentration, making occasional short notes. During the physical examination Empedocles began to talk again, but his examiner was stern and just a little angry, so he subsided and the examination was completed in silence.

At last Hippocrates laid down his pen and smiled. "Now you may speak."

Empedocles began as though flood gates had been opened. "I should have told you that the color on my cheeks is not natural. For over a month I have used pigments such as women apply when age has stolen beauty away."

"Yes, I recognized that as I entered the room."

"One thing more," Empedocles continued. "I am thin, thinner than my wont."

"Yes," Hippocrates said gently, "I know. The skin of your abdomen is relaxed and wrinkled, like a half-empty wineskin. Your loss of weight must have taken place very rapidly since the onset of winter. The evidence is all too plain."

Empedocles nodded and Hippocrates continued. "Let me describe the future for you as clearly as I can, so that you will not reproach me in days to come or say that I was ignorant of your condition. You have pain in back and leg. You find comfort only when you sit erect or stand carefully. There is no trouble that I can discover in the leg itself.

"My conclusion is that you have a malignant disease of the spine. I can feel a lump low down, and the muscles of your back are in constant spasm.

"Now, it is possible that we can cure this disease for you by hot baths, the application of mud, skilled massage, and by extension of the spine on a bed which we shall build for you from an oak plank. My brother Sosander is expert in such matters. It might be that our treatment will succeed. I urge you to live in the light of that hope. In any case, I am sure we can help the pain. But if this disease is too malignant to yield to such treatment, then, Empedocles, there can be only one outcome."

The two men looked at each other. "You believe I will probably die?"

"Yes."

Empedocles' face had turned gray around the artificial color on his cheeks.

"How long?"

Hippocrates threw out his arms. "The gods know. Four months, perhaps."

Empedocles made a little moan and turned away. "It is as I feared. Thank you."

His voice sounded queer and high. Silence followed. Finally Hippocrates said gently, "You must rest now, and you may want to bathe. Following that, I hope you will do me the honor of dining with me, and after dinner you will join me, I hope, in a short symposium with my assistants. Later we will discuss your treatment when we meet as usual in the garden. Treatment will bring you great relief, whatever the outcome — I'm sure of that."

Empedocles looked down at the folds of skin that hung pitifully on his wasted paunch. Then he rose slowly and drew himself up as straight as his back permitted, and clapped his hands to summon his slaves.

Hippocrates left the room while the twin slaves entered and began to dress him. They went about their task with swift, sure movements. A soft woven chiton was drawn over the master's head and a jeweled girdle fastened in place. His white hair and beard were combed carefully and perfume was blown on the pointed beard. At last a small bronze mirror was produced. He looked and nodded, and so, at last, the purple mantle was placed on his shoulders and the slaves withdrew.

When Hippocrates returned, Empedocles was sitting on the bench. He looked up and said solemnly:

"No man outside your circle must know that I have suffered pain or weakness. If I am to leave this body, it must be with dignity. My followers are many. Let no man say he saw me in defeat. If, in the end, you cannot cure me, I will ask you to help me quickly out of this life. If Empedocles is to become no more than a memory, let it be a noble memory."

Hippocrates slipped his hands under the old man's shoulders and helped him ever so gently to his feet. Empedocles took his arm and they walked slowly across the square and into the house. There Hippocrates urged the patient to lie down and rest on his own bed. There was a rather weak protest at first, but finally Empedocles heaved a sigh and obeyed.

The two men had dinner alone, although Hippocrates' mother Praxithea came and went, helping the servant and frequently stopping to talk. When they had finished, the men went out into the garden while the central courtyard of the house was prepared for the symposium to follow. A single tall palm tree grew in the center of the court, on which the rooms of two floors opened. The court was of such a size that when couches were placed around the four walls, each with a little stool for a wine glass, it was ready to accommodate the ten asclepiads and Empedocles, with only one man to a couch. Praxithea had a table placed in the center of the court beside the trunk of the tree, and on it a skin of Coan wine, a decanter of water, goblets, and a large black bowl, beautifully decorated in red with figures of the heroes of Troy.

When Praxithea sent out word that all was ready, the guests came in and Hippocrates assumed the role of symposiarch, pouring wine into the large bowl and diluting it with water until he considered that the strength was suited to the level of conversation desired.

" 'Wine is wont to show the mind of man,' " he quoted as they took their places, and Dexippus, as the youngest asclepiad, handed a brimming goblet to each man, beginning with Empedocles and circling to the right according to long-established rule. They laughed and talked.

Empedocles was brilliant and entertaining, while Sosander and Hippocrates vied with each other in carrying the conversation to many topics and to cities and people all around the Greek world. Empedocles sat upright on the edge of his couch, smiling a little ruefully at those who lay at ease, half reclining on the pillowed benches.

Sosander spoke words of praise and welcome to Empedocles, who made a graceful reply. Then Podalirius whispered in the ear of Dexippus, who left the room and returned in a moment with dark green laurel branches. He wove the leaves into a shining circlet and placed it reverently on Empedocles' head. Then Podalirius, who had been so stern with Empedocles on his arrival, rose to his great height and came to stand beside him. He touched the wreath with a shy smile. "Empedocles, this wreath is well deserved because of your great merit in a brilliant life and your great courage."

Empedocles was silent for a moment, but his handsome old face betrayed his pleasure, and his white beard tipped upward even higher than before.

"A wreath!" he exclaimed. "Yes, it suits me better than a crown. The gods wear wreaths. When I enter strange cities men follow me, expecting miracles. I delight in melodious phrases and in the echoes of my own eloquence. Perhaps that may sound strange. But I am not as other men. I feel within my breast the stirring of strange memories that tell me I was once a god, and will be so again. I sleep little and I think deeply. Poems come to me that I must give to men, and thoughts of the unending rivalry between love and strife all through the universe."

Hippocrates had listened, smiling and stroking his black beard.

"Empedocles," he said, "men do well to call you the Magnificent, for so you are in your vision of the world and your perception of beauty. But you have wandered far away from medicine. Once you were a physician, the most brilliant pupil of that great master Alcmaeon. You made hypotheses of the uses of the heart in the body, and of other body processes. But you could not wait by the bedside to prove your suppositions right or wrong. Instead, you looked beyond man's body to the universe, beyond his life here to his life hereafter, and beyond the mind of man to the mind of God.

"From the valleys where other men live and work, you climbed the slopes of Mount Parnassus where the Muses have their home. You are a shepherd on that mountainside. Your sheep are thoughts and lovely phrases. You open the door of the fold and lead them out to the high pastures, not calling them back at night. They may be no more than dreams, for all you know. You are content when you see that your sheep have beauty and bear on their backs the splash of purple that marks them yours in the sight of men."

The asclepiads stirred and exchanged glances.

"Splendid!" Empedocles exclaimed. "You are a poet, Hippocrates."

"No, I am not that, though I studied rhetoric under Gorgias, your

brilliant pupil. I learned to admire your poetry and I think I learned
to understand your language."

Empedocles laughed. "I can speak the language of a little boy
too, and I learned today how to wait until I am spoken to. That was
the most difficult task of all, but you will admit that I succeeded."

Hippocrates nodded and they both laughed. Then Empedocles
continued: "I can play all roles:

> *'For I have been ere now*
> *A boy and a girl,*
> *A bush and a bird*
> *And a dumb fish in the sea.'*

"That verse was in one of my poems. Sometimes I call my sheep
back, you see."

"Yes," Sosander said, "I know that poem of yours, and many of
your other poems. While I was in Thrace I heard men quoting your
words almost as often as those of the immortal Homer. They considered you a poet rather than a physician, and sometimes a philosopher. What do you say of yourself?"

Empedocles looked through his shaggy white eyebrows at the
listening asclepiads, and there was a light in his eye. One man might
think that light prophetic; another the spark of madness.

"What am I? I am one who has no title. There is some truth in the
picture that Hippocrates painted with his skillful brush. But much is
missing too. I have strayed far, it is true, from the bedside of the sick
to live on the slopes of Mount Parnassus. There I hear the harmonies of the Muses. From there I look down into the valleys of life.
From there I see more than common men can see. You asclepiads
should remember that dreams may have in them more truth than is
to be found in the objects of a physician's study. I shall tell you of
such a dream presently."

He turned to look at Hippocrates, but the sudden movement
brought from him an involuntary groan. The beard tipped downward
as he bowed his head.

"Now that I suffer I come down into the valley. Save me if you
can. Or, failing that, help me quickly to the next life."

He looked up at the sky, which was turning now to sunset colors. "I am an exiled god doomed to pass from life to life. I am the actor in this tragedy. You are the chorus. My part is finished. Now we come to consultation. Let me hear the chorus chant eternal truth."

He turned then, smiling, and addressed Hippocrates. "Good food, sweet wine, good friends and a symposium never to be forgotten! Thank you — and now, since such a time must have its music, I beg of you to let me hear how well asclepiads pluck the lyre. And I, if you will allow me — I shall reply with a poem while my twin slaves play their flutes."

The symposium had ended with the music, and the physicians crossed the open square and took their usual places beneath the plane tree. Hippocrates called on his brother Sosander to open the discussion, and Empedocles listened.

"I know the meaning of back pain all too well," Sosander said. "It was for that very reason my father sent me, with my crooked back, to Thrace to be treated by Herodicus and to study with him as well. Now, thanks to his gymnastics, I am cured.

"Pain in the back can be treated by strengthening the muscles and producing better body posture. Pain in the back when it is accompanied by pain in the leg as well is best treated by stretching the back in various ways. My preference is to lay the sufferer on a ladder and tie his feet firmly, but with great attention to comfort, to one of the rungs, then to raise the ladder gently and place it against a wall so that he hangs head downward. That is most effective, since the pain in the leg is caused by spine pressure, and stretching the spine relieves that pressure."

Empedocles had been listening uneasily. He now made a gesture of distaste, and Hippocrates intervened quickly. Hippocrates was opposed to many of the well-known doctrines of Empedocles, and he wished to avoid a clash at this time and in this place before his disciples. Empedocles believed in magic. He believed that the sacred disease, which Hippocrates had discussed with his followers only the night before, was the work of a demon; that men breathed through the pores of the skin; that life and health could be understood only in relation to some hypothetical explanation of the whole of nature.

"We know," Hippocrates said, "that Empedocles, who is our guest this evening, is a great philosopher, and we hope that at some other time he will discourse on those things that interest him most. But here, by tradition and by rule, we confine our attention to practical medicine. We aim to aid the healing processes within the body and thus to relieve pain. This we will do for you, Empedocles, when you return to the *palaestra* tomorrow."

"A thousand thoughts come crowding into my breast," Empedocles exclaimed, and placed his hand on his heart. "Here in the blood that surges round this thumping heart of mine, here it is that a man's thoughts arise, not in the brain as you have been taught. Egypt's Secret Book of the Physician, written long, long ago, begins with these words: 'Everywhere he feels his heart because its vessels run to all the limbs.'

"Surely you have seen, before the altar of a god, the cloud of vapor that issues forth with the blood when the god's priest plunges his long knife into the heart of a sacrificial animal? That vapor is the spirit leaving the body. It is starting on its long journey before rebirth in the body of another animal or man. Even the Hebrews, whose holy book has been read to me, have always known that a man thinks with his heart. Where else can our thoughts be, then, but in the blood?"

Hippocrates scowled, and his lips compressed themselves into a straight line. But Empedocles, seeing that a storm was about to break, changed the subject abruptly, with a mischievous twinkle in his eye.

"Let me tell you my story now. This pain began quite severely while I was on a secret journey to my former home in Sicily. For almost a month I suffered and remained in hiding, hoping to be better. Then my enemies discovered my hiding place, and I escaped on a donkey, disguised as an old woman and accompanied only by my twin slaves. I thought if I must die anyway, Mount Aetna would be a suitable place, and I knew my enemies would be waiting for me in the seaports.

"When I reached the top of the peak and looked down into Aetna's

fiery crater, life seemed suddenly sweet to me. I decided to escape
death there if I could, and to go for help to the temple of Asclepius
in Epidaurus. Friends brought me word then that I was being followed up the mountain. So I left my golden sandals and my purple
cloak there on the crater's brim, and I hid myself. My pursuers came
and took back word that I was dead, carrying with them the shoes
and the mantle for evidence.

"So we escaped and took ship to Epidaurus. I went to the temple
to offer a sacrifice and I bought an ox, but it came unwillingly to the
altar. That is a bad omen. The beast's bellowing protest echoed
through the shrine until the priest could bury his long knife in the
flank and the river of blood flowed out across the marble. I gave orders that the whole animal should be laid on the altar of Asclepius.
I took no part away with me. I added a gift of gold to the god as well.
I bowed down before the statue of Asclepius and touched his staff,
and the snake that coils about it,with my hand.

"The Chief Priest said, 'Remain here now and you will be well.'
So I did all that he told me to do. I took treatments and baths. I stood
outside the temple and drank the clear, cold water that gushes from
the marble mouth of the son of Asclepius. But it was all to no purpose.

"I returned to the Chief Priest and he said to me, 'One thing more
you must do. Sleep tonight in the temple portico. Dreams will come
to you and I will tell you the will of the god.'

" 'I will do as you say,' I said to him, 'but first answer this question.
Many men throughout the world who have been cured by some phy-
sician send to you a votive offering of thanks to Asclepius, that
through the hand of the physician the god has restored them to health.
Who are those physicians whose skill leads men to thank the god?
And who is the greatest of living physicians?'

"The priest replied, 'We have just received from Perdiccas, King
of Macedonia, a statue of himself because he was cured by a young
asclepiad. I have heard of him before — his name is Hippocrates,
son of Heracleides, of the family of asclepiads on the island of Cos.
He may be called, I think, the first physician in all Hellas!'

"And so that night I did lie down in the *abaton* of the temple portico, side by side with many others, to sleep the sacred sleep of Asclepius. Most of my companions seemed to sleep, but I could not, and I watched the temple priest make his rounds, stopping to talk with those who had slumbered. A large earth snake followed him, coiling along the terrace after him and being fed from time to time.

"Finally, as light began to edge the east, and Orion slanted toward the horizon, I fell asleep. And I did dream, then, a strange dream.

"In it, I stood on a ledge of rock at the very peak of a mountain, and I knew I was close to heaven. Behind me I could hear the bells of grazing flocks, a lovely harmony of sound that told of the valleys of men.

"Before me, and over a precipice, I looked down into the sea, far, far below. I was terrified and tried to shrink back, but I could not, for I found I was bound with ropes. Then I understood. This was the moment that must come to every man. My own life was behind me; the gods above and death before and below.

"But as I waited there bound and helpless, a man came between me and the precipice. He held a long knife in his hand, like the knife the priest had plunged into the heart of the ox. And the man said to me: 'I am Hippocrates of Cos,' and with that, he cut the ropes that bound me. I felt the side of the knife blade cool and comforting against my leg, and the pain was gone.

"Slowly, delightfully, I wakened. Then I started up, for over my leg, where I dreamt the knife blade lay, the great earth snake was slipping, cool and smooth. The priest was standing a little way off in the shadow of the portico, watching.

"I told him my dream. But he shook his head and went away. Later in the day the Chief Priest sent for me and said, 'It is the will of Asclepius that you should go to Hippocrates for help.'

"So I sent a messenger to Aegae, to the King of Macedonia, and when the messenger returned he told me that you, Hippocrates, had gone back to your home in Cos. But he said that King Perdiccas was about to send his own ship to Cos with a message to you. Further, the king sent word that if I would join the ship in Pyraeus, I might make the last stage of the journey to Cos in it. That is how I came to arrive here in a Macedonian trireme."

Empedocles looked about at the asclepiads mysteriously. "There are others aboard the ship who have purposes of their own in coming here. Fame, among the Greeks, brings some men wealth; sometimes it brings them beauty, happiness. The captain of the trireme has a message for you, Hippocrates. Let someone meet him at the harbor in the morning."

Hippocrates went with his guest as far as the shore of the sea and watched him ride away; a proud slave marched on either side of his donkey.

"There goes the man," he mused, "who would know all things by inspiration — always godlike whether in error or in truth. But he dreads the dark passage that lies before him now, as all men must. The boy within holds out a hand for help, and I, his physician, have so little to give, so much to learn!"

CHAPTER EIGHT

Invitation

〜〜〜〜〜〜〜〜〜〜〜〜〜〜〜〜〜〜〜〜〜〜〜〜〜〜〜〜〜〜

THE NEXT MORNING before dawn Pindar left his lodging and passed through the narrow streets of the sleeping city to the waterfront to meet the messenger from Macedonia. There was light on the horizon and an edge of narrow fire toward the east. All about him, men were moving at the tasks that come with the dawn in such a place. Fishermen were landing with the night's catch and others streaming down to the harbor front prepared for work.

Pindar found a vacant seat at a table near a breakfast booth and sat down before a bowl of barley broth and some barley cakes. He pulled his cloak about him and hunched over the steaming liquid, for the spring morning was cold. The harbor policeman passed the table and Pindar hailed him.

"I am here at the request of my master Hippocrates to meet the captain of the trireme from Macedonia. He's coming ashore early."

"Yes," the man replied. "One of his sailors came ashore last night to tell me that."

The policeman passed on and Pindar blew on his barley broth and sipped the hot stuff. Its smell had carried his thoughts far away to his home in the rich farmland of Boetia. His mother was probably stirring by now, and there would be the fragrance of barley broth in the house.

He recalled how his father's brother, the poet Pindar, used to say he would sell his art to anyone who would pay him well. If this messenger on the trireme was bringing an invitation to Hippocrates to return to Macedonia as court physician, could his master answer no? Pindar shook his head doubtfully. Hippocrates, he knew, loved his art. But what Greek could say no to such a king?

The pillars of the colonnade that crowned the island on the other side of the harbor were edged with lines of light now, and the rising sun touched the tops of the masts of anchored vessels with coppery light which moved down to the rigging and finally the hulls. The fishermen near at hand were busy sorting out the night's catch and selling the fish. More boats were rowing through the water passage into the harbor, in slow procession, their brown sails furled along the yardarms high on each mast.

As the light changed from copper to gold, Pindar could see the Macedonian trireme plainly where she rode at anchor. The still surface of the harbor mirrored a shimmering duplicate of the great ship, with the golden spars and gaily colored hull upside down. The bow porthole was painted to look like a great yellow eye ready to glare defiance at the ships of all the world.

A dory was putting off from the ship's side. It made for the principal pier. The harbor policeman beckoned to him with some excitement, and Pindar walked out on the pier. As the dory came alongside, a vigorous old man with bushy graying beard stepped from it up to the pier. Pindar approached him, thinking this must be the captain, but the man turned back to help the other dory passengers.

In a moment a young woman in a white cloak stepped lightly onto the pier. She glanced about her and then looked expectantly at Pindar. This startled and embarrassed him, for she was tall, blonde, and altogether lovely. While wondering who she might be, he nearly forgot the purpose of his own presence on the pier, until the bearded man looked about again and called out:

"I am the captain of this trireme, messenger of King Perdiccas of Macedonia to Hippocrates of the family of asclepiads."

Pindar then came forward. He greeted them, as he did most things, with an air of dignity, in spite of his awkward height and his dreamy preoccupation.

"Welcome to Cos. I am here to conduct the king's messenger to Hippocrates."

The captain was a blunt man of few words. "I will come with you," he said, "and the others too — Empedocles is coming ashore for treatment. This woman is Thargelia and that is her servingmaid over there. The fancy twin slaves belong to Empedocles."

Pindar greeted them gravely and led them to the beach, where the slaves helped Empedocles mount a donkey. The rest of them walked, following Pindar in single file around the harbor front. Even at this early hour, some people had gathered in the hope of seeing the poet-physician. But it was the blonde Thargelia, walking behind him, who excited the muttered admiration of the onlookers. The company came to the asclepiad enclosure and Pindar pounded on the gate. The hinges screeched and the procession filed in.

Praxithea stood in her doorway and beckoned to them. Her gray hair was drawn, smooth and shining, into a ball at the back of her head, and her robe was fastened at the shoulder with a large silver brooch such as Doric women wore on special occasions. She welcomed them with dignity in the sunlit courtyard of her house and sent a slave to call her son. He was busy in the *iatreion,* dressing a wound with the help of Dexippus. When Hippocrates had seen the procession passing through the gate, an involuntary exclamation had escaped him. But he did not interrupt his work, not even when Praxithea's message arrived.

The patient was a sailor. He had had a severe blow on the shin about two months earlier. At first he had paid little attention to the wound. But finally it had grown hot, swollen and painful, and Hippocrates had lanced the swelling to let out pus. That was a month ago. The incision had relieved the young man's pain, and his fever had disappeared.

He sat on the surgeon's table now and Hippocrates inspected the wound carefully. Foul-smelling gray pus was still pooled in the hollow surface of the shinbone. The edges of the bone around the hollow were bare and white, and the margins of the skin were granular and red.

"This wound is indolent," Hippocrates was saying. "The healing process within the bone is sluggish. However, the body is slowly throwing out the putrid material, as you can see."

He took up a curette from the instrument tray and scraped the bone carefully but firmly. Several loose bone fragments came away. "That is dead bone," he said, and removed each fragment with a spring forceps, held delicately between the fingers and thumb.

"There, Dexippus. Put a clean bandage on his leg now and inspect it every four days for further separation of bone fragments. You can remove them as I have done when they are ready. The natural processes will gradually heal this abscession in the end. We can only help Nature do the work."

"But why does it not heal faster?"

"Yes, why indeed?" Hippocrates replied. "Bone disease is always slow to heal. We will discuss this matter again, you and I."

He dropped the forceps and smiled at the bronzed young sailor.

"The wound is improving. It will need another month, perhaps more, to heal finally. But you can carry on with your work. How do you like your new fishing boat?"

"The boat's a good one, but did you know my wife's just given me another son?"

"Good," Hippocrates said. "That makes three, doesn't it? And the oldest about five, nearly the age that you and I were when we used to go octopus fishing down beside the little pier! Those baby octopuses fried crisp in olive oil!" He threw out his hands. "Nothing has tasted so good since."

Dexippus interrupted, smiling. "Did you forget, Master, that someone is waiting for you?"

Hippocrates nodded. But he paused to look about him as though he thought to say good-by. The walls of the surgery were hung with splints of various types. On the shelves were lines of well-made instruments. There was the basket of white wool for dressings, just where his father had kept it, and the fresh, washed bandages hanging on the line. An old woman was coughing by herself in the corner, waiting for the kind-hearted Pindar.

He walked across to the mirror and passed a comb quickly through his hair and beard. He took his cloak from the hook on which the master's cloak had always hung. As he put it on, he squared his broad shoulders, and Dexippus, watching him go through these routine movements, smiled, for he thought there was in his master's eye a light that was not quite routine.

In the meantime Praxithea had continued to talk dutifully with the captain, standing under the palm tree in the courtyard. Thargelia looked about the courtyard with much interest. Then she approached Empedocles.

"May I ask your advice quickly about an — an embarrassing matter?"

She pulled her white cloak over her throat and they walked across the court into the sunshine.

"I am suddenly frightened of these asclepiads and prefer to ask your guidance. I should have spoken to you about this on shipboard." She hesitated and then shrugged.

"First of all, would the asclepiads carry out an abortion for a woman if she asked it, and if she could pay?"

Empedocles looked at her in astonishment. Then he replied:

"I don't know what the practice is here on the Island of Cos. They would do it in Cnidus, that I know. They do not follow the teaching of the Brotherhood of Pythagoras there. The Pythagoreans will do no abortions when the purpose is only to destroy life of the fetus. But why," he asked in a low voice, "did you not go to a midwife in Macedonia if you desired such a thing?"

"Empedocles!" she said with dignity. "I am talking about my slave Sapphira, who stands in the corner over there."

"Oh! Please forgive me!" Empedocles exclaimed.

"You see," she continued quickly, "although I knew the poor girl might be in trouble, we thought she was all right when we left Macedonia. But during the long sea voyage it became quite evident that the operation must be carried out. I saw a friend of mine die in agony once, a few days after visiting a midwife. Sapphira must have a physician." She was silent a moment.

"You have talked with Hippocrates," she said, changing the subject quickly. "Do you think he will accept the king's invitation?"

Empedocles shook his head. "I don't feel at all sure."

"I may as well tell you," she continued, "that the king told me to use what influence I might have to bring Hippocrates back to his court. I do not know him so very well, and I am frightened now."

"Well, well!" Empedocles exclaimed. "Perhaps I know more than you think. The messenger I sent to King Perdiccas brought me stories of how the most beautiful woman in Macedonia had been commanded to catch Hippocrates and bring him back with her. 'If her charms should fail,' he said, 'she is to be forbidden to return to Macedonia.' Is that true?"

"No," she replied, in a low voice, "at least not quite. I told the king that I would come back with Hippocrates or that I would never return. You see, he . . . you see, I love him."

Empedocles shrugged. "You are the widow of the king's chamberlain, who died not so long ago — but before that?"

She looked at him and her blue eyes blazed with sudden anger.

"I see you know something of my past, but perhaps not enough. The man I called my father found me when I was a few days old in the temple of Aphrodite in Corinth. He brought me up, educated me and trained me far beyond the level of ordinary women, so that I might be hired out as companion to men of wealth. He was as fond of me as he might be of his own daughter, so he postponed the start. But at last he found he must have the money.

"The first man who paid for my company immediately bought me, set me free and married me. Ordinarily, fathers who have daughters on their hands are forced to buy husbands for them with a large dowry. We reversed the process, my foster father and I. My beauty was enough, and the dowry went to him." She made an impatient gesture. "I have been educated in rhetoric and music and other arts. I could have made my own way in the world after my husband died, following the profession for which I was trained. But I did not do it; I could not, after meeting Hippocrates."

"A wily monarch is Perdiccas," Empedocles exclaimed. "He offers love and beauty as well as great wealth to the physician he wants."

"Can you help me," she asked, "or guide me in my mission? How shall I persuade him to return to Macedonia?"

Empedocles laughed. "I have been consulted many times, but never by so lovely a patient, and never one with a problem quite like this. You may succeed. Physicians are only men, after all. But Hippocrates," he added thoughtfully, "is not quite like other men."

He looked at Thargelia with undisguised admiration. "You have beauty and grace and wit. The gods can give you no more. Invoke the aid of Aphrodite, and if she comes 'through middle air,' she'll say to you as she said to Sappho: 'Name thine enemy! for whoso flies thee now shall soon pursue.'"

He looked out through the door of the courtyard. "Here comes the unsuspecting enemy."

Hippocrates was coming through the garden, but slowly, with his eyes on the ground. Any man, young or old, might well be excited by the arrival of a messenger from the King of Macedonia — and he was young enough.

It was the arrival of Thargelia here in Cos that astonished him. Was he pleased or was he dismayed? After all, why should it matter to him? During the long illness of her husband, he had been a frequent visitor to their home. She had made advances to him. Physicians learn to deal with that — but she was a difficult woman to ignore. It was a curious coincidence that she had actually been in his thoughts only yesterday.

As he entered his house he walked toward her without seeming to see the others. She held out both her hands and he took them in his and held them for a moment.

"I'm surprised to see you here," he said. "Welcome to Cos."

She did not speak, and he turned away abruptly to greet the ship's captain, who was standing in the shadow of the palm.

"Greetings," the captain replied. "It isn't often that they trust an old sailor like me with cargo as beautiful as Thargelia and as important as Empedocles. I have a message to you from my king."

"Your ship," Hippocrates replied, "has brought us many welcome surprises."

He smiled at Empedocles and went to the door with him. "Sosander will be waiting for you in the *palaestra* over there. We are very glad that you will be one of us now."

Then he turned to his mother. "Thargelia is a friend. She was the wife of the king's chamberlain in Aegae. I will leave her with you while the king's messenger and I go to the *iatreion*."

Praxithea led her guest into the women's apartment.

This, Thargelia thought, is his mother. She must be the kind of woman Hippocrates would want for a wife. I've never known such a woman very well.

The older woman spoke first. "Have you come to Hippocrates as a patient?"

"Yes," Thargelia replied. "And I thought the air of Cos and the famous waters from the Vorina fountain would do me good. You see, I had headaches during my husband's illness and then —"

"No, no," Praxithea interrupted. "You must not tell me your symptoms. Hippocrates does not like it, and it is better for the mother — or for the wife — of a physician to know nothing about such matters."

"Your son," Thargelia continued, "had many medical triumphs in Macedonia and he did his best to save my husband, but no one could have done that. My husband was old. He did not seem so when I married him — but he was."

"How old are you?"

"I am the same age as your son."

"You speak more like a woman from the Peleponnesus than like a Macedonian. Where were you born? — Corinth, perhaps?"

"How clever of you!" Thargelia exclaimed. "I lived in Corinth until I was carried off by the king's chamberlain — and we were married."

"Who was your father?"

Thargelia flushed. "Oh, I was adopted. But my foster father brought me up like his own daughter and gave me a good education."

The gateman came to the door and announced that the captain had gone directly back to the harbor, leaving word that the lady could return to the ship whenever she liked.

Praxithea nodded. "Bring your servingmaid along," she said, and let us go to Hippocrates."

The three women made their way to the small court behind the *iatreion,* and Praxithea left her guests in the waiting room while she entered her son's consulting room. She saw he was reading a papyrus, so she waited, closing the heavy curtains.

"Hippocrates!" At the sound of her voice, he started and looked up. "Thargelia has come to see you as a patient."

He stared at his mother as though he had not heard. Then he banged his fist down on the table.

"Perdiccas wants a permanent court physician. I wish he would leave me alone."

His mother was silent for a moment. Then she said: "What about Thargelia? She seems to be an old friend. Why did you never mention her to me?"

He leaned back and looked at her. "I don't know," he replied. "I don't know why, unless — perhaps I was trying to forget her. But there was never anything between us."

As she turned away he saw a look of anxiety in her eyes.

"I will tell her to come in," she said.

Some minutes passed. Then the curtains opened slowly and closed again. Hippocrates rose. Thargelia stood looking up at him with shining eyes, like a lily, full blown. He wondered why she was here. She would tell him soon. Her beauty made him uneasy and on his guard.

Thargelia looked away and said in a matter-of-fact voice, "I hope you have been happy here, at work with your own people. The three months since you left us have been long and lonely ones for me."

"It is good to see you here," he replied. "Yes, this is where I belong, with Greeks who think and talk as I do."

"Have you read the king's message?" she asked.

"Yes. The king has asked me to return — and to become physician to him, to his court, to his fighting men. He offers a salary that would make me a very rich man. If I cannot come at once, he says, I am to send the most famous asclepiad that I can find in my place."

He reached for the papyrus and read from it:

"The king writes this: *The captain of my trireme will return to Cos in a few weeks to bring you to me. Let my loyal subject Thargelia come with you.*"

Hippocrates frowned and looked down at her. "What have you to do with this?"

She smiled mysteriously. "You left Aegae so suddenly. You did not even come to say good-by to me. After you had gone, I was not well. I went to the king and asked him to send me to you. I knew that only you could help me. He laughed at my request. But when a messenger came to his court from Empedocles asking about you, he decided suddenly that he must have you as the permanent court physician, and he asked me to go to you as his personal emissary. So you see I am a Macedonian official for the moment."

She laughed gaily and then became serious again.

"He was planning to send this ship on a secret mission to Tyre soon in any case. You may guess, if you wish, that he wants to know what position the King of Persia will take when the great war that he expects begins among the Greeks. But he wants you, sincerely, to come to Aegae, and he will treat you well. He is really afraid that he may be ill again as he was when he sent for you before.

"For my own part," she continued, "the reason I did not return to Corinth after my husband's death was partly because of the hope that you would return to Macedonia. But there were other reasons too. If the great war does break out as Perdiccas predicts, Macedonia will keep out of it. I shall be safe in Aegae and you will be safe too, if you are wise enough to return there. Bring your mother with you."

Thargelia had been standing before him with dignity, playing the part of the king's emissary magnificently. As Hippocrates listened, the frown that had warned her to be impersonal had vanished. She sat down and he continued to stare at the wall, oblivious of her for the moment. She watched him and wondered silently.

She loved this man and she wanted him as her husband. What would Praxithea have done in her place if she had been young — and desperate! Perhaps the best way, since the time was so short, was to offer and to take the delights of the body. She wanted that; she wanted it now; that was the kind of woman she was. But she wanted something more.

She touched the back of his hand gently. He started and looked down, embarrassed because he had forgotten her, startled also by something he saw in those lovely blue eyes

"You have not asked me about myself," she said, "nor told me all that has happened to you."

He sat down then and they talked about themselves. He had forgotten how very interesting she could be. She had a very good mind — for a woman; and he was pleased that she should make a genuine effort to help him with his decision.

"I still suffer from headaches," she said at last. "Here, place your hand on the back of my head." They stood up and he felt through the hair at the back of her head. "Is there anything there that should not be there?"

"No." His hand moved down over her warm neck. She put her own hand on his and pressed it hard against her neck for a moment. She looked into his eyes, and turned away quickly.

"I was so glad to meet your mother," she said. "I know you better now that I have met her. She is so strong, so quiet, so wise. I would like to be a woman just like her. Perhaps I could be — if only men would leave me alone. Since my husband died it has been worse."

She laughed gaily, and as she turned back toward him her mantle fell a little way from her shoulders, magnificent curving shoulders and neck, he thought.

"Perhaps you will marry again."

"Yes, perhaps, but this time to a man I love." Her lips trembled a little. "Then at last I could shut myself away from the world. I could have children. How wonderful to bear a son to the man I loved!"

She turned away from him and put her hands over her face. He came close to her and felt the urge to put his arm about her and comfort her. That perfume was altogether delightful! — the same perfume she had worn in Aegae. She felt his tunic brush against her and she stood quite still, waiting. Then she heard him say as he turned away:

"I'm sorry you have had so much trouble. There is no reason you should not marry again. You must find a Hercules who can frighten all men away from you."

He crossed the room and sat down. "What would you like me to do for you?"

She took the seat opposite him. "I want you to treat me."

"Treat you for what?"

"For the pain I have sometimes at the back of my head and in my back."

"If you are a patient I must take a careful history of your past." He turned for the reed pen and papyrus.

"Never mind it today," she said. She stood up and untied the rope of gold that held her mantle about her and stepped out of it. Her chiton was deep blue and he noticed how its color intensified the blue of her eyes.

"I have an ache from my neck down the spine, and even into my leg and foot." She slipped one sandal off and placed her foot in his hand — a warm, perfect foot, beautifully cared for. She passed her hand over it, a hand that had never known work. He wondered about her daily life; how far removed it must be from the toil of household living and the tasks of those who care for the sick!

She took her foot away and smiled at him roguishly. "But the pain is sometimes in the whole leg." She stooped again to raise the hem of her chiton over her smooth shapely calf and thigh, following the path of the pain with her finger.

Hippocrates began to find it a little difficult to catch his breath. He tried to think this was due to her perfume, for she was standing quite close to him. How easy it would be to take her in his arms, how pleasant! Her eyes kept telling him she would not object. But he had a rule about such matters . . . for a moment he could not quite remember what it was. Oh, yes, his rule was to wait until he met the woman he wanted to marry. But this was not the moment to settle such a question; that was clear.

She dropped the hem of the chiton and stood on her tiptoes, laughing at him. "You see," she said, "strange to say, it does not hurt me to move about or even to dance."

She was dancing now, slowly at first, in measured rhythm; then singing a swinging song while she snapped her fingers and clapped her hands:

"*Softly, softly, ever so softly; naked feet on the marble floor; swishing, swishing round and round and back and forth.*"

He knew the music and had heard the words. A dance of the people, as old as time, elemental as love, repeating the cadence, returning the rhythm — "*Softly, softly, ever so softly; naked feet on the marble floor.*"

Hippocrates knew suddenly that he really wanted to dance. How extraordinary! And how absurd! He stood up and turned away, while she whirled past and took up her cloak. Finally she sat down to bind on her sandals and said:

"I'm going now. I want to talk with your mother. There is so much I could learn from her. I hope she'll like me. Perhaps she can tell me how to find a place where my maid and I can live until the trireme returns."

In the doorway she turned and looked at him for a moment. Then she was gone, while he remained standing in the center of the room. He began to hum the music and presently to improvise:

"*Wit and laughter and sparkling eyes; body and limbs sway softly, softly; bidding you follow her round and round and back and forth* . . . Nonsense, Hippocrates, you're playing the fool."

He had spoken out loud. He often talked to himself, though rarely aloud. "I will make up my mind about this matter later. Then perhaps —" He stopped and shook himself. "Then I will either complete this verse or I will forget it and her."

Pindar's voice outside his door recalled him. "Master, I have an urgent message."

"Come in."

The heavy curtains parted and Pindar stooped under the lintel. He looked about him as he entered. "Oh," he said, "— I thought I heard someone talking, singing in fact." Hippocrates did not reply, so the disciple delivered his message gravely.

"Before I tell you the news, may I say that if it is true that you are tempted to return to Macedonia, I — Oh, I — I hope that you will stay here with us. I could do more of your work if you would let me, you know. That would give you more time for the study you love."

Hippocrates laughed and hugged Pindar. "Don't you worry about me," he said. "Now what's the news?"

Pindar smiled, and then, realizing the gravity of the message he had to deliver, looked serious again.

"A runner has come from the town of Halasarna, where your grandmother Phaenarete lives. She is, as I understand it, an old woman."

"Yes, yes," Hippocrates broke in, "but what is the news?"

"I was about to tell you that, for this may be a serious matter. She has had a fall. It was early this morning, apparently about dawn. I questioned the runner carefully."

"Come, come, out with it!"

"When the messenger left her, she was lying on her bed, upon her back. There was pain in her right hip, the one she struck in the fall, and the foot on that side was rotated outward far from the vertical."

"Fracture of the hip," Hippocrates snapped.

"Yes, that is exactly what my diagnosis was."

Hippocrates was disappearing around the corner of the *iatreion*.

"Follow me!" he called over his shoulder. "I must go to my grand‹ mother at once."

He entered the surgery and Pindar followed.

"Take these fracture splints, all of them. I can't be sure what I shall need. Load them on an ass. You are to take charge of the case of Penelope. You will have to visit her at the Archon's palace. Insist on freedom for her, good diet, increasing exercise. Ask Sosander to take full charge of Empedocles."

As Hippocrates crossed the garden he caught sight of Podalirius and hailed him. "How is Nicodemus getting on?"

"He had a big attack this morning, much more serious than the one you saw. He bit his tongue and lost his water. I have limited his diet and he is working in the body-building class. He is apt to work too hard, I find."

"Can you care for all the other patients?" Hippocrates asked.

"Master!" Podalirius exclaimed. "You're not really going to Macedonia? They told me the trireme was preparing to leave the harbor. Take careful thought; we need you here so much."

Hippocrates laughed. "Wait a bit, wait a bit, Podalirius. I've had no chance to think yet. But Phaenarete has broken her hip and I may have to stay with her for some time."

He called to his mother as he entered the house and was surprised to find her emerging from the women's apartment with Thargelia.

"Thargelia is just leaving," Praxithea said. "We have had a good talk, haven't we? I am sending her to a house where she can live quietly."

Thargelia thanked the older woman and left with a quick little smile for Hippocrates.

"Will you come with me to Halasarna?" Hippocrates said to his mother. "Phaenarete has fallen —"

"Yes, I know," his mother interrupted. "I talked with the messenger while Thargelia was with you. My things are all packed and I am ready to go."

Just then, Sosander came into the courtyard, rumbling as he came. "Hippocrates, Hippocrates." He faced his mother and brother, folding his hairy arms across his bulging chest.

"I hear thunder on Mount Olympus. The Island of Cos is quaking again! The gods have sent their messenger Hermes here to offer you the wealth of Macedonia." He raised his hands.

"Against him Apollo has spoken, for he has broken our grandmother's leg just to show you that your duty lies here. But that is not all! For the goddess of love Aphrodite has descended upon the island in person. I have just met her at the gate. I even spoke with her. What golden hair, what eyes! What a lovely bait to hang upon a royal fish hook! A king goes fishing for a court physician! A blonde companion for an asclepiad of Cos! A woman from Corinth, where the perfume of passion blows around the corner of every brothel, and prostitutes have a temple of their own!"

"Take care," Hippocrates warned sharply. "She is the widow of my former patient and thinks to consult me herself — no more."

Praxithea put a hand on Sosander's shoulder.

"Thargelia," she said, "is not just the type of woman I would have chosen for Hippocrates to marry and she has little or no dowry. But she has, nevertheless, a good deal of sweetness hidden beneath her pride and beauty."

Sosander laughed and interrupted her, slapping his enormous hand on his thigh.

"I have the solution. I'll take the woman as my companion so as not to embarrass Hippocrates. An elder brother could do no less! Let me discuss the whole matter with my wife!" His laughter filled the courtyard. "Have you ever heard my wife on the subject of the *hetairai?*" Hippocrates and his mother joined in the laughter.

"Sosander!" his mother protested. "Can you never be serious even for a moment? A great honor has come to Hippocrates in this invitation. He must make his own decisions. He will not forget how much we need him."

Sosander's manner changed suddenly. He nodded, and his voice broke as he said, "Yes, yes, I want him here as Master, more — more than I can say. You know how I feel, Hippocrates. I can't find the words to tell you. It has been wonderful working here together. I don't see how you can refuse this offer, but we certainly need you. There will be no more teaching in Cos if you go to Macedonia."

They stood in silence for a moment. Then Praxithea said, "You are good asclepiads, you two, like your father. Remember, Hippocrates, when you are deciding about your work and your wife, that you physicians are a group apart. You are a strange race. The wife of a physician should be as different from other women as her husband is different from other men.

"She needs more than beauty and poetry to support her through the years of medical practice. She must know how to work. She must have patience. She must be able to understand and to suggest. She must love you, but more than that, she must love your work. Otherwise she will not be happy, nor you. Otherwise you can never do all that you want to do for the sick, never do all that Apollo would have you do."

CHAPTER NINE

Flight of the Nymph

~~~~~~

After Euryphon had halted the ceremony of betrothal between Daphne and Cleomedes, the company about the altar of Zeus watched Hippocrates take his leave and Cleomedes go with him. Then Timon turned to the others.

"I had planned a betrothal symposium tonight," he said, "in honor of Euryphon. And we will hold it just the same, since this is no more than the postponement of a happy event."

Later in the afternoon, Cleomedes found Daphne walking before the villa. He approached her shyly, and when she saw that he was at a loss for words, she smiled and said:

"I see you have had a haircut. Do you know how I can tell?"

He shook his head.

"There is a margin of white skin here." She pointed to his neck.

Silence followed, so she tried again. "Your skin is well tanned. You seem to be in excellent condition. You are in the sun most of the day, I suppose."

"All day," he replied, "naked." He came close to her but said nothing. She drew away.

"Keep your distance this time," she said, trying to smile. "You and I hardly know each other. I wish we might have a good long talk. Talk to me about all the things that interest you, not just boxing."

His dark eyes seemed to devour her. "Talk?" he questioned. Then, after another silence, "I'd like to talk with you; I'd like to talk about you. But it's almost time for evening training. Buto is waiting now, I expect."

She turned her face away from his possessive gaze. "What will you do after the Triopian games?"

"I'm going to be married to you, that's the first thing. Then I shall have to serve my time as a soldier or sailor — two years perhaps, but I will get away sometimes and visit you here." He held out his arms. "Think of it, coming back to you! The young men of Cnidus will envy me. They call you the beautiful, the unobtainable."

"And I," she interrupted, "would live on here with your mother Olympias — for two long years! And after that, what?"

"Oh, we will live at home here, you and I. My father thinks I should interest myself in his shipping affairs. But I like to hunt. The deer are plentiful and there are wild boar in the mountain valleys. The *palaestra* is near at hand. I want to box and box — then perhaps some day I may go to the Delian festival. I might even hope to box at Delphi and finally Olympia. Buto thinks I could win if I get rid of my bad temper. I wouldn't want to kill anyone."

The expression on his handsome face reminded her of a puzzled child's.

"Buto says I ought to forget about you — but I can't."

"Do you read?" she asked.

"Read what?"

"Oh, the plays from Athens, or the poets, or the philosophers perhaps?"

He smiled at her naïvely. "I'd like to read, but I always fall asleep. My mother told me not to let you talk about the poets. She says women do that just to mix men up and dazzle them. I can talk about horses and hunting and boxing and — well, mostly boxing. I know more about that than you do."

"Yes, you do."

"You can talk with my mother," he continued, "about the other things. I used to talk with her, but I don't any more. She thinks I am a child."

Daphne stood silent; her lovely eyes were wide, as though she

were seeing something for the first time. The high clear song of a
nightingale sounded from the wood, and turning with delight, she
exclaimed:

"How lovely!"

"What?" he asked.

She smiled and shook her head at him. He tried to seize her
hand but she pulled it away.

"Cleomedes, you must learn to be gentle. You see, I'd really like to
learn to — to love you. I'm wondering whether I can ever learn to
love your mother. But it's time for you to go to your boxing now."

He watched her disappear into the house, a baffled expression on
his face.

Next morning all was quiet at the villa, and especially so in the
second courtyard. Daphne hurried across it and burst into her father's bedroom.

"Spying, peeping!" she exclaimed indignantly. "Why should she
spy on me?" Then, to her astonishment, she discovered that her father was still in bed, though struggling vainly to open his eyes.

"What a funny sight you are," she laughed.

Euryphon pulled himself slowly into a sitting position and sat
hunched over, rubbing his eyes, his hair standing upward in a
fringe about the bald top of his head. Something, it seemed to him,
was pulling him back with a hundred heavy weights, back to the
hazy world of dreams, dreams of talk and wine, laughter and the
flutes of dancing girls, all whirling round and round.

At last he dropped his hands in his lap and opened his eyes.
"Daphne! You are all dressed."

"Of course I am. The sun's been up an hour — more than that."

"What did you just say?" He was awake now. "Who is spying?"

"She is, Olympias. I can't stand it. I went to the bathing room this
morning. They have a lovely one here, in the women's quarters, just
for women — a marble floor slanting to a drain, and water coming
out of a lion's mouth placed just above your shoulders, like that one
in the public baths — and a bowl of scented soap. When I stooped
to wash my feet, I saw her peeking at me.

"I don't object so much to her seeing me naked, but why should she spy that way? And just now, when I was finishing my toilet, I saw her in my mirror, watching me again. But when I turned toward her she was gone. And you heard the way she spoke to me yesterday!"

"Yes," he growled. "It's the old story. She was being the husband's mother!" He rubbed his burning eyes and yawned again. "She seems to be charming and reasonable in every other way. Who could be more charming?"

He opened his eyes and looked at his daughter sternly. "But you should not be here at all. A well-behaved young woman would not leave the women's apartments at this time of day." He yawned prodigiously and stretched.

"Oh, what a symposium that was last night! The wine was good, but it was that heavy white Coan wine and I drank more of it than I really wanted. There was light in the east before we went to bed. That's why I'm so — so sleepy."

Euryphon laughed reflectively. "You should have heard me play on Timon's lyre! He had the most remarkable conjuror there, and how we laughed!" He smoothed down his hair and looked at her.

"Have you seen Cleomedes again?"

"Yes. We talked for a little while."

"Do you like him any better?"

"Perhaps." She started for the door but turned back. "Please talk with me later, Father, when we can be alone. I'll meet you on the terrace."

"Very well, later on. But do go away now. I don't know what to do about my beard. There was no time for the barber before we left Cnidus. Does it look well enough — or does it need trimming?"

She put her head on one side and laughed. "It does indeed! I'll run and get my own scissors."

"Go away, young woman, and stay away. Leave your father in peace."

It was midday before Euryphon and his daughter met on the terrace.

"How long you were!" she exclaimed. "I've been for a walk to Apollo's temple." She put her hand affectionately on her father's arm.

"Do you realize," she said, "what living here with Olympias would be like after I married Cleomedes? I don't see how I could."

"You would soon become friends," Euryphon said seriously. "I am sure of that."

Daphne made a disagreeable face. "I've had a great deal of time to think this morning, with Cleomedes safely out of the way boxing. While I was in the temple I made a small offering and I prayed to Apollo. Then I walked home through the cypress grove. In the grove I seemed to be in the temple still."

Euryphon looked at Daphne and smiled. But like a wise parent, he waited to discover the direction of her thinking. In a moment she continued.

"We worship Apollo, as they do in Delos and Delphi. Athenians worship the virgin maid Athena, and in Olympia it is Zeus. But beyond the beauty of Apollo, the wisdom of Athena and the might of Zeus, there is something more. I seemed to feel that this morning."

"You are a strange young woman," Euryphon said. "You should have been born a man. You would have been a philosopher like Thales."

She shook her head. "No. If I had been born a man, I would have become an asclepiad, like you. But now I can think of something even better than that — to be the wife of an asclepiad, to look after him the way I've looked after you, and to bear him sons and bring them up to be asclepiads too.

"Cleomedes," she continued, "is young and alive. I like him well enough. Couldn't you take him, Father, and teach him to be an asclepiad?" She laughed and continued, "He never reads. He told me that he would like to read but he falls asleep. Don't you see what I miss in him?"

"But, Daphne," her father said impatiently, "we have to be practical. The money Timon's son would bring you would be useful.

You'll be as happy with him as with any other young man. It's time to stop this nonsense. My mind is made up."

Daphne took her father's arm and put it about her, laying her head on his shoulder.

"I wish that Hippocrates were not so old. Sometimes he seems as old as you. But he doesn't forget to trim his beard."

Her father only grunted.

"Look there!" Daphne exclaimed. "Who is that turning in here from the highroad? I think it is — yes, I'm sure, Hippocrates." She leaned out on the terrace parapet. "Isn't it strange that he should come as we were talking about him? He is leading an ass, and a woman is following him on a second ass."

It was indeed Hippocrates, followed by his mother. They came up the road and he tied the asses to the hitching posts. Praxithea remained below while he came running up the steps two at a time. As he did so Olympias appeared from nowhere and welcomed him with her full, flutelike voice.

"*Chaire!*" she cried. "How good of you to visit us. If that is your mother down there, do bid her to come up also."

"No, thank you," Hippocrates replied. "We cannot stop. We are on our way to Halasarna to my grandmother Phaenarete. She has broken her hip, and I have come to ask a favor of Euryphon." He turned to him. "I hope you will come with us. I shall need your skill and advice."

"Of course I will go with you," Euryphon said. "But I must return to Cnidus tomorrow. I shall send word to the boat that waits for me in the harbor here to sail around the island to Halasarna and call for me there."

"I will go with you, Father," Daphne broke in. "Poor Phaenarete. I can help care for her. We must hurry."

She had started for her room, but her father called her back. "No, Daphne, you must stay here and come down to the harbor of Cos and join me there. I shall land at Cos Meropis tomorrow afternoon and pick you up on my return journey. Meantime, Xanthias will remain here with you."

"You must stay," Olympias agreed. "Think how disappointed Cle-

omedes would be if he should come from the *palaestra* and find you
you gone."

Daphne turned away and said no more. When Euryphon returned
from his room with his personal belongings, she remained alone on
the terrace, watching him pack his things into a mule's saddlebags.

She realized that Hippocrates' mother was glancing up at her from
time to time with a good deal of interest. His mother, Daphne
thought to herself, somehow reminds me of my own . . . If only
my mother were with me now! Hippocrates might at least take the
trouble to look up at me —

Her father beckoned to her to come down the steps, but she shook
her head. Shyness, added to pride and disappointment, kept her on
the terrace. She felt lonely and afraid . . . afraid of what? Of
Olympias, of love . . . and of many things.

The travelers started down the path that ran through the garden,
Hippocrates leading the way. Euryphon, sitting erect on his long-
legged mule, turned to look back at the lone figure on the terrace.
He knew how reluctant his daughter was to remain behind, how
reluctant she had always been to consider this marriage and other
marriages he had proposed. Why was she so shy and elusive? He
loved his only daughter deeply, but he could not altogether understand her.

When she was younger he had understood her well enough. She
had been a leader then in the children's dance and in music. She
had even competed at racing with boys of her own age. He could
picture her now with hair flying, running in her short skirt like a
swift fawn, outdistancing everyone. He smiled and then sighed. He
had no son. As the little group turned into the sunlit highroad,
Euryphon raised his arm in a final farewell. She waved back.

"Well named," he thought, "my little Daphne, my laurel. You
must forget me now. Cleomedes is as beautiful as Apollo. I wish I
could say as much for his mind. But don't run away. Don't turn to
leaves and tree trunk at his touch."

Daphne stood gazing out from the terrace long after the travelers
had disappeared from view. A cuckoo's call came from far off in the

shadowy aisles of the cypress wood, and near at hand, quite close, quite loud, an answering *Cuckoo, cuckoo.*" Back and forth, back and forth, call and answer interminably . . . She wanted to cry out, to silence these sounds of mating.

Well, she would do her best — probably a part of life comes this way to all women. But she had so hoped it would be different! The cup was here, she must drink from it. Too bad one could not taste marriage, and throw the rest of the cup away if it proved to be too horrid! . . .

"Come, come!" Daphne was startled from her reverie by Olympias' voice behind her. She whirled about. "You must not dream away the day!" Daphne realized that Olympias had been watching her again. "Come with me," the older woman said, and led the way into the house.

They crossed the courtyard and climbed up two flights of stairs to the roof of the villa. Olympias went to the far end of the roof, and when Daphne joined her at the parapet she pointed up the mountainside.

"On this side of the *palaestra* you see the open place that can be used for boxing, and I have told Buto to bring Cleomedes out there so I can keep an eye on the boy. There they are, coming out of the *palaestra* now, all ready to box."

"But they are naked!" Daphne exclaimed.

"Of course." Olympias laughed, a deep-toned gusty laugh like that of a man. "Come on, my dear, the parapet hides us, so no one can see us here. You might discover what your future husband really looks like! He won't look quite that way when you see him on your wedding night. I suppose you are so innocent you never heard of the work of Priapus, the son of Aphrodite." She laughed again and continued to watch the boxing. "Don't worry, my dear. I'm only the mother of your future husband. I won't be jealous of you. But we'll have no secrets between us, woman to woman, you know. I'm the one who realizes how lucky you are. After all, I went to bed with his father —"

Back and forth the boxers moved in rapid lunge and parry. They circled round and round. Cleomedes broke through Buto's guard and reached his face with his left fist. Olympias laughed, and turning, found herself alone on the rooftop. "Daphne! Daphne!" There was no answer. She ran to the top of the stairs and stood trembling with anger.

Daphne had fled down the stairs and along the gallery to her own room. She had never known a woman like Olympias, and she had only half understood her talk, but something about her filled her with loathing. She had run away before she stopped to think. Now she felt confused. She wanted to make friends for her father's sake, if such a thing were possible. At last she left her room and walked along the gallery. She heard Penelope singing and playing her lyre, so she joined her until it was time for lunch.

Olympias appeared then and was most amiable and pleasant. Cleomedes and Buto, she told them, were planning to return to the Triopian training grounds late in the afternoon. She would send word to Daphne when Cleomedes was ready to say good-by.

"Cleomedes," she added, "is now in the stable. He misses the horses when he is away, and he will probably exercise them in the chariot before he comes in." Daphne wondered if Olympias ever talked of anything but her son.

When Daphne returned to her room, she found her father's old servant Xanthias waiting for her. He asked now what he might do for her.

"Oh Xanthias, I'm glad you are here! I feel so lonely."

When he left, he patted her hand. "I won't be far away."

Daphne gave some time to her toilet and then sat down to her mending. Presently Xanthias returned. He spoke in a low voice and his face seemed troubled.

"Cleomedes has come from the stables and finished his bath. He is with his mother and Buto now. I heard her say they would send for you soon."

Daphne sighed. "Xanthias, when I was a little girl I used to come to you with all my troubles, and after my mother died you were very good to me."

The old man smiled.

"Xanthias, what would life be like for me in this house if I were to marry Cleomedes?"

The old man shook his head. "I don't know, Daphne. When love comes it can make up for many things. But — I can only tell you what I hear and see.

"Just now, before I came to you, I overheard Buto talking to Cleomedes' mother. He was angry and Olympias tried to quiet him. She was frightened, I think. Buto said — but I can't believe I heard him right —"

"What did he say?" Daphne asked. "Tell me what you think you heard."

"I wasn't very near, and of course I wouldn't spy, you understand. But I thought I heard him exclaim, 'Cleomedes is a fool! If you get a girl in your arms once, she's yours. That's the way I got you.' Then he laughed."

Daphne looked at Xanthias. "I think you must have been too far away to hear clearly."

"Yes," said Xanthias. "I must have been mistaken. After that, Cleomedes joined them. He seemed to be angry at his mother. Finally I heard her say she would send for you, so I came up quickly to warn you."

They heard someone now coming along the gallery; then Olympias' voice outside the curtain asked if she could come in. Daphne drew the curtain aside and Olympias entered, smiling at both of them. Then she embraced Daphne.

"I saw your servant crossing the terrace just now. He does move about quickly, for his age. And now, my dear Daphne, Cleomedes is waiting for you. Let us go down. He is so sad that he must return this afternoon. We have all learned to love you dearly."

On the terrace Olympias left the two to what she called their "fond farewell." They walked along to the end of the terrace and a little way into the cypress wood; then Daphne stopped. The great dark wood filled her with misgiving now.

"If I remain away from Triopion any longer," Cleomedes was saying, "the Chief Judge will bar me completely from the men's boxing competition. I saw him before I left. 'You may take two days away,' he said, 'but train yourself. Apollo expects the best that you can give him in strength and speed and effort.' "

He grinned at her like a boy, standing there in kilt and sandals while the magnificent muscles of young manhood rippled under his bronzed skin. Her beauty and the thought that at last they were alone made him fall silent for a moment.

She drew her cloak more closely about ther. "Is the competition strong in the men's boxing?"

Cleomedes laughed. "Is it strong? It's the strongest in years. Peisirrodus, grandson of Diagoras of Rhodes, is in. He won the crown in the boy's boxing class at the last Olympic contest, and he steps up into our men's class now — long arms and very fast. He's just like his grandfather Diagoras, and his uncles — they were all Olympic champions. You know his mother is Diagoras' daughter. She trains him, and what a woman she is! What a woman!"

Cleomedes threw his head back and his laughter echoed through the wood. When he could control his mirth, he went on.

"They say that one day some fellow tried to get too familiar with her — you know what I mean? Well, she just hit him once, just once. That man dropped to the ground and he stayed there!"

Cleomedes laughed again and danced about on his toes as he loved to do, shadow-boxing. Daphne looked at him in surprise. She had never seen him excited like this. Perhaps, she thought, he is waking up, in his own peculiar way. He stopped suddenly in front of her.

"Why did you run away from me in Cnidus when I tried to kiss you? You did the same thing yesterday. Why?"

"I couldn't help it. It was so sudden."

He came a step nearer.

"I don't know much about women, but I've always heard that the way to get one is to grab her. That's why I did it. Anyway, I wanted to . . . and I want to now."

Daphne laughed a cold little laugh and stood her ground. "That may be how men get their women in — in a brothel. No man can woo me that way."

He flushed. "Don't make me mad. You asked your father not to make the marriage contract. I've been told there's one way of making a woman beg for it."

She turned pale. "Please," she said. "Can't we learn to be friends?"

He stepped closer, and she backed away. "I'll show you how a boxer makes love. And you'll not run away this time!"

Daphne's eyes flashed with sudden anger. "Don't you dare —"

"If you get a girl in your arms," he laughed, "she's yours."

It flashed through Daphne's mind that those were the very words that Xanthias had heard from the lips of Buto. She broke away from Cleomedes as he reached for her, leaving her cloak in his hands. She was off, running like a deer through the woods while he followed at full speed. They flashed out onto the terrace, where he overtook her and caught her in his arms. She cried out, and turning, scratched and bit, bit so deeply that he dropped her, and she escaped into the villa. She heard someone scream, "Cleomedes!" She thought she passed Olympias, but she was not sure. She rushed on headlong, not stopping until she reached her own room. There she threw herself on her bed and wept bitter, angry tears.

After a time she lay quiet. Penelope came to her room bringing her cloak. Daphne took the cloak and sent her away, saying that she wanted to be alone and that she would not come down to the evening meal. After that she heard the voice of her father's servant outside the door and she called to him, "Come in, Xanthias."

The old man stepped through the curtains and she sat up. "I'm so glad you've come." He looked at her with a slow smile.

"Xanthias," she said, "there is a back door to the villa and a path leads from it past the stable. Does that path enter the highroad?"

"Yes," he replied.

"Can you find the way to Halasarna, where my father has gone with Hippocrates?"

"Yes — but surely, Daphne, you are not thinking of going there so late in the day. It must be a good three parasangs away — unless, perhaps, you are willing to borrow the Archon's mules."

"No. I'll borrow nothing. We will walk."

The old servant smiled again as though to himself. "I thought so," he said quietly. "I know you very well. I was watching for you and I saw you when you came out of the forest. I was surprised and disappointed in you as a runner! I didn't think there was a boy or man living who could catch you when you really wanted to run."

Daphne had been packing her things. Now she stopped, and putting them down, she hugged him. "You have always understood without being told, and I love you." She went back to her packing. "We will leave at once and stop in Pelea for the night. If the pack sack grows too heavy for your shoulders, I'll carry it. I'll leave a writing here in my room to tell them we've gone to join my father in Halasarna. But I hope no one will discover the writing until it is too late for them to overtake us.

"Aeneas lives in Pelea. You remember him, he was the very old asclepiad who was here at the villa the day before yesterday, and he has been a guest in my father's house in Cnidus."

Xanthias nodded, and she continued. "I am sure he will take us in. Pelea is, I believe, a little way off the road to Halasarna. We should be able to get there before dark, although it may be a long climb up the mountainside."

As the sun was setting that evening, Daphne and Xanthias toiled up a stony road along the rim of a deep ravine. Far down at the bottom of the ravine, a mountain brook was rushing and tumbling toward the sea. Across the ravine, and towering high above, was a mighty cone of rock, and perched on its summit they saw the white pillars of the acropolis of Pelea. Up and up they went, as the ravine curved around the rock. At last the road slanted downward to a bridge that crossed the torrent of foaming water.

Here they rested a little while and parted the tall reeds that grew on the bank to drink the cold clear water and to wash in it. Xanthias drew his knife and cut a purple thistle. He removed its thorns and gave it to Daphne. She smiled and put it in her hair.

They crossed the bridge, and climbing a short rise, found themselves in the little city of Pelea hidden on a shelf behind the acropolis. Far above the shelf the mountain wall still rose steeply to its final pinnacle.

And so the old servant and the young woman came to the door of

Aeneas, "the good physician," who took them in and gave them food and bed with all the gracious hospitality for which true Greeks have always been justly famed.

Early next morning they made ready to leave. But Aeneas said, "Stay a little while," and he gave Daphne a present, a shawl of finest wool.

"Before you go," he said, "come up with me to the rooftop." And he took his staff and hobbled ahead of her up the stairs and then on up the second flight, for his house, like many others in Pelea, had two floors above the entrance but only one at the back, because of the mountain slope.

At the top of the house Daphne cried out in wonder, for she found herself looking down, down, down the mountain to the fertile plain of Cos. Beyond was the sea, deep blue in the morning sun, with its islands all spread out as though they were pictured on a map. And from the rising slopes of the mountain behind them came the sound of distant bells of grazing flocks, like music in the clear, cold air.

The old man was out of breath. He sat on a stone bench to rest, stooping over, so that his white beard rested on his knees. Presently, when he was breathing more easily, he looked up at her and nodded his head.

"Stay a little longer and talk awhile, for I see you are troubled." So she sat beside him while he questioned her, and she talked freely.

At last he said: "It was long ago that I was trained as an asclepiad in Syrna. I may have forgotten some of the things I learned. But I know life as only a physician can come to know it. Throughout the many years that I have lived and practiced here, my patients have opened their hearts to me, knowing their secrets were safe — women and men, wives and husbands, and children.

"You are troubled about love and about what life holds for you. I learned the ways of love from my wife, who died long ago, and from watching others and listening to the good and the bad in their lives as they tell it to me.

"Love is not a hateful duty nor a passing pleasure. That is something else. Love is a happy bond for a man and a woman, a helpful harness for living and working together. It is possible that love would have united you with Pyramus if he had lived, but don't look back. Look forward now.

"Somewhere there is another Pyramus who needs you and wants you. Don't hide yourself away and expect the gods to tell him where you are. Go, live your life and watch. You will know him, I have no doubt, before he discovers you. The man must pursue the maid, it is said, and fathers must arrange. But the maid most often starts it off. It is she who provokes the chase with word or gesture or meaningful glance, for she has the quicker wit, the surer sight.

"Come," he said. "I'll walk along with you as far as the bridge."

Xanthias was waiting at the door of the house. He shouldered his pack and they walked through the streets of Pelea together. The wind blew Aeneas' long white beard back over his shoulders and he stamped his staff on the roadway stones as he trudged along. Daphne watched how the people who passed turned and smiled and greeted him — men and women and little children — and he called them all by name.

They came to the rushing brook and stopped on the bridge. Daphne kissed Aeneas there and continued on her journey with Xanthias. She was gay again and reassured since sharing her thoughts with the wise old man. He waved as they climbed the opposite side of the ravine and muttered his blessings into the wind.

CHAPTER TEN

Halasarna

~~~~~~

THE TWO PHYSICIANS stood at the bedside of Hippocrates' grand-mother in her home at Halasarna.

"No, Hippocrates, I think you are wrong," Euryphon was saying. "You're wrong to attempt what you cannot do."

Phaenarete seemed to be asleep. Only her thin, weatherbeaten face showed above the coverlet; it gave an impression of strength and dignity. The many wrinkles told their tale of storms and sun-shine, of kindness and resolution.

Hippocrates and Euryphon were reconsidering, in the light of day, their handiwork of the night before. They had found the upper thigh of the right leg broken very close to the hip joint. Two strong men had been called in, the one to hold the old woman's body, the other to pull with all his strength on the leg. With the palms of his hands on either side of the thigh, Hippocrates had felt the bones click into place at last. After that, he knew, the problem was to keep the thigh muscles from contracting too strongly. That would pull the bone ends past each other and produce a short leg.

Then bandages had been applied with skill, layer after layer. Collars of Egyptian leather were placed around the thigh in the groin, and also above the knee and about the ankle. Six or more splints of cornel wood, no thicker than a finger, were inserted into the collars. These springy splints served to draw the collars at the ankle and the knee away from the collar in the groin, and so exerted a continuous pull upon the bones in the thigh to prevent overriding.

The physicians had provided carefully against sores of the skin which might be caused by uneven pressure. Pads made of clean raw wool were pulled out smooth and placed so as to protect the vulnerable points, such as heel and lower back. The leg was then cradled in a hollow splint.

"This hollow splint," Hippocrates said, "is what people see and call for. But it is no more than a convenience for handling the patient in bed and at stool."

Euryphon's eyes twinkled. "Never has one old woman been the subject of more learned discussion and argument. But I predict some shortening of this leg, even if you do say that shortening is a 'disgrace to the physician.' You are energetic and hopeful, but I am still gloomy. We find in Cnidus that the less we do, the better our old women get along."

Phaenarete stirred and opened her eyes. "Where are all the old women you are talking about? I'm certainly not old. If I had been, then how could I have climbed up on the table I fell off of? You have worked all night on me. I suppose you couldn't help hurting me. But I never heard so much unnecessary talk in all my life.

"Go away now and let me have a word with Praxithea. She'll do the important things for me. I told my son Heracleides when he said he wanted to marry Praxithea that he was getting the finest young woman in Halasarna, whether she brought him any dowry or not."

Hippocrates leaned over the patient. "Is the bandage still too tight?"

The countless wrinkles in Phaenarete's leathery face formed themselves into a smile, and a soft expression came into her sunken eyes. "It's not too bad. You've done the best you could." Her eyes closed again. "Run away now."

The two men smiled and left the room. But they stopped in the court to continue their discussion.

"If I can hold the leg as it is now," Hippocrates said, "there will be no shortening. This promotes the natural process of healing, I believe. You Cnidians don't realize how much better the results are if you can keep the fracture reduced, one end against the other, and without movement at the site of the break during the first ten days. That is when the local thickening appears about the broken ends, which will hold them in place.

"She has a gay spirit, my grandmother, but she is old — very old and frail. I may not succeed, but I shall watch it and rebandage and keep up the extension with those wands of cornel wood day and night."

There was a knocking at the great wooden doors and Hippocrates went to open them, while Euryphon followed him, still expostulating.

"You try to understand what cannot be understood. That's the trouble with you, Hippocrates. It is better to treat the symptoms. If the leg hurts, move it. If she is comfortable, leave her alone. I repeat that fractures of the hip are different from fractures of other bones."

Hippocrates slid the bar back and swung the double doors open.

"By the gods, Euryphon!" he cried. "Look who's here!"

Old Xanthias was standing before the door, about to knock a second time. He had a large pack on his shoulders. Behind him was Daphne, carrying a smaller bundle.

Xanthias stepped aside but Daphne did not move. She was looking at Hippocrates as though she had never seen him before — as though she were asking a question. He realized with a thrill of surprise that her eyes were only for him.

"Daphne!" her father cried. "What are you doing here?"

She threw her arms about him and clung to him in silence. Hippocrates' mother came hurrying across the courtyard.

"Welcome to you, Daphne!" she said in a matter-of-fact voice. "I'm glad you've come. I hoped you would. I half expected you."

Daphne raised her head to look at Praxithea. Her eyes were filled with tears.

"I had to leave the villa," she said. "There was no other way. But how could you know?"

Praxithea laughed. "I watched you on the terrace and I have asked some questions. Come with me now."

"But will you let me stay and — help you with the care of Phaenarete? My father will tell you I've had experience."

"She would rather care for the sick," Euryphon said, "than do anything else, and she's very clever at it, even though she is such a little thing and not much good at lifting."

"I can lift much more than you think," Daphne objected.

Her father laughed. "No, Praxithea, I'm afraid my daughter will have to return to Cnidus with me. The ship for our return voyage is drawn up on the shore. They are waiting for the word to launch her." He looked at Daphne severely. "To say I am surprised to see you here, young woman, expresses only half of what I would like to say to you."

"Daphne is tired," Praxithea broke in, "and footsore and dusty. And look at your poor old servant. He is too tired even to put down that heavy pack. No, she must come with me. She will return presently to talk to you, Euryphon, while I prepare a meal for all of us."

Euryphon watched the two women disappear across the court. Then he shook his head and turned to Hippocrates.

"When you marry," he said, "as I suppose you will some day, my advice to you is to pray the gods for sons. No father can plan the life of his daughter or understand what she thinks."

Hippocrates smiled, and Euryphon began to pace up and down the courtyard in silence. It seemed a long time before Daphne returned — "Unnecessarily long," Euryphon muttered to himself. At last she came, glowing and fresh and dressed in another tunic. She smiled at Hippocrates.

"I love this old house, and your mother tells me that you were born here."

Hippocrates nodded and led father and daughter to the reception room.

"Daphne, Daphne!" Euryphon exclaimed in exasperation as soon as they were alone. But before he could go on, she put her fingers on his lips and said:

"Please, Father, I did try to do as you wished. I tried very hard. Please, wait until I tell you what happened."

When she had finished the story, her father said, "I was afraid of this. Cleomedes is a little stupid. He made the wrong approach."

"He certainly did! But it isn't only Cleomedes. I can't tolerate his mother."

"Well, we will stop at Cos Meropis this afternoon on our return voyage and I shall talk with Timon."

She shook her head, and he saw her slender body stiffen. "With your permission," she said, speaking slowly, "with your permission, I intend to remain here to help care for Phaenarete. After Hippocrates leaves us, I shall stay on to help still longer, unless there seems to be danger of a visit from Cleomedes. I am afraid of him, Father."

"Nonsense!" Euryphon exclaimed — but again she cut him short and continued with slow emphasis:

"Hippocrates' mother told me just now that she was delighted that I might become acquainted with her son. I'm sorry you feel differently. Hippocrates interests me, that is all."

"Hippocrates!" Euryphon exclaimed. "Oh, but — I never thought —"

"Don't think," she interrupted. "Don't — Just go back to Cnidus and leave me alone, I beg you. I haven't been able to think either, not yet. There's been so little time. I need to be quiet here with these two women, women I like, women I understand and who understand me."

Euryphon sat down very suddenly. Just then Praxithea called. They saw her crossing the court.

"Come," she said, "we will eat our meal together as one family. Hippocrates says he will be with us in a moment. I hope, Euryphon, that you will leave Daphne with me as my guest."

He nodded and gave Praxithea a rather sad smile. "You remind me a little of my own wife. I can pay no woman a higher tribute."

They were very gay at the meal, but Euryphon did not remain with them long afterward. He said he must get back to his work in Cnidus.

"When Daphne is ready to come home, send her back by the

Cnidus fish boat. It makes the round trip, as you know, every second day."

His eyes twinkled as he looked at Praxithea. "If she should run away from you, just let her go. She'll probably swim home, with Xanthias on her back. Meanwhile, I will leave him here also. He may help in the household."

A week later Hippocrates stood beside his grandmother's bed. His face was drawn with fatigue. The patient was mumbling words that made no sense. Daphne stood beside him, dressed in the coarse white tunic commonly worn by those who nursed the sick.

"Did she take her barley gruel?" he asked without turning round.

"Yes, she took it quite well. And she talked all the time. She said things that almost seemed to make sense. But she called me Hippocrates. I don't think she meant you — I think she meant your grandfather, because sometimes she called me darling, and begged me to come and take her away. 'Take me out of this prison,' she said. 'Take me out. They are killing me.'"

Hippocrates grunted and nodded his head.

"Why does her mind wander so?" Daphne asked.

He made no answer but stooped and, opening the bedgown, watched her rapid breathing. There were hollows between the ribs. They sucked in still further with each breath, and the wrinkled breasts hung down on either side, pitifully thin. The left side of the chest moved more than the right. He knelt down and placed his ear against the ribs on one side and then the other.

"She has a pneumonia, as I feared she would. She is so thin and old." He put his hand on her forehead. "She is hot," he said. "The heat comes from the *coction* of the crude humors that is going on in her body. It is that which has affected her brain, and so she has these strange fancies and understands nothing that we say. I expect that the crisis will come today or tomorrow. At the time of the crisis, *concoction* occurs and she will be better suddenly, or —" He turned away and added, "Or else she will die quickly."

"The trouble," he said, coming back to the bed, "is here in the lungs. The leg is all right, so far. We must still keep fresh wool under her so that she is always dry. I will help you, or Praxithea, every time she needs to be turned."

As they left the room, Hippocrates' mother was waiting for them in the peristyle.

"The healing forces of nature," he said, "are strong in Phaenarete. She has gained a little. But the crisis of this pneumonia will come soon — then we will know. The gods may yet smile on her, as they did on me when they gave me two such helpers as you are."

" 'The gods help them that help themselves,' " his mother quoted.

Hippocrates passed along the peristyle and turned into the *oecus*, where he liked to sit. The principal family rooms were arranged in a line along one side of the court. The master bedroom, or *thalamus*, where Phaenarete lay, was between the large room called the women's apartment on the right and the reception room — *oecus* — on the left. Beyond the *oecus*, farther to the left, was the kitchen, and beyond that a well-concealed privy with cess-pit. All of these family rooms faced south across the sunny court, being separated from it only by the columns of the peristyle. The roof of the peristyle protected the wide doorways from the direct rays of the sun.

Praxithea nodded to Daphne and they walked away toward the kitchen. Here Praxithea used the flame of a small oil lamp to light a pile of dried reeds on the open fireplace. She swung an iron pot over the quick fire. Soon she dipped out hot soup into a bowl.

She gave the bowl to Daphne and said, "Take it to him, and stay awhile to talk. You must not work all the time. I will go to Phaenarete, and the servant will prepare the evening meal."

Daphne carried the steaming bowl into the *oecus* and set it down on a stool before Hippocrates.

"Your mother's command: You are to drink this and I am to make sure that you do so while it is still hot."

He looked up at her. "You have helped us more than I can say, much more than our distant family relationship would call for."

"I wanted to do it." She looked into his eyes, and this time she did not look away. He felt a strange thrill pass through him. He had felt that thrill when he opened the gate and found her standing outside. Her eyes had lingered then too, seeming to say something to him.

"Your eyes puzzle me," he said. "Since the first day we met at Timon's villa, I have tried to decide just what their color is. I thought then that they were blue. Now I think they are a greenish-brown."

He walked out into the court and broke off a small branch from the plane tree there. Returning, he gave it to her. "I used to call these buds kitten's paws when I was a child. The fuzzy, furry jacket is opening now to let the round blossom emerge. Golden brown and a tinge of green. That is something like the color of your eyes."

"Interesting," she said, but she blushed. "You believe that a physician should describe and classify everything, don't you? Then you would have him write these details down in the notes of the case and forget them."

"Some things I shall never forget." He tried to look into her eyes again, but she turned her head away.

"Tell me about the house. There is so much room in it and it must be very old . . . Sit down and drink your soup now before you reply."

He obeyed, but finding it hot, he put it down again.

"Yes, the house is old and many tales are told of it. Some member of the Heracleides family has lived in it for I don't know how many generations. There is a temple to Heracles here in Halasarna, and you remember that in the Iliad, Homer tells how after the sack of Troy the goddess Hera was angry at Heracles. When he sailed away, she sent him winds that drove him off his course and so he landed in Cos. He lived here, after killing King Eurypylus and marrying his daughter."

Hippocrates stopped and smiled at her.

"Go on," she said, and leaned toward him, like a child eager to hear a story.

"Well, we only know that Halasarna has many members of the Heracleides family who claim descent from Heracles, just as the asclepiads in Syrna and Cnidus claim their descent from Asclepius.

"Phaenarete was an only daughter, and she lived here with her father and mother. Her father commanded a ship under Queen Artemisia of Halicarnassus, and so he fought for Xerxes against the Greeks. After he was wounded by an arrow he was brought home to this house and to the bed in that *thalamus* to die. Phaenarete was then about to become a bride. She and her asclepiad husband, who was my grandfather Hippocrates, came to live here and the room became theirs. My father was born here. In due time he brought his bride to live in this house with his parents, and here I was born.

He was silent for a time, looking out through the doorway. "That plane tree in the center of the court was planted by my great-grandfather just before he sailed away to war. The slave who opens the gate and his wife were living in that same room beside the gate when I was a boy here. I was only about five years old when my grandfather Hippocrates died, and then my father moved to Cos Meropis and took the house where we live now."

He looked at her and changed the subject suddenly. "Most asclepiads seem to marry women much younger than themselves. That may be because of the long period of preparation. Perhaps you are wondering why any woman, old or young, should be so lacking in wisdom as to marry an asclepiad."

"Wisdom," she replied, "seems to have very little to do with the making of a marriage." She paused. "How old is Thargelia?"

He looked at her in surprise.

"What do you know about her?"

"Your mother told me something."

"Thargelia is my age, I believe." His mind slipped back to her golden hair and dancing feet.

"I'll take your bowl away," she said, rising.

He handed it to her and their eyes met again and lingered. "Are you expecting —" He hesitated. "Are you expecting Cleomedes to come here to visit you? You have hardly mentioned him since you came."

She made a sudden gesture of resentment. "I never want to see him again. Perhaps I shall change my mind, but at the moment, I don't like boxers." Then, after a moment's pause: "I like old wrestlers much better!"

She turned in the doorway and looked back at him, laughing. Then she disappeared and he stood still, listening to the slap, slap of her sandals till the sound died away and all was silent in the house.

So, he thought, she was turning away from Cleomedes. If there was trouble between them, would Olympias be counting on his help to bring them together again? He recalled her morning visit to his consulting room. She had certainly tried in her own strange way to get medical advice about Cleomedes. He had promised her that he would help her with him, "somehow, if he needs it." Did he need it? Why had Daphne run away from the villa?

It is curious, he mused, that Daphne should have mentioned Thargelia. Daphne was all the things that Thargelia was not, yet both were exciting. Why should his mind be running to these matters now? Perhaps he was losing his defenses. Perhaps he was so far away from his usual associations that there was nothing else to fill his mind. Perhaps there was a longing within him for something men and medicine could never satisfy. His mother seemed to believe that he was missing something in life. Perhaps she was right.

When Daphne entered the sickroom next day, Hippocrates was there before her, his hand on Phaenarete's forehead.

"The heat has lessened," he exclaimed with a lift in his voice, "after a night of fever. This morning she recognized me. Didn't you, Grandmother?"

The old woman opened her eyes, but she did not answer directly. "Who is this young woman? I never saw her before."

"This is Daphne," he said, "the daughter of Euryphon of Cnidus. She has been helping you for days."

"Never saw her," Phaenarete quavered, looking at Daphne with deep sunken eyes. "Turn your face, my girl, to the side — that's it! I thought so. She has the profile of the Heracleides women — a good Greek profile." She closed her eyes.

Daphne said, "The strong man has come, the man who helps you with the splints."

"Good," Hippocrates replied. Then, to the man who was entering the room, he said, "Raise up the foot of the bed and put the high block under it. Then pull on her foot. Keep the leg extended while I remove the splints and bandages. Now, Daphne, you get the clean bandages and a bowl of warm water and some soap. Then stand by. I shall need you."

In the afternoon Hippocrates announced to his mother that Phaenarete had passed her crisis and that there was no further reason to fear for her life. Also, the bones of the thigh were still in their proper position! The gods had been good!

"What is more," Daphne added, "Phaenarete seems to have lost all proper respect for the fame of her grandson! She scolded him steadily all the while he was replacing her splints. He was 'awkward,' she said, 'slow,' even 'stupid.'"

They all laughed as though an inner tension had been released, and Praxithea shook her head. "That's the way she used to be! My mother-in-law must be well again. When I first came, a bride, into this house, she was good to me, very good, but she scolded me and she spoke her mind to me, and in those days she spoke that way to all the world.

"And now," she continued, "I am going to speak my mind to you, Hippocrates. You have succeeded. I realize it. Apollo might well be proud of you. But now the time has come for you to turn your eyes away from the sickroom.

"Out of doors spring is waiting; the birds are building their nests; the early rye is ready to harvest. Daphne does not know the beauty of the hills and valleys that lie between Halasarna and Mount Oromedon — Elysian fields for those who can open their eyes! I know — I remember."

She left them abruptly and Hippocrates looked after her, startled. He turned back to Daphne and was startled again, for her eyes were wet and as bright as two stars.

"Would you," he said awkwardly at last, "would you care to go for a little walk? It may be dusty."

"I'll just change my costume," she said, and walked demurely across the courtyard. But before the first of the columns she made a little bow. Then, light as a leaf in an eddying wind, she danced the length of the peristyle and around each pillar in turn.

Just as they left the house, Praxithea called to them:

"We have planned a special dinner just before sundown. So bring back good appetites when you come, and also some thin cheeses. And Hippocrates, if you can get it, bring me some of that honey they sometimes sell at the roadside in the high meadows."

The door closed behind them. Hippocrates looked about at the familiar scene with a feeling of exhilaration. It was good to be out of doors and to know that all was well. The path from the house, running down toward the highroad, was arched over by a double row of olive trees, the trunks writhing like tortured bodies. The new gray-green olive leaves were fresh and fuzzy. The sky above was very blue.

"You are my guide," Daphne said, "and I want to see everything. But I think I hear the oven. It may be our evening meal."

She was off in the direction of the sound and he followed. Just around the corner of the house stood the large stone oven from which came the roar of the fire. The gatekeeper's wife, a kindly old witch of a woman, was tending it. She showed them proudly the great metal pot filled with meat and spices ready for the cooking, and the vegetables in another bowl to be added later.

As they watched, the roaring fire died down suddenly. "It's hot enough now," she said. She opened the door and swept the feathery ashes out of the oven. Then she set the pot on the oven floor and shoved it in cautiously with a long wooden paddle, using her other arm to shield her face from the oven's hot breath. When she had the pot in place, she pushed in metal trays, each bearing a flattened lump of dough. Then she banged the oven door shut, and straightened her back slowly. She gave them a toothless grin as they turned away and walked together down the arching aisle of olive trees.

But a black cat ran swiftly across the path, almost under Hippocrates' feet, and the woman cried out, "Turn back! Turn back!" They stopped and she came around and stood in the path in front of them.

"This journey you are beginning will not be smooth," she said. "There's trouble, danger in the way. Best for you to turn back."

"But we are not going on a journey," Hippocrates laughed. "We are just going for a walk, to get some honey."

She shook her head slowly.

"If it's the truth I see in your eyes, and I think it is, you've started the journey that has no end this side of the grave." She opened her tunic at the neck and spat on one of her breasts, then on the other. After that she held her hands above her head and stood aside. They passed on, and as they passed they heard her crooning:

> "Go on your way; be steadfast, true.
> The gods have honey for such as you."

"Hippocrates," Daphne said, when they had gone part way down the aisle of arching olive trees, "don't you believe, just a little bit, in such signs and such words? When she spoke to us, her voice seemed the voice of a Sibyl. Don't you think, perhaps, we had better turn back from this walk, this 'journey' — before it is really too late? Something may happen — to you and me."

Hippocrates smiled. "That dear old woman has always been full of superstitions of all kinds. She knows all the unlucky days in the calendar. Her whole life has been devoted to averting evil, for herself and for others. Nevertheless, I've always felt that there was something mysterious about her.

"I know the superstition about cats. But what can that poor cat know of the fate that is waiting for us on the highroad? Or, if there really was no cat beneath my feet, what oracle or god was it that made us think we saw it?"

When they came to the well, where the path joined the roadway, Daphne leaned against an olive tree, putting her hands on its gnarled trunk.

"The sun is hot," she said. "I'm thirsty. I'd like to stop here a little while."

Hippocrates turned to the well. A rope, fastened to the wooden crossbar over its wide mouth, passed downward into the cool, dark depths below. He pulled it up hand over hand, and the rope slipped smoothly through a groove in the marble brim, worn by years of use, while the bucket, bumping and splashing its way up the wall of the well, made sounds that struck familiar chords in his boyhood memory.

They stood with gourds of cold water in their hands, and Hippocrates continued his discussion.

"In the minds of most Greeks, nothing is so certain to break an evil spell as spitting into one's bosom, and especially so if an old woman does it for you. So we may accept this act from her as her blessing, meant to bring us good in place of evil.

"But in general, such things are no more than silly actions because of wrong beliefs. Most men spit in their bosom when they see a madman or some luckless person in a falling fit. In Athens, I saw a poor woman fall down in the Agora, groaning on the ground, and shaking and frothing at the mouth. All the people shuddered. They cried out 'The sacred disease!' and opening their mantles they spat upon themselves! How absurd it is when there is no god, no devil, no spirit that is responsible for such things, only natural causes acting within the body."

"You see such things," Daphne said, "so clearly, so logically. That is what makes you a great physician, I suppose. And yet you do not seem to see the meanings that I see. Is a woman's world so different? There are many things a woman could tell you, ways in which a woman could guide you, to happiness if not to knowledge."

"You talk the way my mother does," he said. "Come along now. We must be back here when that stew is done — the witch's stew. I suppose you'll be afraid to eat it for fear of a mystic spell."

They laughed and entered the highroad, turning away from the town. The sweetness of jasmine was in the air. Men and animals were streaming past, some to the fields to work, others returning to their houses in the town . . . shepherds in their long cloaks and broad-brimmed hats, farmers and women in short tunics clacking along on their wooden sandals, children scampering here and there with dogs and lambs and kids and calves, donkeys clicking smartly over the gravel and sober goats and sheep and cattle on leading straps.

The passers-by were gay and life was good for them, or so it seemed to this physician free from care for the afternoon and this woman no longer frightened by the thought that love might come to her.

"The best honey," Hippocrates said, "comes from the wild *thimari*. I know a place where the hills used to be purple with it at this time of year." So they went on till the road was deserted and the plain slanted smoothly up to the foothills of rugged Oromedon.

As the road rose they stopped to look back to Halasarna's lines of white houses, like little boxes in the trees that bordered the ocean. Over to the right was the acropolis on a hilltop and the pillared temple of Heracles. Below the temple the upper rows of seats of the theater were visible.

Hippocrates turned to watch Daphne thoughtfully, while she continued to look at the distant scene.

"I shall remember your words," he said, "as we stood beside the well — that a woman could guide a man to happiness. I suppose it is true that some women could guide a man in the way he should go. Others would certainly lead him into confusion." For a moment Thargelia, with her painted nails and heady perfume, was there between them.

"It may be that physicians need a woman's guidance and companionship more than other men. Happiness comes to them as a reward, secondarily. There are other urges than the pursuit of happiness that keep them going. But what can a physician do? No woman would marry him if she were in her right mind."

Daphne did not reply, but she looked at him as though about to laugh, and they walked on until he broke the silence again with:

> "*While we are young. Now is the moment, now*
> *To take what happiness the gods allow.*' "

She looked at him in surprise. "Those words — are they from Alcaeus?" He nodded. "I have not heard you quote the poets before. I am learning more about you all the time."

Soon they reached the rolling hills, which were purple with thyme as Hippocrates had predicted. In a little hollow they saw a collection of small boxes. These were the beehives, arranged in rows like a small Greek village. They walked across the fields, smelling the pungent odor of the *thimari* beneath their feet. She picked the stiff stems with their tufted ends and tiny feathery lavender or purple blossoms.

Hippocrates called to a shepherd on the hill above them.

"That honey," replied the shepherd, "can only be bought in the city from the wife of Krisamis. She used to let me sell it to passers-by on the road, but not now. She doesn't trust me any more, and if I so much as take a part of a comb to make a shepherd's lunch more tasty, she finds the broken comb every time. There's no pleasure at all now in a shepherd's life."

"Oh, but you have your flute slung over your back," Daphne laughed. "Play for us now."

Not unwillingly, the young shepherd took his flute in hand, and leaving the sheep and the frolicking lambs to graze as they pleased, he came down to them and sat on a stone.

"This is something that came to me this morning — from the Muse, you know." He smiled at them. "She keeps me company up here."

He placed the long bamboo flute between his knees, fitted his fingers to the holes, and putting his lips over the end, he blew and fingered with a will. They listened to the soft husky tones, the wandering cadences and recurring refrains.

Hippocrates sat down a little way off and looked at Daphne while she listened. She seemed to be unaware of his admiration. Presently she took off her warm gray cloak and spread it out on the ground and sat down on it. Then she smiled at him and they looked at each other, lingering as though in an embrace.

What joy it would be, Hippocrates thought, to sit on the cloak beside her, just to be near to her. How could he have been so blind before — not to see the halo of tumbled curls, the delicate flush of her cheek, the moist ripe lips and the teeth of pearl, and her neck, smooth as ivory, curving with modest invitation, down to the breasts that swelled beneath her chiton.

Here was a woman a man might love through life! She had spirit and wit and sweetness. What a mother she'd make, and what a wife! Suppose he were to ask Euryphon for her. Euryphon, he was quite sure, would prefer the son of Timon. And yet if Daphne were to

ask him too, he might be persuaded. Would she want to ask him?
Surely not!

This woman, he said to himself, was what he had been waiting
for. This was why he had denied himself all these years. Without
realizing that he had done so, Hippocrates came closer and sat on the
corner of the cloak. Daphne held out her hand as though to welcome
him, and their hands almost touched, but not quite.

The shepherd looked up and stopped his piping. He was pleased
when they praised his playing. And, as they started back toward
Halasarna, he called to Hippocrates:

"Bring your wife back tomorrow — I'll have something better to
play for her."

Daphne blushed. "Yes," she whispered, "couldn't we come back
tomorrow?"

Hippocrates smiled at her and then called to the shepherd:

"She's not my wife. She's not anyone's wife, not yet. But I'll try to
bring her back again. Will you have the Muse here with you?"

The shepherd laughed. "I'll do my best," he shouted. "It's hard to
promise when it comes to women."

Daphne looked up at Hippocrates. "When we first met I never
suspected that you could be like this. You seemed so old and serious.
I told you then that I liked boys and didn't like men, and I hoped I
would grow old very fast. I don't want to grow old, now that I've
met a real man who is young in his heart."

He laughed, and she laughed too, although the cause of their
laughter might not have been apparent to a third person if one had
been present. But these were moments never to be forgotten by
them and never to be shared with a third person.

They found the wife of Krisamis. She had the honey of *thimari*
to sell, and cheeses too. And so they came back home, and stopped
outside the house while the wife of the gateman opened the oven
and let them smell the steaming, bubbling contents of the pot and
admire the crusty brown loaves of bread.

But the gateman himself had unexpected news for them when he
swung the great doors open.

"There is a woman here from Meropis. She asked to see you both."

"Olympias!" Daphne exclaimed.

"Yes, that's her name."

Praxithea came hurrying across the court.

"Olympias is in the *oecus*," she said. "Hippocrates, you can go in and talk with her. Let Daphne come in later."

The Olympias that Hippocrates found waiting for him in the *oecus* was full of dignity and charm.

"I am distressed," she said, "by the impulsive behavior of my son Cleomedes. We were astonished to discover that Daphne had come here. Then we thought of course that she would have returned to Cnidus with her father. But it has been so nice that you two could become acquainted with each other — nice for you, Hippocrates. I'm sure you must have been missing your friends in Meropis. Thargelia and I have become quite well acquainted.

"Cleomedes," she continued, "has not been working very well at his training, I am told. If he should learn what is happening here, you might be in real danger — he might do what the mad Cleomedes did. I dream of his doing something like that almost every night. But I take reassurance in the fact that you have promised to help me with him, as a physician."

"Olympias," he interrupted, "I know nothing of what you call your son's impulsive behavior. I have not discussed him with Daphne. My promise to help you with him depended entirely on whether or not he needed the help of a physician. My diagnosis up to the present, based on what you have told me and on what I have observed, is that he is slow in mind and depends too much on his mother. I have seen no evidence that he is either sick or mad."

As he talked, Hippocrates became aware that Daphne had entered the room and was standing behind him. But he continued without interruption:

"I am not concerned with your son's love affairs, nor with his success at the Festival of the Triopian Apollo. It is my rule to speak plainly in medical matters and I shall do so now.

"Your daughter Penelope developed an illness because of your unkind treatment. Your fears for your son and your efforts to protect him may well have a bad effect on him. Whether he is in himself abnormal in any way, I am not yet prepared to say."

"I am so glad that you are frank," Olympias replied, with a disarming smile, "especially in the presence of my son's future wife."

Daphne stepped nearer, but stood silent while Olympias continued:

"I have come here, Daphne, to tell you that my husband and I have just returned from a visit to Cnidus. We expected to find you there. Your father has now promised us that he will do nothing to discourage Cleomedes in his belief that you may yet marry him.

"We beg you, as we begged your father, to give Cleomedes another chance in spite of what may have happened that last afternoon at the villa. Cleomedes would never tell me what did happen. I thought perhaps you would."

"I would rather not discuss the matter with you," Daphne replied. "My father has already made it clear to you that we will make our decision after the Festival. You can send that message to Cleomedes."

Olympias smiled. "I suppose you will have to marry someone sometime. Well, I am sorry I must hurry back to Meropis now. Here, Daphne, is a message which your father asked me to give you." She drew a small scroll from beneath her cloak.

Then she turned to Hippocrates and spoke with a knowing smile. "I will tell Thargelia that you are well and happy. She is waiting for news of your return, you know. The trireme is waiting and I must return home now."

When she had gone, Daphne broke the seal and read her father's brief message. She sighed and said without taking her eyes from the papyrus, "Tomorrow afternoon I must return to my father on the fish boat. I am sorry that you should be involved, against your will, in my father's plans to marry me off."

Hippocrates was aware that something had come between them. Or was it that she was distressed now by memories and unsolved problems?

"Come," he said. "We must go to see Phaenarete." They crossed the court, but she walked beside him with her eyes on the ground.

"Sometimes it helps to share your thoughts with someone, someone who will listen. Would my mother do? Or can I help you?"

She flashed a brief smile at him as they turned from the peristyle into Phaenarete's room. The old woman opened her eyes.

"Where have you been, you two? I missed you."

Daphne bent down. "We've been climbing on the purple hills where the scent of wild *thimari* fills the air."

Phaenarete nodded and put a bony hand on Daphne's. "Teach him to pick the flowers," she murmured, and then in a stronger voice: "I know these asclepiads well. I wived one and mothered one. Teacher and pupil, they've been about me, in and out of my house, ever since I married this man's grandfather. 'Work today and be happy tomorrow' — that's the physician's rule of life."

She looked at Daphne and smiled. "I wish you could teach this grandson of mine how to live a happy life."

The old woman shifted her position and winced with pain. Hippocrates lifted her gently, while Daphne rubbed her back and arranged the bed with pillows and wool, laughing and talking as though there had been no visit from Olympias.

When it was over and she lay again in a comfortable bed, Phaenarete looked at Hippocrates with a calculating eye.

"You are a Hercules. I feel your strength when you lift me. Well, you have just as much of his blood in your veins through the Heracleides on my side of the family as you have from Asclepius through my husband's side. I think it is thinned out to nothing on both sides, if you ask me to speak the truth. But you are different from any asclepiad I've ever known, Hippocrates. You've brought something new into the family, something you get from your mother.

"I suppose you've saved my life, but that is nothing to boast about. It's what men and women do with their lives while they have them that is important. When will physicians learn that?"

CHAPTER ELEVEN

A Crown Denied

~~~~~~

THE OIL LAMP hanging in the little dining room filled it with warm mellow light that evening, and Daphne's quick appreciation roused Hippocrates to his best as a conversationalist. His mother added overtones of approval. The stew was steaming hot, fragrant and tasty — as they all testified when the smiling face of the gateman's wife appeared in the doorway. And the crusty fresh bread sprinkled over with sesame seeds, the butter and cheese, the cakes with honey and the watered wine left nothing for a hungry man or woman to desire.

It was Daphne's custom to retire early, and Hippocrates had realized that he saw her disappear each evening with increasing regret. As she was about to go this evening, he said:

"We must lay our plans for the time that remains to us in Halasarna. Daphne leaves tomorrow afternoon, and I shall return to my work the next morning. Such times as this must have an end — the gods grow jealous. But if Daphne will go back to the hills with me, we can use the morning to appease Apollo and listen to the music of his Muses. Those are the orders, in fact, that I heard my grandmother delivering to Daphne. There seems to be a conspiracy of women in this house. You might think a man couldn't be happy without them."

They all laughed, and Hippocrates said, "Do you remember, Mother, how my father used to plague you by quoting from Hesiod?

> *'Bring not a wife to your home too soon or too late.*
> *Wait till you're thirty but don't thereafter wait . . .*
> *Choose out a virgin, and then you will be obeyed . . .*
> *but watch if people grin when you name her for wife.*
> *She's best of all prizes or worst of all horrors in life!'"*

"I think Hesiod was a horrid bachelor!" Praxithea exclaimed. "He was probably so ugly that no nice woman ever went near him. But I have something to add to this conspiracy." She left the room and returned with a lyre in her hand.

"Phaenarete wants to give this to you, Hippocrates. Your great-grandfather brought it back from the Persian wars. See, the crossbar and the sound box are inlaid with shell, and both of the curving arms have delicate gold figures on them. I had all twelve strings renewed today with the best hemp."

Hippocrates made a gesture of resistance, but his mother coaxed: "It's a very small lyre, nothing like the big ones that the professionals use. You must take it with you tomorrow. Perhaps Daphne can teach you something new on it."

Hippocrates shook his head: "Conspiracy leads inevitably to tyranny, and tyranny must be resisted by free men. Otherwise the Greeks will become no more than the husbands of Amazons."

Daphne smiled. "Wise tyranny is the best government of all."

Next day not long after the sun rose, Hippocrates and Daphne set out gaily toward the slopes of Mount Oromedon. Men and women plodding toward their work watched the two and wondered who they were. Two men passed them, somewhat better cloaked than the average. One said, "Beautiful woman, that."

The other said, "You know who the man is, don't you?"

"No."

"Remember the boy wrestler who won the crown for Cos at the Triopian games? It must have been ten years ago, probably more. Hippocrates his name was, Hippocrates, son of Heracleides. The family is still here in Halasarna."

"By the gods!" the other replied, turning to look back. "I believe you're right. He is quite a lot older now but he has the same way of holding his head. That was eleven years ago. I remember the contests very well that year. You know I was competing myself in the javelin throw. Well, I'd gladly change places with him right now. I think he is carrying a lyre under that cloak. Lucky fellow! Is there a wedding somewhere today?"

The mimosa on the roadside had come into golden bloom, and here and there from green hedgerows the hibiscus hung out lovely flower heads, ruby and black with yellow pollen powdered on. In the dense thickets of rustling bamboo, the young shoots were capped with gay feathery plumes.

As Hippocrates and Daphne climbed higher, they looked down on orchards of fig trees in orderly rows — the trunks gray-blue in the distance, the branches misty with leaves in tiny bud — and on groves of olives, peaches, oranges, apples, *musmula*.

They came at last to the purple hills, but the shepherd was nowhere to be seen. So they climbed on, up to a terrace on a shoulder of the mountain. There was a ruined tower there, probably a watch tower and fortress built in the nearly forgotten days when the Dorian invaders from Epidaurus had first occupied the western end of the island. The road from Astypalaea in the west joined the road from Halasarna here, and the road from Meropis as it came around the mountain.

"So much has happened," Daphne said, "since Xanthias and I came along that road from Timon's villa. We stopped right here to rest."

The air was cool, but they laid off their cloaks with the feeling of triumph that rewards the climber. A rocky cliff rose steeply at the end of the terrace. From high above they could hear the deep-toned whistling calls of the rock nuthatch.

"Listen," Daphne said. "What a haunting sound it is echoing down the cliffs. A little like the voices of the nightingales in the cypress wood at the villa."

"Yes," Hippocrates said. "You hear these birds on the cliffs at

Delphi — above the sports stadium there. It sounds as though mountain spirits were laughing at men."

They walked across the platform to a broken wall and leaned upon it, standing close, side by side. They gazed in silence at the wide panorama below, but each was turning an inward eye on things unheard and unconfessed.

Daphne's mind at that moment was not something that a man would understand. She had a feeling somehow akin to weakness, and she knew that in this man, so close to her now, there was great strength. She knew she was happy, very happy. She wanted no change. She wanted things to remain as they were — until — Oh well, why try to think? She gazed at the horizon and wondered which one of the twin mountains on the distant island of Ialos was the higher.

Hippocrates had done a good deal of thinking since his astonishing discovery of yesterday that he loved Daphne. About one thing there remained no doubt in his mind whatever — he wanted to marry her with the least possible delay. But he saw clearly that he could not, in all honor, go to Euryphon to ask for his daughter — not until the decision had finally been made as to her marrying Cleomedes. Also, he could not, in all honor, take a promise of marriage from her now before that time. Her father and Timon would have a right to think ill of him if he did.

And yet it was only fair to Daphne to let her know, or at least suspect, that he loved her, so that she might make her choice with her eyes open. But was it fair to let her even think of marrying so unworthy a man as he thought Cleomedes to be? She would not be happy. Shouldn't he take her in his arms now and leave the future to take care of itself? No, no, that would not be right.

They were standing close. She came a little closer, touching him and looking up into his eyes. They stood thus while feeling seemed to swell and overflow, uniting them as though they were one, not two.

Suddenly — crunch, crunch, crunch — steps were sounding on the gravel behind them. They started apart and turned. Daphne cried out, frightened. Cleomedes was striding across the terrace, naked to the waist except for a cavalry cap swinging at his back, fastened by a cord about his neck — a splendid figure that could have modeled for a statue of Heracles. Sweat glistened on his forehead.

He stopped, dumb with astonishment.

"Daphne!" he cried. "Hippocrates! I was coming to see you in Halasarna, Daphne. But I thought you were caring for a woman with a broken leg. What are you doing here on the mountainside? Playing with him, eh? Is that the kind you are? Couldn't you wait to be married? Well, I'm your man — I, Cleomedes. You won't run away from me again!"

He started for her, but Hippocrates stepped between them.

"Wait, Cleomedes!" he said. "You're wrong about her and you're wrong about me."

"Wrong, am I? I'll show you!"

He hurled Hippocrates to one side and seized Daphne, pulling her toward him.

"Stop that!" Hippocrates cried. "Don't touch her! Listen to me!"

He pulled Cleomedes back by one shoulder, forcing him to drop Daphne. But Cleomedes whirled and shot his fist out low and straight, a knockout blow to the abdomen. Hippocrates groaned, doubled up, fell to the ground and lay there, unable to draw in his breath.

Daphne screamed and beat with her fists on Cleomedes' back.

"Ha, ha, ha!" he laughed, turning about and catching her. "You bit me once, you little cat. But you'll behave now! If you don't, I'll kill you." He laughed again.

Hippocrates lay quiet, watching through half-closed eyes. Little by little his breathing grew deeper, but he did not stir. Cleomedes started off, carrying Daphne in a grip of steel.

Suddenly Hippocrates was on his feet; he tore off his chiton and flung it to the ground, standing naked except for the loincloth.

"Come back, you coward, come back! I'll give you time to take that fine cape from around your neck. Otherwise I might strangle you with it."

Cleomedes let go his hold on Daphne and turned back, his face twisted with anger. The two men approached each other warily.

"Keep well away from us, Daphne," Hippocrates said quietly. "Keep away till I teach this boy a lesson."

They were circling about each other now — a young boxer, heavy-muscled and as quick on his feet as a wild boar, and a wrestler who stooped and moved with lithe power, his arms curving forward and hands open in the attitude so well know in the *palaestra*.

Hippocrates laughed, a taunting laugh.

"This poor boy, Daphne! He has no mother now to come to his rescue."

Cleomedes roared with rage and came boring in at his adversary. He led with his left fist, and Hippocrates jumped back. He swung with his right and caught the jaw, but only with a glancing blow.

That was what Hippocrates was hoping for. As Cleomedes passed, Hippocrates pivoted, catching the boxer's head and neck in the crook of his arm. He threw him high in the air and brought him down to earth on his back with a crash, holding the head and neck securely under him. Tightening the stranglehold, Hippocrates watched Cleomedes' face, caught as it was in the vise of his upper arm and chest. For a time, Cleomedes struggled, while his color gradually turned blue, then purple, and finally his movements stopped. Hippocrates relaxed his hold instantly and watched the face change back from purple to blue to red.

"Don't struggle any more, Cleomedes," he said. "You are beaten."

But Cleomedes made a supreme effort to throw him off. The vise tightened again, this time without shutting off the wind, but applied so as to produce pain, in a way that wrestlers and *pancratiasts* understand. Cleomedes finally cried out and his lips trembled. The vise relaxed again. Cleomedes whimpered.

"Now will you be quiet," Hippocrates asked, "and listen to me?"

Cleomedes nodded, being quite unable to speak. Without changing his position, Hippocrates called out: "Daphne, you had better come and listen to this."

Daphne discovered then, to her surprise, that she had a large stone in her hands. She threw it down and came near, tears running down her cheeks.

Hippocrates talked quietly and deliberately to his fallen opponent, but he kept his head-hold firmly in place.

"What on earth were you thinking of, Cleomedes, to come here shouting like an ignorant Barbarian, roaring insults at the woman you hope to marry, and mistreating her? You know very well that Daphne's father will keep his pledge to give you your answer after you have won the boxing crown — or lost it. If you keep on behaving like this you deserve to lose her.

"My advice to you is to go back to your training with Buto. You have an expert opponent in the grandson of Diagoras, and you shouldn't be wasting time here.

"Now, Cleomedes, I want you to answer this question. Has someone been telling you that you are the kind of man who kills people?"

There was no answer. The hammer lock tightened.

"Has your mother told you that?"

Cleomedes nodded reluctantly.

"I thought so. You and I know you're not a killer. You want friends, you want people to like you, and you can control your anger. When you let it go, you lose the friends you want to make. Your only chance to win Daphne is to show her that you are a Greek who does nothing in excess, that you are gentle with women and would make her a kind husband."

Hippocrates let go his hold, rose to his feet, and walked away without looking back. Cleomedes turned slowly over and lay on his stomach, hiding his face on his arm. Then he got to his feet slowly and faced Daphne.

"I came here today," he said in a very hoarse voice, "to ask you to forgive me for grabbing you. I thought women liked that, but I guess I was wrong. Will you give me a chance to show what I can do?"

"Yes," she said faintly. "Yes, until after the Festival of Apollo. That is my father's wish."

Cleomedes walked over to Hippocrates, who had dressed and stood looking out over the slopes of Halasarna, rubbing his jaw.

"What shall I do now?"

"Walk back to your father's house," Hippocrates replied, picking up Cleomedes' cape and handing it to him. "Get the first boat back to Triopion and start serious training again. There is no time to lose, you know. In the future, be careful not to swing too soon with that right arm. There's plenty of power in it."

Cleomedes nodded. "Yes I know. But what you said made me mad."

Hippocrates laughed. "I meant that it should. I had to bring you in quickly, for I'm out of practice and would not have lasted long. You see, it shows that not getting angry will even make you a better boxer. Now, listen to me. Only you and Daphne and I know about this — this contest. We might call it a *pancration*, since it included boxing and wrestling! If you behave like an honorable Greek, we will keep this *pancration* a secret. Go now. *Chaire.*"

Cleomedes started off toward Meropis, but hesitated, and then came back slowly.

"You were telling me the truth?" he asked.

"Yes," Hippocrates replied, "nothing but the truth."

"All right then. I wish you would come and see me on the training grounds. No one has ever talked to me like that. And I think it is too bad you didn't try the Olympic wrestling when they wanted you to go. You're good."

"In boxing and wrestling," Hippocrates said, "we have to take the decision of the judge."

Cleomedes nodded.

"It's the same way in love," he continued. "You and I may hope for the crown, but someone else will decide."

Cleomedes cast a quick glance toward Daphne, and then said shyly:

"Tell Daphne for me that I'll come to see her after the games. She'll be proud of me then, I hope, and I'll be gentle."

Cleomedes squared his beautiful shoulders, swung his *chlamys* over them and fastened it at the throat. Then he walked away down the road with a jaunty air.

When he was out of sight, Daphne sat down suddenly on a large

rock and shook her head, as though she could find no words. Hippocrates came and sat on the other end of the rock.

"This is the first time I ever had to fight with a patient before I
could begin to treat him. He seems to be my patient after all. It's a
strange case. He has the mind of a bewildered boy. He should become a normal man, and yet just now he was dangerous — mad, if
you like. After all, what is madness? Something goes wrong with the
brain, of course. But does the cause come from outside the brain, or
does it arise within?"

"Hippocrates!" she exclaimed.

But he continued, ignoring the interruption. "I should tell you,
Daphne, that his mother asked me to take him as a patient, and I said
I would if he needed it. Today we have had our interview, and I
have a sore jaw." He put his hand to it and grinned.

"Hippocrates!" she exclaimed again, but again he went on. "Speaking as Cleomedes' physician, I would prescribe that he marry you.
All you need to do is to wean him from his mother. Then you can
lead him about as you like. You said that a woman can lead a man.
What a wonderful opportunity to prove your hypothesis. And don't
forget, he has lots of money."

"Hippocrates!" she cried, jumping up from the rock. "What utter
nonsense! Oh Hippocrates, he might have killed you! And you were
— oh, there are no words to describe what you were. Wait a minute.
I know what I should do. Sit there where you are. What can I find?
Let me see."

She ran across the terrace to a laurel tree, and wove some leaves
quickly into a crown. Then she stood in front of Hippocrates. "I am
going to crown you now with the victor's crown."

Hippocrates started up. "Oh, no! I'd like the crown, and all that
might come with it. But no! The judge must wait and be fair to all
contestants."

She paused. Then she threw the crown away.

"Very well. Let me see your jaw —"

He stooped, and before either of them knew what she was about,
she had kissed him. She drew back instantly, and they looked at each

other for a bewildered moment. "I —" he began. "I . . ." His voice trailed into silence; finally, he turned and crossed the terrace toward the highway.

Daphne looked slowly about the terrace. She saw the marks in the dust where the fight had taken place and the stone she had dropped from her hands. Then she looked away across the sea to the twin peaks of Ialos. At last she called after Hippocrates.

"The lyre! Would you leave it behind? And me too perhaps?"

He turned back and picked up the lyre, and they walked away in silence. Finally she said, without looking at him:

"You have thought about Cleomedes and what would be best for him. Isn't there someone you have forgotten?"

He stopped still in the roadway and said very gently, "Yes. But let us sit over there on the hillside, where no passers-by can come upon us." Then he added with a shrug, "One roadside consultation is enough for today."

They left the road and started up the slope.

"The person I seem to forget," he began, "is you, Daphne. There is another person too who seems to be forgotten, a young asclepiad by the name of Hippocrates. I want to tell you something about him and about her, but I don't know how to do it. I want to tell you without saying the thing I tell. . . . Sit down here," he said, and began to pace up and down.

There was the beginning of a smile on her lips as she took a seat on a broken tree trunk. It was a smile which many men have seen and some have even painted, calling it inscrutable — the smile of a woman who knows she is loved and who waits.

"You can see, of course, that since Cleomedes is my patient now, and since you are in a way pledged to him, and since I cannot talk to your father, there are certain things that I cannot say to you. That is, I mean, I cannot say them until after the Festival of Apollo. But when that time comes —"

He shook his head and sat down near her, while she watched him with that faint smile still on her lips. It seemed to him less a smile than a reflection of light from within.

"Daphne," Hippocrates began again, but he fell silent, and picking up the lyre, he began to play, hesitantly at first and then more surely.

Daphne leaned forward. After a while she said, "Put the words to it."

Without looking at her, he began to sing:

" *'Like the sweet apple which reddens upon the topmost bough,*
Atop the topmost twig — which the pluckers forgot somehow —
Forgot it not, nay, but got it not, for none could get it till now.' "

Her eyes glowed. "And am I that apple?" She read his answer in the look he gave her. "Oh Hippocrates," she whispered, "you are —"

He handed her the lyre. She set it on her knee, bowing her lovely head to the crossbar. After a time she began to pluck the strings. He watched and listened, breathless. At last she raised her head and looked at him — her eyes were like stars, he thought.

She sang the opening lines of one of Sappho's songs, then stopped too shy to sing it all:

" *'In loveliness the dew spills over*
And with new strength revives the rose,
Slim grasses and the flowering clover.
But sadly up and down she goes —' "

That afternoon, Daphne and Hippocrates left Phaenarete's house and followed a lane that led to the shore. They walked in silence, but the silence told of the feeling they knew they shared, a feeling too wonderful for words.

To Daphne even the commonest things seemed strangely fraught with meaning — a tethered sheep with crumpled horns and a lamb at her side turned her head to watch them pass. A little cock darted swiftly into their path. His head was low and he ran with might and main, but the feathery object of pursuit fluttered ahead of him, delightfully near but out of his reach.

So they came to the shelving beach of yellow sand. The water near the shore was shallow and vivid green. A long wharf ran out to where the green changed to purple, and the shallow bottom dropped away to the deep.

The fish boat had come. It had been made fast, and men were shouting and running along the shore and crowding out on the pier. It was always like that when the fish boat came — excitement came with it and seemed to spread to the town. Some citizens came to the shore to buy fish, but many came to see and talk and hear the news.

Daphne and Hippocrates crossed the beach as though walking in a dream. Old Xanthias hailed them and followed them out on the pier as best he could. He was carrying bulging bags on his back, with the lyre, Hippocrates' parting gift, tied on top. People laughed to see him totter and almost fall along the edge.

When they reached the side of the ship, Hippocrates looked at Daphne. His look was like a kiss, but the words he wanted to say to her were left unsaid — the things she longed to hear, and had never heard.

He watched her jump to the deck of the ship and turn to him again. So many things he wanted to say . . . He knew what they were, but he could not speak. He must not speak, not yet. He must only bid her good-by.

Men shouted. The ship cast off. The sails came rattling down. They bellied out in the offshore breeze, steady and square and brown. Daphne was high on the afterdeck. But higher still the helmsman stood, and swung the tiller over, taking the ship across the green to the purple deep beyond.

Smaller and smaller the vessel grew, rolling and plunging along the waves, while the splash of the bow was white in the sun like a galloping horse's mane — a horse on a purple plain.

When Hippocrates took his leave next day, his mother walked to the gate with him. "When you get back to Cos Meropis," she said, "many will be waiting for you, Thargelia among them. She is not a woman to be ignored. And what are you going to do about Daphne?"

"What indeed?" he replied. "There is nothing at all I can do for the time being. I cannot carry her off without her father's consent like a conquering Barbarian. And Daphne may care little for wealth, but her father, I suspect, cares a great deal. Timon, too, is a hard man to refuse; Cos has never had such a leader.

"Remember that I only met Daphne by chance at the consultation, when she was there to be betrothed to someone else. Olympias invited me back to the ceremony only because she had a strange scheme to make Cleomedes my patient. Even though the betrothal plans fell through, and Daphne ran away for some reason, Euryphon and Daphne are still pledged to give Cleomedes first consideration. The only honorable thing for me to do is to wait."

"Men can be so stupid!" Praxithea exclaimed. "I suppose it never occurred to you that your presence at the villa had something to do with Daphne's change of mind? Perhaps my prayers to Apollo helped."

She walked impatiently to the well and pulled up a bucket of water. "Don't waste your sympathy on Cleomedes. You'd better take Daphne as your patient. Help her to get the man she loves. I understand her better than you do. She is a woman of determination. Euryphon will find it hard to force her into a match against her will, and he knows it. The danger is that with your pride and your idea of honor, she may not be sure you love her. In any case, she will certainly have many doubts. There is trouble ahead, Hippocrates, tragedy perhaps. I feel it. You must send her messages somehow."

Hippocrates shook his head. "No. I can't do that."

Then Praxithea burst out angrily: "I want Daphne as a wife for my son as much as Olympias does! And beware of that scheming woman! I knew her before she married Timon — I've heard how she caught him in her net. There are many stories about her. Timon wasn't the only man in her life."

Hippocrates looked at his mother in amazement. There were tears of anger in her eyes.

"You asclepiads! You're too — too honorable. Don't resign yourself to your fate, the way your cousin Podalirius did. Don't let yourself be a stupid bachelor like him."

She turned away impatiently and stumbled back up the path beneath the olive trees. He heard the great door of the house close with a bang.

CHAPTER TWELVE

Love in Strange Clothing

BACK IN COS MEROPIS, Hippocrates was plunged at once into that never-ending stream of other people's problems which constitutes the practice of medicine. As he entered the asclepiad enclosure, Podalirius hailed him.

After warm words of welcome, he said: "I need your help as soon as possible with a serious medical problem and a difficult family situation."

"A hungry man can give you only half his mind," Hippocrates answered. "You had better allow me a little time to eat and wash. It's a long walk in the wind, all the way from Halasarna. But I won't be long."

Hippocrates turned to the gatekeeper, who was waiting for a word of greeting.

"*Chaire*, Elaphus! What news? Where is the dog?"

"My wife has taken Bobo out on a leash to wash him. He's been running away again. The crowds that follow Empedocles seem to make him nervous."

Hippocrates looked surprised, and Elaphus added:

"Every time Empedocles comes to the gate riding on his donkey, there is a crowd following, and some of them wait on the seashore until he comes out again. Bobo doesn't understand — or it may be the perfume on the twin slaves."

Hippocrates laughed as he turned towards his house. But when he reappeared, Bobo came bounding with ungainly speed to greet him, and might have knocked him down if he had not been quick on his feet. Elaphus came running. He looked at Hippocrates, fresh and handsome after his bath and a change of clothing.

"Halasarna's done you good, Master. You show the health and strength you used to have. Perhaps you had time for wrestling in their *palaestra*."

"Well, not in the *palaestra*, exactly. But I did wrestle in spite of myself." Hippocrates chuckled.

Podalirius emerged from the surgery and began at once:

"This is my problem. Cephalus, as you probably know, is a young man of good family here in Cos. His slave fell ill and I treated the boy, but without success. Now he has an acute fever. He is getting worse in spite of all my efforts. But there is something more — it is hard to explain to you about the wife and household. That is part of the trouble. I wish you would go there with me."

"I'll come with you," Hippocrates said. "How is Empedocles?"

"He was much relieved by Sosander's treatment at first, but he seems to be losing ground now. You will see him when we come back, and there will be many other patients waiting for you as well."

Podalirius talked as they walked. "I will try to explain this household to you. Cephalus is about thirty-five; his wife is somewhat younger. There are no children and there have been no miscarriages. The slave who has the fever was a beautiful young man. There is war between man and wife. The wife is handsome, as you will see. But there is much discord in the family and — well — when we are alone she seems much too fond of me."

Hippocrates realized that this aging bachelor physician was somewhat embarrassed, and possibly also a little gratified. So he replied in generalities.

"A warring household is a stage for tragedy. When a physician steps on that stage, the wife sometimes welcomes him — for her own purposes. Some would attribute this to unsatisfied bodily urges. More often, I suspect, it is to make the husband jealous, and to assist him in the rediscovery of her own forgotten charms."

"Oh no," Podalirius said. "This goes deeper than that. I've been called to their house before, and I used to see her sometimes before they were married. She noticed even then that I was different — so she says now. And I can't help liking her. I'm very sorry for her, really very sorry."

Hippocrates glanced at his companion and then looked ahead of them along the road that ran between the crowding houses. He realized that the credulous boy who lurks on in most men had spoken out unexpectedly in Podalirius, the experienced and indefatigable physician.

The house of Cephalus was a white, boxlike structure a single story high, built about a large open court with rambling connections to other courts. In one of these secondary courts they came upon Cephalus, pacing up and down and stroking his curling black mustaches with an air of gloom. "I'm glad you've come, Hippocrates," he said. "I don't believe my poor slave even knows me any longer."

It seemed to Cephalus a very long time before Hippocrates emerged from the slave's room, looking grave. "This acute fever has gone beyond the power of the body to resist," Hippocrates said. "Podalirius is staying with him now to do whatever is possible, but I believe that the young man will die nevertheless."

Cephalus could not speak at first. Then he said in a husky voice, "My slave is such a beautiful boy, well educated too. I shall miss him more than you can know."

As they went on talking, Hippocrates led the conversation into the past — to Cephalus' early life and his marriage. In the end, he confided in Hippocrates, his hopes, his disappointments, his resentments. This much-loved boy, dying of fever, was not the first male to whom he had been attached. When he married, he had hoped for a changed life and for sons. But things had gone wrong. His wife was unreasonable and combative, he said, and there were many points of friction which extended to include his wife's mother. He was relieved when Hippocrates suggested that the two women should visit him in his *iatreion*.

By the time Podalirius joined them, Cephalus had brightened up considerably. As he ushered the physicians to the door, he said to Hippocrates:

"The time has come now for a very pleasant duty. I could almost wish that I were a physician myself! You must stop to see Thargelia, who lives in the little house that belongs to me next door. I understand that you were great friends in Macedonia. There is Thargelia's servant now." He pointed down the street. "She's standing before the door, waiting for you. She will make sure that you do not escape."

Cephalus twirled his mustaches as he watched the servant speak to Hippocrates. And he laughed as she led him into the house next door, while Podalirius hurried back to the *iatreion*.

Others who watched along the street saw Hippocrates emerge again in a surprisingly short time. When he reached the asclepiad enclosure, Podalirius was waiting for him. "If I may say so," Podalirius said, "you were wise not to linger with Thargelia. There are many eyes in the streets of Cos. But I have waited to ask you how you could be so sure that the slave is going to die?"

"Come into my consulting room," Hippocrates said. When they were seated there he began: "It was the slave's face, above all else, that made me sure. I've seen that appearance before, and so have you. But the face must be considered together with the history to give the prognosis.

"In the case of this slave, there is no preceding chronic illness to explain the sunken appearance of the face, and there has been no strong diarrhea or starvation or sleeplessness to contribute to it. In the absence of these things, such a facial appearance points to a fatal ending. If one of these conditions exists, it may be necessary to wait a day and a night before deciding how serious the situation is.

"The face of a man at the approach of death speaks for itself, but I have made these further observations also: In acute fevers, pneumonia, phrenitis and headache — if the hands move to and fro before the face, seeking in the void, gathering the straw of the bed into pellets, picking at the coverings, detaching objects from the walls of the room — these movements constitute so many signs suggesting a fatal termination."

"Yes," Podalirius said. "I've seen the movements and I've seen that facial appearance many times. Often the patient dies, but sometimes he does not. I can remember several who got well. But" — Podalirius struck his fist into his hand — "now that I stop to think of it, I believe they were suffering from severe diarrhea — By the gods! I believe you are right! I am older than you, Hippocrates. I've seen many more sick people, and yet you reach conclusions as I do not."

"Perhaps it is the short summaries I write of each case," Hippocrates said simply. "They help me to review and conclude."

"Master," Podalirius said haltingly, "don't go back to Macedonia. Stay with us."

Podalirius, who was afraid of any show of emotion, turned away abruptly and pulled back the curtain. He called to Nicodemus, who came running across the courtyard.

"This young man," Podalirius said, "has worked very hard in the gymnastic classes since he first consulted you."

"I'm so much better," Nicodemus broke in. He pushed forward and started to kiss Hippocrates' hand, but caught himself and stood erect.

"I feel better!" he exclaimed. "I'm growing strong. I've followed the diet, and the fits are rare and very light; sometimes just a sensation in the stomach and the bitter smell. Then the attack is all over and there is no loss of consciousness."

Hippocrates looked at him with approval. The Hebrew wore no mantle. He was dressed only in a kilt, and the sun had tanned his body. He held his handsome head high as he continued:

"I am learning to breathe deeply, and to use my muscles according to the teaching of your brother Sosander." He straightened up. "But my greatest help comes from the fact that I know now there is no evil spirit in me. There is no curse, no need to beat my breast and search for forgotten sins.

"I say thank you with all my soul. I kiss your hand in spirit, I bow to you in spirit; but since I am in Greece learning to act as a Greek, I neither bow nor kiss your hand. I stand like the pillar of Hermes. I walk about like Podalirius here with my head in the air. Some day I expect to see the gods on Mount Olympus, if they are really there." He laughed. "But soon I shall have no attacks. Then I can return to my people to worship Jehovah and be like other men."

Hippocrates chuckled as the young Hebrew left the room.

"Does he try to make fun of you?" he asked.

"No," Podalirius replied, without a smile, "no, never, but he does talk a great deal, mostly nonsense. At times, he flies into fits of anger."

"Yes," Hippocrates said. "Those who have attacks of this type may have uneven tempers, more often than those who have epilepsia in other forms."

Through the rest of the day, Hippocrates saw a long succession of patients. He picked up the threads of many lives, concentrating his attention on each patient in turn, then moving quickly to the next, dismissing success and thanks with a fleeting feeling of pleasure, and turning to consideration of failure and the unsolved problem.

When evening came, he walked along the shore of the sea to be alone and to think of his own life. He was not the man who had hurried away to care for a broken hip ten days before. He was aware of a strange excited feeling which he examined now by careful introspection. It was located, he realized, in front just under the border of his ribs. It was relieved momentarily by a deep breath, a sigh. The diagnosis was clear enough. This was the reaction of his body to what had happened in Halasarna. This was what it was to be in love. He had never guessed what it would be like, this lonely longing, this hunger. For treatment it might be enough, he thought, to be near Daphne. In ten days he would go to the Triopian Festival, and he might at least see her then. But this was a case for which he did not dare to venture a final prognosis.

The next days were busy ones for Hippocrates. At the urgent request of Cephalus, he visited his house daily. And each day Thargelia was waiting for him in Cephalus' courtyard, as though she had known in advance of his coming.

On the day after the slave's death, Cephalus came to the *iatreion* by appointment, bringing his wife with him, and his wife's mother as well. Hippocrates talked with the wife at some length. Then he examined her and carried out an operation. The procedure was painful, but very quickly and skillfully accomplished.

After the operation Hippocrates talked with Cephalus. "When

your wife has fully recovered from this operation," he said, "she will be able to carry out the marital act without pain. This was not possible for her before. Her pain was real, and she did not understand, nor did her mother. Now they do. Be patient with her. I believe she will be a good wife, and I see no reason why she should not be a good mother of your sons and daughters. Give her no cause to be jealous. Her behavior, which you found so unreasonable, was due to misunderstanding and to a deep longing to be loved."

"I had never seen her until the day of our marriage," Cephalus replied. "She brought me a very good dowry and I expected to learn to love her. After the first night she would not let me come near her and she would not tell me why. So I turned to the slave. I am sure now of one thing. There is room for only one love in a household. My wife and I have talked since you came into our house, since we began to understand. I am sorry I hurt her. I want sons to follow me. We are very grateful to you."

Hippocrates rose, thinking to put an end to their talk, but Cephalus persisted:

"There is something else I think I should tell you. Thargelia left our house this morning for Cnidus. She left suddenly and did not give us any reason. But Olympias, who went with her, hinted to me that she was going for medical reasons that you would understand. It was only at Olympias' request that I let Thargelia move from her first lodgings into my house here, so you could see her when you attended my slave and no one would be the wiser."

"By Zeus and all the gods of Olympus!" Hippocrates exclaimed. "She is a friend, no more than a friend! What are you suggesting?"

"Of course," Cephalus replied. "Of course."

When it came time that evening for the gathering of the asclepiads, Hippocrates and Podalirius crossed the garden together, each absorbed in his own thoughts. Podalirius heaved a sigh. No more secret messages, he thought, no exciting requests are likely to come from the wife of Cephalus. And a very good thing that is, of course. But her glances had brought him pleasure, he could admit that to himself at least.

When they reached the plane tree, Hippocrates looked around at the group of asclepiads waiting for him. They seemed unusually silent. He had no heart for discussion himself this evening, but he knew they expected it. He had not even thought what to say, which was quite contrary to his custom. He glanced at Sosander, hoping for help from him, but his back was turned.

He sat down in the cathedra seat. "From time to time," he began, "it is our custom to discuss with the younger asclepiads the conduct of the physician who enters men's homes to care for the sick." He turned to Podalirius. "You have had a long experience, Podalirius. You are counselor as well as physician to many households here in Cos. You open the discussion for us."

Podalirius rose slowly from his seat beside the Master. He knew Hippocrates was thinking of their recent experiences in the household of Cephalus. He also knew that no reference was to be made to that household. Some matters are better not told, even within the secret circle of medical discussion.

"An asclepiad," he said, "who is summoned to treat the sick at home should never mention outside the house those things which the master of the house does not want known. This is the conduct called for in the ancient asclepiad oath. Also, the master of the house is much more apt to pay the fee of a physician who keeps silence."

Sosander, who was sitting on the other side of Hippocrates, interrupted. "Some men pay the house visit fee just to keep the physician still. They can buy silence, if they can't always buy cure."

He laughed, and the others on the benches about the tree joined him, all but Podalirius. Podalirius held his head high; the setting sun, shining on his gray hair and beard, changed them to gold.

"It is better," he continued, "for the physician in the house to be blind and deaf to all except his patient. In any case, he should forget what he knows regardless of fee."

He sat down abruptly. Hippocrates smiled.

"There is much more to be considered," he said. "So many things are not mentioned in the ancient asclepiad oath. I think the time has come now to rewrite it."

He glanced at his brother, who nodded his agreement. Then Hippocrates continued.

"A physician should preserve as secrets all those things that should be secret, but when he enters the home he should inquire carefully into whatever may affect his patient in any way. After all, it is easier for a physician to change what he finds indoors than it is to alter such circumstances as the weather and the movements of the stars. The cause of disease and the cause of unhappiness are often to be found in the patient's immediate environment as well as in the climate, the season, the air and the place."

He fell silent then, until one of the younger asclepiads spoke up.

"I have wanted to ask you a question for a long time. How would you define love?"

"That is a difficult question!" Hippocrates exclaimed. "A question that the sophists would relish. It would keep them busy for a whole symposium."

"And at the end," Sosander added, "there would be no clear-cut answer. Only sleep and pleasant dreams, very pleasant dreams."

Hippocrates hesitated. "The mysterious urge that comes to a man in regard to one woman — that is love. It has elements of the mind in it as well as of the body. It seems to establish a bond of the spirit that is present even when the body is forgotten. You might say that love is the urge that Aphrodite instills in men and women. It has wedlock and the rearing of children as its goal. But perhaps a woman's definition of love might be different from mine, a man's. I do not know."

"But," the young man persisted, "I have learned of strange sensual practices between women themselves and sometimes of women alone. The same is true of men — is this love?"

Hippocrates shrugged. "Love is much more than sensual acts and the satisfying of sexual appetites. Empedocles would say that love is the force throughout all nature that brings opposites together: the man and the woman, the dry and the moist, the hot and the cold. Strife, or hate, according to him, is the opposite force. It drives similars together and opposites apart.

"A patient said to me recently, 'There is room for only one love in a household.' There is much truth in that saying. There is room in a house only for the love of a man for a woman and a woman for a man. That love is the reason the home exists. The love between parent and child is strong and of great importance. But it should be given another name — tenderness perhaps, or affection. And the bond between others still another name — such as friendship, comradeship.

"Under conditions that are normal, there is nothing else. Hidden forms of self-gratification are not part of the normal order of things. You see exploratory sensual movements in young animals. They disappear with maturity. The same is true of man — they disappear with adequate exercise, full occupation, normal relationships."

Sosander growled his approval. Then, after a silence, he cleared his throat and began to speak.

"The conditions in an army," he said, "are always abnormal. Conditions in some households are abnormal, especially when the master of the house is absent or turns his attention elsewhere. Love goes out then and strife comes in. Yes, Empedocles' word 'strife' is very apt. In army or household, when man turns to man or woman to woman or when the individual turns to himself, the conditions are abnormal.

"I agree that these things are not to be defined as love. I can give no better definition of love than the one Hippocrates has given you. That was a man's definition. He suggested that a woman's might be different. But no woman would bother to define love, however well she may understand it.

"But there is another aspect of this whole problem," Sosander continued, looking gravely at his brother, "an aspect that no one has mentioned. Whenever a physician enters a home to care for the sick he is exposed to real danger, the danger of personal slander. Even when he conducts himself with the utmost purity, as you did, Hippocrates, in the house of the chamberlain of the Macedonian court, he exposes himself to evil-speaking. You may as well know that false stories are being circulated about you and Thargelia. There is even absurd talk of a fight between you and her husband!"

Hippocrates smiled. "You should have seen the old man, not a very lively antagonist!"

Sosander brought the palm of his huge hand down on his knee with a crack. "I wish I could discover who spreads these lies!"

Hippocrates shook his head at his brother, but Sosander was not to be silenced.

"I know you want me to ignore it. I know that there is nothing you can do about it. Nevertheless, I think we can do something, all of us. We can go about denying the lies when we hear them." He jumped up from his seat and his voice became a roar: "If I catch the liar, I'll strangle him — or her!"

He lumbered away across the garden, while a sudden silence fell on the company. They wanted to shout their applause. But here was a strange situation, a situation that called for great tact. And so, not knowing what to say, they said nothing. One by one they walked away in awkward silence. Hippocrates remained behind, sitting in the twilight beneath the tree, amazed.

After a time he heard footsteps and, looking up, saw Pindar returning.

"Those stories are utter nonsense, Master. No one in Cos believes a word of them. Don't think of it."

"No, Pindar," Hippocrates replied. "I will try not to. There are so many more important things. Only two days remain before the Triopian Festival — Tell me how you have succeeded in the case of Penelope."

CHAPTER THIRTEEN

Empedocles and the Gods

~~~~~~

On the following afternoon the sons of Heracleides crossed the enclosure together. "Empedocles has asked us to hold our gathering under the tree earlier than usual today," Hippocrates said. "He is coming to it to say good-by. I'm not quite certain what he means."

Sosander shook his head. "He has reached the limit of endurance. The malignant disease in his back has advanced and we are losing ground. I invited him into my house and he had a bad attack of pain. My wife heard him groaning and she is furious now with us that we should let him go on suffering. I wouldn't want the disciples to hear me say this, but I've been wondering myself if the gods would not forgive us if we gave him the poison for which he begs."

They joined the asclepiads in the dappled shadow beneath the plane tree. Seeing that Empedocles had not arrived, Hippocrates answered his brother while the others gathered around.

"Our task," he said, "is to save life, not to end it. The gods may snip the thread of life at will, perhaps. But if physicians should take up the shears, where would it all end? This is another matter that should be introduced into the physicians' oath when we rewrite it."

Sosander nodded assent, but he added: "There are times when the turn from life to death does rest in our hands. Pity because of the patient's agony may cause us to withhold the treatment that would only prolong life. How much further freedom would the gods allow?

We boast that Greeks are free to think for themselves, while men in other nations must bow to king and priest."

"Wait a moment," Podalirius objected. "We are far from free as I see it. We are bound to defend the state, preserve and obey the laws, obey the judges, honor the gods. We fear the vengeance of the gods on Mount Olympus if we break divine law against incest, disloyalty to parents, and murder."

"Very well," Sosander replied. "But compare our lot with that of the physicians of Egypt. They are bound in their practice by the Book of the Dead, and if they depart from it in treatment ever so little their own lives may be forfeited. For a thousand years and more there has been no advance in medicine there. The same is true of all the arts. Look at sculpture and painting there and compare it with our own! The difference is due to the fact that our gods have granted us freedom to grow and improve."

"While we wait for Empedocles," Hippocrates interjected, "let us take our seats."

He turned to his brother. "Tell us what Herodotus has to say of the gods, Sosander. You have been reading a copy of his recent scrolls."

Sosander smiled and nodded. "Herodotus argues that Hesiod and Homer created the Greek gods by their writings. He shows quite clearly how this came about. He has written a history of the gods."

At this point, young Dexippus interrupted impetuously. "If we created our own gods, then why must we obey them? And why should you not give Empedocles the poison he wants? We all know he has asked for it."

The company was startled by this blunt question from the youngest disciple. They turned to Hippocrates, but he motioned to his brother.

Sosander's face lit up as he answered, speaking slowly and thoughtfully. "Wise men believe in the gods and pray to them. Nevertheless, thinking men know that if they were to climb Mount Olympus they would not find them there; they know too that these Greek gods do exist, for the gods are but different sides of the eternal god — different faces.

"The Greek gods help the Greeks and hear their prayers. It is heresy to speak against them and you must not think that I have done so. But it is nonsense for intelligent men not to understand their true nature. Greeks are free to understand, if they only will.

"Take, for example, what the Greek storytellers have done to our ancestor Asclepius. He has been made into a god now, with nearly a hundred shrines where men and women worship him and sacrifice to him. He was once only a good physician, as Homer described him. Through Asclepius, as the god of healing, men catch a glimpse of one aspect of the eternal god."

Sosander was walking back and forth now, waving his long arms in his excitement, for this subject was very dear to his heart.

"The Greeks," he exclaimed, as he brought his argument to a close, "must thank the Greek gods for their freedom. When I say that the Greeks made up the stories of the gods on Mount Olympus and that they created the gods, that does not mean that the gods do not exist. You might as well say that a certain truth is not the truth because a Greek discovered it."

"Magnificent argument!" Hippocrates exclaimed. "If Socrates were here we would discuss this subject until the dawn. But if you lived in Athens, Sosander, the Athenians might decide to exile you or give you hemlock to drink for teaching heresy to the young. Now, Pindar, I see you holding a scroll in your hand. What have you there?"

"I have a papyrus from Empedocles," Pindar replied. "I think he means it to be his parting gift to you, Master. Part of it he wrote himself, and he has treasured it from the days when he was a disciple of Alcmaeon in the school of Pythagoras."

Hippocrates started to unroll the scroll but paused and asked, "Have you read it, Pindar?"

"Yes."

"Give us its meaning."

"This manuscript," Pindar said, standing before his master, tall and confident, "contains an illuminating description of the hidden structure of the heart and the passages connected to the heart that contain the blood.

"Empedocles has also described here the *pneuma,* or air. He proves this to be an actual stuff that is present throughout the universe in all those places where men have thought that there was nothing. He has pointed out, for example, that in a water clock the air occupies space, just as water does. In the body of man, he says, the air passes by way of the heart and the blood passages into all of our parts."

Hippocrates nodded. "These are important contributions," he said. "Why can he not stop there? Why must he pass so quickly to unprovable hypotheses?"

"Yes," Pindar continued. "The scroll also presents certain teachings that you would have us discard. He states that the source of innate heat is in the strong left chamber of the heart. Innate heat and thought, he would have us believe, are one and the same thing. I find it strange that Empedocles should be deaf to your arguments that the brain is the home of the mind, the dwelling place of the intellect. Especially so since Empedocles' own teacher Alcmaeon was of the same opinion as you in this regard. I have talked a good deal with Empedocles while you were away.

"Perhaps," he added with a smile, "it would be more accurate to say that I have listened to him at great length. He is not a man who hears other people's points of view, as you do. But I have learned now to admire him as all men do, and — to feel sorry for him. Perhaps you don't know it, but here in Cos crowds follow him through the streets calling on him for miracles and asking him to cure their diseases.

"One more thing — but perhaps I have talked too much already —"

"No," Hippocrates said, smiling. "Go on."

"What I want to say is that when I look at him critically, with the eyes of a physician, I realize he is growing thin and haggard. The tumor on his back has enlarged. There is swelling of his legs. He has to be lifted on and off the donkey on which he rides through the streets and —"

Hippocrates held up his hand. "Here he comes now."

They could hear the distant shouting of men and women on the shore, and near at hand the music of lyres. Someone was walking toward them. It was Empedocles, but strangely changed in dress and manner. His handsome face was radiant. Like a king, he wore a golden crown and a golden girdle. His robe was purple and his staff was jewel-topped. When he raised his hand to greet his friends, light flashed from the purple ring.

No one spoke as he approached. But Hippocrates, rising from his high-backed seat at the base of the plane tree, stepped aside and motioned him there. Empedocles sat down slowly, cautiously. The solemn music came nearer. The twin slaves, approaching side by side, stopped beyond the spreading branches of the plane tree. They lowered their lyres, while the sun through the trees lit up their yellow robes and flaxen hair.

Hippocrates and the others took disciples' seats and waited to hear what the man in the master's chair would say. Empedocles looked about the circle.

"I have come to say farewell. I begged for cure or death, but the cure it seems is not to be found and the drink of death the gods forbid, or so you believe. Well, you've done what you thought was best for me. Your kindness has smoothed my path of pain and you used such art as medicine knows. But even with the best of will and the greatest skill, none can rebuild this broken house."

"Nonsense," Sosander interrupted. "We have only just begun. You know yourself, Empedocles, that your posture has improved greatly."

Empedocles laughed, a little ruefully.

"No, Sosander, you've done your best. My tragedy draws to its close. Only the chorus is yet to be sung, after the hero goes."

A wind stirred in the great plane tree above their heads, making last year's seed balls swing like silent bells on the fraying threads. Hippocrates watched as the flying seeds came settling down on Empedocles' robe and crown — a promise that birth would be following death, birth of another sort. He realized that the kingly pose of this philosopher who was sitting in his seat was not quite the mad pantomime that it might appear. Had Empedocles really convinced himself that he was a god? Or was he acting a part so that posterity would think him one? Inspiration and madness may seem to have much in common, and the mind of a genius is still creative even when confused.

"Like Prometheus," Empedocles was saying, "I am a god condemned to linger on in agony. Like him I have given rich gifts to men. The penalty for my ancient sin is to wander through eternity — as man and beast and tree. I must live a hundred lives and die a hundred deaths, while my soul puts on new cloaks that are soon worn out and cast aside."

"Empedocles," Pindar said, "you have described to us four elements that make up all that there is in the universe: air, water, earth and fire. But you have said that they are also gods: Zeus, Hera, Aidoneus and Mestis. You have said also that the forces that move in the universe, love (*philia*) and hate (*neikos*), are also gods.

"Is there, then, in your philosophy another god, a great god even above Zeus and above Apollo and Aphrodite? A god that has some greater power?"

Hippocrates looked about at the listeners and saw that they approved the question. Smiling to himself, he turned his attention back to Empedocles. Pindar's question was a searching one, and logical as always. Anyone who spoke in this symposium must expect to face such questions.

"Yes," Empedocles answered. "The spherical plenum that embraces the All — that is the great god. *Sphaeros* we may call her. Parmenides called her Dike."

Empedocles raised his resonant voice, and the asclepiads stirred in their seats.

"Once there was a golden age. I described it in a poem:

> *There was no War, no Battle din,*
> *No kingly Zeus, no Kronos, nor any Poseidon*
> *But Love alone was queen.*

"The sun and earth and air and sea, four roots, were bound together. And Aphrodite's power of love was able to hold them so. But although nothing could be destroyed nor taken away, yet change was possible.

"So it was that Sphaeros created all. Dipping her brush in every hue, she painted trees and men, women and beasts, fishes and birds and the long-lived gods. Some forms she made that could not survive, and others changed with the passage of time. So, by the long process of evolution, the forms that survived are with us today and we are here. We are the products of this evolution, survivors because we were fit to survive.

"The golden age has passed now and we enter a second stage, a time of grief and strife. A sinister force is splitting the world, splitting the spherical plenum with hate. Now love withdraws while discord grows."

Empedocles rose from his chair. "This is enough for mortals to hear —"

But he could say no more. He bowed his head and groaned. He slipped down into Hippocrates' seat again, but only for a moment. The crumpled man straightened himself and rose slowly to his feet. With Hippocrates and Sosander holding him by either arm, he walked to the gate. They lifted him gently and put him on the mule that his slaves had brought, shifting the saddle until he was as comfortable as could be.

"The scroll that you have given me," Hippocrates said, "will be preserved among our most precious manuscripts. It will be a memorial of all that you have contributed to medicine."

Empedocles' face lit up with pleasure and he removed the crown from his head. He looked about at the asclepiads, smiling. "Those were my happiest years, those young years in medicine. But now — I say farewell. You remember the words of Aeschylus:

> 'Oh Death the Healer, scorn thou not I pray,
> To come to me: of cureless ills thou art
> The one physician. Pain lays not its touch
> Upon a corpse.' "

Hippocrates watched Empedocles ride out through the gate and heard the people shout.

"When will we learn to kill pain," he said to Sosander, "without killing the man? When will we learn to cure malignant growth?"

Then he turned to Pindar. "Empedocles, I discover, is going to Pelea. Follow him there — I'm afraid he might need your help. You can stay with old Aeneas."

When the asclepiads gathered the following evening, Pindar had not yet returned from Pelea. But he arrived before the teaching hour was over.

"Yes," he said, in answer to Hippocrates' question, "there is news. But what the meaning of this news may be, and whether it is good news or bad news, you must be the judge.

"I arrived in Pelea shortly after Empedocles yesterday evening. He was housed as an honored guest in the acropolis there. But when I went this morning at dawn to find him, they told me that he had left long before with a guide and his twin slaves to climb the mountain in back of Pelea. They told me there is a path that his mule could climb all the way to the top, and a favorite ledge there for those who wish to look out southward over the sea.

"I followed after them and came on the guide and the slaves with Empedocles' mule, a little below the peak. He had told them to wait. I went on, following the path that he had taken. It passed around and between jagged rocks, and I came at last to a lonely ledge. His clothes were lying there — folded neatly and placed in a pile: chiton and sandals, and on them his staff and girdle and the crown of gold." Pindar choked and stopped.

"And is that all?" Hippocrates asked. "Didn't you look further?"

Pindar nodded, and controlling himself with an effort, he continued. "Yes. I listened first. Then I called. But there was no answer. So I walked farther on along the ledge until I came suddenly upon him. I almost stumbled over him, and I thought he was dead. He was lying on his face, naked. Only his purple cloak was spread out between him and the rocky floor. I spoke his name softly, and he raised his head and looked at me quietly, supporting himself on his elbows.

"There was a strange light in his eyes, but all he said was: 'Well, Pindar — you've come.' He turned his head and looked out over the sea — he was lying very near the edge of the cliff.

" 'I've been thinking back over this life,' he said, 'back to my boyhood and my young manhood. It was a good life, a magnificent life until I was banished, and then my wife — but I need not tell you that.'

"I tried then to reason with him and to lift him up, but he asked me to leave him alone. The morning was very cold, though the sun was rising over Cnidia and it shone on the ledge. He just lay there, naked and flat on the ledge."

Pindar shook his head. "Empedocles looked at me and said: 'There is a little more that I want to say — and I have always liked an audience, you know.' He smiled when he said that; then he went on. 'Asclepius sent me to Cos. But Hippocrates could not save me. It was not the will of the gods. And so this body of mine will die; not I, for I live on. . . . What do you think, Pindar? What will it be? Shall I be housed in a man, or a beast, or a creeping thing? Or shall I be free in Olympus at last?'

"He lowered his head and was silent for a moment. Then he groaned with sudden pain. 'Go, Pindar,' he said. 'Get my sandals so I can walk. The rocks hurt my feet.'

"So I did it, as quickly as I could. But as I was hurrying back, I heard a great shout. I ran on until I came to the ledge where I had left him. Empedocles was gone."

Pindar turned away as though the tale were told.

"Gone!" Sosander roared. "What do you mean, gone?"

"His robe was there. I shouted, and shouted again. But no answer came back at all. Behind me, down the slopes toward Pelea, I could hear the bells of grazing sheep and soon the sound of lyres. The twin slaves were playing a hymn to guide their master home, as he had asked them to do. The precipice toward the sea is very high and sheer. The sea was very far away and no sail in sight."

"You saw no more?" Hippocrates asked.

"Nothing — nothing except a snake that slid away, and a large, slowly moving turtle making off along the ledge."

The asclepiads were silent and looked at one another. At last Hippocrates spoke. "There comes a time in the evening of life when the lights are dim behind and death is dark before — Then every man must face the gods alone."

When Hippocrates returned to his house, he found Nicodemus waiting for him outside the door. The young man bowed.

"May I speak to you?" he asked. "I want to take my leave and to thank you with all my heart for the help you have given me. A ship for Tyre is expected soon and I have been told that you are leaving for the Triopian games tomorrow."

"Yes," Hippocrates replied. "I may be gone four or five days at least. They tell me, Nicodemus, that you have shown great interest in the teachings of Empedocles."

"Oh, yes," the young man replied eagerly. "I was educated to be a priest in Jerusalem, and only the falling fits kept me from the priesthood. I have followed Empedocles about and listened when he talked to the people. You see, I haven't many friends to talk to in Cos."

"I'm sorry to have to tell you that you can listen to him no longer. Empedocles is dead."

"Alas!" Nicodemus exclaimed. "I shall miss him."

Hippocrates, seeing tears in Nicodemus' eyes, said kindly, "I suppose you are lonely here sometimes?"

"Yes."

"Come in. I am alone. If you have not had your evening meal you must dine with me."

They entered the house together.

"Over there," Hippocrates said, pointing, "is the toilet. And here is the water for washing your hands and feet. Leave your sandals and put on these red slippers. They are like the ones men wear in the East, are they not? You will find me in the *oecus,* which is over there across the court. Meanwhile, I will tell the servant to prepare for two. I hope you will like my simple fare."

After they had finished the meal and Hippocrates had poured out the wine, he turned to Nicodemus.

"Tell me," he asked, "why did your education for the priesthood make you so interested in Empedocles?"

"He seemed to me," Nicodemus replied, "a man of great insight, a man of inspiration. There have been many such men in the history of Israel. Some of them were called prophets; and others, I suppose, were stoned because their teachings were not in accordance with our religion."

Hippocrates looked at him with interest.

"Have your people preserved their ancient religion?"

"Yes," Nicodemus replied. "The Hebrew religion is preserved unchanged. It cannot be altered, except by interpretation, because of the writings; we call them the Scriptures. We preserved them even during our captivity in Babylon. Now we can speak openly again of the Scriptures since our return to Jerusalem. They are the writings of prophets, poets, scribes and others who listened to the word of God. I know many of the writings by heart."

"What would Hebrews think of Empedocles's story of the creation of the world and the gods?"

"Let me answer you," Nicodemus replied, "by quoting from the Scriptures:

'In the beginning, God created the heaven and the earth.

'And the earth was without form, and void; and darkness was upon the face of the deep. And the spirit of God moved upon the face of the waters.

'And God said, Let there be light: and there was light.' "

Hippocrates regarded his guest thoughtfully, but he said nothing, and Nicodemus continued.

"David, the Hebrew poet and king, wrote:

'Lord, thou hast been our dwelling place in all generations.

'Before the mountains were brought forth, or ever thou hadst formed the earth and the world, even from everlasting to everlasting, thou art God. . . .

'For a thousand years in thy sight are but as yesterday when it is past, and as a watch in the night.' "

Hippocrates smiled with appreciation.

"Is your God, then, like a man," he asked, "made in the image of men?"

"No. But it is written that man was made in the image of God, and David sang of us as sheep in the care of a shepherd:

'The Lord is my shepherd; I shall not want.

'He maketh me to lie down in green pastures: He leadeth me beside the still waters.

'He restoreth my soul: He leadeth me in the paths of righteousness for His name's sake.

'Yea, though I walk through the valley of the shadow of death, I will fear no evil: for thou art with me; thy rod and thy staff they comfort me.' "

"Beautiful!" Hippocrates said. "If he is a shepherd, do you see him or hear his voice?"

Nicodemus' eyes were shining with pleasure in this discussion. "Jehovah," he said, "is also a still small voice. It is written that when Elijah went up into a high mountain and called upon the Lord:

'Behold the Lord passed by, and a great and strong wind rent the mountains and brake in pieces the rocks before the Lord; but the Lord was not in the wind: and after the wind an earthquake; but the Lord was not in the earthquake:

'And after the earthquake a fire; but the Lord was not in the fire: and after the fire a still small voice.' "

Hippocrates nodded. "Socrates," he said, "teaches that men have souls and that they communicate somehow with the spirit of God. He might question you as to how you know these things, but his thinking seems to run along with yours."

He walked to the door with Nicodemus, and went out with him to stand under the stars. Remembering that he could help this patient with his future, he spoke with him about his father in Jerusalem and about his plans for life.

"All men," he said, "have handicaps that they must overcome and learn to live with. Your epilepsy is no more than that. You will be better, I think. In any case, life lies before you. You must go to work. Perhaps, when you return, you can help to build the walls of the new Jerusalem."

CHAPTER FOURTEEN

Festival of Apollo

〰〰〰〰〰〰〰〰〰〰〰〰〰〰〰〰〰〰〰〰〰〰〰

It was still dark next morning when Hippocrates crossed from his house to the enclosure gate, carrying his travel bag. Bobo's soft whine of recognition came to him out of the dark and a warm tongue licked his hand. While Elaphus was lighting a torch from the small oil lamp that burned in the gatehouse, Hippocrates crouched beside the dog and stroked his smooth head and warm flank.

"Good old Bobo. How would you like it if I should bring back a lovely young mistress for you from Cnidus? Don't wag your tail — there's not much chance of that."

Elaphus shouldered his master's bag and walked out, holding the torch aloft. Hippocrates followed in the circle of light, while Bobo bade farewell with a subdued bark, his head down on his forepaws and his tail wagging with slow regret.

This was the first day of the famous festival of the Triopian Apollo. Every man on the Island of Cos who could find passage would be sailing today across the Ceramic Gulf and around the Cnidian headland to Triopion. They had done it for centuries. How many centuries no one knew, not even Herodotus, their own historian.

The two men walked in silence to the sloping beach of the harbor. Here Hippocrates told Elaphus to set the bag down. The servant hesitated, but obeyed. The old gateman knew that all was not well. He could not know the cause.

"May the gods give you good gifts," he said.

Hippocrates thanked him and watched his torch grow small and disappear. When its light was gone he could see nothing for a time. There was a sharp smell of fish in the air which brought back Halasarna to his mind. A chill wind was stirring. The lanterns before the open shops on the waterfront had begun to swing. Between the shops he could see, in the feeble light, the drooping limbs of the tamarisk trees. They were swaying back and forth, like a woman's hair in the wind — or the garments of mourners, marching and dancing to the grave. He thought of his mother's words when he left her ten days before: "There is trouble ahead, tragedy perhaps."

"Hippocrates!" someone called and he shouted back. Soon he saw the squat figure of his brother Sosander lumbering toward him out of the darkness.

"I've found you at last!" his brother cried. "I thought you might have started to swim to the mainland, you've been so absent-minded lately. If it weren't for the fact that I never saw you look at a woman, I'd think you were in love. I'm told that the trireme is anchored just offshore somewhere, and we are to be on board and away before the sun is over the mountains of Caria."

They walked along the waterfront past tables where well-dressed citizens sat drinking bowls of steaming barley broth or tea. The eastern horizon was tinged with gray light now, making sharp silhouettes of the pillars on the island across the harbor. On the water, they could see the lights of moving boats, and the little harbor resounded with lusty shouts.

"What a crowd!" Sosander exclaimed. "I've never seen more enthusiasm than there is this year. Some people say Cleomedes is sure to win the boxing. Others say he broke his training. If he has to face Peisirrodus from Rhodes, the grandson of Diagoras, he'll need to be fit.

"The Coans," he continued, "are pleased that you are going to represent them again when you speak from the temple steps, Hippocrates. They say you're a far better speaker than Euryphon, though how anyone could know that, I can't imagine. In any case, that's the news as I heard it at the barber's alcove yesterday. Is Podalirius coming with us?"

"No," Hippocrates replied. "He will remain here to look after the work in the *iatreion* and do as well as he can with the patients in the city. The younger asclepiads will help him. But Pindar is coming."

As he spoke, Pindar himself appeared, and at the same time they heard a shout: "Out of the way, out of the way!"

The three men moved quickly out of the path of a long boat that was grating its way down the sloping gravel, pushed by grunting men. The boat slid into the water, the grating stopped, and the anchor was dropped with a great splash.

"This way," Pindar said. "The tender for the trireme of the City of Cos Meropis is farther along the shore. I've agreed to pull an oar myself today, since many of the regular oarsmen are being replaced by those who want to go to see the festival. We get free passage this way."

As they were rowed out from shore, the trireme loomed above them, with its high decks forward and aft. In between were the three levels of rowing seats and the heavy mast with its cross spars. Coming nearer, they could see the pointed metal horn that projected from the bow just at the water line. It had a sharp iron cap at the tip. A city trireme must be ready for war, ready to ram and sink enemy warships. Through the openings in the ship's side they could see the oarsmen taking their seats.

"There are eighty-seven oarsmen on each side," Sosander said, "but we are sure to have a following wind, so our sails will bring us there long before noontime, and there will be little for the oars to do."

They climbed the ladder to the afterdeck.

"Come here, Pindar," Hippocrates called, "before you take your place in the rowing seat. Come and look carefully with me at the light in the east. Notice the color that edges the tops of the mountains of Caria. It is deep orange. Now look higher up in the sky. The color is violet there, and as your eye moves downward you see the other shades: blue, green, yellow, orange. If you look at it again, just before the sun rises, you will see pink and red appear below the orange. That makes all the colors of the rainbow and they are arranged in the same order."

"I see what you mean," Pindar replied. "I suppose Empedocles would have said that those are the colors into which Sphaeros dipped her brush when she made the world and us. There is meaning in Empedocles' poetry, and I can't get his words out of my mind."

"You are a poet yourself," Hippocrates replied. "But beware! Don't trust the wings of poetry or of philosophy when investigating the facts of nature and man and disease."

After Pindar left them, the two sons of Heracleides stood together on deck under the gay canopy. The boatswain shouted his commands. The anchor came up, the oars began to swing, and the ship took a curving course across the harbor and into the water passage to the open sea.

Standing on the high deck as the ship slipped along the passage, the brothers could look down on the enclosure. Through the branches of the plane tree they could see the stone seats about the trunk, for the leaves are slow to come out in the spring.

"Why," Hippocrates asked his brother, "when our father moved from Halasarna, did he come to live here instead of at the old capital of Astypalaea? Astypalaea was so much larger then."

"He was determined to form a teaching center," Sosander replied, "like the one in Cnidus, and not to wander from place to place like so many physicians in other parts of Greece. The physicians in Astypalaea were hostile to the building of an *iatreion* there. I think too that he wanted his family to be near this defensible harbor in case of future war with Persia. He found that he could buy this walled enclosure, and it was remarkable how soon students began to come. But I am afraid our parents almost starved in the first years here. Praxithea didn't bring him much dowry, but they had courage, both of them. Cos Meropis grew from a town to a city in his lifetime. Our father's wisdom has been amply justified. But his ambition to rival the center of medical teaching at Cnidus is yet to be fulfilled."

The ship was moving out to sea and the wind was strong from

the northwest. They pulled their cloaks about them and leaned on the rail.

"At the time he died," Sosander continued, "he was placing his hopes on you, the younger son, to make his dreams come true after he was gone."

"You are much more important in our common undertaking than I am," Hippocrates said. "You do the work that counts. And I seem to have accomplished little since my return, except perhaps to bring false scandal back from Macedonia. It is false, Sosander, completely false."

Sosander nodded his shaggy head. "I believe you, you have never lied to me. But why is it false? That is the question. If Odysseus had met Thargelia on his wanderings, he would never have returned to Penelope. I marvel when I see this beautiful woman hurling herself headlong at my younger brother while he steps aside! Oh, I know it would not work very well. But it would be an exciting experience at least."

After a pause, Sosander continued, "You have never told me what your answer to the King of Macedonia is going to be."

Hippocrates straightened up and turned his back to the sea.

"The day the captain of the trireme brought the invitation, I had no time to make up my mind. I wanted to talk with you about it, but the invitation to Macedonia arrived together with Thargelia, and was followed almost at once by news of our grandmother's broken hip. So I sent word to the captain that I would give him his answer when he returned from Tyre. You see, Sosander, while I was in Halasarna, I thought a good deal. I thought perhaps I ought to get married after all."

Sosander raised his eyebrows. But Hippocrates continued. "That should be considered before making the decision about Macedonia, especially now that war is threatening like thunder in the distance. The salary the king promised would make my wife and me rich; rich, I suppose, for life. What do you advise?"

"Advise? What can I say when Aphrodite seems to be meddling so mysteriously in your affairs?"

Sosander often changed suddenly from banter to sober reason. He did so now. "Don't leave us, Hippocrates. Who else could carry out the dream of Heracleides? Our dream it is now! Without you there will never be a teaching school in Cos. With you — just think of what we might do together, all of us, just think! Reason tells me you will go. But I hope from my heart you will stay."

Hippocrates smiled and put a hand for a moment on his brother's shoulder. The two had never been demonstrative, although they were very close to each other in understanding and affection.

"Recently," Hippocrates said, "I have been excited by reading the scrolls that our father was working on at the time of his death, the ones called Aphorisms. Some of his writing in them is splendid, really splendid. But the work is incomplete. The papyrus on fevers is quite unfinished too. I long to add to those writings, but it calls for a good deal more study, more experience."

Sosander nodded. "That is exactly what he hoped you would do for him and what I cannot do."

He held out huge, hairy arms and opened his hands. "I am a man with arms and hands for gymnastics, massage, surgery. These hands were not made for the reed pen, nor this head for philosophy."

"Don't talk such foolishness. You are the best philosopher of us all. And in medical treatment, I ride on your back like — like Anchises on the back of Aeneas."

"My back!" Sosander laughed a little bitterly. "My back is the back of an ass. It would be fit to carry a man out of the walls of burning Troy, perhaps. But as part of a man, it is crooked and ugly — a jest for the gods!"

The sail had been set and the ship was sailing fast before the wind, the oarsmen sat idly talking and laughing back and forth while the oars were pulled high up in their leather slings. The peninsula of Cnidia showed only a bare and rocky range of mountains, as they approached it from the north, across the Ceramic Gulf. It was long and narrow with only two fertile valleys, both of them on the southern slope. Cnidus, the capital city, was in the larger fertile area at the center of Cnidia. Triopion, west of it, was in the other valley. The temple of Apollo was located at Triopion, and in the temple precincts were the gymnasium and stadium for the games of the five Doric cities of the east.

As the Coan trireme rounded the towering island of rock at the tip of the peninsula, Sosander, who had been talking with his many Coan friends, rejoined his brother. Hippocrates had moved to the bow of the ship and was standing there alone.

"The captain is cutting in closer to the rock than usual," Sosander said. "But the water is deep here, very deep. Look how still the surface is behind the island. It's like a mirror."

As they came into the lee of the land, the wind dropped and the ship's sail flapped. Then the oars began to swing and the ship slipped smoothly on.

"What a magnificent harbor that would make!" Sosander continued, "behind that island mountain."

Hippocrates nodded absently and changed the subject.

"I wish I could avoid speaking tomorrow," he said. "I have written a formal address, but it is poor. My heart is not in it. Timon has arranged this as an oratorical contest with Herodotus speaking first, followed by Euryphon and me. I am very much surprised that he could get Herodotus here all the way from Italy. He has not dared to return to his birthplace for years. But our Timon even persuaded the Tyrant of Halicarnassus to invite him to visit his native city again."

"I shall be delighted to hear him," Sosander said, "now that I have read his writings. I knew him when I was a boy, although he was older than I. He has read his history at the Olympic games, and he was invited to read in Athens, as you know. But the people will not compare your oration with his in any case; they will compare your oration with Euryphon's."

"That's just the trouble!" Hippocrates exclaimed. "I wouldn't want to speak better than Euryphon, even if I could. At the same time, I don't want to lessen the honor of Cos."

Sosander grunted. "Speaking in public is like throwing the discus. You do your best and wait for the result. The applause of the audience will decide the matter as to who is the best speaker."

Hippocrates shook his head, and Sosander looked at him questioningly.

"Oh well," Hippocrates said, flushing, "you may as well know why it would be a misfortune to beat Euryphon. He has a daughter. Her name is Daphne."

Sosander whistled. "By Zeus! So that's it — of course! But isn't Daphne to marry Cleomedes? Isn't the marriage contract completed?"

"No," Hippocrates replied. "It is not, and Euryphon has told her he will not force her to it. But Timon is a hard man to say no to, and Cleomedes is young, handsome, rich."

Sosander nodded and looked serious. "Yes, Crates, I see." The older brother had slipped back to the boyhood nickname. "I see. Euryphon is a good physician, but he is fond of his fees. He likes wealth and wealthy people. He never appears in the agora at Cnidus, I am told, without at least one slave in attendance. He likes to make a proper impression on the world. On the other hand, we are simple folk from Cos — you and your misshapen brother. Don't be too disappointed if Euryphon should choose young Cleomedes for his daughter."

Sosander held his head as high as he could and looked up at his brother with a grim smile as he continued: "Perhaps, Crates, Daphne has a little sister who would be good enough for us! But to be serious, and to speak as your older brother, my advice is not to bow too low to Euryphon. Don't bow at all."

It was nearly noon when the trireme rounded another headland and Triopion's island came in sight. The waves had smoothed into glittering rollers. From time to time, shoals of flying fish soared into the air ahead of them. They appeared in groups and sailed off in straight diverging lines, borne up by their winglike lateral fins. Occasionally they touched the surface of the water and sailed up again without entering it, thanks to a kick from the tail fin.

What a spectacle they saw that day! Proud ships and sailing craft scattered over the purple sea, all moving toward the golden beach that curved like a well-drawn bow. It was the call of Apollo that brought them back. The men on these ships were Greeks, proud of their Doric blood, proud of the fact that their "hollow ships" had sailed to the siege of Troy so many years ago.

Slowly, steadily the great fleet converged on Triopion Bay. The smaller boats drove straight on, to beach themselves on the sloping yellow sand. The triremes and the larger ships turned away to the left and so came into the lee of a sickle-shaped island. The far end of the island was connected to the land by a sea wall four or five stadia in length, providing safe anchorage even against the dreaded southerly storms.

The trireme from Cos Meropis had furled her sails and the banks of oars were swinging now in time to the boatswain's call: "*Op — o — op! Op — o — op!*" while the oarsmen answered, "*Rhup — pa — pai! Rhup — pa — pai!*" As they neared the shore, a company on the forward deck played on their flutes the ancient song of rowing men, piping the proud ship in. And those on the land gave a rousing shout for Cos Meropis.

Then the helmsman shoved the tiller across. The rudder blades made a rushing sound and the ship swung round in a graceful arc, heading back to the island's lee, till anchors splashed and the ship was still.

The days of Apollo's Festival at Triopion were the days that men remembered through the years. What happened there might serve to identify one passing year from another during the lifetime of any man who lived in one of the Doric cities washed by the Aegean Sea.

While they waited for the tender, they looked at the green valley, rising upward to the height on which the temple stood with its white pillars shining in the sun. They could see the platform before it and the parallel terraces of the stadium below. The gods might well have placed the little mountain there at the head of the valley as a site for the temple, where men might look down on the lush green slopes and out to sea.

When the passengers reached the shore, a great crowd gathered about the tender, some shouting out the cost of a donkey ride to the sacred precincts of Apollo, some offering food and parasols, pillows and blankets, all at a price. A half hour's climb past vineyards and farms brought the brothers and Pindar to stairs that led steeply up to the town itself.

In the evening, shortly before sundown, Hippocrates and the other judges gathered in a small room in the gymnasium, where they were welcomed by the Chief Judge.

"I must give you my report," he said. "I have eliminated one of the contestants because it was proven that his mother was not a Greek. Most of the others have worked faithfully. For a time one of the boxers, Cleomedes, was irregular, and twice he was absent, although it is said he continued his training. I propose to you that he be allowed to enter the boxing, not because he is the son of Timon of Cos, who has given money and has worked for the good of the festival, but because the young man has changed and worked as he should for the past ten days.

"You will remember that Peisirrodus of Rhodes won the boys' boxing crown here two years ago with a splendid performance, and that he was trained by his mother Pherenice, the daughter of Diagoras, the greatest of all boxers, and sister to Acusilas and Damagetus and Dorieus, all of whom also won the men's crown at Olympia. This family of the Diagoridai has no equal in the history of the Greek games.

"You probably have heard that Peisirrodus himself won the crown in boys' boxing at the last Olympic festival and that this remarkable woman, his mother, was present at the games dressed as a man among the other trainers. She is a magnificent boxer herself, if you can believe it. I have seen her.

"I need not tell you the rest of the story at Olympia." The judges nodded and smiled at each other. Everyone in Greece had heard that story: How it was reported to the Olympic judges that the trainer of Peisirrodus was a woman, not the man she seemed. Her clothes were taken away from her and she was condemned to death as a woman who dared to watch the games before Zeus. But she stood before the judges and argued her case, explaining that she was the daughter of Diagoras and the sister of three who had won the Olympic crown. The judges relented then and pardoned her, but passed a law that henceforth at Olympia all trainers must go naked during the games, like the contestants.

"Peisirrodus," the Chief Judge continued, "appears this year in the men's boxing class. I have told this woman that she cannot be present during the contests before Apollo. Have I your support?"

The judges agreed with some shouting and laughter.

"I have, however, allowed her to continue to train her son, since the training is not carried out in the presence of the god, and also because all three of the Rhodian cities requested me to do so."

The judges moved out in a body and stood under the arch at the top of a broad flight of stone steps. Below them was an enormous open court, bounded all around by a covered colonnade, and several hundred young men and boys were standing naked in the court and along the colonnade. As the judges appeared, the trainers came out of the room reserved for them, and each joined his charge. The boys arranged themselves under the portico on one side of the court, the men on the other, divided according to events: the sprint, the long jump, the discus throw, the javelin throw, wrestling. Next came the pentathlon contestants who would have to compete in each of the preceding events. Pentathlon was followed by boxing, the long race, the race in armor, and finally the savage *pancration*, which permitted both boxing and wrestling.

The judges walked in a body around the court, stopping before one group after another. Each trainer would give the name of his pupil and the names of his father and mother. This statement was duly checked by a scribe who followed with his list.

When they reached the men's boxing group, Hippocrates looked with interest at the daughter of Diagoras. She was dressed exactly like the male trainers, with her hair cut short. He noted with amusement a few black hairs on her upper lip and chin. Nature seemed to be helping her in her attempt to masquerade as a man. Her features were coarse, her expression defiant. Her shoulders were broader than those of most women and her chest was flat. Her arms were long and beautifully muscled. As she moved, her slow grace reminded Hippocrates of a tigress he had seen in Macedonia. Her son moved with the same lithe deliberation.

When the mother had given her son's name and his parentage, the Chief Judge turned to the boxers and wrestlers. "The ode of Pindar," he said so all could hear, "which is inscribed in gold in Athena's temple at Lindus describes this young man's grandfather as a 'straight fighter,' one 'who walks in the straight path that abhors insolence.' Let all who box or wrestle here fight straight like Diagoras."

It was Cleomedes' turn next. Buto shuffled forward with the trainer's forked staff in his hand.

"Cleomedes, son of . . ." Buto cleared his throat with a rumbling sound . . . "son of Timon and Olympias of Cos, both of them Greek."

At last, when all had been examined and the scribe had checked his lists, the trainers left the gymnasium and the contestants gathered about the Chief Judge, who stood on the steps to speak to them.

"All of you here are accepted for the contests. If you have exercised and trained in a manner worthy of our Triopian tradition, and if you have been guilty of no ignoble act, go on with courage. What you do in these games will be done in the presence of the Triopian Apollo. In the agony of contest give him your supreme effort. That is *aretê*. In *aretê*, Apollo takes delight."

The young men drifted out of the court toward their dressing rooms. Hippocrates watched them go, admiring the naked beauty of their tanned bodies. They were graceful, sure, alert, with a zest for living.

Later in the evening he joined his brother and Pindar and they watched as much as they could see of the formal opening of the festival. It was a relay torch race. The runners were stationed at intervals along the course, and flaming torches were given to each of the starters. The runners must be fast and yet not let the torch go out. So the flaming lights moved along the length of the stadium; then up the steps to the acropolis; across the square to the temple steps; up the steps and into the temple. The first to arrive with lighted torch lit the fire on Apollo's altar.

Next morning the three asclepiads from Cos walked through the town of Triopion, which was completely given over to the gay throng of visitors. The musical contests and the orations were scheduled to take place later that morning, and the athletic games did not begin until the afternoon. Women would therefore not be excluded from the precincts until that time, and women seemed to be everywhere now. Hippocrates wondered whether Daphne was there too. Surely she would be listening when her father spoke.

Here and there they found tricksters and jugglers of all sorts, the majority of them women. There were sword swallowers and fire eaters, men shouting their wares, and eager buyers. There were beggers too and countrymen, rich and poor, and thieves. Even the sick and the lame had come for miraculous cures at the nearby temple of Asclepius.

A large circle of onlookers had formed around five women jugglers who kept an incredible number of balls in the air, catching and throwing them and dancing all the while. But Pindar was fascinated by a woman who stood on her hands and shot an arrow from a bow that she held with her feet and toes.

They climbed the flight of stairs to the acropolis gate, but they were unable to enter because of the crowd that had come to hear the music competitions. Presently there was a great burst of applause, and people dispersed while judges awarded the prizes to the players of the flute, the harp and the lyre.

Then a herald went about announcing that all who would hear Herodotus, Euryphon and Hippocrates should gather in the portico before the steps of the temple of Apollo. A messenger came to Hippocrates and warned him to be ready when the master of ceremonies should call on him. When at last the music-lovers had gone and others had come, Timon of Cos ascended the stairs. He called for silence. Then he beckoned to Herodotus.

As Herodotus followed him and took his place on the steps there was great applause. Then the priest of Apollo appeared above them, on the top step.

"I used to know that priest," Hippocrates whispered to Sosander. "We wrestled against each other for the boys' wrestling crown. A fine lad he was, from Cnidus, and afterward for a time he was a pupil of medicine under Ctesiochus. I knew he had given up medicine but I didn't know what had become of him."

The priest's white robes and his long hair blew out in the wind as he looked down. "Welcome, Herodotus," he said. "Welcome back to the Triopian Festival."

Then he gave Timon a wreath of laurel leaves like the wreath he himself was wearing, and Timon placed the wreath on the head of Herodotus, who turned about and began his oration.

"Today I speak to you as Herodotus of Halicarnassus, although I am now a citizen of Thuri, far to the west in Italy. There I am writing a history, hoping thereby to preserve the remembrance of what men have done. Man's memory is short. Even heroic deeds come soon to oblivion, unless there is a record like the record of Homer. I am writing such a record of the great and wonderful actions of the Greeks and the Barbarians. Thus they may receive their due meed of glory for all time. My researches have been many, my travels long, and my writings have been rewarded by Athens; I have been honored by Olympia; and I rejoice today that you should honor me in the presence of Triopian Apollo.

"I am a man, like you, from Doris-beyond-the-sea, for I was born here in the city of Halicarnassus. Dorian Greeks from the Peleponnesus founded Halicarnassus and the five cities that now celebrate this festival. In the history of the past, the greatest leaders in Hellas have been drawn from this eastern coast. By that I mean the coast and the islands of this our Doris, but also the coast and islands of Ionia and Aeolis, north of us.

"The asclepiad physicians who trace their proud descent from Asclepius of Thessaly developed their art in Caria. Now they are teaching medicine to all the Greeks through their ancient center of instruction in Cnidus, and more recently, I am told, in Cos.

"No Dorian city here in the east, however proud it may be of its ancestry, is pure Dorian. Your ancestors married Carian women. The learning of our Doris-in-the-east is shared with the Ionian cities along the coast to the north of us, and by that greatest of Ionian cities, Athens.

"Pericles, their famous first citizen, speaking to his fellow Athenians, said recently: 'We follow philosophy without loss of manliness.' His argument was that the Ionians to the north of us are soft and unmanly as the result of Persian influence. I say today that we Dorians have kept our manliness as well as any Athenian. At the same time we may claim that we are teaching Greece too, teaching them the meaning of history and of medicine today.

"History shows that learning has moved from east to west. Miletus is only a little way north at the mouth of the Meander River, and did not Thales, with whom philosophy began, teach the world from there? I have told in my writings how he predicted the sun's eclipse one hundred and fifty years ago. Did not Anaximander, his pupil, maintain that this world of ours and other worlds swing rotating in the void? Was not Pythagoras born on the island of Samos nearby? He led his followers far west across the sea to Croton in Italy. But the theory of numbers, arithmetic, and geometry which they have developed began in the east. Did not Homer come from the island of Chios, and Sappho from Lesbos?"

It was a brilliant audience of men and women who stood among the pillars of the portico. They were richly dressed and highly educated. They listened to all Herodotus had to say with keen interest, and Hippocrates listened with them until the mention of Sappho, after which he heard no more. The speaker, the temple and the people about him faded and Daphne was there instead. He heard Sappho's words: "Like the sweet apple which reddens upon the topmost bough, atop the topmost twig," and Daphne's whisper: "Oh Hippocrates!"

He turned away and looked out toward the sea. But instead of the sea, he saw Daphne herself. He realized in a flash that she had been looking at him. She smiled; then she looked down quickly. She was standing on the outer limit of the portico, with her back to a railing that separated the portico from the stadium far below.

"There she is," he said to his brother Sosander, Sosander watched with astonishment as Hippocrates sidled away through the crowd. When he saw his brother stop beside Daphne, his astonishment was followed by delight.

"Lovely," he muttered to himself. "Yes, really lovely." Pindar saw also, and understood.

But Hippocrates seemed to be aware of no one except Daphne. When he reached her, she looked embarrassed and made a little gesture to one side. He looked beyond her then, and saw Euryphon standing beside her, and beyond him Olympias. Euryphon looked at him but gave no sign of recognition. Olympias smiled graciously and then whispered to Euryphon.

Hippocrates turned back toward the speaker, but he did not listen to what Herodotus was saying. After a time he turned again and murmured to Daphne, so that only she, he thought, could hear.

"The apple on the topmost bough is still the reddest. It's still the sweetest — but the gardener beside you seems to frown. He doesn't speak."

She looked at him. "You must not . . ." She was blushing, and her lips trembled. Her eyes were wet as she looked away.

Hippocrates moved a little way off, thinking to himself that he had been too headlong. The audience laughed. Herodotus must have been amusing.

"Yes," Herodotus was saying, "you Dorians of the east are proud and exclusive. You will allow no other Greeks to worship in your temple. You do not admit other Greeks to enter your athletic games. Elsewhere all the world is welcome. Any well-born Greek may enter the games at Olympia, Delphi, Nemea, Corinth; but not here at the proud festival of the Triopian Apollo.

"Boxing was born here, and you have trained and sent out mighty boxers to capture the boxing and *pancration* crowns at all of the pan-Hellenic festivals.

"Years ago this league, which was then the Doric Hexapolis, became the Doric Pentapolis. Halicarnassus was expelled just because one of our athletes carried away the tripod, his prize for victory, instead of dedicating it, as he should have done, to Apollo. Let me read to you from my history just how this came about, since there are many stories of this affair and some of them are wrong.

" 'Now a man of Halicarnassus whose name was Agasicles, being declared victor in the games, in open contempt of the law took the tripod home to his own house, and there hung it against the wall. As a punishment for his fault, the five other cities, Lindus, Ialyssus, Camirus, Cos and Cnidus, deprived the sixth city, Halicarnassus, of the right of entering the temple.' "

A whispering and a muttering swept through the audience. But Herodotus held up his hand.

"I do not say," he cried, "that you should take Halicarnassus back, nor that you should welcome all the world to your athletic games. That is your affair. But one thing more I have to say, speaking as a historian.

"Be not blind as well as proud, you who live in island cities — and Cnidia, too, is almost an island. Beware, I say. You are no longer free from the threat of conquest, as in the ancient time. The history of the past is not the history of tomorrow. The Persians have learned how to strike by sea. Move your cities. Follow the lead of Cos. Build harbors that you can defend from attacks by sea — attacks by modern vessels of war! I have finished."

Herodotus walked down the steps amid deafening applause.

After a short interval, while discussion hummed on all sides, Timon mounted the steps again and beckoned to Euryphon. The priest appeared as before, and Timon placed a wreath on Euryphon's head, who then began to speak. His words came nervously at first, then slowly and clearly, telling the story of the asclepiads in Caria and dwelling at some length on his own work in Cnidus and that of his kinsmen Ctesiarchus and Ctesiochus.

During the applause that followed, Sosander turned to Pindar and said, "He did not even mention the asclepiads of Cos. Can you see Hippocrates?"

"Yes," Pindar replied from his great height. "I've been watching him from time to time. I don't think he listened to the speech at all."

Timon climbed the steps again and looked in vain for the next speaker. Daphne took a step toward Hippocrates and said:

"Timon is searching for you." Hippocrates looked at her as though he had not heard. "It's your turn to speak," she said. Then she added, "I want you to do well."

"Oh," he replied, as though dazed.

"Hippocrates!" Timon called. The crowd about him opened a path and Hippocrates passed through it and up the steps. The priest of Apollo stood above, waiting for him and smiling. He even took a step down to meet him and placed the crown of laurel on his head with his own hand.

"Once as a wrestler," he cried, "and now again as an asclepiad you have pleased the Triopian Apollo!"

A loud shout went up from the crowd, for Hippocrates' fame had gone out through the cities of the Pentapolis during his stay in the Macedonian court.

Hippocrates, turning back toward the audience in the portico, smiled when he heard the unexpected shout. It was like the old days when he wrestled in the *palaestra*. He stood for a little time, realizing that he had not listened to what Euryphon had said.

At last he held up a scroll. "I have written a script to read to you," he said, "but now I know it will not do. Euryphon, who spoke before me, is master now of the medical teachers of Cnidus. I am master of the teachers of Cos, although my brother Sosander is older and wiser than I. When I am asked to speak here today, what do you men of the Doric Pentapolis expect of me? That I should strive with Euryphon? Show Cos superior to Cnidus? Outrun him, outbox him with words, throw the javelin of my thought a little farther? Outdistance the discus of his argument? Once in this magnificent festival I wrestled before Apollo, striving to throw my opponent to the ground, with all the strength of boyhood.

"But as I climbed these stairs just now, it came to me that since those days are past, I should speak the simple truth before Apollo; set before him something more than skill and the agony of bodily effort. Apollo means many things to many men. It is Apollo the healer to whom I offer these words. But how shall I begin?"

He looked in the direction of Daphne, still struggling to collect his shattered thoughts.

"I am a physician, not an athlete. I am not a philosopher who might bring you unprovable hypotheses of disease. I am not a priest of Asclepius who would heal with the blessing of the god, nor a miracle worker. I cannot drive out devils that men believe in error to be the causes of disease. Nor am I a lying merchant, selling false medicines.

"I am a physician and a teacher of young physicians. Only the Greeks have called their healers by that name. It is a new word and physicians must look to new horizons. *Physis* means nature.

"A physician is a naturalist, a man who strives to learn what he can about nature, especially the nature of the body, in health and growth, in disease and death. He is a man who would use this knowledge to heal the sick. There are some who would practice the art because of greed or idle curiosity or delight in chambering. Such men are charlatans and they remain so even though they may learn skills from the teaching of the past. Beware of them!

"Medicine is an art. Knowledge of this art has been handed down from teacher to disciple since the days of Asclepius. The asclepiads, living here along the shores of Caria, have guarded the secrets of ancient medicine and taught them to those who took the oath of secrecy. But in that teaching, as it comes to us today, falsehood and truth are intermixed. Authority is not to be found in ancient medicine, but rather in the working of nature and in the face of disease.

"There are many arts, and Greeks, turning to them, have discovered truth never dreamed of by the teachers of the past. They have done this in sculpture, painting, music, poetry, philosophy. We have listened to Herodotus talk of the new art history. Pythagoras has made of numbers and lines an art of a different sort, an exact knowing, a science. The time has come for physicians to add something new to the teaching of medicine. The time has come to test the guesses and superstitions of the past by critical observations.

"What brings a worthy disciple to the teaching physician? It is most often the urge of pity and the desire to comfort. It is curiosity too, no doubt, about the human body and disease. He learns in time how to help the sick and comfort them. He serves men and women, but he is not responsible to them as a slave is responsible to a master. He is responsible to the gods for all that he does as physician. The good disciple, when he becomes a physician, comes to feel something more than pity. There is a force that draws him on, stronger than the urge to pleasure and the hope of happiness, a force that is stronger than the love of woman. Seeing how much there is to learn, how much to understand, the urge is born in him to discover in nature a new science.

"What, you may well ask me, does the word science mean? To know is science. To believe, one knows without inquiry, to teach the past without trying to test its truth is ignorance. Here and now I dedicate my life to the physicians' art and the science of medicine. With those who are of like mind, I will begin the climb that must lead at last to the secret truth of life. Will Apollo be content with this? Is this enough when the art is so long and life so short?"

Hippocrates stopped speaking. There was no applause. Instead there was complete silence. The priest came forward again to the top step.

"Seek truth," he said, "for truth is more than victory. Climb well, Hippocrates, and know that Apollo goes before."

Hippocrates and his brother followed the crowd through the great stone gates at the end of the portico and down the steps that curved around the mountainside toward the stadium.

"I am sorry," Hippocrates said, "that it was such a poor speech. As I stood there my mind cleared suddenly and I spoke as I had been thinking."

Sosander nodded. "I understand. At least I think I do."

Pindar was waiting at the foot of the steps. His only words were: "Master! Magnificent!"

"No," Hippocrates replied, "not that. But suddenly I knew that I was going to remain in Cos, to practice medicine and to teach, and I knew why."

"Yes," Pindar replied. "I realized your words meant that."

"Yes," Sosander added, "and we thank the gods for that."

CHAPTER FIFTEEN

The Games of the Doric Pentapolis

〰〰〰〰〰〰〰〰〰〰〰〰〰〰〰〰〰〰〰〰〰〰〰〰〰

THE ATHLETIC GAMES were scheduled to begin an hour after midday. Before this time Hippocrates made his way to the gymnasium and joined the other judges in a room the gymnasiarch had set aside for them. The gymnasiarch had complete authority within this large building. In addition to the great open central court where the contestants had been reviewed the previous evening, there were small courts and rooms for such purposes as bathing, dressing, lectures, small games and a large room for the trainers.

The judges were briefed by the Chief Judge on their duties for the two and one half days to be devoted to sports. On the last half-day, women would be admitted to the stadium while the girls had their sports. At that time the stadium track would be shortened by movable markers. On the last afternoon also it was planned to hold the temple ceremonies at which the victors would receive their prizes, the bronze tripods. Each victor would then dedicate his tripod to Apollo and thus leave behind him the record of his triumph in the temple for all to see, while he carried away only the fame of his achievement.

Each judge was given a staff to carry during the games. This was the mark of his authority, but it might be used on occasion to punish or control a contestant, just as the trainers were empowered to do with their forked staffs. Before the parade of athletes should begin, the judges crossed the open space between gymnasium and stadium and took the special seats reserved for them along the track.

The track was straight, not round, one stade (about two hundred yards) long, and only wide enough for ten or fifteen runners abreast. Thus the stadium was very long and quite narrow. It was situated on a level strip of land at the foot of the acropolis hill. Along the track on either side there were several rows of stone seats for important people. Behind the seats on the right and at the far end was a steep hillside along which ledges had been cut, and where thousands could stand in rising tiers and have an excellent view. On the other side, and around the entrance end, a lower stand was built.

Hippocrates looked about and listened. This was a familiar but always stirring sight to him. The track had been raked and rolled and sprinkled with white gravel. And at the far end the jumping pit had been dug to make it soft and was sprinkled with white sand. Under the brilliant Aegean sun, most of the men had removed their cloaks and many their tunics. Hippocrates listened to the deep tone of male talk and laughter.

These were the sights and sounds he had known so well when he had been a competitor, rejoicing in the chance to match his skill and strength against all comers. But they were no more than background then, contributing to the exultation a contestant feels in such a place at such a time.

Suddenly silence fell. The trumpeters had taken their places beside the entrance at the end of the stadium; they raised their trumpets now and blew. The stirring sound echoed along the stands and from the hills above and down to the ships on the yellow beach, as it had echoed each year for centuries in honor of Apollo. Then the contestants appeared five abreast, and the men who watched gave a mighty shout that also echoed through the hills and out to the sea. The boys came first, marching in companies, and after them the men. Everyone knew the order in which they walked — It was always the same from left to right: Lindus, Cos, Camirus, Ialysus, Cnidus.

First the company of boxers came, the wrestlers next; then the short-distance runners and long-distance runners, the jumpers and

discus throwers and the pentathlon contestants. Each group walked
the length of the track and back again and out.

The boys had the beauty and natural grace that youth bestows.
Among the men specialized power and posture showed itself. Hippocrates, watching them pass, remarked what nature does to the
bodies of men — nature and use and the passing years.

The javelin throwers carried their javelins and the runners-in-
armor their shields. It was hard to descibe a body type for them or
for the speed runners either. Speed, he thought, seems to depend on
the timing system that is born in a man rather than on any particular
body shape.

On the other hand the pentathlon competitors, who must contest
the sprint, the long jump, the discus throw, the javelin throw, and
wrestling, had a suppleness of movement and a grace dependent on
a smooth muscular development of the body in perfect proportion.
The boxers were heavier, since there were no weight limits in Greek
games. These men were long of arm and strongly muscled in shoulder and chest. The faces of the older ones were thickened with scars.
The older wrestlers were bull-necked men with bulbous ears. The
pancratiasts came last, scarred, heavy-muscled, ugly.

As the naked men passed by, the Chief Judge leaned over to Hippocrates. "There you see why no soldier in the world is a match for
the Greek. One of these men on the battlefield is worth ten soft
Persians. What do you think of the condition of the contestants this
year? I've been working hard with them."

Hippocrates nodded. "Splendid, splendid!"

"In my opinion," the Chief Judge continued, "Cleomedes of Cos
has the finest physique of anyone this year. What magnificent shoulders and arms! But he has a queer trainer and he is hard to control.
Here he comes now. Most of these men have trained faithfully for
six months at least, and many of the boys as well have worked that
long."

"There is a danger," Hippocrates said, "that training may be too
continuous. There should be periods of rest and change. Otherwise
you may bring a man to his final test lacking the fire and speed that
he possessed perhaps a month earlier."

The Chief Judge nodded his head thoughtfully. "Yes, I've heard it said that you hold that view. You may be right. Yet the contestants at Olympia are called upon to swear at the altar of Zeus that they have trained faithfully for ten months."

Cleomedes was passing now. He looked across at Hippocrates, coming up on his toes and tensing the muscles of his arms to show how fit he was.

Hippocrates turned to the Chief Judge again. "Is it your experience that the wit of athletes is dulled by too much use of muscle continuing beyond the time when the beard begins to grow?"

The Chief Judge laughed. "That is a difficult question. It may be a matter of what interests the athlete. The man who continues as an athlete in later life has made a choice of what interests him. Perhaps it is only that."

Hippocrates nodded. "He who is busy using the mind has no time for training, and he who trains is too tired to think. But the boxers seem to me especially slow in mind, and I wonder if that is not due to the constant blows on the head."

The Chief Judge nodded vigorously. "Old boxers and pancratiasts too — they all have foggy wits."

"All things in life," Hippocrates concluded, "may be good when due proportion is preserved, balancing body and mind, work and play, discipline and relaxation."

When the parade was over, ten boys came back into the stadium prepared to run the dash. Each took his position beside a post which bore a letter that all could see. The runner fixed his eyes on the post at the other end which bore the same letter. He must pass that post on his left to end the race. The runners stood erect, poised with one foot a little ahead of the other, waiting for the signal. At the cry "*Apite!*" — Go! — they were away, flying down the smooth white track. The first and the second to dart through the line of posts were given branches of laurel. They would run again in the final heat.

Next came the longer race, for men this time. This was the *diaulos,* the hardest race of all; for it was a dash all the way down and back. Each runner turned around the post that bore his letter and then raced back again and through the starting posts.

When the time came for Hippocrates to officiate at the wrestling, he made his way to the *palaestra*. It was upright wrestling — strong and clean and fast. When one contestant struck the ground with any part of his body except the knee, he had lost a fall. It took two falls out of three to win a match.

Next morning the judges gathered in the stadium before the start of the contests. The long-distance runners were making ready. A single post, around which they all must turn, now replaced the line of posts at either end. Sosander came down and called to Hippocrates from just above the judges' seats. Euryphon was with him.

"Can you come to Cnidus tomorrow?" Euryphon began without greeting. "Your brother tells me you do not need to be present here tomorrow."

Hippocrates' heart leaped up at first. Did this mean that he would be able to ask this man for Daphne's hand? But he saw soon that the physician's attitude was anything but cordial.

"I have been called back to Cnidus," Euryphon added, "to see a very sick patient. I want you in medical consultation on the problem. Will you come to my house tomorrow? I will explain everything to you then."

"Yes, of course," Hippocrates replied, "with pleasure."

Euryphon turned abruptly and walked away. Sosander looked after him. "What a strange way to ask for a consultation! Do you know what all this means?"

"No."

"Some people," Sosander continued, shaking his head, "thought you were attacking the Cnidian asclepiads in your oration yesterday. Perhaps that explains it."

Hippocrates made a gesture of protest. "But how absurd! I wasn't thinking of them any more than of physicians everywhere. By the gods, I don't understand why he should be rude, and I don't like it."

Sosander shook his head. "I wouldn't give Euryphon a second thought — if he were not the father of that beautiful girl. Daphne is worth working for — I'm glad I've seen her. Well, I'll see what I can discover." He moved away into the crowd.

In the boxing competition for men that year, there was only one contestant from each of the five cities. Lots were drawn so as to pair off four and let one draw bye. Peisirrodus was the one to draw bye; he passed thus to the next round without having to box. On the afternoon of the first day, Cleomedes won his first qualifying match easily. Then he and the other qualifying winner, with Peisirrodus, put their hands into the silver urn again and each drew out his lot with a letter on it. Again Peisirrodus drew bye, and on the morning of the second day Cleomedes fought a long hard match. But he won, and so he was scheduled to meet Peisirrodus at the end of the afternoon.

When the last wrestling match was over that afternoon and he had finished his work as judge, Hippocrates left the *palaestra* and hurried to the great court of the gymnasium. He was glad to discover that the boxing had not yet begun. The discus throw was still in progress there, and the portico that ran around the great court was crowded with men, but they stood aside to let him pass through when they saw his judge's staff. He made his way to the corner where the discus contestants stood. In that corner of the court there was a small triangular stone floor. Here each thrower in turn stood and whirled about to send the discus on its long, graceful flight.

Before long the gymnasiarch came up to speak to the discus judge. Then he said to Hippocrates, "This is nearly finished — I think I'll send for the boxers now. There is a great crowd waiting for this final boxing event."

Hippocrates followed the messenger out a side door and stopped there, thinking to speak to Cleomedes as he entered. To his astonishment he found Olympias waiting, evidently for the same purpose.

"I'm allowed to come as far as this," she said. "I've been waiting and waiting. Was that the messenger for the boxing that just went into the contestants' quarters?"

"Yes."

"I don't see why men keep women out of these games," she continued indignantly. "That woman Pherenice is in the quarters over there with her son, but they would not let me go in to see mine. Men let women bring them into the world. There is no cloak to hide their naked bodies then. But when they enter the games to contest before the god, then they must be naked and women must not look. Nonsense!"

Her white arms came out from under her cloak and she touched her hair and necklace while bracelets tinkled and clicked over her smooth skin from wrist to elbow.

"Men seem to like to look at us whether they think the god is watching or not. They don't mind our seeing them naked either, in private. Oh, that reminds me, Hippocrates. I took Thargelia to Cnidus, you know. She will be longing to see you. You will go to Cnidus before you return, won't you? Oh!" she exclaimed, not waiting for his answer. "There he is!"

Buto was coming out of the quarters, followed by Cleomedes. Pherenice and Peisirrodus followed. Hippocrates saw that Cleomedes' face was red and bruised. Olympias hurried forward to meet her son. She tried to kiss him, but he would not stoop. He frowned, and Buto growled something.

"Cleomedes!" she exclaimed. "You're bruised — you've had to fight twice, poor boy. You're tired. You can't fight again so soon, and this young man is rested. Look at him, no cuts on his face." She glared at Peisirrodus, then at Pherenice.

"You are his trainer!" Her lips curled. Then she laughed as her eye traveled from close-cropped hair to heavy sandal and big dirty foot. "It is too bad your son isn't able to win by fighting instead of by the draw."

Pherenice raised her head, so like a man's, and squared her shoulders. Slow anger showed itself in her face and her jaw came forward.

"My son won the Olympic crown fighting with his hands when he was a boy. Now he's a man and he'll do the same here, and in other games. He'll do it fighting straight the way my brothers did and my father. As for Cleomedes, who, I'd like to know, is his father? Not that little shipowner from Cos! He couldn't father a son like that."

She gave a hoarse laugh. "Come on, now, who was it? You know that bastards are barred from these games." She turned and looked at Buto and laughed again, a manlike laugh.

"I'm not blind, even if the judges are!"

Olympias did not scream, but her voice slipped into a very high pitch.

"Why — you common, ugly, hateful slut. You —"

Pherenice raised her right fist and moved swiftly forward. But the two sons intervened. Cleomedes seized his mother by her shoulders, and lifting her from the ground, he shook her.

"Be quiet! Why do you do this? Always, always!" He held her in the air as though she were a doll, staring at her.

The anger in Olympias' face had vanished and sudden fear was there in its place. "Don't! Don't kill me, your mother!"

He set her down and she shrank away from him. Meanwhile Peisirrodus had caught his mother and put his arm about her, laughing.

"My mother's right hook would kill any woman that ever walked, or any man either if she could land it square." He laughed again.

Hippocrates had watched as Olympias roused this angry outburst. He felt an undeniable thrill of pleasure to see her shaken. Buto, he observed, seemed to freeze into immobility when Pherenice laughed at him.

"They will be waiting for you two," Hippocrates said. "Are your knuckles wrapped and ready?"

Peisirrodus held out his long arms toward his mother. She inspected the ox thong that was wrapped many times around the base of the four fingers of each hand. The binding crossed the palm and the back of the hand diagonally and passed well up on the forearm, leaving only the thumb uncovered. These thongs protected the boxer's fist in a straight blow to the head. They were also heavy enough and rough enough to make a side blow from the open hand quite effective. She asked him to close his fist several times while she felt the thongs. At last she nodded.

"Go on," she said. She made no gesture, but there was tenderness in her eyes as she looked into her son's face.

"Don't touch that woman after we go," he said to her. Then he stooped and kissed her and walked away through the door into the gymnasium.

Cleomedes did not turn to Buto, but inspected his own hands. He looked up at Hippocrates. There were pain and bewilderment in his eyes. Hippocrates reached out and felt the thongs and nodded.

"Get your mind on the fight now. Don't rush him too soon."

Cleomedes looked at him for a moment, but it was as though he had not heard. Then he walked without a word into the gymnasium and Buto padded after him like an enormous cat, looking sidewise at Hippocrates as he passed.

Olympias turned and walked away. Pherenice remained, looking speculatively at Hippocrates. Presently she came toward him, rolling easily from side to side as she walked.

"You're one of the judges?"

"Yes."

"You couldn't just let me slip into the gymnasium, could you? No one would notice me now. It will be a good fight. Cleomedes is the toughest opponent my boy has ever faced."

"Everyone knows you," Hippocrates said.

She smiled as though the remark pleased her. "Yes, I guess they do around here."

"Is he your only child?"

She looked at him with interest and answered, "Yes."

"Was your voice always like this?"

"No. It began to change and get more like a man's some time after he was born."

Hippocrates nodded and looked into the distance. "Your monthly flow never amounted to much, I suppose." He seemed to be talking to himself.

"Ah — you must be an asclepiad. No, they never did amount to much. Then they stopped, almost — Wait, I know who you are, you're Hippocrates."

He nodded, smiling, and left her, not quite closing the door as he passed into the gymnasium.

The match had just begun as Hippocrates re-entered. The large central portion of the court was clear and the two boxers were moving with speed round and round and back and forth. The Greeks used no ring to limit the boxers' movements, and since body blows were never employed, the head and face were the only targets for their fists. There were no rounds and no intermissions, so the match went on until one contestant fell unconscious or confessed defeat by holding up his index finger. At this sign the judge would interfere and stop the fight.

Each fighter extended his left hand, bound with the ox thongs, toward his opponent's face, making this his guard and his lead. He carried his right fist at shoulder height ready to strike when he could get past the opponent's guard.

"This is a magnificent match!" Hippocrates heard a spectator exclaim. "Just look at that strength and speed."

As they circled, each kept his left foot forward pointing straight toward the opponent, the right foot at a right angle to this. At each lunge the right leg drove him forward with power.

Hippocrates noticed again how curiously long were Peisirrodus' arms. He moved with ease, sidestepping and giving ground, as Cleomedes pushed the pace. But as he did so, that long outstretched left hand often struck Cleomedes' face from the side or chopped down on it from above. The blows were not heavy, but they were frequent.

Cleomedes was faster on his feet than his opponent. He was clearly the more powerful of the two. When he did drive or hook with his right, the fist was carrying deadly power. But his blows were usually short, as Peisirrodus pulled back, or they passed the face as he sidestepped. Once he caught the cheekbone a glancing blow and Peisirrodus staggered. There was a shout from the onlookers and Cleomedes rushed for him, but Peisirrodus recovered his control and got away.

After that Peisirrodus was even more cautious, giving ground and shifting from side to side.

"Cleomedes will wear himself out," Hippocrates said to the spectator who had spoken. "No one can keep up such a pace." He thought to himself that if Olympias had stayed away and not caused that scene outside the gymnasium, her son might have kept his head. Instead of going into this match with a cool head and a carefully considered plan of attack, he had gone in confused and angry. One of his eyes was swollen shut now. He changed his pushing tactics

and began to stoop and follow. Suddenly he ducked below Peisirrodus' left and rushed in. But Peisirrodus, sidestepping, caught him
with his right fist square on the jaw. It was almost the first time during
the match that he had used his right. Cleomedes slumped to the
ground and lay quite still.

There was a great shout. The judge declared Peisirrodus the winner and handed him a laurel branch. Slowly, Cleomedes got to his
hands and knees, then up to his feet. He staggered, then walked
unsteadily through the crowd toward the baths. Buto went with him,
saying nothing. At the entrance to the room he gave him his cape as
usual, and left him.

Hippocrates made his way to the room. Large shallow marble
basins were set in a line on blocks of stone along one wall, and a
groove in the floor in front of the basins slanted to the corner of the
room and to an outside drain. Above the basins was a line of marble
lion heads and out of the mouths spewed curving streams of water.
Hippocrates picked his way across the wet floor. Men and boys were
splashing the cold clean water onto their glittering bodies. They
dipped their hands in the soap and washed themselves and each
other by turns, shouting and laughing.

At last he found Cleomedes slumped on the floor in a corner,
leaning against the cool wall. He looked dizzy and dazed. Blood
dripped from his chin and ran down his heaving chest.

Hippocrates stood beside him unobserved for a little time. Then he
spoke. "Peisirrodus has a very long reach, like all the Diagoridai. But
you certainly looked like the winner for a while."

Cleomedes looked up in surprise, tilting his head so he could see
with the untouched eye. He grunted. Then he said slowly: "I never
did reach him with my right, his left was too long. It held me off —
Finally, I knew I was getting winded — I had to do something, so
I think I tried to charge in low to get under his left — I don't remember anything more. What happened?"

"It was his right."

"Hmm," Cleomedes grunted again, wiping the blood and sweat
from his face with the cloth Hippocrates offered. "I remembered
what you said about using my right — but I never could land it fair

— What'll Daphne say now?" Cleomedes got to his feet slowly. "Are you going to Cnidus?"

"Yes," Hippocrates replied.

"May I go with you? I don't want to see my mother until I have to, nor Buto either."

"Yes. I'll meet you at the bridge."

Hippocrates left the baths and went to say good-by to Sosander and Pindar. Then he shouldered his belongings and strode off along the broad highroad that ran from Triopion to Cnidus. At the first bridge Cleomedes was waiting for him. They walked along together in silence for some time, each occupied with his own thoughts.

Many men in Hippocrates' position rarely appeared in public unless accompanied by a slave or servant, and many of those who were returning now to Cnidus rode on mules or asses. Some, who were wealthy or desirous of being thought so, rode on horseback. But Hippocrates looked upon walking as an opportunity to be alone with his thoughts and had little pride in such matters.

The road was arched with mighty oak trees, *haroup* trees and olives. The rays of the setting sun behind them sent shafts of light along the road. The two crossed over rushing streams on widely arching stone bridges and skirted deep ravines. The talk of those on the highroad about them turned on the races, the boxing, the wrestling.

After two hours of walking they reached the city of Cnidus and found an inn. Here they were given a small room off an open courtyard. The good smell of frying fish guided them to a fish booth nearby, and here they stretched their legs on the benches and satisfied a hunger and a thirst too long denied. Returning to the inn, each man rolled himself in his blanket, and Cleomedes, too exhausted to think, dropped asleep at once. Hippocrates lay awake and watched the stars through the open doorway. Why, he wondered, had Euryphon asked to see him, and what was Daphne doing and thinking?

CHAPTER SIXTEEN

Thargelia

~~~~~~

NEXT MORNING, Daphne climbed the stairs to the roof of her father's house in Cnidus. Over the parapet she could look down through the treetops to the asclepiad enclosure and watch for Hippocrates to come through the gate. Her father had told her he was coming, but he had also told her to put this man out of her mind now and forever. Well, she could do that, she supposed, if Hippocrates really loved the woman from Macedonia. Seven days ago Thargelia had come to consult her father, and Daphne had seen her then. She thought of her now with a little feeling of envy, thought of her blonde beauty and her manner that seemed to bid all men to follow. I suppose, she mused, that men buzz about such a woman like bees about ripe fruit.

Daphne laid her smooth flushed cheek against the cold surface of the parapet. I hate Olympias! she thought. I hate the way she smiled when she said Hippocrates visited Thargelia in her lodgings every day after his return to Cos. He couldn't do that! She must be lying! And yet when I kissed him that morning on the mountain, he turned away. Was he thinking only of his honor? Or did Thargelia step between us then? And when we parted and I sailed away, he said nothing, nothing but good-by.

If Hippocrates did not care for her, what would life be like? Probably after all Cleomedes might make a good enough husband, as husbands go. If only he were not so deadly dull! But one thing she could not do; she could not live in the same house with Olympias —

never! Never! No. Her father would have to find another husband for her — or she would live on and die a virgin. Perhaps she could become a poet like Sappho.

But there! She heard the sound she was waiting for, the squeaking of the entrance gate. There he was! Hippocrates was coming through. His dignity made her think of an actor coming onto the stage before he speaks for the first time. He looked serious. So did her father, who was coming to meet him. They crossed the enclosure together and disappeared into the *iatreion*.

Olympias must be lying! But — of course, men are different from women. Why had he not kissed her when she gave him the chance?

As Hippocrates approached the entrance to Euryphon's enclosure, he had been recalling early days, the days when he had come for a few months of medical study under Ctesiochus, the former master of the Cnidian asclepiads. The greeting he exchanged with Euryphon was formal. When they were seated in the *iatreion*, Euryphon began abruptly.

"It is Thargelia I want you to see. You knew of course that she was pregnant."

"Thargelia!" Hippocrates exclaimed. "No. She told me that her handmaid was pregnant. There must be some mistake."

"Very strange," Euryphon said. "This beautiful woman is obviously in love with you. She asked me to carry out an abortion, so that she would be ready to return with you to Macedonia."

"But," Hippocrates said, "I have decided not to go to Macedonia. Isn't there some mistake about this? Are you sure she is pregnant?"

"Mistake!" Euryphon exploded. "No, there is no mistake, and I think it was your duty to handle the whole affair yourself. Olympias has very generously befriended the girl and brought her here in Timon's trireme. She tells me you saw Thargelia every day after Daphne left you, and yet you say you know nothing about her!" Euryphon laughed.

Hippocrates flushed with anger and controlled himself with difficulty.

"I saw Thargelia on certain days only because I had to visit the house of Cephalus to see a slave who was dying. Please explain yourself."

"Very well," Euryphon said. "This is what happened. Thargelia arrived here a few days before the Triopian Festival began. She complained of a swelling in the lower abdomen, and my assistant brought her to me. She lied to me, said there was no possibility of her being pregnant, and that her monthly periods had continued and were quite regular.

"On examination I found her womb large and soft. In spite of the findings, I thought she was telling the truth. I should have been warned by Olympias, who said she was a professional *hetaira* and famous as a companion of men in the court of King Perdiccas."

"She was the wife of the court chamberlain," Hippocrates objected.

"Yes, I know," Euryphon replied impatiently. "The patient told me that too. In any case, I decided to empty the womb. Perhaps I would have done so even if I had diagnosed pregnancy — I do not know.

"The fetus was living. It was between two months and four months of age. The woman is in love with you and has been unhappy since you left Aegae. That was almost four months ago, wasn't it? Perhaps I have done you a good service without knowing it."

Hippocrates was looking at Euryphon, amazed, hurt, angry, wondering if Daphne had been told this and what she thought.

"Your love affairs," Euryphon continued, "are not my business. Many men settle down after such episodes. But Daphne told me how happy she was with you in Halasarna. I gather you — what shall I say? — you almost made love to her. After those ten days with my daughter, I find it hard to understand how you could see this woman Thargelia every day as soon as you returned to Meropis. You saw her privately, I'm told. Daphne seems to think it was all right, but . . ."

Hippocrates interrupted him, exclaiming: "Daphne knows about Thargelia, then? And you think Thargelia was my mistress? It is not true. I cared for her husband until he died. After that I avoided her. She came to Cos recently to consult me about headaches.

"It is your daughter I love, Euryphon. There is no other woman for me, there never has been."

"Daphne knows," Euryphon said. "She even knows why I have asked you to see Thargelia with me."

"Why have you done so?" Hippocrates asked.

"Because she has a fever. I think she is going to die."

"What!" Hippocrates exclaimed. "Oh, poor woman."

"Yes," Euryphon said. "I am sad too, very, very sad. But come with me and we will see her. She is not far away. I put her in the house of a widow who takes in our patients from time to time."

He shook his head as they crossed the tree-shaded enclosure. "I had another woman staying in that house. She had a fever due to a swelling of the throat. She died two days after I sent Thargelia to the house. My assistant came to Triopion during the games to tell me that Thargelia, whom I had left there, was in a critical condition. The gods seem to send us one misfortune after another sometimes."

"The gods," Hippocrates said, "or perhaps something else. It may be something we do. I saw a similar situation in the case of a woman who had given birth to a normal child. She was living in the same house with a boy who had erysipelas. He recovered and she died. The same asclepiad treated both."

Euryphon stopped short and straightened up, a thing he rarely did. It made him almost as tall as his square-shouldered younger companion. There was nothing about Euryphon to suggest an athletic past. His shoulders were sloping, his neck thin, his long face impassive. Ordinarily the direction of his nimble thinking could be guessed only by the expression of his eyes, and those who knew him best watched for the twinkle that gave warning of some sudden sally of his wit.

There was no twinkle now.

"Since you did not take care of your woman friend," he said coldly, "I did the best I could for her, and for you. Now, even before you have seen what has happened to her, you are ready to show me my error."

"Oh, no! I didn't mean . . ."

But Euryphon held up his hand. "Wait!" he said. "I am sorry this

case involves you personally. It involves me too, professionally. To
Daphne it must have brought surprise, although she will say little to
me about it. Let us ignore our personal differences, you and I. As
physicians we understand each other, I think.

"When you spoke to the people during the Festival of Apollo, some
of my friends did not understand your meaning. They thought you
had gone mad and were attacking the Cnidian asclepiads. But I
understood. I knew you were sincere. You said what I believe,
what I would follow if I could. We have ambitions here in Cnidus,
and ideals too."

As they spoke a tall, stooped man with a long white beard came
out of the *iatreion* across the square from them. Hippocrates recognized him as the famous old physician Ctesiochus, once his teacher.
He was followed by a group of young disciples.

"There goes the old master now," Euryphon said. "Since I became
master in his stead, he no longer lives in the enclosure, but he likes
to come back to teach, and I like to have him. We will not speak to
him now, but I will show you how the asclepiads of Cnidus live and
work and teach today. Thargelia was sleeping when I left her a little
while ago. You have never visited us since you came here as a pupil
years ago. Let me show you the changes I have made since I became
master."

The asclepiad buildings were set about a level space on top of a
small hill, and a wall ran all around the hilltop. Euryphon stood now
with his back to the gate and pointed.

"Over here," he said, "on my right, is the house where Daphne and
I live. The surgery and the treatments are still carried out in the
iatreion opposite us. Over to the left, you see, is the same old
palaestra."

They walked over to it and looked in through the open door. "We
don't give as much gymnastic treatment as your brother Sosander
does. We use this building largely for massage, and have good results
rubbing the skin with olive oil to which we add certain medicaments. Those amphoras are filled with oil. We pour it from them
into that vat and add the medicaments to the oil there.

"The small building here next to the *palaestra*, you remember,

used to be the outer court of the master's house. We have altered it
and placed all the papyrus writings in it. It is now a sort of manuscript house where pupils, as well as asclepiads, can read quietly."
His eyes lit up, and pride spoke out in his voice. "We have all the
writings of Alcmaeon, and many other treasures.

"The old master used to live in the house beyond. Now his son
Ctesiarchus lives there with his invalid wife. They have only one
child. Here he comes now. You see, there is a door at the back of
the manuscript house into the home, and the boy runs through it
when the door is unlocked to spend most of his time in our house
with Daphne.

"What have you there, Ctesias? Let me see."

Ctesias was carrying a turtle in his hands with obvious pride.

"Daphne and I found him in the fields yesterday." The boy looked
up with a radiant smile. "I took him into my room last night without
letting Mother see him. I tied him by one leg where I could reach
him from my bed. But he got away and made everything wet. My
mother doesn't like him. He is going to live all his life now in
Daphne's courtyard. She and I are going to build him a house. Do
you want to hold him? Be careful, he may make you wet. Daphne
says he carries his house on his back. If he has a house already, perhaps we might build him a manuscript house."

The two men smiled, and Ctesias ran across the garden and stood
before the door of Euryphon's house, calling. The door opened and,
suddenly, Hippocrates' heart seemed to stand still, for Daphne stood
there. She waved, and the door closed again.

"No doubt," Euryphon continued, "the boy's home is quiet with
his mother confined to her bed. Her legs have become almost use-
less. I'd like to have a boy like that of my own. I have no son."

The expression in Euryphon's eyes altered. He looked toward his
home. "I've only my daughter . . ."

After a moment Euryphon resumed briskly: "My chief pride here
is in this library of papyrus scrolls, and also in the excellent results I
have had with the oil massage. Do you think the medicaments pass
through the skin to the bone? But we must not start an argument
now. Let us go to Thargelia."

The two physicians walked down the path to the lower town. They made their way past the harbor and up a steeply rising street to a little house on the mountainside. As they stopped before the door Hippocrates said:

"Didn't you ask Thargelia who was responsible for this pregnancy?"

Euryphon's expression hardened. "Yes, I did, and she refused to tell me. When I insisted she finally said, 'It was a man who is above all others.' "

Euryphon shrugged and knocked on the door. "I concluded that she was referring to you, Hippocrates. You are certainly the man above all others in her consideration."

"By all the gods!" Hippocrates exclaimed. "I swear that I have never been her lover, although I admit I admired her, as any man might."

"Very well, very well," Euryphon said testily. "I make no accusations. Whatever I may believe is my own affair."

The widow Lycia, fat and rosy, opened the door. "I'm glad you've come," she said. "I don't think she is so well. She has a terrible headache and she feels so hot."

Euryphon nodded and turned to Hippocrates. "I'll go in first and do what I think is necessary. You may examine her when I have finished, and then we will consult. It is better for her that way."

Hippocrates nodded. He looked inside, and seeing how small the house was, he said: "I will remain outside here in the street until you are ready for me."

When the door had closed, he walked back and forth before the house. He was furious that Euryphon had spoken to him as he had, and that he obviously did not believe his statements. He understood now Euryphon's aloof behavior at Triopion. He was depressed at what he had learned of Thargelia. Was she no more than a clever and beautiful prostitute? He was embarrassed, too, that she had misled him so successfully. Most of all his heart ached for Daphne. What must she think and feel if she knew what Euryphon believed of him? He would demand an interview with her. Surely she would believe what he told her, if her father did not. But first he must do what he could for Thargelia, alone here, perhaps facing death.

The road that passed the house curved sharply down the moun-tainside and he could see down it into the harbor. A trireme was moving slowly into the still protection of the breakwater, its brown sail furled on the yardarm and the oars swinging back and forth. He could hear the captain shouting his orders to poise the oars on the starboard and pull hard on the port side. The ship turned and he heard the forward anchor splash into the water.

He recognized suddenly that this was the Coan trireme that be-longed to the mighty little Archon Timon. The woman in a crimson cloak on the afterdeck was probably Olympias and the short man who stood by her side was certainly Timon. They had come, no doubt, from Triopion to ask Euryphon for his decision, to ask that Daphne should marry their son Cleomedes. Hippocrates was angry but felt himself helpless.

He heard his name called, and turning back, he saw the widow Lycia standing in the doorway.

"Euryphon would like to have you come in now." As he passed through the door the widow said: "It is good that you have come. Thargelia talks of no one else." She had an expression on her fat face that Hippocrates resented, and she shook her head as much as to say: "You are responsible for all this." He had a feeling that he would like to strike her. But he entered the house without a word, and a moment later stood in the doorway of a little room that opened on an inner courtyard.

On a bed before him was Thargelia, her golden hair in braids on the pillow, her face flushed, her great blue eyes staring at him.

His anger vanished and he stepped toward her and put his hand on her forehead, without noticing Euryphon, who stood at the foot of the bed watching.

Thargelia closed her eyes. She spoke softly: "You've come at last — at last." She opened her eyes and looked at him.

"I'm afraid, Hippocrates," and then, in a louder voice, "I'm afraid I'm going to die. I wanted so much to be well, so . . . so we could go back to Aegae together."

"Nonsense," Hippocrates said. "We'll soon have you better."

He caught sight then of Euryphon, who shrugged and said:

"I will leave you two — to renew old times. When you have examined her, you will find me in the *oecus*."

When he had gone Thargelia said: "Please don't take your hand away. My head aches. Oh, how it aches!" Then, after a moment of silence: "You know now, don't you, what Euryphon found when he operated? I hoped I could keep you from knowing and Olympias suggested this way of doing it. She was very kind to me and brought me here. They have asked me who the father was. I heard Olympias tell Euryphon that I had been your mistress." She paused. "I wanted to be. Is that wrong?"

Her lids drooped slowly over the large eyes, but without quite closing, and she was quiet. His practiced hand told him that the fever was very high. Her skin was dry. His fingertips on the temple felt the rapid hammering of the temporal artery. Her blue eyes opened and she looked at him, staring just a little.

"Am I going to die? I've had time to think about so many things. I tried to win. I staked my happiness on the rolling of the dice. But since I lost, perhaps it is just as well to die."

Her eyes closed slowly.

"No, I'm not asleep. I must tell you before it is too late. I loved you. I wanted to be a woman like . . . like your mother. A woman you could love forever. After you left Macedonia I wanted to follow you. Only the king could make that possible. So I begged him, and begged again. At last he sent for me and we made a bargain. He swore and I swore, by Aphrodite, to keep the bargain secret. Please do not tell.

"Then I gave him his pleasure and in return he put me on the ship for Cos. I did not know till then that he planned to bring you back to his court anyway. The voyage was very long. My monthly periods stopped, alas! I had lost the casting of the dice. The father of what might have been my son was King Perdiccas."

She opened her eyes and tears stole down her cheeks.

"That's all over now," Hippocrates said. "Euryphon and I will do everything possible. Don't worry."

She smiled and spoke softly. "Only you can make me want to live. I've no one else in all the world."

He took her hand for a moment. Then he said: "Have you any pain?" She motioned toward the lower abdomen. He slipped one hand under the covers. The abdominal wall felt tense, hard. "Open your mouth, put out your tongue." He looked and nodded.

"What have you had to eat and drink? What medicine?"

"Only water," she replied, "and hydromel for the last two days. The widow did what she thought best, with Euryphon away."

Hippocrates joined Euryphon in the *oecus* and the widow left them to talk.

"Did she tell you the name of the man?" Euryphon asked.

"Yes, but she asked me to keep it a secret."

"I thought so." Euryphon's eyes were cold, calculating.

Hippocrates flushed, but kept his temper. "What she told you about the man was correct."

Euryphon looked up in surprise.

"But," Hippocrates continued, "there are more important things to be considered. She has an ardent fever and, unfortunately, she has fasted. She has had no remedies as yet."

Euryphon's eyes warned him not to proceed with his criticism.

"I'm sorry," Hippocrates said. "My prognosis is like yours. She will probably die. But we must use every remedy that is suitable to her case."

Euryphon rose, and going to the door, called the widow Lycia. When she came, he said, "Now, Hippocrates, will you be good enough to give us your recommendations for treatment in detail."

"Such pain as she has," Hippocrates said, "is below the diaphragm. I should therefore recommend black hellebore to soften the bowels, mixing with it a fragrant herb such as daucus, seseli, cumin or anise. I recommend also that you continue the hydromel that you have started. I should keep this up throughout the course of the acute disease. I suppose your hydromel is made of the finest honey, dissolved simply in water? It is apt to act in such cases as a mild diuretic.

"Oxymel, on the other hand, even though it is made of the purest vinegar and honey, is less suitable for her, since vinegar, it is said by many, causes women to have pain in the womb. I should hesitate to bleed her or to use fomentations on the body, as it would be of little benefit. Since she has been fasting, however, it might be better to begin with barley water and later use barley gruel carefully strained."

"I hope," the widow said, "that Hippocrates will not leave us until Thargelia is out of danger."

Euryphon nodded. "Yes, stay on here and support the patient. I give you a free hand with her."

Hippocrates hesitated. To remain would reinforce the suspicions of Euryphon. He had so much hoped to plead his own suit for Daphne before returning, but he must postpone that. He could really help Tharegelia, he knew; even save her, he hoped. She had looked so forlorn when she said, "Only you can make me want to live. I've no one else in all the world."

Hippocrates nodded. "I will stay as long as I can really help."

Euryphon prepared to go. "Be good enough to give the widow your further instructions." He left the house abruptly, but Hippocrates followed him out into the street. There the two men faced each other. Euryphon's manner was reserved, his long face impassive; Hippocrates was flushed and distressed.

"I thought you'd stay," Euryphon said, "regardless of what people will be saying about you. I admire you for that, at least." He looked Hippocrates in the eye as he spoke, but there was no smile on his face.

"Euryphon," Hippocrates exclaimed, "you must believe me! What I have told you about Thargelia is the truth, and I must talk to you about Daphne. Don't let her condemn me unheard. If she loves Cleomedes and if you conclude that she will be happy married to the son of the Archon, you will of course arrange that marriage without considering me. I want Daphne to be happy. Cleomedes is taking his defeat at Triopion well.

"This is not the time I would choose to propose marriage with your daughter, far from it! But since you and Daphne have discussed the friendship that developed between us while she was in Halasarna, I must speak now. If the time comes when Cleomedes is no longer considered, I shall ask your permission to marry her. I love her. I ask you to tell her that, since I did not do so."

"Very well," Euryphon said. "Leave it that way. But do not try to see her! Stay away from her unless you hear from us." He turned to go, but Hippocrates stopped him once more.

"One thing more," he said. "Time will hang heavy on my hands here. May I have permission to read in the asclepiad manuscript house? You spoke of Alcmaeon's writings."

Euryphon smiled in spite of himself. "Yes. If you find the manuscript house locked, just ask the gateman for the key."

Hippocrates re-entered the widow's house and discussed with her the preparation of barley water, hydromel and medicines, as well as other matters of the patient's care. Finally he left the widow and her servant in the kitchen and re-entered Thargelia's room. She was sleeping, so he sat down quietly beside her.

Her perfume came to him delicately as though to greet him and recall the times when they had met before. She was still beautiful, for illness had not robbed her of her charms, not yet. Fever had only put color in her cheeks, and sleep had added peace and dignity to her features. The curving neck and shoulders were the same and the breast half shown above the silken sheet, "her own luxurious sheets that she carries with her," the widow Lycia had said with a touch of envy in her voice.

Thargelia stirred in her sleep and whimpered like a child, reaching out her hands. Her eyes opened.

"Hippocrates! It is you — really you! I found you in my dream." She raised herself and then dropped back on the pillow, resting her hand on his arm. "Now I am awake, and you are still here.

"I had such a dream . . ." She looked at him with wonder in her eyes. "Such a dream!" She laughed a little. "I was in a beehive. I must have been the queen bee, I suppose. And I went into one tiny room after another. There was a man in each room. Each man tried to lay hands on me. It was hard to escape, and some were rough, until I came at last to a room and found you in it. I begged you to take me out of the hive. I think I cried — then I woke up, and here you are!

"Lycia told me you had promised to stay in Cnidus to be near me. Everything is changed now because you care enough to stay. I can face death now. I wonder, if it should go the other way, whether I could face life."

She looked at him and smiled sadly. "Am I going to die? You wouldn't tell me, I suppose. You say nothing. You just sit there. But your spirit talks with me. I've had time to think about so many things.

"I knew when you came back from Halasarna that I had lost — lost to that girl Daphne who followed you there. Was she more beautiful, or was she more your kind, more like your mother? I would like to see her before I go away.

"If I could only have had a mother and a father, as she did! But I didn't. Some man left me, a little red baby in a pot, at the shrine of the Goddess of Love. So my foster father let Aphrodite plan my teaching. My mind was trained like that of any man so that I could in time excel in the trade of the *hetairai*, the companions of men. But I had no mother's arms, no father's affection. I knew there was a better love where trade and commerce did not enter in. I dreamed of it. I longed for it. With you I thought that I would find it."

Her eyes closed slowly. After a while she said, "No, I'm not going to sleep. Perhaps I've talked too much and wearied you. But I think and think, and long to tell my thoughts to you — Yes, it is better to die. The child I carried in my womb is dead. I failed to win, and failure for the *hetairai* is worse than death. Failure means the horrid life of common prostitution — Sophocles it was, I think, who wrote:

'A wise gamester ought to take the dice
Even as they fall, and pay down quietly.'

"I'll pay. But a good gamester should do more. He should laugh at failure, as at success." She smiled at him. "I think it will be great fun; if you will go with me to the end, and I can tell myself that Hippocrates is mine for all my life!"

She laughed. "No, the fever has not touched my mind. You think it strange, no doubt, but I am happy. Bring Daphne here to see my triumph. Surely she'll not begrudge me these few days of friendship?"

She put her hand in his, but still he did not speak. "What was it Antigone said when she was about to enter her tomb? Do you remember? It began this way:

'Only a little time to please the living,' "

She looked at him and he finished the couplet:

" *'But all eternity to love the dead.'* "

She laughed a little. "There are tears in your eyes, Hippocrates, and I made you speak in spite of yourself, at last. Yes, this way I shall have you — always, all of my life that is left, and all my death." She was silent for a moment.

"What lies beyond the tomb?" she asked. "You must have sat with many who were about to enter the land beyond."

"We cannot know," he answered. "For you, I suppose, there will be peace and perhaps a better love than you have known."

"Yes, that is what I wanted, a better love, love in which the body is not first and last. And when there is no body at all — what then — will God love me? Since you have spoken of peace and a better love, I believe he may. I seem to slip in and out of dreaming."

Her eyes closed again, and her breathing changed to the rhythmic whispering of sleep. Hippocrates put her hand back on the silken sheet and left the room on tiptoe. After a word to the widow Lycia, he left the house and walked aimlessly through the streets of the old city. The pathos and the calm courage of Thargelia stirred him deeply. And who was to say that what Thargelia had done with the life she was given was wrong?

What does lie beyond the grave? Does the love of God receive those who pass beyond, as Thargelia hoped? Socrates too, he recalled again, so often passed swiftly over the gods of Olympus and talked of God, as she had done.

Hippocrates walked through the city as these thoughts passed

through his mind. And so, hardly aware of where his feet were taking him, he came to the hill on which the asclepiad buildings stood.
He climbed up to the gate and knocked. The gateman let him in,
and he went directly to the manuscript house. As he passed the
palaestra next to it, he looked in. Men lay on each of the rubbing
tables that lined the walls and masseurs were working on them,
rubbing and slapping their naked bodies and limbs. By the side of
each table was a bottle of the rubbing oil that Euryphon evidently
prized so highly.

He caught sight of Buto the boxer, stripped to the waist, working at one of the tables, kneading the muscles of a flabby, middle-
aged man. Buto saw him, and to Hippocrates' surprise, came out to
speak to him.

"They've given me work here," he said. "I'll do this until Cleomedes starts training again. He'll win next time, after he has married
Daphne and can forget her. She made him lose. If anyone stands
in the way of his marrying Daphne, it will go — it will go hard with
him."

Hippocrates passed on into the library, wondering if those words
were intended as a threat. He stood in the court and looked about
him. The rooms that opened on the court were filled with carefully
made boxes. A young man who was reading in one of the rooms
recognized him and came to help him.

He led Hippocrates to a large box, and opening the lid, showed
him many papyrus scrolls. "Here," he said, "on the outside of the box
Euryphon himself has written a list of the writings of Alcmaeon."
Hippocrates selected a double-handled scroll which bore the title
"On Nature."

He laid the scroll on a table in the open court. Then he threw off
his cloak, and sitting down, let the warm sun bathe his neck and
shoulders as he prepared to read.

Presently the young man rolled up his own papyrus and rose to
leave. He cleared his throat and, as Hippocrates looked up, spoke
shyly:

"I have heard your opinions discussed by many teachers and it is
my ambition to come to Cos to join your disciples. My father will

send you word." Then he left the library abruptly, not waiting for a reply. Hippocrates smiled and turned back to his reading.

During health, he read, there is a balance of the elements within the body, the moist and dry, the bitter and sweet, the hot and cold. In disease, however, there develops a preponderance of one element over the others. This destroys the elemental harmony. It establishes a *monarchia* of one element, replacing thus the democracy of health.

He raised his head. This, he thought, is explanation by hypothesis. Heat, it is true, is an element in all living bodies. In Thargelia's fever, heat is present in excess. Yes, but —

The thread of his thought was broken by the squeaking of hinges. A small boy was closing the little door in the far side of the court, the door, he thought, that must open into the home of Ctesiarchus. The boy crossed the court and stopped beside him, looking at him with a friendly grin.

"I know who you are," he said. "You are Hippocrates. I saw you this morning. Do you know who I am?"

Hippocrates smiled. "You are Ctesias, son of Ctesiarchus, grandson of Ctesiochus. How is the turtle?"

"Very well, thank you, but do you know what he did? He laid an egg. Daphne has it. She says it might hatch out a baby turtle if we keep it in the sun. We put him in a box with sand in it. Daphne found the egg in the sand. He hid it there. Did you know he came all the way up from the water just to lay his eggs? Daphne said so."

"I suppose it must be a girl turtle," Hippocrates said.

"Perhaps." Ctesias shook his head in doubt. "I'll ask Daphne when she comes out. She's busy now." The boy smiled at him again. "I'm going over to her house now." He walked on, closing the main door of the library with a bang.

Silence reigned again and Hippocrates laid the scroll down on his lap.

Thargelia had asked to see Daphne. Was it only curiosity? How could he take her there? He certainly did not want the two women to meet! That would be the worst thing he could think of. He sighed and realized he was hungry. But he thought he had better look in at the widow's house before he found an eating place. As he passed out through the gate of the asclepiad enclosure he met Euryphon coming in. Euryphon greeted him coldly.

"Thargelia," he said, "seems slightly better, but, whatever happens, it is understood that you will make no attempt to speak to my daughter."

When Hippocrates would have replied, he shook his head and passed on.

Hippocrates knocked at the door of the widow Lycia's, and the servant opened to him. He handed over his cloak and strode into the courtyard. There, to his astonishment, he came face to face with Olympias, and beyond he saw someone — it could not be, but it was — Daphne! She was just entering Thargelia's room.

Now, he thought, the worst has happened.

The widow came bustling up. "We have visitors!" she cried. "This is the wife of the Chief Archon of Cos."

"He knows me." Olympias laughed in her rich contralto voice. "We are fellow Coans. How sad to find Thargelia this way! It must be heart-breaking for you, Hippocrates."

She gave him a smile of sympathy, or was it, he wondered, amusement? Or spite? "Go right in. Thargelia would want you to. I'll remain outside here. But afterward, I should like a word with you. Daphne talks as though she had decided never to marry. I cannot get the girl to discuss it with me. She's quite unreasonable."

Hippocrates had a sudden impulse to run away. He hesitated. Finally he made a sound in his throat that was suspiciously like a growl. Olympias thought it was a curse. She smiled as she watched him cross the court and enter the room.

He found Daphne standing at the foot of the bed, exquisite — dressed with special care. The angle at which she held her head suggested that she was on her guard, to say the least.

"Hippocrates!" Thargelia exclaimed, turning her head toward him with obvious surprise and pleasure. "How nice you've come!" Then she looked back at Daphne and seemed bewildered. "Who did you say you are?"

"I'm Daphne, the daughter of Euryphon," Daphne said. "Olympias told me you wanted to see me." Daphne turned to Hippocrates and added, "She was asleep when I came into the room. When she woke I explained to her who I was. I think I should not have come."

"Daphne?" Thargelia said. "Oh yes, I did want to see Daphne. Come near me — you are the woman who has had all the things in life that I missed and will have all the things I tried to make my own. When you came in I was having such a happy dream and I suppose I didn't want to wake up."

She looked at Hippocrates. "Perhaps," she added, "I'm still dreaming — no, no, this is real. There was something I wanted to say to Daphne. What was it, Hippocrates?"

"I don't know," he said helplessly. She took his hand and placed it on her forehead. "Hold it there," she said. "That's better."

"I think I'd better go," Daphne said.

"No, no! Please don't go!" Thargelia exclaimed. "There was something . . ."

"Perhaps," Hippocrates suggested, "it would be better for you to finish your sleep."

He was finding it difficult to think clearly, caught as he was between two overpowering emotions — compassion for Thargelia and love for Daphne; two emotions that called within him for opposite reactions. Daphne seemed cold and kept her eyes averted from him. He longed to cry out to her: "It is you I love — you, you!"

But he could not hurt Thargelia now, not now. He was somehow awed by her confident courage. Most men and women he had seen face death were brave, but this was something more. To tragedy she had added the appeal of a hurt child and the beauty of a woman's insight. He must play the role she had cast for him until the tragedy was over, the audience gone home.

He did not dare to look at Daphne. Suddenly he could bear it no longer. Without a word, he burst out of the room. As he strode across the court, he caught a glimpse of Olympias shrinking back out of sight in the room next door. He realized she must have heard every word. What did it matter? This was all as she had planned it — for Cleomedes. She must rejoice in it. He continued his headlong flight, stopping only for his cloak, until he was well outside.

Meanwhile Daphne moved to go.

"Oh, please don't be in such a hurry, you two," Thargelia said. "These are my most precious days. Perhaps you don't know, Daphne, that I am going to die."

Daphne turned in the doorway and took a quick step back. "Oh, don't say that!" she exclaimed.

"It's true," Thargelia said. "And I'm content to have it so. I wanted you to see how happy I am in my few days." She looked about. "Hippocrates has gone, hasn't he? But he will be back. He won't leave me now."

Her eyelids closed. Then she stirred and opened her eyes.

"I remember what it was. There is something else, something I may do for you. I heard Olympias telling your father Euryphon that I had been mistress to Hippocrates. Have you been told that too?"

"Yes," Daphne said, "but I don't think I believed it."

"It is not true." Thargelia said. "I was pregnant, but not by him." She laughed a little and added, "Unfortunately, not by him."

Olympias, listening outside, stood dazed, shocked. How could Thargelia — ! She stepped nearer so she could see as well as hear. What she saw was Thargelia holding out her hand and Daphne crossing the room with a quick birdlike movement to take it.

"You might not believe him if he said that," Thargelia was saying. "But me, you must believe. I have never been his mistress, only an admiring friend — desiring but never possessed."

Then a curious thing happened: Daphne burst into tears. If Hippocrates had remained, he would not have believed his eyes, for he would have seen the two women in each other's arms.

Olympias saw, and she left the house as precipitately as Hippocrates had done, without even taking leave of the widow Lycia. When she reached the street outside, her waiting slave heard her muttering, "Curse that woman Thargelia! Curse her! Curse her!"

Next morning Hippocrates was wakened early by Cleomedes, who, apparently, had not been in bed. He said he must talk with him. Hippocrates guessed what the young boxer had on his mind. But he kept him from talking about it until they had breakfasted. When they had finished the meal of porridge and barley cakes and sardines, Hippocrates smiled at Cleomedes.

"Tell me now," he said, "what you want to discuss."

"Daphne has refused me!" Cleomedes blurted out. "I've been waiting all night to ask you what I should do now. My father says I can come back home and go hunting. Old Buto says he'll go to Euryphon himself and come back with a yes or find out why. He gets rough. You might think he really was my father instead of just a tough old trainer. My mother — well, she says lots of things. But I don't listen to her any more."

"What do you think you should do?" Hippocrates asked.

"Well, I'm not sure what I should think. I know I've got to show Daphne that I can be gentle and that I would make a good husband — the way you said after our fight. I'd sort of like to stay on here in Cnidus for a time. Maybe I won't go back to Cos."

Hippocrates nodded. "That sounds reasonable. Women do sometimes change their minds. My brother Sosander says I don't understand women." He smiled reflectively. "I'm only a man, you know. But I consider that one thing is well established in regard to women; perhaps it is the only thing we know about them with certainty: they do change their minds.

"I suppose you will have the best chance to win Daphne if you can do the thing she might admire. The hardest thing to do after losing the boxing crown would be to go to work quietly like an ordinary citizen. Perhaps your father can give you real work to do in connection with his shipping until your turn comes to enter the Navy. I admire the way you have taken your defeat, and others will too."

Hippocrates rose to go. Cleomedes remained in his seat but looked up at him with doglike admiration.

"Thanks," he said. "I wish I could be an asclepiad like you. I suppose I'm too slow for that. Olympias said last night that I was as stupid as Buto. She says lots of things when she is angry." After a pause he added, "I hear you've had trouble too. I hope Thargelia doesn't die. May the gods be good to you and her."

Hippocrates stopped and looked down at the boy, putting a hand on his massive shoulder.

"That's kind. Thank you. It's false what they say about her and me. She's not the woman I wanted to marry. You'll understand all that I mean some day. You and I must both remember that in athletics and in love, men should accept defeat or victory as it comes, and accept it calmly. The good Greek does nothing in excess."

When Hippocrates reached the house of the widow Lycia he found that Thargelia was worse. "She does not know me now," the widow said, "and she says strange things."

Hippocrates stooped over her bed and put his hand on her burning forehead. The artery in the temple was pounding almost faster than he could count. "One leg," the widow said, "is swollen badly."

Hippocrates looked and frowned and shook his head. "You had better send someone to call Euryphon," he said to Lycia. "Do it at once."

Thargelia stirred and looked up at him. She smiled and whispered something. He stooped over to hear.

"I knew you would come," she said.

He watched her as her eyelids drooped. Her hair lay in golden waves about her face. Suddenly she roused and looked up at him. She struggled to sit up.

"Don't go, Hippocrates! Please don't leave me now."

He took her hand. "Of course I won't."

She dropped back on the pillow. "So," she said, "you are coming with me."

Hippocrates saw her smile and close her eyes. He waited until she seemed to be asleep. Then he left the room to prepare a medicine while Lycia returned to the bedside. But Lycia called:

"Come Hippocrates! Come! Hurry! Hurry!"

He came, only to discover that Thargelia had gone before him — she knew by now "what lies beyond" . . . Beautiful nymph of

Aphrodite! A woman who gambled and lost with courage, a woman who hoped for better love.

Then Hippocrates the physician pulled at his beard and muttered to himself: "When a leg swells up in the course of an ardent fever — I've seen it before — there is danger of sudden death like this."

Telling Lycia he would return, he left the house and climbed the mountain path above the city. As he climbed, he wondered why Thargelia's passing had moved him so. He had watched many die. He had learned to hide his feelings, but this sense of defeat and sadness was always there like a weight on his chest. Today it was somehow worse.

"Pity, it seems to me, is the quality that most distinguishes physicians from other men." Those were Daphne's words. She had said that on the terrace before the Archon's villa.

He reached the height and stood there, the busy little harbor open before him. He looked, but he did not see it, nor feel the wind as it came cool against his face, nor the cloak that flapped on his legs, nor the sun that warmed him. Instead he listened to a gentle voice, Thargelia's words like echoes in the mind.

"Only a little time to please the living, but all eternity to love the dead . . . There are tears in your eyes, Hippocrates . . . Yes, this way I shall have you — always, all of my life that is left, and all my death . . . What lies beyond the tomb? . . . That is what I wanted, a better love, love in which the body is not first and last. And when there is no body . . . will God love me? . . . So, you are coming with me."

Hippocrates walked down into the city. Later he returned to Lycia's house. Euryphon, she told him, had come and shaken his head and gone away again.

Hippocrates nodded. "I want you to do those things for her that men think right and proper for the dead. Thargelia would have wanted it that way." Then he added, "I shall not go with her to the grave. It is better so, but I will pay what is needed. You may hire the usual mourners."

When he returned to see that all had been done, he found

Thargelia wrapped in the blue chiton and lying in a good coffin. There was a honey cake for Cerberus in her hand and an obol between her teeth, the fee for Charon's ferry. About her head were the waves of golden hair, and the peace of death was on her face.

And Hippocrates wondered, as men have always wondered, What is life? Where from? What lies beyond the tomb?

CHAPTER SEVENTEEN

Buto

~~~~~~

Next morning, aboard his trireme in the harbor of Cnidus, Timon of Cos was stirring very early. He and his wife and a few servants had spent the night on board. The oarsmen had been sent to lodgings on shore. In the first gray light of dawn he stepped out on deck. It was cold, and the rigging was wet with heavy dew which dripped from the spars. Olympias followed him, shivering.

"I could not sleep last night," she said. "I was thinking about our poor Cleomedes all night long. It is Hippocrates who has caught the eye of Daphne. If you can get him out of the way Euryphon will give his daughter to our son, but not until then. What do you propose to do about it?"

"I have plans of great importance for this day," Timon said. "I'll set it right."

"You've had important plans," Olympias replied, "for every day that I can remember since we were married. That is why, my dear, you have grown so great and achieved so much."

Timon smiled with pleasure and would have thanked her if she had given him the opportunity. But she went on.

"You've never had time, however, to spend on our son. Cleomedes has been acting strangely toward me ever since Buto came to train him. But still you've no time to spend on him. Even Buto found him strange. That is why I asked Hippocrates to study him and treat him. I had another reason for that too. When you asked Hippocrates

out to the villa for that ill-timed consultation about Penelope, I saw
him meet Daphne before Cleomedes arrived — a very bad omen. I
thought then that if I called him in as a physicain, his code of
asclepiad behavior would keep him from meddling in our family
affairs. But it was too late, it seems. I tell you —"

"Wait," Timon broke in. "Let me talk. I plan to see Euryphon
again today about the marriage. That's the very thing I am busy
about. Euryphon is a sensible man and I'll arrange everything, no matter what it costs. The plan I have will make Euryphon rich. He
can't refuse. Cleomedes will settle down all right when he marries
Daphne. She'll keep him busy when he is not in service to the
State."

"But I tell you," Olympias exclaimed, raising her voice, "that you
can't make Daphne see reason until you get Hippocrates out of the
way. I wish his blonde mistress had taken him back to Macedonia
and kept him there."

"Thargelia?" Timon interrupted. "Oh — that reminds me. I heard
yesterday that Thargelia is dead. She died yesterday. Too bad!"

"Too bad, indeed!" Olympias cried. "A curse on the woman. She
died just when she was serving our purpose best."

"Olympias!" Timon exclaimed in surprise. "It is wrong to speak of
the dead that way."

"Wrong?" Olympias exclaimed. "Wrong? What is wrong and what
is right?" She laughed. "The right is what helps me and mine. The
wrong is whatever helps those against us."

"Olympias! Have you forgotten the gods?"

"Gods! Nonsense! There are no gods. Or if there are then they
must be against us." From her husband's expression she saw she had
gone too far in angry impulse.

"Forgive me, Timon; it's our son; I'm worried about him. I could
not sleep last night."

"Yes, I know," he replied. Then, after a pause: "It is impious for
us to deny that the gods exist. But you may be right when you fear
that they are angry with us. You know what ignorant people say
about the grove of Apollo in which our villa stands. I cut down some
of those trees about the house because you were afraid of the dark

forest. I had bought the grove and paid for it. But perhaps it was wrong in the eyes of Apollo to cut the trees.

"It was then that Penelope had her first falling fit, remember? Now Cleomedes loses the boxing crown that he should have won, and Daphne draws back when the marriage contract was ready to be signed. But leave it to me, I'll arrange everything somehow, and we will take steps to appease Apollo when we return to Cos."

"Do what you can to persuade Euryphon," she replied, "and I will see what I can do. Hippocrates is our stumbling block."

Olympias allowed her husband to embrace her. She watched, like a dutiful wife, as he climbed down the ship's ladder and was rowed away. The water was still; down through it, she could see a broken amphora on the bottom. Timon looked back as he stepped out on the beach and she waved to him.

"I need you, Timon," she murmured. "I've always needed you. You think I love you. . . . Well, so I do, with my mind. There must be more than one me."

She drew the folds of the woolen cloak together and hugged herself. "This body craves other satisfactions. Buto started me off wrong, perhaps. Timon I've always loved with the mind, and a little with the body. Can a woman love one man with the mind and others with the body? Loves and hates? I hate Buto. I love the strong bodies of athletes. I'm afraid of Buto."

She put her hands on the cold wet rail and scanned the waterfront. Soon she saw what she waited to see. Buto the boxer was slouching along the causeway. He crossed the little harbor-island and came to the shore. Olympias moved to the other side of the deck to be out of sight, and to think.

Why should she start, she thought to herself, when she saw that man on the shore? Was it fear of what he might do to her, or something more? She would never catch her breath, she thought, if Timon returned to the shore.

The months since Buto's return, she mused, had been months of fear for her. She had hoped that his coming would bring success, success to her only boy, her love, her joy. Now Cleomedes had lost his match, and might lose his woman too. And she herself was losing her son in spite of all she could do. Timon still believed in his wife. He gave her the comforts she wanted in life. She might lose that too, if Timon should learn what Buto knew — what Buto knew, what Buto did — if Timon should learn . . .

Suddenly she cried out in anguish, "There it is again! My mind goes round and round, round and round! Am I going mad like my cousins?"

In a moment Buto would be on the deck with her, and they would be alone. The feeling of fear was gripping her now, like a pressure below her ribs, like a hand that clutched at her heart.

"What is it I fear?" she said aloud. "He may kill again — let my secret out? I must send him away. But will he go? Do I want him to go?"

She heard a voice from the water below and footsteps on the ladder. Then Buto stood on the rail above, outlined against the sky; straight and still he balanced there and scanned the deck below. She did not speak; he had come like that, she recalled, in her dreams, to hold her tight in his mighty arms, till she woke and found him gone.

He jumped to the deck and came toward her, like a ponderous cat approaching its prey.

"There are men below," she said nervously. "They'll come to me if I call."

He looked at her and did not speak. Just then the cook came up with a steaming pot of broth, but she sent him back. They walked to the bow of the ship and stood where none could hear. The deck was wet and water ran down the ropes and dripped on them. She shivered and, reaching out, she touched the mat of graying hair on Buto's bare chest; then she pulled his cloak across it. Her white arms disappeared under her own cloak and she shivered again.

Buto turned his little eyes on her, but still he said nothing. There was a sullen expression on his scarred face. She glanced back along the deck to make sure they were alone.

"You've done nothing but run away from me ever since I came from Sparta," he said slowly. "Why'd you send for me now?"

"Because I wanted to talk about Cleomedes."

"Why do you keep yourself away from me?"

"Because I'm afraid."

They were silent for a time. At last he said: "Have you forgotten the time when I was in hiding on Astypalea? — That was twenty-one years ago. You remember those days in the cave on the shore, the cave where I hid?"

"Yes," she whispered. "I remember — all too well."

He opened his enormous hands as though about to seize her.

"No!" she cried, shrinking back. Her face flamed with color and she trembled a little. Then something hard came into her voice. "When did you last see Cleomedes?"

He dropped his hands at his sides and turned away.

"I saw your son this morning."

"Our son," she said in a low voice. "You know that. Timon thinks he was named for his ancestor. You know he was named for you. What did he say to you this morning?"

"He wants to stay here," Buto growled, "here in Cnidus. He won't go to Cos and he won't go to Sparta. He wants to wait and wait, like a dog outside the gate, till the bitch comes out in heat."

"Buto!" Olympias protested. Then she gave way to a gusty laugh.

"Cleomedes says," Buto continued, "that Daphne may change her mind. Hippocrates told him that women do change their minds! Hippocrates says this; Hippocrates says that. I hear too much about Hippocrates — curse him!"

"Yes," Olympias echoed, "curse him!" After a silence Olympias said, "Buto, Cleomedes won't box any more, not now. Later on he will, perhaps, and he might even go with you to Sparta for training then. Timon would pay you well, very well. Please return to Sparta now. I'm afraid to have you stay."

He shook his head. "If I could just get Cleomedes away from that girl — or if he would marry her, then I could make something out of him right now, and this is the time to do it. He's young, strong, he has everything that a boxer needs to win." A strange light came into his face. She watched the muscles writhe in his mighty arms as he closed his fists.

"I can make him the greatest boxer of all. He'll get the crown that they would not give me. I am the first Cleomedes. They took my crown away, but he could go to Olympia and win that crown and keep it — Cleomedes the Second!"

"Don't," she whispered — "don't talk so loud. I'm afraid." Then she continued in her ordinary voice:

"You probably don't know what I've been trying to do. When I visited Halasarna, I realized Hippocrates had been making love to Daphne. Following that, I laid excellent plans so that Thargelia might spoil his attempt to catch Daphne. Thargelia, blonde and pregnant! That was exactly what I would have hoped for. Then, the day before yesterday, I took Daphne to see Thargelia — expecting them to fight, expecting Daphne to hate Hippocrates."

"That was an awful good idea," Buto drawled.

"Yes, it was," she said bitterly. "But what do you suppose they did?"

Buto had turned his little eyes on her with an expression of delighted admiration. Now he shook his great head.

"They fell into each other's arms and kissed!" Olympias slapped her thigh, like a fishwife. "The two women kissed each other! And now Thargelia is dead and no use to us at all."

Buto grunted. The light that had appeared in his moon-shaped face while he thought of Cleomedes' future triumphs was fading slowly. The look of sullen discouragement returned. They stood in silence for a little time, a strangely matched pair — Olympias black-haired, handsome, well-groomed, and Buto, his hair and beard uncouth — ugly, powerful.

She looked at his scars and the distorted features, recalling the boyish face she had known, the Herculean neck and shoulders, and rippling muscles under the smooth hot skin of youth.

"Well," she said, as though thinking aloud, "you must go back to Sparta sometime. But if you will not go now, let us consider what we can do for Cleomedes. He must have what he wants. He might be different to me then. His wife would live with me in my house. Perhaps we could get Daphne for him after all. He won't have anyone else. I wouldn't have chosen her for him. But no one can change his choice.

"Perhaps, now," she continued reflectively, "if we could just make trouble between Euryphon and Hippocrates, Cleomedes might still win. You told me Hippocrates spends his idle time reading among Euryphon's papyruses. Now, if he would only steal those manuscripts — or perhaps burn them — that could make trouble all right."

Olympias looked out across the harbor.

"The oil room," she mused, "and the rubbing tables, where you work, are next to the building in which the manuscripts are kept. I noticed that."

She paused and watched him. Slowly, slowly, Buto's face wrinkled itself into a cunning grin. He placed a huge hand over his mouth for a little time.

Then suddenly he said, "I have to go to work," and moved away down the deck. "I must not be late. I must start my work."

Olympias followed. He leaped up on the rail and, turning, started down the ladder. But he stopped when he was partly over the side, and leaned on the rail, looking at her with a delighted open-mouthed grin on his face.

"It takes me and you together to do things. What a plan!"

He threw back his head and laughed a great laugh. The sound, she thought, echoed back from every ship in the harbor and from the hills beyond.

In the still surface of the water the other triremes and the hillside houses above were reflected as though in a mirror. The level rays of the rising sun seemed to touch their outlines with gold. The sun shone on Buto too, turning his shaggy hair into a bristling halo. He laughed again like an evil satyr.

"Buto, be quiet," she said in a hoarse whisper. Then, reaching over the rail, she held him by a hairy hand.

"Buto!" she whispered. "Buto! What are you going to do? Be careful, don't hurt anyone, don't — kill anyone, not even Hippocrates. I'm afraid of what you may do."

CHAPTER EIGHTEEN

Ctesias

~~~~~~

HIPPOCRATES too was awake early that morning, after a restless night. He sat up and rubbed his eyes, and looked out into the courtyard. Sleeping men were scattered about the court, each rolled in his blanket.

He felt thwarted and disconsolate. Now, since Daphne had rejected Cleomedes, his hopes should have been high. Instead of that, his heart was heavy, and he was angry that Euryphon should believe the slanders that Olympias had put on him. He could not approach Euryphon now. That was plain enough. And Daphne — he wondered what she thought after her visit to Thargelia. He felt he could not tell either of them that Perdiccas had been the father of her child — that was the deathbed secret of a patient. Even if they did know that, they would probably still believe that he had been Thargelia's lover in Cos.

He straightened up. This would not do! He would not bend the knee to Euryphon, but bide his time instead. A boat was scheduled to leave for Cos at sundown. He must be on that boat . . . and somehow, before then, perhaps —

He rose to his feet and folded up his blanket, moving quietly so as not to waken Cleomedes, who slept on the mat beside him.

He looked down at the sleeper. In spite of his massive frame, he was only a boy and he had the beauty of youth. His face was more delicately chiseled than that of Buto, and yet it bore a startling re-semblance. Hippocrates marveled now that Timon had never noticed how much this boy he thought his son resembled the boxing in-structor.

Cleomedes stirred and muttered something unintelligible. It would seem, Hippocrates thought, that Daphne does not keep him awake as she does me. But Cleomedes, as though to answer him, rolled over and spoke quite clearly.

"I can be gentle too." Then, after a silence, "Daphne, Daphne." This was followed by a long sigh and presently heavy breathing again.

The brain, Hippocrates mused, is beginning to rouse and to set the stage for dreaming. The curtains of sleep still shut out the light of day, but within, in the room of memory, lights are glimmering. He sees Daphne there with his inward eye and speaks to her.

He picked his way among the sleepers on the floor of the court and entered the washroom. Then, leaving his belongings in the care of a sleepy attendant, he breakfasted and set off for a long walk into the country to be alone with his thoughts.

On his way he passed the house of the widow Lycia, and acting on sudden impulse, he stopped and knocked on her door. It occurred to him then, as it should have done before, that it might be far too early for a call. But he could not take back the knocking, so he waited. Eventually the maid opened the door.

He apologized for the hour. Then he asked if the widow was awake yet. The maid was hesitant, but a cheery voice from across the court called out:

"Tell Hippocrates I'll be with him soon. Bid him be patient; I'm on my way."

He stepped inside, and as he waited for her he heard her singing: "I'm on my way, I'm on my way, a daughter of Aphrodite today."

This is rather different, he thought, from the hush in this house only yesterday. It was not long before Lycia came sweeping across the court. She was trying, not very successfully, to keep an overlong white cloak from dragging on the floor. Hippocrates observed that she seemed somehow different. Her cheeks were as round and as red as ever, redder in fact. Her hair was somewhat in disarray. She smiled as usual, but more so.

"How good you are, Hippocrates, to come to visit me before I take my rest. You remember you told me to keep Thargelia's things. It was very kind of you. I had one or two friends come in last night to taste her wine. She had only a few bottles, alas, but of such fine quality!"

Lycia laughed and he smelled the wine on her breath, and garlic too!

"My friends have only just gone home. They would not go before. But after great sorrow men should be gay, you know, and women too, by the gods."

Hippocrates turned back to the door, resentful, intending to leave.

"Oh, don't you go," she said. "You came to hear about the burial. I understand. All went as you would have had it. The mourners you asked me to hire were here, and it was all very sad. We all wept for Thargelia — poor Thargelia!"

Her voice choked and a sudden tear stole down her cheek. She wiped it on the border of her cloak.

"Yes, we wept for her — but her life was not so bad, at least while it lasted. And she did have lovely things! Hippocrates, I'll tell you a secret."

She came close and placed a hand on his arm. He drew away. He could smell Thargelia's perfume now, and he realized that this woman was wearing her cloak. It was as though Thargelia herself had whispered to him. Surely, he thought, a perfume should go to the grave with its owner and not walk abroad like a ghost recalling other days.

"Thargelia and I," she said, "had much in common." She lowered her voice to a whisper. "I was once a *hetaira*. I was educated for that profession. I can quote from the poets as well as she could. Before I got fat I was something to see."

She stopped and regarded him. He was standing silent, but his eyes were looking beyond her. He was no longer listening.

"But," Lycia continued, catching his eye after the silence, "I gave up that life and I have a new profession now. I learned to be a midwife first and now I keep this house to care for the sick. And I do very well with it. Sometimes the house is full of Euryphon's patients who cannot be kept at home. I love them all and I give them good care.

"You asclepiads should develop such homes, homes like mine. I would like to train young women to learn the art of the care of the sick, the art that Euryphon is teaching me. A woman's role in the care of the sick might be made an art in itself."

"Yes." Hippocrates looked at her thoughtfully. "This is a part of the art of medicine, a part in which we will always need the help of women, women who have learned the skill."

"Perhaps," Lycia said, "I ought to tell you what I did with Thargelia's most valuable possession, her mirror — I sent it to Daphne."

Hippocrates looked at her in astonishment. "Did she accept it?"

The widow smiled. "Confidentially, I wouldn't have been quite so generous, but I thought it would please Euryphon. I need his goodwill, especially after two deaths in the house and having no patients to care for now. But why shouldn't Daphne accept it? You needn't be so surprised. You think Daphne is different . . . She is the sort of woman you would take for a wife. But how little you men know women! Any woman might envy Thargelia that face and form, that hair and wit; any woman might be what Thargelia was and be glad of it."

Hippocrates shook his head and smiled. "Each woman I meet seems to teach me something unexpected, and you are no exception, Lycia. Women! A fascinating subject for study — but medicine is so much simpler!" He turned to leave. "Good-by, Lycia. It's time for you to go to bed. I'm sorry I called so early."

"Never too early for men to come," she laughed as she closed the door. "Never too early and never too late when you're trained in the art of *hetaira*."

Lycia yawned and stretched and turned toward her room.

"Well, I'll sleep between Thargelia's sheets. What adventures they must have known! Yes, I'll sleep in her lovely silken sheets, and dream of her loves — and my own."

Hippocrates continued on his way, passing over the shoulder of the mountain. He looked down on the rooftops and into the courts and crooked streets of the city, watching the people as the gods must watch. And he seemed to see his own life and problems in long perspective with the lives of other men.

The intimate sounds of a city's life came softly up to him: the crowing of cocks in many keys, the barking of dogs, and the sobbing sound of a braying ass, and children's cries, and the tremulous bleat of kid and goat; and the song of those who hawked their wares — familiar sounds, like voices chanting a distant hymn. And he smelt the smoke of the burning reeds in the still, cool air of the morning, sweet incense from the breakfast hearths of a thousand homes below.

At the end of the morning Hippocrates had made peace with himself. He had begun to plan his work in Cos. He was not happy, but he was content to return. Happiness, he thought as he sat at his midday meal in the town, is something else. When he had finished he walked through the streets, stopping to buy a new cloak for his mother. He hunted up a barber's booth and found it crowded. Talk among the waiting men turned to the events of the Triopian games. When his turn came and the barber was trimming his beard, he heard his own name.

"I didn't think much of Hippocrates' oration. I didn't know what he was talking about."

"Neither did he," another voice replied. This was followed by a laugh. "I'm told he can think of nothing but this woman who came to be treated by Euryphon. She died, you know."

Hippocrates walked away through the town. He turned his lonely steps to the asclepiad hill, and asking for the key at the gate, he went to the manuscript house. The *palaestra* next door was closed, since treatments were carried out there in the morning. He read for some time in the silence. Once he heard a sound and looked up. There was an opening like a window in the wall between the *palaestra* rubbing room and the manuscript house. The sound that had attracted his attention seemed to have come from the window. He saw now that a shutter was moving slowly across the opening without further noise. He wondered whose was the unseen hand that was closing the window. Why should anyone care to spy on him? But what did it matter?

What was it, he mused, that had killed Thargelia? He put the papyrus scrolls away and paced back and forth in the library courtyard. Suddenly he stopped pacing and struck his fist into his hand. "Here are related conditions. Some cause must run through this sequence: fever in the first woman, an opened womb in the second, fever in the second, painful veins and swollen leg, sudden death!

"What passes from one woman with a fever to another woman to give her that fever? I wonder if I am not near to a clue. What strikes so suddenly from swollen veins, perhaps through the veins, to kill in an instant of time? I will not take the easy way and say that an evil spirit enters the body. No! There are natural causes. There must be!

"One experience is often deceptive. But if I see these same relations often enough, perhaps some day I shall discover the cause, the basic cause. For the present I can only record, remember, compare."

He was interrupted in this soliloquy by the squeaking of the door that led into the home of Ctesiarchus. The small figure of Ctesias dressed in a kilt appeared in the doorway. He walked directly to Hippocrates and looked at him as though there was something he wanted to say. Hippocrates smiled and sat down so as to reach the boy's level.

"How old are you?"

"I'm almost seven. Let me feel your muscle, please."

Hippocrates did as he was told, flexing his biceps strongly. The boy put both hands on his upper arm; then nodded gravely.

"Daphne told me that you were just about as strong as Heracles. He was your great-great-great-grandfather, wasn't he?"

Hippocrates shrugged. "Some people like to say so. Are you on your way now to see Daphne?"

"Yes. We are going to give the turtle his bath."

"Will you take something to Daphne for me?"

Ctesias nodded assent. There were writing materials on the table. Hippocrates cut a very small strip of papyrus and wrote: *I am re-*

turning to Cos. I shall remain there as a physician and a teacher. If I may hope for your love, send me word. Send Ctesias back with it; or just tell him to say the word "yes."

He rolled up the little scroll and sealed it.

"Will you take this to Daphne's house and give it to her? Not to anyone else, remember. Do it right away."

Ctesias took the scroll and put it in the little bag that hung at his belt, along with pebbles and food for the turtle. Hippocrates opened the big door and watched him as he ran across the enclosure to Euryphon's house.

He waited. Finally he closed the door and paced back and forth again in the court. When Ctesias did come again, he entered by the small door from Ctesiarchus' house. He had a box in his arms which he set down in an alcove.

"My turtle is in that box," he said.

"Did Daphne tell you to tell me something?" Hippocrates asked eagerly.

Ctesias shook his head in the negative.

"Did you give her my writing?"

Ctesias nodded assent.

"And didn't she tell you to say yes to me — or perhaps no?"

"No," Ctesias replied, "but my mother told me to tell you something. She wants to see you, upstairs in our house. I said to her that I wanted to ask you to tell me a story. So she told me that I could ask you to tell me just one story first. I like stories."

Hippocrates turned and walked away from the boy. He sat down heavily. Ctesias ran to him and stood expectantly, leaning against his knee.

"Tell me a story about Heracles — please."

Hippocrates shook his head. "I'm not a good storyteller. That is something I've never done."

"Never mind. Tell me just a little story — please. It doesn't matter how bad you are."

Hippocrates leaned back against the wall. Finally he made a gesture of despair, or resignation. Then he sat upright and began his tale.

"Heracles was the son of Zeus, you know. Zeus is the king of all the gods up on Olympus, and he promised that if his son Heracles would work very hard and use his strength in many labors throughout his life, he would at last take him up to Mount Olympus to live forever with the gods and goddesses there.

"Now, one day when Heracles was a baby, sleeping in his cradle, two serpents came and coiled about the cradle. They hiss-ss-ssed and hiss-ss-ssed until, at last, Heracles woke up. He saw the serpents above him about to bite. So he grabbed one serpent in one hand and the other serpent in the other, and he squeezed and squeezed — just like this. So, when his mother Alcmene came to the cradle, what do you suppose she found?"

Ctesias shook his head.

"She found both serpents dead, and little Heracles was kicking his heels in the air."

Ctesias drew in a long breath. "Tell me some more."

"Well, when Heracles grew older, he was sailing home from the overthrow of Troy. But there was a great storm, and the ship was wrecked on the island of Cos, where I live. Then the Coan people took their spears and came against him with their King Eurypylus to drive him away. But Heracles was so strong that he overcame them and killed the king.

"After that, the king's daughter Chalciope came down to the shore and she danced before Heracles. She was very beautiful — like Daphne, you know. So she and Heracles were married, and they lived happily on our island for years. That is why some Coans believe, even today, that they are the sons and daughters of Heracles."

"Tell me another."

"I should go back to Cos before long, you know."

"Just one."

"Well, this is the one I like to remember myself. When Heracles was a boy, like you, his teacher was the good centaur Chiron. And as Heracles grew older Chiron taught him to tame wild horses, and to wrestle. Soon the boy was faster of foot and stronger of arm than any boy or man.

"You know it was Chiron too who taught the healing art to Asclepius, and Asclepius became the blameless physician. All that Asclepius knew about medicine he taught his sons, and they handed what they knew down to their sons, and so Chiron's healing art has come down to us. We, the asclepiads, are his sons."

"Yes," Ctesias said soberly, "and when I grow up I shall be an asclepiad too."

Hippocrates nodded.

"Heracles knew that his father Zeus expected him to use his strength for every task that came his way. So, when he had learned all that Chiron could teach him, he killed the great Thespian lion that lived in the nearby wood. He did this with his bare hands, and made himself a cloak of the lion's skin. Then he set out to see the world, wearing this cloak on his shoulders.

"But he came to the place where the road divides and he wondered which to take. He had passed so many men on the road living a life of ease. Why use my strength in contest, he thought; why struggle to right the wrong?

"Then he saw two women approaching him, one on either road. And the first one laughed and arched her neck. The light shone through her cloak. He wanted to touch her lovely form and hold it in his arms.

" 'Come along my road,' she sang. 'There are no tasks, no labor here. This is the road of idleness; no struggle here, no work, no sweat. This is the road of happiness, to a land of no regret.' And he thought he would go with her.

"Then the woman on the other road approached with flashing eyes. 'A man of strength and courage,' she cried, 'should seek his work in the world. Come with me on this road. It's a rough road for the strong. Joy comes to men in contest, happiness with success. Labor wins men's praises, anguish the smile of the gods.'

" 'What is your name?' Heracles asked."

" 'Aretê,' " she replied."

Hippocrates looked at the boy. "Do you know which road Heracles took?"

"Yes," Ctesias replied, "the hard one with Aretê. Heracles had many, many labors," he continued, "and he finished every one."

Hippocrates nodded. "You will understand all that I mean when you are older. Aretê has led the leaders in Greece from Homer to men of today. She makes them want to excel, each at the labor he chooses in life."

Hippocrates stood up. "Did you say your mother asked to see me?"

"But," Ctesias persisted, "I was going to tell you a story. Don't you want to hear it?"

"Well — yes," Hippocrates said, somewhat doubtfully.

"Do you know who Poseidon is? He's the King of the Sea." Hippocrates nodded.

"Once he was chasing Polybutes, a big big giant, and he threw his trident at him. Do you know what happened? He didn't hit the giant but he cut off a big piece of Cos, your island. Then he took the piece and threw it after the giant and it covered him up. That is why the little island beside Cos is always smoking."

"Yes," Hippocrates said soberly. "We call the island Nisyros."

"I saw it," Ctesias said, "when I went in the ship to Rhodes. The giant is still underneath. He can't get away, but he growls. My mother says if he got away he might shake all our houses down."

Ctesias smiled proudly. "Now I'll take you to my mother." He led Hippocrates out of the manuscript house through the small door into the house of his father Ctesiarchus. They climbed a creaking flight of stairs and passed along a short hall to a veranda.

"Welcome, welcome!" his mother called. She was lying on a couch at the end of the veranda, a dark-haired, delicate woman with pale, lined face and appealing dark brown eyes. "I thought I should never see you."

Hippocrates greeted her and tried to explain the delay. But she interrupted him.

"Yes, yes, I know before you tell me. Ctesias insisted that you should tell him a story about Heracles, and then he asked for another, and another! He is a very determined child, this son of mine. I am sorry my husband is not here. He told me about you when he returned from Triopion. He heard you speak there. But he was called away today to see a sick man in Syrna. I have heard so much about you. Can you help me? You see, I am paralyzed."

She made a gesture to her servant, who turned down the soft white coverlet of lamb's wool, exposing her legs. Hippocrates looked at her with a practiced eye: her arms, he saw, moved normally, but the legs lay still and stiff. When he stooped and lifted one leg it vibrated rapidly in his hand, shaking the wooden couch.

"Can you cure me?" she said, holding a bony hand toward him. "My husband spoke of asking you to see me, after the festival. But Euryphon said no. That was because of the woman Thargelia. She has just died, I know. I am sorry. But can you help me? Ctesias and I thought we would ask you now, without waiting for my husband's return."

She put her arms about the boy and drew him close to her.

Hippocrates continued to look at her, passing finger and thumb over the hair of his mustache. He ignored her reference to Thargelia, focusing his mind on the problem she presented.

"Have you had pain?"

"Yes, like a knife coming from my back around the chest and into my breast, here."

"How long?"

"For almost a year."

He asked no more questions, but he smiled at her and she knew he understood.

"I will talk with your husband," he said. "We can devise some way to help you. But I cannot promise to cure you."

He took his leave and walked down the stairs and across the court, entering the manuscript house through the small back door again. And Ctesias walked back with him, sober and half understanding that medicine had no cure for his mother. Hippocrates said good-by to the boy and left him standing in the library, as he closed and locked the front door.

Outside, Hippocrates realized that sunset was not far off, so he gave the key to the gate keeper and hurried away to his inn. There he shouldered his pack-bag and stopped to take leave of Cleomedes. The young boxer had been waiting for him. He was stripped to the waist.

"I'm going to run as far as the asclepiad hill and on up the mountain. I might perhaps see Daphne there, and I want to keep my legs in condition." He danced about, shadow-boxing. Then he stopped and looked at Hippocrates, his boyish face suddenly serious.

"Buto asked me to leave Daphne and to go away with him. Did you know that? He wants to take me to Sparta to train for boxing there. He says Daphne loves you — does she?"

Hippocrates set his bag down. "I don't know," he answered quietly. "Her father has told me not to see her. So I'm going back to my work."

Cleomedes nodded. "We'll have to 'wait for the word of the judge,' both of us."

"You have changed," Hippocrates said, looking at the young athlete with undisguised admiration. "You're growing up. But after all, her father may not choose either of us. Who knows?" He smiled and shouldered the bag. "Good-by. We will meet again soon, I hope."

Hippocrates made his way to the harbor and was rowed out to the trireme. It was one of the freight and passenger boats that plied between Tyre, on the Phoenician coast, and Piraeus, the seaport of Athens. The anchor came up, the oars began to swing and the ship slid smoothly across the harbor.

He climbed the afterdeck. Six days had passed since he had sailed from Cos, days of decision, disappointment, tragedy and sorrow. The ship rounded the breakwater and headed out. Now he could look back at the city of Cnidus, white houses crowding along the curving beach with the pillars of the acropolis beyond. In the middle distance, not far from the shore, was the little hill crowned by asclepiad buildings where Daphne lived. . . . There was more smoke, he thought, than usual over the city. The ship passed close to a small rocky island, and further view was cut off suddenly, as though a curtain had been drawn. He must turn his mind back to Cos, he thought, and make plans for the future, a lonely future for him.

Some hours later, when night had fallen and the only light on sea and ship came from the moon and from heaven's vast dome of twinkling stars, they rounded the headland of the Cnidian peninsula. The captain of the ship came forward looking for Hippocrates.

"Beautiful night," he said. "With stars as bright as these, sailors don't need the sun. We will anchor at Cos before dawn and take on a cargo of wine skins and Coan honey for Athens." After a pause he continued:

"The commander of the king's trireme from Macedonia, who is an old friend of mine, says he knows you. I saw him in Tyre and we talked of war among the Greeks — Athens against Corinth and Sparta. You know, don't you, that Athenian troops have landed in the north, near Potidea?"

Hippocrates nodded and the two men talked gravely of what war might mean to Greece.

"War among ourselves," Hippocrates said, "will mean death for so many young men who might in time have contributed to the splendor of Athens. Sparta has prepared so long for war that Spartans have been able to add little to what is good in Greece. But Sparta can destroy the good things that Spartans never learned to appreciate. War among ourselves could change great Greece, with her competitions and her arts and her achievements of hand and mind, into a vast Greek desert — a place where Barbarians will find no more than the shells of former life and thought. But perhaps I talk this way because I am gloomy tonight."

They stood silent, looking out to sea, until his companion said, "The Macedonia captain told me he planned to stop at Cos to carry you back to the court of King Perdiccas. He should be arriving there about now."

Hippocrates shook his head. "I shall not go with him."

The captain looked at him and scratched his beard thoughtfully, waiting for an explanation. But when the famous physician showed no desire to talk, he continued himself.

"You'd be safe there, and you'd have great wealth. But after all, you're a Greek, not a Macedonian, and money is not everything."

"You have summarized my reasons very well," Hippocrates said, smiling, "and with few words, like a sailor. Medicine is more than wealth to me."

"Your fame as a physician," the captain observed as he turned away, "is well known, I can tell you, in all the ports. Those who need you will find you wherever you go, even in Cos. It has an excellent harbor and good wine. But it's a windswept little island."

They drew away from the Cnidian headland, turning north. Before them the mountain mass of Cos was plain to see in the moonlight, and off to the left, the volcanic cone of the island of Nisyros. Hippocrates smiled to himself, remembering how well Ctesias had told the tale of Poseidon and the giant. The sails were furled, and the ship swished forward, to the rhythmical creak of oars and the grunting song of the oarsmen, *"Rhup-pa-pai! Rhup-pa-pai!"*

As he stood alone on the afterdeck, Daphne seemed strangely near. A wave of shimmering silver followed the ship and Hippocrates watched it through the night.

CHAPTER NINETEEN

Purkaia!

~~~~~~

AFTER HIPPOCRATES had left the manuscript house and hurried down the hill, Olympias knocked on the gate. She asked for Daphne, and the gateman admitted her and watched her cross the square and stand before the door of Euryphon's house. He noticed, however, that instead of knocking there at once, she stood for a little while looking back toward the *palaestra* and the manuscript house.

Meanwhile, inside the house, Euryphon was preparing to leave. He called to Daphne from the court. He knew she must be in the spinning and weaving room, for he heard her voice and the sound of the loom and the voices of her maids. At his second call, she appeared on the gallery.

"I'm leaving now," he said. "There is urgent illness in the house of Timotheus, the rich merchant."

Daphne saw that her father looked stern. She could read his moods at a glance. Taking the skirt of her chiton in her hand, she came running along the gallery, down the stairs and across the court to him. His expression softened as he watched her. They crossed the court together.

"You are worried," she said. He nodded.

"What is it?"

"Timon has been calling on me again. It's about Cleomedes — But I don't want to talk about that now. If a messenger comes from the house of Scyllis with news about his old mother, let one of my assistants go to see her. She is to remain at home and not to go to Lycia's house — two deaths there are enough for the present."

"Oh! Father, you should see the mirror Lycia sent me. It was Thargelia's."

Her father frowned in surprise, but she continued before he could speak. "Don't say anything. I have some important news to tell you about her, and about Hippocrates — when you have time for it."

Daphne mounted the stairs again, singing as she went, while old Xanthias brought his master's best cloak.

"The young slave," he said, "will accompany you to the house of Timotheus. Here is your staff."

Euryphon nodded, and Xanthias opened the door. To their surprise, Olympias was standing there with her back turned.

"*Chaire!*" Euryphon exclaimed. "*Chaire!*"

She was so startled that she swayed and almost fell, but she rallied quickly.

"Oh! You gave me such a fright! How good to find you here, Euryphon. I really came to see your daughter. We have had so few opportunities for friendly talk. I want to make myself a good mother-in-law to her, you know."

"Come in, come in and be welcome," Euryphon said. "Xanthias here will take care of you. You will excuse me, for I must hurry away to visit a patient who is dangerously ill, the daughter of a most important citizen of Cnidus."

The smile with which he had greeted her was gone now.

"Your friend Thargelia," he said, "died yesterday. No doubt you have heard the news."

"Oh, yes," she said. "I am so sad, and her going will be a bitter blow to Hippocrates."

"I wonder," he replied, staring at her. "I wonder if it will."

"Oh, yes," she exclaimed. "I was talking with your gateman just now. He said Hippocrates had hidden himself away this afternoon among your manuscripts. He was very depressed and he left in a great hurry just before I arrived — I saw him going — a great hurry, and not a word out of him."

"I'm sorry he's gone," Euryphon said. "I wanted to see him again, but I have been so busy."

Olympias watched him cross the enclosure and pass through the gate, swinging his staff and followed by the young slave, a fine-looking Scythian youth. She turned back, and Xanthias smiled as though to apologize for his master's abrupt disappearance. He ushered her courteously into the waiting room, asking her if her servant had not come with her.

"No," Olympias said. The old man made a gesture of polite surprise.

"No," she repeated, with sudden anger. "No. I left in a hurry. After all, it's not your affair. A slave should not ask such questions — Anyway, she's not very well. She has a headache. Even slaves have headaches, don't they, Xanthias?"

Xanthias' head was bowed by many years of service and by something else, in the joints of his neck, that gave him pain and made a grating sound. But he raised his head quite high now, without feeling the pain. He looked directly at Olympias.

"Even slaves have headaches," he repeated quietly. "I will tell Daphne that you are here."

He paused in the doorway and turned back.

"I am a freedman, Olympias, not a slave. There are other questions I could have asked."

The old man shuffled off, his head still high.

"What does Xanthias mean?" Olympias muttered. "What does he mean? Does he suspect our secret?"

She went to the door of the waiting room and listened, her lips compressed to a line. From the courtyard came the sound of a loom — clack, clack, clack — and women laughing, then Daphne's voice.

Olympias glided across to the house door and opened it wide enough to see out. She glanced back furtively, then looked again, putting her face against the edge of the oaken door and whispering, as though the door might understand.

"I'm so afraid. If I could only stop him. I must stop him."

She returned to the court to listen. The sound of the loom had stopped. Suddenly Daphne's voice was heard loud and clear:

"That is a lie, made up and spread about by Olympias. I know who the father was —"

Olympias could not hear what followed. She flushed in sudden anger, and turning back to the outer door, she disappeared from the house.

Meantime Xanthias had climbed the courtyard stair with heavy tread and clumped along the gallery. He stopped before the spinning room to watch the scene. The spinning maid, a graceful lass, held with finger and thumb the thread she spun, and held it high to keep the whirling spindle free. The distaff covered with raw white wool was in her other hand. She laughed to hear what Daphne said, and some of the wool slipped off the staff to the floor.

Daphne, standing with her back to the door, was talking about Ctesias and his turtle. On the other side an older servant, Anna, sat weaving at the loom. When the laughter subsided, Daphne spoke seriously.

"The things Ctesias does and says are sometimes very, very funny. And yet no one could laugh in his presence. He has the dignity of a grown man, and also a remarkable mind. That comes, I suppose, from being alone so much with his mother. He tries so hard to understand everything and he's so thoughtful and sweet and utterly lovable."

Xanthias stood waiting for his mistress's nod. She turned and smiled, but let him wait. Her eyes, he saw, were quite blue again, as they had been when she was a child. The blue band that bound her hair let curls escape about her happy face.

Anna, sitting before her loom, was watching her mistress too.

"Daphne," she said smiling, "what a change I see in you. The day before yesterday, when Olympias came to take you to Thargelia, you were sad and silent. But since your return, the house is full of laughter. You have opened your chest, with all its lovely marriage things, for the first time in a year! You've started me weaving for it again. What did Thargelia do for you?"

Daphne blushed and did not reply. She stooped to pick up the wool from the floor. Old Xanthias smiled, then he looked away. As she stooped, he had seen her breasts, and sadness came into his eyes and his thoughts slipped back through many years, to the breasts of another maid. He felt her kiss on his lips again, remembered her voice, and saw her kneel by another wedding chest — remembered the tears they wept together so long ago — when he was taken away, a slave.

Daphne, half reading the mind of the old man she loved so well, smiled at him. "Where have your thoughts gone wandering now? Is it far away and long ago?"

He nodded, unable to speak for a moment.

The spinning woman picked up her spindle. She wound the twisted thread about it, round and round, and fastened the thread in the notch. Then she took the thread between finger and thumb, drawing it from the distaff's wool as she set the spindle to spinning again.

"I know the widow Lycia's servant," she said. "She told me about Thargelia. Thargelia was a *hetaira* and had become pregnant by the great asclepiad from Cos. She said they had lived together in Macedonia."

"That's a lie!" Daphne whirled about as she spoke, and her eyes flashed. "That is a lie, made up and spread about by Olympias. I know who the father was, the father of the child Thargelia lost. She told me herself before she died. It was — it was a king."

Xanthias cleared his throat discreetly, and Daphne turned to him, her face still flaming.

"Oh, Xanthias! I forgot. What is it?"

"Olympias," he said, with a slight bow and a faint smile, "the wife of Timon, First Citizen of Cos, is waiting for you below."

"What a coincidence!" Daphne exclaimed. "I must go down to see her. At least, I suppose I must. She is a guest in the house. But Xanthias, isn't it almost sunset time?"

"Yes, Daphne, the sun is setting now."

"Then it is time for me to go to Ctesias. I promised to sing to him tonight. I could not disappoint him. Will you get me my lyre and bring it to the house door? You know which lyre."

Xanthias smiled. "You mean the one that I almost dropped into the sea at Halasarna?"

Daphne laughed gaily. "Get it, while I stay here a little longer to talk with Anna about the pattern of her weaving."

When she came down to the waiting room, she found Xanthias in the doorway with the lyre. He set it down.

"Olympias is not here," he said. "She seems to have disappeared."

They looked and asked for her through the house, but she was not there and no one had seen her.

"Olympias didn't look well," Xanthias observed. "She was pale, she might have been ill. She became suddenly angry and rude when I asked if her servant had not come with her. I'm afraid I showed my resentment in return."

Daphne smiled quietly and picked up the lyre. As Xanthias swung the door open they heard a hubbub of voices. Daphne set the lyre down and they stepped out.

"*Purkaia! Purkaia!* Fire! Fire!"

They could hear the gateman's voice repeating the cry. Dense black smoke was pouring up from the court of the manuscript house.

"Oh, my father's papyrus scrolls!" Daphne cried. "Xanthias! Water! We must carry water!"

They turned back into the house, and then they hurried out, each carrying an amphora full of water. People were pouring in through the gate. A woman's voice cried:

"It was Hippocrates! Hippocrates set fire to the manuscripts!"

Other voices took up the cry. Daphne staggered under her load, and a man coming through the gate lifted it from her shoulder. She could see flames now, leaping high in the air from the court of the manuscript house, and as she watched, the *palaestra* next to it seemed to burst into sudden flame. She knew it was the vat of rubbing oil that burned there. No water could stop that.

Daphne stood quite still, trying to take it all in. A sudden fear clutched her. Ctesias! And his mother, who could not walk! And Ctesiarchus was away — She looked beyond. Yes, there was smoke rising from the courtyard of Ctesiarchus' house too! She ran across the open square and around the *palaestra*. People stood before the entrance to Ctesiarchus' house. The door was open and she started to go in, but a servant caught her and held her.

"You must not go in!" she cried. "It is death in there." The servant sobbed. "Alas, alas! I tried to carry my mistress out. I was not strong enough. I did try — and then I ran back and tried again — the smoke came, she told me to leave her, she said to go."

"Where is Ctesias?" Daphne cried.

"He would not leave his mother. I called him, but he would not come. They are in there, in her bedroom. The smoke, it is awful!"

Daphne threw off the servant's hold on her arm and rushed again toward the door, but someone stepped in front of her and a strong hand stopped her.

It was Cleomedes. Beads of sweat were standing on his face and on his naked chest, as though he had been running. Behind him came Buto. Buto's face and arms were black.

"What is happening, Daphne?" Cleomedes shouted. "Is someone there in that house?"

"Ctesias and his mother are there!" she cried in anguish. "I must go in and get them out!" She struggled with him.

"No, I'll go, you stay here. I'll get them for you. Where are they?"

"Up there in her bedroom, off the gallery — that's her window!" Daphne pointed.

Cleomedes looked at the sheer wall; there were no windows in the lower rooms by which an agile man might climb; smoke poured up from the court beyond; it coiled out of the doorway and out of the windows above. Slow-minded Cleomedes was quick in mind now, and quick in action.

"I'll get to them by the gallery inside!" he shouted.

He started for the door and would have entered the house, but Buto barred his path.

"Too dangerous!" Buto roared. "I've been in there. I tried to keep the fire back so it would not spread to the house."

Cleomedes tried to push him out of the way, but the giant Buto held his ground. As they struggled, Buto continued to bellow. "You cannot go! The peristyle, the gallery, they're on fire. I'm your father and I say you cannot go!"

Cleomedes drew back, then lunged at him. There was a smacking sound and Buto, reeling backward, fell to the ground. Cleomedes had struck him with his driving right jab to the jaw, the blow that Buto himself had taught him. Cleomedes leaped over him and on through the doorway. He disappeared in the smoke.

Daphne, tense, waited and watched. The roar of flames grew louder. It seemed a very long time. Then someone shouted:

"There he is!"

It was Cleomedes. He was on the veranda, and — yes — he was carrying someone. It was little Ctesias, lying limp in his arms. Cleomedes leaned over the railing and dropped the lad into the up-stretched arms of those below. Then he stood up again and called out, gasping:

"Don't worry, Daphne, he's alive. I'll get his mother if I can. Don't worry, whatever happens." He waved. It was, Daphne thought later, as though when he waved he knew he was saying good-by.

"Cleomedes! Cleomedes!" It was Buto calling now. He was getting to his feet with difficulty. "Wait for me!" he bellowed. "I'm coming to help you." Buto staggered, but he reached the door at last. He set his hand on the opening, his feet wide apart, wavering. "Wait for me!" he bellowed again. "Wait for me, my son."

Then the crowd heard a ripping, smashing, crashing sound, ending in a boom — then a second boom. Buto was blown reeling back from the door. Then all was still, still except for the roar, the roar and crackle of hungry flames.

Someone shrieked, "The roof fell in!"

Daphne knelt on the ground with Ctesias. His face was black with smoke and he gasped and gasped for air. But soon the gasping stopped. He opened his eyes. Daphne sat on the ground and took him in her arms, whispering to him and rocking him back and forth.

Presently she heard a woman's voice above her, pitched in a strange high key. Daphne looked up and saw Olympias standing beside her. Above the crimson robe, her face was pale like the face of death, and she pointed a finger at the flames.

"Is it true?" she cried. "Did my Cleomedes die in there?"

"Yes," Daphne said sorrowfully, "it is true."

"No!" Olympias shrieked. "No! No!"

Then she fell unconscious on the ground. Daphne watched men

carry her away. One said, "I think she's dead." Another said, "No, she's breathing now."

Old Xanthias came to Daphne's side and stooped down.

"Is the boy all right?"

"I think so."

Ctesias opened his eyes and sat up on her lap.

"Where is my mother?"

"I don't know — perhaps she'll be coming soon — would you like to sleep in my house tonight?"

Daphne set the boy on the ground gently while she stood up. She looked about, dazed, and stretched her cramped arms.

"Oh Daphne, don't leave me!" the boy cried out in terror and he put his little arms around her legs and wept. "Don't, don't, don't leave me!"

She lifted him and held him in her arms. He clutched her with all his strength and buried his face on her shoulder. Anna came to her mistress's side.

"Let me take him," she said. But Daphne shook her head.

Xanthias cleared a way for them through the crowd. The whole enclosure was choked with people now, and they were still streaming in through the gate. Daphne listened to the shouting and the talk as she stumbled after Xanthias with her precious load.

"How did the fire start?" she heard someone say — and then the answer:

"Haven't you heard? It must have been that Coan asclepiad Hippocrates; they found the manuscript house burning right after he left. Then it spread to the *palaestra* and Ctesiarchus' house."

"No. I don't know why," someone else was saying. "Some say he was jealous of Euryphon. He's gone back to Cos. Lucky for him he did. These people would kill him. Lucky too that there's no wind blowing."

Daphne took Ctesias to her room and washed him and comforted him. When she tried to leave, he cried and clung to her. At last he fell asleep suddenly, as children do.

Daphne tiptoed out, and then ran down the stairs intending to look for her father. She knew he must have returned long ago from his consultation. Then she heard his voice calling her name. He had just come in the door, and she ran to him. His cloak was gone, his chiton partly burned, his face and hands smudged with black. Xanthias brought an oil lamp. Euryphon looked at his daughter.

"They told me that you and Ctesias were safe. Thank the gods for that."

He stood still and seemed to be confused, a man without a plan, Daphne thought. She led him to the reception room, and he sat on the edge of a couch — a tired, thin, aging man. His long face was pale, and the whites of his eyes were red as he turned to her.

"They're gone." His voice was flat. "All gone. It's still too hot to get very close, but we raked some ashes out . . . Not one bit of papyrus left. Those scrolls of Sappho's poems that I collected for you, Daphne, must be gone with the rest."

"I have one in my bedroom," she said. "It's my favorite."

"Curious," he mused, "to see how thoughts can burn and blow away in smoke — and knowledge — and beauty. The only medical manuscripts left of any value are those I gave to Hippocrates when I thought that you were going to marry Cleomedes and become a Coan. Hippocrates will burn those too, I suppose."

"No, Father. He will never do that. Hippocrates did not start this fire."

"Don't you think so? Everyone seems to be saying he did." Euryphon put his face in his hands, his elbows on his knees, and looked at the floor.

"After your mother died I had two treasures left; you were one, and the medical writings were the other. I could have no more children, so I turned to the task of increasing the collection. It was the finest and the largest collection of medical manuscripts in all the world, do you realize that? It's gone, and soon you will be gone. That is as it should be. But I'm not old, not yet."

"Lie down, Father."

He obeyed as though he were a boy, and rolled over on his face. She looked at Xanthias.

"You may set the light down." He nodded and shuffled away.

Daphne knew that this was no time for words. She bent over

him as though she had been mother, not daughter, of this man, and put a comforting hand on his shoulder.

Could it be? Yes! He was sobbing silently, her father!

"I'm going to leave you now," she said. "And after a while I'll bring your supper here, and we will have it together."

CHAPTER TWENTY

Hippocratic Oath

~~~~~~

As THE CAPTAIN had predicted, it was still dark when Hippocrates' ship came to anchor off the entrance to the harbor of Cos. He was rowed ashore and walked along the gravel beach under the stars which blazed with even greater brilliance now that the moon had set. He listened to the slow recurring pound and hiss of rollers from the sea. Even now, when no ripple roughened the water's surface, there was movement and force within that depth. It was like the pulse, Hippocrates thought, that tells of the life and strength in the body when muscles and mind are stilled in sleep.

Life seemed to him a dull and stupid round but he was ready now to take up his work. He would put the broken pieces of his life and thought together again. He knocked on the enclosure gate and it swung open silently. Elaphus greeted him.

"What's happened to the squeak?" Hippocrates exclaimed.

"You noticed it was gone?" There was pleasure in Elaphus' voice. "I put water in the hinge cups, as you asked me to do. I hope your mother will forgive me, but you're the master now. They have all been hoping you would get back before morning. Your brother Sosander is spending the night here waiting for you. He is asleep in the *iatreion*."

Hippocrates felt Bobo's cold wet muzzle in his hand and then his warm tongue. In the darkness beside the gatehouse the dog was wagging his tail in joyful silence.

"Bobo never barks when I come, does he?"

"He knows the sound of your step on the shingle," Elaphus said. "And so do I. So do the others. It's a welcome sound to all of us."

Hippocrates stopped to pat the big dog, then he walked to the house. The outer door stood ajar. He pushed it open and crossed the court. A light was streaming from the weaving room. He went to the doorway and looked around the screen; then he stepped inside. His mother was dressed and sitting at the loom, but he saw that she was asleep. Her hands lay in her lap where they had fallen; her head rested against the warp. He looked at her and a wave of tenderness swept over him. Her graying hair shone smooth in the light of the lamp. Her face was so calm and strong. How much help and strength had come from her to him! How much support and joy she had given his father through many years!

"Mother," he said softly.

She started up. "Oh! I must have fallen asleep!"

She put her arms about him and held him tight, not saying anything for a time. He bent his head and his lips touched her hair. The clean sweet smell of that hair brought back in a flash the boy he had been when memory first began.

"Oh," she said, standing back and looking at him, "I'm so glad you're home! Sosander told me about your wonderful speech at Triopion and how, as you stood on the steps of the temple, Apollo's priest returned and said to you, so all could hear, 'Seek truth, for truth is more than victory. Climb well, and know Apollo goes before.'

"Since Sosander told me that, I've repeated it to myself many times. I'm proud of you, my son. I'm happy you are to stay with us in Cos."

Hippocrates smiled at her. "It's good to be wanted here, good to have work to do. But I thought you would still be in Halasarna. How is Phaenarete? Did her hipbone stay in place? I must go to see her soon."

"Your grandmother is well and I think the bone is in place. I left her in good hands. But she commanded me to come back here and to go about getting a wife for you. One might suppose that neither you nor I had given this matter a thought. When I left Halasarna, she said to me, 'I've decided that Daphne is the nymph for him.' — Well, son, what have you to tell me about Daphne?"

"My grandmother," he said, ignoring the reference to Daphne, "should have been born a queen in a woman's world. What a tyrant she would have made. Can't you see her taking the throne from Queen Artemisia?"

"Hippocrates!" his mother expostulated. "Tell me about Daphne. You know I can't wait to know what has happened."

"Oh, Daphne! She is well — not married yet, so I understand. According to your friend Olympias, Daphne intends to be a virgin all her life."

He laughed bitterly and his mother shook her head. She knew that he chose this means of hiding the hurt he must have received.

"You speak of my friend Olympias!" she said with quiet disgust. "Was it your brother Sosander who taught you how to be so maddening? Answer me now — did you inform Euryphon's daughter that you love her or did you not?"

"Yes, I did. I sent her a written statement that I did love her and I put my name to it. She could have replied so easily, but she did not do so. Her father does not believe that I speak the truth. Perhaps she is of the same opinion — I don't know. He asked me not to talk to his daughter, so I wrote to her. That is all.

"But Mother, I've come back to Cos to practice the art of medicine, not to weep nor ask for sympathy. I've come back to teach medicine and to learn it."

"Would you like to know," she asked, "what I intend to do?"

"Yes," he said.

"I'm going to Cnidus at the break of day."

"You!" he exclaimed.

"Yes. I laid my plans as soon as Sosander returned from Triopion and told me that Euryphon had been unfriendly to you. We thought you might come tonight. If not, I was going anyway. I have hired a swift boat and it will wait in Cnidus for my return."

He shook his head. "You waste your time."

She smiled and smoothed her hair.

"You are my son. You have not succeeded very well in arranging for your own future happiness. What I do in Cnidus is my own affair — until I return."

His mother smiled as though to herself, "You must answer me one question before I go . . . Are you willing to send Euryphon to Macedonia in your place?"

Hippocrates smiled bitterly. "Don't be asburd."

"Answer me," his mother insisted. "Yes? Or no?"

He looked at her, suddenly serious. "Yes, if he cares to go. Let him have it. Perdiccas would be lucky to get him as court physician. And Euryphon might discover for himself who was the father of Thargelia's child. I suppose he would take his daughter with him."

"I suppose *not.*" Praxithea spoke emphatically. Just then the house door burst open.

"Hippocrates!" It was Sosander's voice. "Hippocrates, where are you?" Sosander came clumping across the court as though following the sound of his own voice, and Praxithea left them together.

"By the gods, Hippocrates, you came through those gates quietly! Or did Hecate lift you over the wall? Here I was in the *iatreion,* waiting for the well-known squeak of that gate. But Elaphus, I find, has done away with the ancient squeak, the squeak our mother loved so well."

He stopped in front of his brother and laughed. They embraced each other. Praxithea came back with a tray of cakes and sugared fruits.

"I'm glad that you have come, Sosander. I can't make your brother talk sensibly. But I've told him I'm going to Cnidus today. He does say he is willing to send Euryphon to Macedonia."

Sosander nodded. "You see, Hippocrates, that Macedonian trireme is back in the harbor of Cos, and the commander won't wait long. If you are not willing to go, and if you do not appoint someone else, he will sail away without a physician. Our mother is of the opinion that a voyage to Macedonia would be good for Euryphon's health and also for his disposition. I don't think he'd dislike the wealth that would come to him. I say let Praxithea go with our blessing. She is determined to go with or without it, and if she cannot teach common sense to Cnidians, no one can."

Hippocrates shook his head.

"There are some things you two plotters may not understand. But I don't care what physician goes to the court of Perdiccas so long as it is not my brother Sosander. I need him here."

"Me!" Sosander laughed. "My wife would never hear of my going. She'd be afraid Thargelia's younger sister might catch me there. Ah, if she only would!"

Praxithea held up her hand. "Listen, my sons. The cocks of Cos are crowing now; do you hear? They are crowing the coming of day. Apollo is stirring before the dawn, and men should be in their beds. Good night."

"I must tell you," Hippocrates said, when she had gone, "that Thargelia died as the result of an abortion carried out by Euryphon."

"No!" his brother exclaimed. "So she was the patient he wanted you to see."

Hippocrates nodded soberly.

"I plan to rewrite, in final form, the asclepiad oath. We have discussed the oath before, you and I. I am clear in regard to most of it, but I want a word with you about abortion as carried out by physicians. Our decision should depend on medical evidence, it seems to me, not on political expediency or religious arguments.

"There will always be women who try to terminate pregnancies by jumping down on their heels. It does succeed occasionally, I am told. And midwives will continue to carry out abortions. Fathers will continue to destroy unwanted newborn babes. There is nothing that we as physicians can do about such acts. But the life of a pregnant woman who is in our care is another matter.

"I watched Thargelia die, and I have seen other women die like that. Could it be, do you think, that physicians bring death to such patients because they are handling so many other patients with fatal fevers and with wounds from which the pus is pouring? Could it be that we transfer something from one to another that brings death?"

Sosander grunted. Then he said, thoughtfully:

"I have seen a number of deaths after pessary abortions carried out by physicians, but now that you mention it, I agree that death produced by a midwife in this way is rare, though not unheard of. Yes, you may have a clue to something there. What that something is, I can't imagine. Most men would say a devil and be done with thinking. I'll give it further thought. Good night, Crates. Get some rest."

Hippocrates fell asleep as soon as his body touched the mattress, and he did not stir until he heard the voice of his mother's second slave calling to him outside the heavy curtains of his door. The first slave had already left for Cnidus with her mistress.

"Podalirius is here," the servant called. "He says he must know now whether you intend to hold the discussion under the plane tree this evening."

Hippocrates sat up and stretched. The servant called again.

"Are you awake?"

He finished a yawn and then answered, "Yes, yes. Tell Podalirius that we will have the gathering as usual. But why does he have to wake me so early to find out?"

"What?" the servant called. "What message did you say for Podalirius? I cannot hear you."

"Tell him I said yes."

"What?"

"Tell him we will have the gathering!"

"What message for Podalirius?"

Hippocrates sat up and roared:

"Tell Podalirius to run out to Pelea to the ledge where Empedocles stood and jump off!"

"What did you say about Empedocles?"

"Oh, nothing, nothing."

He threw off his rug, and leaping up, he pulled the curtain aside. The servant was old and stooped. She was cupping her ear at the curtain. She looked up now and cackled with sudden laughter to see the master naked in the doorway.

"Tell Podalirius that the gathering will be held as usual under the plane tree."

Hippocrates retreated precipitately, but the old woman peered into the room after him. "I understand now," she said, still shouting. "I'm a little deaf, you know." Then, as she hobbled away, she called back, "I'm sorry I had to waken you. There's fresh honey for your cakes this morning."

Life might be "a dull and stupid round." But something — perhaps it was the fresh honey — something began to give him zest for the task he had set himself that morning. If it was not the honey, it might have been the hot bright sunshine or the bracing wind that tossed the palm branches above his head. More likely it was the balm that most men find in the work they want to do. He had planned the clauses of the asclepiad oath so long. Putting it in final form would mark the true beginning of his medical teaching and study. He was content now to return to his chosen work. His hoped-for happiness had been put out of his mind.

He entered the *oecus*, put some scrolls on the table, and drew out some earlier drafts of the oath. He set out fresh papyrus and ink and selected a hollow reed which he cut slantwise to make a fresh reed pen, a calamus. The beginning was easy enough, he could follow the form his father had used for pupil contracts. He began to write:

I swear by Apollo Physician, by Asclepius, by Hygeia and Panacea and by all the gods and goddesses, making them my witnesses that I will carry out this indenture —

"No," he said aloud, "that won't do. It will be more than an indenture, I must add the word 'oath.'"

He began to write again:

— making them my witnesses, that I will carry out according to my ability and judgment this oath and this indenture.

He laid the calamus down and his eye traveled over the boxes of medical manuscripts. Some of them were his own. More had been collected by his father, and there were a few that had belonged to his grandfather Hippocrates. And there were the two large scrolls Euryphon had given him. This was the Coan medical collection. It was small indeed as compared with the treasure in the Cnidian manuscript house where he had spent the hours of yesterday afternoon. Disappointing hours, he thought. Daphne could have so easily sent him an answer to his message. But he must not let his thoughts drift away in that direction.

A shadow fell on the table. Podalirius stood in the doorway, erect and austere.

"You wondered," Podalirius began abruptly, "why I called you early this morning. I must explain that while you were gone I received messages from physicians outside of our group to say that they wished to be present at the first teaching hour after your return."

"Why?" Hippocrates asked.

"Because they have heard of your invitation from the King of Macedonia, and some of them heard you speak at Triopion. I have sent them word now."

"That is good of them," Hippocrates said, "but very awkward. I propose to read the new oath, and I would have preferred the smaller group. I wish you had discussed this with me before you sent them word. Well, no matter!"

He looked up at Podalirius. He had seen him stand before his father many a time as he stood now before him, serious and stubborn. "I shall be busy here all day until sunset," he continued. "Then tomorrow I must go to Halasarna to see Phaenarete. After that I will be ready to work with you again, Podalirius."

Podalirius frowned. "I think you do wrong. Your first duty is with the patients and all who wish to see you. You must take time for teaching, of course. But the master's place is in the *iatreion*. I have a list of patients for you to see today, a long list. It would be easier for us all if you would stay here in Meropis the way your father did and do your work."

"Podalirius!" Something in his voice startled the older man.

"Oh, I am sorry," Podalirius said. "I didn't mean . . ."

Hippocrates rose abruptly, kicking the three-legged stool on which he had been sitting across the room. Podalirius retreated to the peristyle and Hippocrates followed.

"Podalirius, you have gone too far. I plan to remain in Cos as master, not slave —" He lowered his voice, struggling to regain control of himself, and continued: "I will play my part as I believe I should with patient and pupil. But I must have freedom to study too. The master needs it most of all."

He paused.

"It is so easy to do what is wrong in medicine, Podalirius, and to do it over and over again."

The flash of anger had passed now.

"There are many sick who need our help today, and there will be tomorrow, and the day after. We must do what we can, but we must also take time for those things which will make for greater knowledge and wisdom. Don't you see, Podalirius?"

"Yes, I understand. I do understand. Forgive me. I didn't think . . . But could you help Dexippus for a moment?"

"Yes, of course." As the two men crossed the court together Hippocrates looked at his companion. "You do a great deal for me, Podalirius. I'm grateful for it, but you must help me, too, to have some time alone. A teacher cannot do without it."

Dexippus came out of the surgery, a welcoming smile on his handsome face. "Master, I know you are busy, but will you look at something?"

Hippocrates turned into the surgery.

"You remember your friend the young sailor with the abscession on his leg? I wish you would see the leg with me."

Hippocrates hailed his former playmate. Then he turned his attention to the open wound.

"You see," Dexippus said, "there is a great deal of matter still coming from the bone. It is increasing."

He dipped his finger into the puddle of slimy greenish-white pus and held it up for his master to see and smell.

"It has developed an awful odor," he said, as he wiped his finger off on the edge of the table.

"I think, Dexippus," Hippocrates said, "You should take care not to get that matter on your hands. Wash them well now. It's a benefit to the patient himself to have these abscessions drain out, but . . ." He paused and pursed his lips. "Perhaps what comes from one wound might do harm if put into another."

He picked up the curette and scraped out some dead pieces of bone. "Yes, it has changed, but it will heal in the end, I think. Keep on with your regular dressings." He tossed the instrument on the table. But he stopped and looked at the instrument and then back at the wound. "The table," he said, "and the instruments should be washed well now with soap and water. I'll explain to you what is going through my mind another time."

No one saw Hippocrates again during the day, except his brother Sosander who came to discuss the writing. Not long before sunset, Hippocrates left his house and crossed the enclosure alone. An expectant group was waiting for him. In addition to those usually present, there were physicians from Cos Meropis and from distant parts of the island. Old Aeneas was there, he noticed. And to his surprise, there were physicians who had come all the way from the old capital of Astypalaea. They gathered around him.

"We hired a boat," one of them said, "and came very fast with a west wind behind us. We only needed to use the oars for the last hour."

Hippocrates sat where his father had sat, his back to the trunk of the plane tree while Sosander placed old Aeneas beside him.

"I am pleased to see so many old friends here," Hippocrates began. "Take seats if you can find them. Many of the Greek teachers — the philosophers for example — walk about, and talk as they go. But medicine is not philosophy. In medicine we must see the man who is sick, see him well in a shaded light that is not too dim and not too bright. That is why we spend our teaching hour in a half circle under this tree. In medicine, nature and disease must be made to teach. Before physicians begin to treat they should learn to observe, compare, remember, record.

"You may have heard of my invitation to leave Cos. But I have decided to remain here on this island where I was born. This is where my father taught. Here my brother and I can work together. Here we may draw about us, I hope, men of like minds and interests to learn and to practice the art of medicine.

"I have chosen this quiet, simple life rather than the wealth and the ease of a foreign court because I am at heart a Greek. This work lies before me and I shall undertake it, striving to follow the example of Heracles. I hope your presence here today means that we may work at a common task together, toward a common goal."

"Hippocrates," one of the physicians from Astypalaea interrupted. "We have asked Aeneas to speak to you on our behalf. He was practicing the art in Pelea before some of us were born."

"Yes, yes," Aeneas quavered in his high-pitched voice. He was getting to his feet slowly, pulling himself up with both hands on his staff. "These physicians did ask me to speak for them. Because I'm old, perhaps, or it may be because of my descent from Heracles. You mentioned him just now."

His listeners laughed. Aeneas was standing as straight as he could, looking about him with twinkling eyes and wagging his long white beard.

"I may not look it now, but my mother did tell me that I was a son of Heracles. She didn't exactly give me his lion's skin, nor very much of his muscle. But I'm one of the Heracleidai just the same, and I'm just as much like Heracles as some asclepiads I have known are like Asclepius."

His listeners laughed and shook their heads with glee — all except Podalirius — for Aeneas was a great favorite. He chuckled and tugged on his beard as he turned to Hippocrates.

"Forgive me for these ramblings; I have something more serious to say. First, we have heard stories about you and a woman. We want to tell you that we know they are false, false scandals." His hearers growled their agreement.

"Don't be sad," he went on, "if men speak evil of you. Be patient, be of good heart. Lies dissolve away in time. Truth triumphs in the end. I knew your father well and loved him. We welcome you in his place.

"Something else I was to say — what was it now? Oh, yes!" He turned to the men from Astypalaea. "Old age forgets the lessons others teach. You say it for me."

One of the group stood up. "Hippocrates," he said, "most of us who have come here today were once your father's disciples. He taught us the art of medicine under this same tree. We were at

Triopion too, and heard you speak on the temple steps. In the silence that followed your words, the Coans there were filled with pride that such a man should come from Cos.

"You offered to give your life to the physician's art with those, you said, 'who are of like mind.' We knew very well that you were turning away from great wealth and ease to do this. Then we heard the priest, who had placed the wreath of the god around your head, say: 'Climb well, Hippocrates, and know that Apollo goes before.'

"We have come to tell you that we are asclepiads of 'like mind' with you, and we rejoice that you will stay with us and work with us here on the island of Cos."

Hippocrates was embarrassed but profoundly pleased. After a silence, he looked at his brother, who nodded. So he began simply, remaining in his chair:

"It was my intention today to discuss the art of medicine with those who are beginning to learn it. Many arts have been created in Greece. The sculptors labor at one, the builders at another, musicians, poets, and writers of plays, athletes, dancers, mathematicians — they have all developed special skills. Each art has its own techniques that must be taught, and must be learned during years of labor. That is the Greek way.

"But the art of medicine is different. Skill and technique and knowledge are needed for it, but these are not enough. The physician must know the meaning of pity and compassion. He must make answer to the gods for his acts in the practice of medicine as well as to man.

"Let me give you one example. You remember that when Empedocles left us, he reproached us because we would not give him the cup of death after we had failed to cure his pain.

"But we could not do this, not even for him. We are servants of men, we care for them. But our allegiance is to something beyond them. Men who are aware of this, trust us because of it. But the time has come when the physician's code should be stated as clearly as is the indenture with which he begins his training. Through such a statement, men may come to know the code and we may not forget."

Hippocrates stood up now and drew from beneath his mantle a roll of papyrus.

"In preparing this oath, I have reconsidered the indenture with which my father bound his disciples. I have studied too the rules of entrance into the school of Pythagoras. This that I have written is what my brother and I believe to be good. We will swear to live by it ourselves, as best we can. And we expect those who follow us to do likewise. Here it is."

Hippocrates began to read:

THE OATH

I swear by Apollo Physician, by Asclepius, by Hygeia and Panacea and by all the gods and goddesses, making them my witnesses, that I will carry out, according to my ability and judgment, this oath and this indenture.

To hold my teacher in this art equal to my own parents; to make him partner in my livelihood; when he is in need of money to share mine with him; to consider his family as my own brothers, and to teach them this art, if they want to learn it, without fee or indenture; to impart instruction written, oral and practical, to my own sons, the sons of my teacher, and to indentured pupils who have taken the physician's oath, but to nobody else.

I will use treatment to help the sick according to my ability and judgment, but never with a view to injury and wrongdoing.

Neither will I administer a poison to anybody when asked to do so, nor will I suggest such a course.

Similarly I will not give to a woman a pessary to cause abortion. But I will keep pure and holy both my life and my art.

Into whatsoever houses I enter, I will enter to help the sick, and I will abstain from all intentional wrongdoing and harm, especially from abusing the bodies of man or woman, bond or free.

And whatsoever I shall see or hear in the course of my profession, as well as outside my profession in my intercourse with men, if it be what should not be published abroad, I will never divulge, holding such things to be holy secrets.

Now if I carry out this oath, and break it not, may I gain forever

reputation among all men for my life and for my art; but if I trans-
gress it and forswear myself, may the opposite befall me.

No one spoke when Hippocrates had finished reading. He looked about him, wondering at the silence. Then he looked at his brother, who nodded soberly.

"What we have heard," Sosander began, "is much more than an indenture between disciple and master, although the disciple does promise to help support the master. He does this because the master devotes his life to teaching and study, rather than to the pursuit of wealth.

"The rest of the oath is a special code of behavior for physicians. It applies to their lives inside the profession of medicine and outside of it. The oath calls on each physician to dedicate his life to the good of the sick. What he asks, in return, is that he may hope to gain for himself and for his art a good reputation."

Again there was silence, and Hippocrates asked if the pupils of medicine had any questions. Pindar spoke up then.

"We have had discussions among ourselves, knowing something of what this oath might contain. The teachers of other arts do not call for any such promises. The learner pays his fee and hopes to become a pcet, or a philosopher, sculptor, painter, musician or public speaker. His teacher does not ask him to swear an oath of dedication. In what way then is medicine so different from other arts?"

"The other arts," Hippocrates answered, "do not deal directly with man himself, but rather with such subjects as ideas, thoughts, beauty, democracy, and with objects such as marble, paints, musical instruments and building stones. These are inanimate things. Medicine has to do with men and women and children. It is concerned with their diseases, their mistakes, accidents, sorrows, dementias. The oath is needed as a code of conduct because the physician must practice his art on man. He serves man, but in his service to man he, more than others, must serve God. That is why the oath I give you is more than a teaching contract.

"In future years the art of medicine will change, but not the need for the oath. Discovery will alter the practice of medicine, but not the oath, for in it there are eternal values that time can never change. Write it on the tables of your heart and mind."

He unrolled the papyrus and read again: *"I will keep pure and holy both my life and my art.* Here is the beginning of it all, and the end. A good physician may swear to that and strive to keep his oath — today, tomorrow and always."

CHAPTER TWENTY-ONE

Hippocratic Teaching

~~~~~~

THE MEDICAL PRACTITIONERS who had attended the teaching hour that day lingered on to talk with Hippocrates and to tell him of local happenings. Perhaps some of them guessed the truth, that the teacher himself had need of friendship and reassurance. When they were gone at last, Hippocrates returned to his house alone. There outside his door he saw in the gathering darkness a group of men. Coming nearer, he recognized them as his apprenticed disciples, all of them. It was Pindar, as the senior member of the group, who was first to speak.

"Master, we have come to tell you that we are ready to take that oath now, or whenever you think the time for each of us has come."

They saw at once that he was pleased, for he smiled and made a quick gesture, as though to embrace them all.

"You must learn to be familiar with it," he said. "You should have copies now. Here, Pindar, you take this first draft." He handed over the little roll of papyrus from which he had read. "Copy it and let each of the others copy it. I will call you, one by one, to swear to it later on."

Then Dexippus, who never missed an opportunity, asked the master a question. Dexippus was the youngest, but also the most impetuous of the group. He was the clever son of a wealthy citizen of Ephesus, and he hoped still for clear-cut rules, facts to which no postscripts of doubt need be added. Students have always hoped for this. And why not? If only the truth would stand still! If understanding were absolute and knowledge were final and complete!

"Tell us," Dexippus said, "the perfect course of medical training, so we may follow it."

Hippocrates was not in the mood for this; he wanted very much, just then, to be alone. He had a vague awareness that he was unhappy, as though there were a sad something at the back of his mind. He wanted to examine that sadness. It was late, too, and past the time for the evening meal. He hesitated. But after all, he reflected, the time to teach, man or child, is when that man or child asks the question. The pupils saw him frown. Then suddenly his quick smile came back

"Come in and we will sit in the court while the stars come out."

When they were gathered about him, he began.

"He who is to acquire a competent knowledge of medicine should 'have a natural talent, instruction, a favorable place for study, early tuition, love of labor, leisure.' "

He paused and was silent, while other thoughts came crowding into his mind. But Pindar prompted him.

"How would you advise the young physician who goes to a city where he is not known? How should he behave?"

"When he begins to practice for himself," Hippocrates said, "he should not try to dazzle the patient with brilliant exhibitions of skill, which are not really necessary. He should not hold public lectures for the purpose of increasing his own reputation, and especially lectures tricked out with quotations from the poets.

"Physicians should observe scrupulous cleanliness. They should cultivate an elegance removed from all signs of luxury, using perfumes if desired but only with restraint.

" 'I urge you not to be too unkind, nor to consider too carefully your patient's superabundance of means. Sometimes give your services for nothing — and if there be an opportunity of serving one who is a stranger in financial straits, give full assistance to all such. For where there is love of man, there is also love of the art. For some patients, though conscious that their condition is perilous, recover their health simply through their contentment with the goodness of the physician.'

"Make no pretense to infallibility. When you are in doubt you should always ask for medical consultation. Learn when you can from others, but place no reliance on the unprovable hypotheses of the philosophers. Turn first and last to nature itself and to observation of the body in health and disease to learn the truth.

"But record your observations. Have a system of your own. Here is the important thing. Make a careful history of your cases. Begin to do it now. Be brief but faithful. Come with me!"

He jumped to his feet and crossed the court.

"Come on!" he called. "I keep a small sheet of papyrus for each case, and when I return from the visit I make a note."

He disappeared into the *oecus*, where a small lamp burned. He lit the big hanging lamp and opened a box, while the young men came crowding in after him.

"Here on these sheets are the more important of my cases. I record them so that I may remember details, and later compare one with another. Thus I can hope to make a sure prognosis when I see such sickness again. If you can know in advance, then men will trust you. Many of these records are of patients who died, unfortunately. But it is important to recognize the signs of fatal termination. Let us take examples from these records."

He picked up a sheet and read:

"The man lying sick in the garden of Delearces had for a long time heaviness in the head and pain in the right temple. From some exciting cause, he was seized with fever, and took to his bed.

"Second day. Slight flow of unmixed blood from left nostril. The bowels were well moved; urine thin and varied, with particles in small groups, like barley meal or semen, floating in it."

"Here, you see, I have made a note for each day up to the eleventh. But I will not read them now. After that I saw him at longer intervals. Here, on the seventeenth day, the record reads as follows:

"Extremities cold in the early morning; would wrap himself up; acute fever, sweated all over; was relieved; more rational; some fever; thirst, vomited bilious matters, yellow and scanty; solid motions of the bowels; after a while they became black, scanty and thin; urine thin, and not of good color.

"Eighteenth day. Was not rational; comatose."

"Here then is the last note:

"Fortieth day. Passed motions full of phlegm, white and rather frequent; copious sweat all over; a perfect crisis."

"After the crisis he had no more fever and recovered his health. Throughout this illness, of course, we supported him with good regimen and carefully planned diet. That was the treatment he needed.

"Now here is another example, the case of a woman who died in five days with erysipelas." He picked up a second sheet from which he read:

"The woman suffering from angina who lay sick in the house of Ariston began her complaint with indistinctness of speech. Tongue red and grew parched.

"First day. Shivered, and grew hot.

"Third day. Rigor; acute fever; a reddish hard swelling in the neck, extending to the breast on either side; extremities cold and livid; breathing elevated; drink returned through nostrils — she could not swallow — stools and urine ceased.

"Fourth day. General exacerbation.

"Fifth day. Death."

Hippocrates looked away over their heads and, for a moment, he seemed to have forgotten the young men who stood at his elbow. He pulled on his short beard with finger and thumb.

"When a pregnant woman," he said, "dies following abortion,

she dies fast, like that. For example, take this case." He reached for a sheet in another box and read:

"*A woman who was one of the house of Pantimedes, after a miscarriage, was seized with fever on the first day. She had delirium and died on the seventh day.* And here again," he went on, picking up another sheet and reading:

"*Another woman, after a miscarriage about the fifth month, the wife of Hicetas, was seized with fever. At the beginning she had alternations of coma and sleeplessness; pain in the loins; heaviness in the head.*

"*Second day. Bowels disordered, with scanty, thin stools, which at first were uncompounded.*

"*Third day. Stools were copious and worse; no sleep at night.*

"*Fourth day. Delirium; fears; depression. Squinting of the right eye; slight cold sweat about the head; extremities cold.*

"*Fifth day. General exacerbation; much wandering, with rapid recovery of reason, no thirst, no sleep . . . And so, on the seventh day, death.*" He thought of Thargelia. "So it was, too, in the case of a pregnant woman I saw recently," he continued. "A physician emptied her womb while she was lying in a house where another woman was dying with erysipelas. On the sixth day after her abortion she died.

"I am forced to conclude," he said slowly, "that abortion, by operation or pessary, is dangerous to the mother when carried out by a physician — much more dangerous than spontaneous abortion. That is why it is forbidden in the oath."

Hippocrates looked around at the eager faces of his pupils in the circle of the lamplight.

"You are wondering why a physician's abortion is dangerous?" They nodded. The master shook his head.

"I don't know," he said suddenly. "Perhaps you will discover the secret. Try to be detached observers of disease. Do not allow pity to distort your vision. Thus, reason may teach you the answers."

"You speak of many unsolved questions," one of the pupils said. "What facts can we be sure of now?"

Hippocrates smiled. "From old time, our fathers have set the humors of the body at four: blood, phlegm, yellow bile and black bile. A man's health and mood depend upon the balance of these fluids within his body. The temperament, or constitution of each of us differs from that of his neighbor. For one is sanguinous, due to a plethora of blood; another is phlegmatic due to overbalancing phlegm; a third, having too much yellow bile, is bilious; and a fourth, alas, is melancholic because of much black bile within.

"Even these are not final facts. They are hypotheses that come to us from ancient medicine, hypotheses which we must test as we watch the unfolding of life, the progress of disease.

"It is self-evident that there is a constant interplay between the body and its environment. There is a *physis* going on within the body so that it may readjust itself and bring dyscrasia of hormones into more perfect proportion. That is to say, there is a constant balancing of body elements. The physician's treatment should serve to assist the body readjustments. This brings cure.

"The Cnidian physicians concern themselves too much with a vain effort to separate disease into many groups, separations which no man can recognize with certainty and so they fail to treat their patients adequately. Even in acute disease, they employ little more than purgatives, milk whey and milk."

A young man who had recently come from Cnidus said, "That is true. But talk to us, then, of Coan therapy. What more is done here?"

"There is so much that you can do," Hippocrates replied. "Teach the sick and his attendants what to do and not do. Arrange all circumstances to his good. Use purgatives as needed, and cupping and blood-letting on occasion. Order the diet; arrange for the patient's rest; do all things for the good of the sick and not for the effect upon observers.

"You must, of course, learn the detail of medical treatments and their several uses: baths, inunctions, clysters, warm and cold suffusions, massage, the gentler exercises and gymnastics. You must treat broken bones, each according to its shape and position. You must learn details of surgery, how to help the wounds to heal, and how to deal with aches and pains; how and when to cut to let abscessions flow. Learn to listen to the lungs within the chest and to recognize the splash of fluid so that, in desperate cases, you may open the chest and let the fluid out. You must even open the skull at times when blood has gathered beneath it after a blow and paralysis appears in the opposite arm and leg.

"By your treatment, you must strive to help the body at its work. Dis-ease is a difficulty of body elimination. The innate heat within the body carries out coction, or cooking or ripening, so that crude or waste products may be eliminated. After that there is return to health. In acute conditions the patient recovers by crisis, or else he dies then; in chronic conditions by lysis; in local conditions by abscession. In any case, failure to eliminate, or to obtain a normal balance of the humors, may mean death.

"Consider this simple example of how the body carries out its work of elimination each day of your life: You eat food and drink liquids and your body eliminates the irrelevant matter. You give the process no thought. The body does it, preserving balance and health.

"In conclusion, the physician must study each disease so he can predict its course and help the body to succeed in its own curative reactions."

Hippocrates turned to his case records and put them back in their boxes. He looked around at his pupils. There were no more questions. Even Dexippus was still for the moment.

"Make your own records of disease," he said. "Observe! Compare! Learn to prognosticate! Diseases have natural causes and they follow natural courses. Neither gods nor evil spirits enter into men to make them sick. Treat them, then, by helping nature in the working of the body. The gods established how the body works, and much more as well. We physicians must answer to them for what we do. That is the reason for the physician's oath."

His disciples took their leave of him as usual. But that evening, quite contrary to habit, each of the young men stopped in turn to thank him. They knew very well that the master was sad and that he had his own reasons to be disturbed. He sensed their friendship and felt new strength come to him from them

He was beginning to experience, too, what he had suspected in Athens while he watched Socrates teach. The teacher who makes no false claims to final knowledge, but who instead sets out the evidence for others to consider, discovers himself much unsuspected truth.

CHAPTER TWENTY-TWO

Return to Halasarna

LATE THAT EVENING Pindar returned alone to Hippocrates' house. He found him sitting in the court, muffled in a heavy cloak and reading in the light of a lamp that hung from the peristyle above him.

"I'm reading Sappho," Hippocrates said, putting the scroll down on his knees. "What other Greek poet, do you think, can compare with her? What would your uncle have answered to that question?"

"My uncle considered her highly. He might have placed her first, at least as a writer of love lyrics. But . . ." He broke off for a moment and then continued. "I want you to know that your friends here will believe in you always."

The wind sighed and rattled through the palm fronds above their heads, as though a storm were blowing in from the south.

"Why do you tell me this now?" Hippocrates asked.

"Because I have bad news, and Sosander asked me to come and tell you quickly before someone else should do so."

As he spoke, the servant was opening the house door, and Podalirius came striding in.

"I have news, Hippocrates," he blurted out, "bad news. And you must hear it." Pindar made a gesture as though to stop him, but Podalirius ignored it and continued.

"Timon has arrived in his trireme from Cnidus. His oarsmen have spread through the city telling many tales. Euryphon's manuscript house was burned yesterday evening, and with it the *palaestra* and the home of Ctesiarchus."

"No!" Hippocrates exclaimed. "But it can't be true! I was reading there myself until nearly sunset time."

"That is exactly what the people of Cnidus are saying," Podalirius continued. "The wife of Ctesiarchus was burned to death and Timon's son Cleomedes was killed in the fire."

Hippocrates turned pale.

"Daphne," he said. "Is Daphne safe?"

"Yes, Daphne is safe."

After a pause Hippocrates asked, "And Ctesias, the little son of Ctesiarchus? I left him in the manuscript house."

"Cleomedes rescued Ctesias, they say."

Hippocrates stood up. "I must return to Cnidus. I will take these manuscripts that Euryphon gave me back to him. It may encourage him to begin on his scrolls again."

Podalirius shook his head.

"No, Hippocrates. That would not be safe. There is worse to tell you. The people of Cnidus are saying that it was you who set the fire in the manuscript house. The oarsmen say that Cnidians are shouting threats against you."

"Against me!" Hippocrates said softly. "They say I set fire? Who says that? Who said it first? I wonder —"

"It seems to me," Podalirius continued, "that you ought to be able to tell us something about how that fire started."

At last Pindar could contain himself no longer. He stepped close to Podalirius, his fists clenched and his voice trembling.

"You fool! You stupid, childish, blind fool — to repeat that cursed lie and to do it in that way! Have you no sense at all? Can't you understand anything?"

Hippocrates sat down suddenly on a couch against the wall of the court.

"Wait, Pindar!" he said. "It's all right. I want to hear all they are saying. What other news have you for me, Podalirius? Tell me now."

"No," Podalirius said. "That's all. That's really all." He seemed embarrassed now. "I'm sorry if — but that's all." He wondered what he had done that was wrong and tried to think of something to tell Hippocrates that was pleasant.

"You might like to know about the happy outcome of your operation on the wife of Cephalus. Cephalus is enthusiastic."

"No, Podalirius," Hippocrates said, "I don't want to hear about them!"

He put his head down in his hands and laughed. Then he sat up suddenly and looked at the two men — the one bewildered, the other angry.

"You see, Pindar," he said, controlling himself and speaking very slowly, "what Podalirius wanted to know was whether I actually did burn the manuscript house or whether I did not!"

"Yes, that's it," Podalirius exclaimed, "exactly; so I can go out and deny it. You didn't burn it, I suppose, did you?"

Hippocrates shook with laughter again. The laughter quieted down slowly, ending in a sound that was suspiciously like a sob. He leaned back against the wall of the court again and looked up at the palm branches. They were snapping and sawing now, as though in a rising storm. The flickering lamplight showed the lines in his tortured face.

"Gods!" he exclaimed. "Why do I laugh? But it's better to laugh than cry, and I well might weep for young Cleomedes, for the paralyzed wife of Ctesiarchus, for what Daphne must think of me now."

He sat up again. "No, Podalirius, I did not burn the manuscript house, but I know who did. It was a woman and her onetime paramour."

"Who?" Podalirius said. "Who did you say set the fire?"

Hippocrates shook his head. "I have no proof. Just tell them that I do not know."

"Very well! I shall go now," Podalirius said, "and I shall deny the lies they tell about you. I shall go through the whole city."

Podalirius left the house as abruptly as he had entered it. Hippocrates sat in silence.

"Podalirius was mistaken," Pindar said. "Timon did not come back in the trireme; he remained in Cnidus. Only Olympias and Buto

returned. They went directly out to the villa. Your brother Sosander
has called some of our Archons together and he is with them now.
He told me to tell you that they are planning a meeting of the Council of Cos to investigate this matter tomorrow."

"I shall not be here tomorrow," Hippocrates said. "I'm going to
Halasarna. My friends — if I still have any friends — must discover
the truth for themselves. I see it all now."

After a silence he looked up at Pindar.

"How does the physician's oath end . . . ? 'Now if I carry out this
oath, and break it not, may I gain forever reputation among all men
for my life and my art — if not, may the opposite befall me!"

He smiled bitterly. "The opposite, it seems, can befall one without
transgression."

Pindar put his hand on his master's shoulder, but he said nothing
more. After a little time he crossed the court and passed out the door,
leaving him alone.

Hippocrates spent a restless night. It stormed, but the rain had
stopped by morning and he was off early. It was just as well, he
thought bitterly, to get away before people were about, to look at him
with accusing eyes. He reached the highroad and set off with his
swinging stride for Halasarna. What would his friends and acquaint-
ances think when they heard the stories about him in the barber stalls
of Athens? In half an hour he was walking through Apollo's cypress
grove. He looked up at Timon's villa and saw someone in a saffron
tunic running down through the garden. He recognized Penelope
and stopped at the gate.

"I saw you from the top of the house, Hippocrates," she panted.
"But I never thought I could catch you. Won't you come in?"

He shook his head. "I must go on to see my grandmother in
Halasarna."

"It's so sad up there," she said, "since Cleomedes' death. Poor Cleomedes!"

"Yes, poor Cleomedes!" he said. "But he died like a good Greek."

She glanced back at the villa. "My mother frightens me, and Buto
just walks about like a cat, looking with his little eyes and saying

nothing. It makes me feel — the way I used to feel before you made me well. I hope my father returns from Cnidus today."

"You must go in to Meropis this morning," Hippocrates said. "See Pindar and tell him all about it."

She nodded eagerly. "I was watching for him from the roof just now when I saw you. He comes to see me often, you know. I think he's wonderful.

"You find him so?"

"Oh, yes! And he's such a good physician."

"I'll remember that," Hippocrates said with a faint smile, and started off along the road.

"Wait !" she called and ran after him. "I've heard the terrible things people are saying about you. I know they're not true — I could kill them."

She threw her arms about him impulsively. "Don't be sad, Hippocrates, Everything will come out all right for you in the end."

Farther along the highroad, he overtook old Aeneas riding home to Pelea on his donkey. They went along together, but Hippocrates had little to say and Aeneas understood. He had heard the accusations, he also remembered Daphne's visit to him; he could guess a truth without all the evidence.

"My wife," he remarked, "died many years ago, and I've lived alone up there since then."

Hippocrates looked up. Far above them on a jutting cliff, the acropolis of Pelea shone white against the rising greens and browns of Mount Oromedon.

"But I have never been really alone. People are always calling for me. I share their happiness and their secrets. Long years in the practice of medicine does something to a man; it gives him a special kind of philosophy, I suppose. Anyway, it's a happy life in itself. I don't understand all of the things you hope to do in medicine, Hippocrates, but you can be sure it will bring you compensations."

Hippocrates looked at him and nodded. They had come to the crossroads now where Aenas was to turn off.

When they parted, Aenas said, "Good-by, Pyramus."

Hippocrates walked on. How strange that the old man should call him Pyramus. Old men probably grow confused. He wondered what old age would bring to him. As he swung around the shoulder of Mount Oromedon, he passed the place where he had wrestled with Cleomedes, and the wall beside which he and Daphne had stood and looked across the slopes of Halasarna, so close together — so close! The whistle of the rock nuthatch echoed down the cliffs, derisive and mocking as ever.

As he continued on down the slope toward the sea, he thought, "I can live like old Aeneas. The sick will ask for me too, as they do for him. I'll share their sorrows with them and their happiness too perhaps."

At last he came to his grandmother's gate and entered. As he looked at the well and saw the empty drinking gourds, and the twisted trunks of the olive trees, he felt a sudden pang of remembrance and Daphne seemed to rise before him. There she stood, her black curls like little waves of light about her face. Her eyes were saying something to him, her lips smiled. Oh, to hold her in his arms!

He turned and ran up the path to the house and hammered on wooden doors. He might escape from his thoughts inside — but he had to wait, so he turned about. The olive trees that arched above the path were all leafed out now. There were only fresh fuzzy buds on those branches when he had stood with Daphne here. A wind blew up the hillside and ripples of silver gray flowed upward through the dark green.

"The gods have honey for such as you" — that was what the gatekeeper's wife had said to them after she spat in her bosom to keep away the curse. He smiled bitterly. Daphne had called her a sibyl.

Someone was fumbling with the locking pins, and now the bolt was being drawn back slowly. The door swung open and there stood the sibyl herself, peering at him through wisps of hair.

"Hippocrates, Hippocrates," she cackled. "I told the mistress it would be you. She's waiting now."

He gave her his cloak and bag and strode across the court. A quavering voice was calling his name as though the caller were

short of breath. As he entered Phaenarete's room, he saw that the
thin old face above the coverlet was thinner and paler than before; her eyes were as black and as bright as ever, but they peered at
him out of shadowed caverns.

Her hand trembled as she held it out. He took it in his and looked
at it. It seemed very small and thin, and the mottled senile pigment
on the back of the hand contrasted sharply with the pale transparence
of her skin. He stooped and kissed her.

"At last," she whispered. "At last you've come." She took some
quick breaths and then spoke again. "It's hard to be in bed alone.
Why didn't you come before? I'm so alone."

Tears ran down into the wrinkles of the sunken cheek. He dried
them and changed her position in bed and put a pillow under her
head. She smiled.

"When I'm alone," she said, "do you know what I do sometimes? I
talk to your grandfather. That's only when no one can hear, of course.
They'd think me mad if they heard, when he's been dead so long."

Hippocrates lifted the blankets from her leg and began his examination. But she continued to follow her own train of thought, seeming to ignore him.

"We have a good time together, your grandfather and I. I can still
scold him and it does me good. I always used to say that scolding
did him good, and he would laugh." She laughed a little herself.
"There's no one left around here who's worth scolding. You would
do, but you are not here. Your brother Sosander came to see me when
he returned from the games. Now there's a man worth scolding. What
a delightful day we had!"

She smiled reminiscently. Then she continued: "The neighbor
comes in and they all do their best, I suppose. The gatekeeper lifts
me about the bed. I don't need a Hercules for that any more, I'm
such a thin old bird.

"But whenever I want to do something nice, no matter what it is,
they say: 'Oh no! Hippocrates wouldn't like it; Hippocrates this and
Hippocrates that.'"

Her voice came stronger. "Look here, young man! Listen to me. I
want to get up. You are to give them those orders. If it kills me —

well, that is my affair, not yours. I'm ready to go. There's just one
thing more I'm waiting for."

She struggled up and supported herself on her thin arms, panting
a little. "What I'm waiting for is to see that sweet nymph from
Cnidus. I told you to bring her with you. I told your mother to go
and arrange it. Is Daphne outside now?"

Hippocrates did not answer. He had taken the splint from the leg
and was measuring it. He looked up and smiled.

"It's in position," he said. "No shortening, not yet anyway." He
drew back to look at it and at her wasted body.

Hippocrates!" she exclaimed, still staring at him. "Hippocrates,
you didn't bring her with you! You left her behind when she
wanted to come. I know she wanted to come. And you're unhappy
too. My poor boy! You go back and — Oh!"

Her words were interrupted by a groan of pain and she fell back
on her pillow. "Go back and get her," she gasped.

As he bent over her, she put her hand on her chest. "It's here it
hurts — here — but — it's nothing. Don't be worried."

He placed his hand over her heart. Then he put his ear against
her chest. When he stood up again, she said to him:

"It's all right. But I did want to see her. Leave me alone now. Go
— get something to eat. Don't make me talk any more. The pain will
come again — please go."

Hippocrates left her to rest. But he stopped outside the door stroking his beard. Then he shook his head and straightened up and
walked along the peristyle. He sat down in the *oecus* and stared
through the door at the plane tree in the court.

Presently the gatekeeper's wife brought him hot food and he ate
with relish. When she came to clear away she said, "I'm glad you
arrived before her time to die."

Hippocrates looked at the old woman. "Is there a time to die?"

She set the little table down and pushed her hair back. "You don't
know much about old age. Yes, there is a time to die. She's only
waiting for Daphne now. There's a time too for sleep, a time to forget
your troubles. You just lie down on that couch right now."

He stretched his tired legs on the couch and closed his eyes to think awhile. But his fatigue was due to thinking, not to walking, and the house was quiet. He slept the deep sleep of exhaustion, and when he woke the sun was setting. He got up and walked along the peristyle to the *thalamus*. He sat down to talk with Phaenarete and told her the news of the festival and of the doings of the asclepiads.

She put her scrawny hand on his and said, "There is something I have been thinking about, Hippocrates. I wish I could teach it to you. Physicians don't seem to understand old age, not until it is too late, perhaps, and they are old themselves. Maybe a woman who has lived a long time can teach you something.

"You saved my life, I suppose, when you came to mend my broken leg. Now when you return to view your handiwork, there are two things that you should study, the leg and me. You're a good craftsman, and like all craftsmen you're proud of the result that all can see. 'No shortening yet,' you said, and you wished that Euryphon had been here to see it. I know, you wanted to prove him wrong. I was the wife of an asclepiad.

"Would you still be proud of what you have done if I said I do not thank you for saving my life? I did not enjoy these endless days in bed. My time had come to die, I was ready to go, you see. Do you do these things to please the gods, or me, the patient? Or is it the praise of other men and of other physicians that physicians seek?"

Hippocrates was listening thoughtfully, his head tipped to one side, the fingers of one hand moving slowly over his lips and down to the tip of his beard.

"Very good questions," he said softly. "I must have time to think about them before I dare to answer." Then he added with a smile, "Go on with your lecture."

"Youth never knows," she said, "what age is like till youth is gone forever. You scan this body of mine, this wrinkled ruin. But me inside you cannot see. Within the ruin I am the same. I have not changed at all. I am the child that ran to her play, and the maid that your grandfather loved. Sight grows dim and hearing fails. It's hard to remember at times. But the girl in this house of closing doors remains the same at heart."

Her old voice had quavered at first, but now it grew strong. "Your grandfather left me long ago, and I know quite well it was better so. Yes, I'm glad he went ahead of me if one of us had to go. The boy within an aging man finds it harder to live alone.

"A woman has her cooking, her spinning and her weaving. She need never know the lonely hours of idleness at home. The housewife's door stands open, and the world looks in and nods to her as she works amid the echoes of the past — not unhappy at the last — unless, Hippocrates, she breaks her hip and someone keeps her alive beyond her time."

Phaenarete smiled. "Just remember this: Death, our enemy all through life, comes in the end as a friend. Look at him when you hear him knocking, and look at the woman who waits for him. He may well be her long-awaited suitor whose wooing would be welcome — so welcome in the end."

She closed her eyes and put her hand on her heart.

"I think he's knocking now. Leave me, please. Just be glad for me, when he does come through the door —"

CHAPTER TWENTY-THREE

Archons Investigate

~~~~~~

Before Daphne returned to her father, he had regained control of his emotions and was pacing up and down the room. She saw that he had washed away the soot, although he still wore the chiton which had been burned and blackened by the smoldering ruin of his buildings. She handed him a warm woolen cloak. He put it on without a word and watched Anna as she brought in the evening meal and set it out on small tables. When all was ready, he made for his dining couch with the alacrity that is characteristic of physicians in the presence of food, regardless of what harrowing experiences they may have had.

"Well, daughter," Euryphon said, rubbing his hands and sampling the steaming dish on the table at his elbow, "you and Anna have prepared a feast worthy of a king tonight. Roast hare! And cooked in a way to make the mouth of Dionysus himself water! And what is this? Caviar!"

She laughed. "Oh, Anna ran down to the market for the caviar. And it just happened that one of your patients, old Malthus who came in from the country today, brought you this hare as a present; he never pays you anything otherwise. I must confess that I smelled it before I saw it. But Anna said it was only a wild smell, and she started to roast it at once."

"It is good," he said. "You know the hunter's saying: 'To taste good it must first smell dead.'" He reached for a cube of meat with his fingers and put it in his mouth. "Just savor that flavor! And why shouldn't we live as well as we can? There's not much left to us after the fire!" He turned to his daughter. "I might as well tell you, Daphne, that I had spent all I could save from my years of work as a physician on the manuscript house and the scrolls — all vanished now in black, billowing smoke."

When they had finished, Anna brought water and a towel and they washed their hands. The dishes were carried out, and Euryphon and his daughter began to talk about what had happened during that dreadful day. He listened while Daphne told him all that Thargelia had revealed to her before her death. Finally he summed up his conclusions as follows:

"Thargelia lied to me about her condition. I believe she may have lied to you about who caused it. But let that be forgotten now. Someone set this fire which destroyed our buildings and our medical manuscripts. Whoever did it must answer for it. He must answer, too, for a double murder. The Archons of the Council of Cnidus will be here tomorrow to inquire into the cause of the burning. Since Hippocrates has been accused, and since he is now on his way to Cos, Cos should be represented. Therefore Timotheus, who is now the First Archon of Cnidus, has urged Timon to be present at the investigation here tomorrow. Timon has agreed."

"Hippocrates is not guilty," Daphne said. "I know he's not. He could not do such a thing. It's that woman Olympias who is back of all this — she and probably that awful boxer Buto."

Euryphon made a gesture of exasperation. "I realize that Olympias was here at the time the fire broke out. But why should she want to set the fire after Hippocrates left, or Buto either?"

"She would do it," Daphne answered, her face flushing with anger, "for the same reason that she accused Hippocrates of being the father of Thargelia's baby, just to make us hate Hippocrates. That's enough reason for that kind of woman. She would do it so that you would let Cleomedes have the bride he wanted. She knew very well that I was beginning to love Hippocrates. I do love him — and I will love him, no matter what he has done."

Euryphon saw angry tears in his daughter's eyes. He hummed thoughtfully. Then he said:

"I see what you mean. I hadn't thought of it quite that way. But I am astonished to hear you say you could love the man who burned my manuscripts."

"He didn't burn them!" she cried.

"Well," Euryphon countered, "there are reasons why he might want to. And I have always found Olympias kind and charming. I can't believe she would do such a thing." Then Euryphon's face hardened and he stood up.

"No more now, Daphne. You may tell the Archons what you believe tomorrow, if you insist. But I warn you now that you must have real evidence — something more than a woman's intuition or your personal dislike of Olympias. No more tonight! Go to your room now and get some rest.

When Daphne went outside, she discovered that the court was filled with feathery light, and she paused a moment to look at the moon and to wonder how it could flood the streets and courtyards of Cnidus with so much mysterious whiteness — and a hundred seaport cities as well, all round the sea. And she thought of the ship that had sailed at sunset. It too must be bathed in the moon's soft light as it moved across the sea to Cos.

It might have been an hour later when Euryphon appeared in the court on his way to bed. He found her still standing there where she had stopped to look.

"Daphne!" he exclaimed. "You still here?"

"Father! Did the moon ever make you feel — I don't know — as through you could almost talk to someone?"

Her father grunted and continued on his way, but at the door of his room he stopped.

"Yes — I know," he said.

The next morning as Euryphon left his bedroom and crossed the courtyard, Daphne called to him and came running down the stairs.

"I have it! I have it!" she cried excitedly.

"You have what?"

"I have the evidence! You said I must have some real evidence to present to the Archons, not just a woman's intuition. You must ask them to let me come before them as soon as they arrive. I shall bring Ctesias with me."

"Don't be absurd, Daphne. This is not a matter for a child to settle. I have no time to talk with you now. Women are bad enough," he complained as he continued on his way, "without bringing children into this affair. There must be stern justice. I hardly slept at all last night."

"Father!" she called after him.

"Yes." He stopped.

"Have you had anything to eat this morning?"

"No."

"I thought not. Come back just for a moment. I left some cheese and olives for you in the *oecus*. Come back with me. Anna has hot broth and I'll get some barley cakes."

"There's no time for that," he grumbled. But he followed her back into the *oecus*. "What a nuisance a woman can be!"

When he left the room a few minutes later, he turned and looked back at Daphne, and she saw the familiar twinkle in his eye.

"Women," he declared, "are an eternal nuisance, and children too. But what a sad world this is for anyone who has to live alone without them!"

Later in the morning, old Xanthias came hurrying across the court to find his mistress.

"Timotheus has sent for you to present to the Council any evidence you may have about the fire."

"Ctesias must come with me," she said. "He is busy on the roof with the turtle. It was very good of you, Xanthias, to find him a new one. You must have been up very early! He believes it is the same turtle, changed a little by the fire. I didn't contradict him. I want you also, Xanthias, to come with us to the Council and to bring the gatekeeper."

The Archons of Cnidus sat in the open square in the warm spring sunshine. Daphne left her house and walked toward them across the enclosure. Little Ctesias walked beside her and held her hand tightly. She saw that the Master's chair had been brought out and that the Chief Archon, Timotheus, was sitting in it. The others sat on benches arranged on either side of him in a half circle. Her father was on Timotheus' right and Timon on his left. Beyond them stood the blackened shells of burned buildings. Pale wisps of smoke still rose here and there from the ruin.

As Daphne and Ctesias approached, they were followed by Xanthias and the gatekeeper. Outside the circle they stopped. Timon had risen from his seat and was addressing the Archons.

"Buto, I am told," Timon was saying, "behaved creditably. He tried to keep the flames from spreading from the manuscript house to the house of Ctesiarchus. After that, I understand, he tried to hold my son back as he rushed into the burning building. He was about to follow in after him when the roof fell and killed my boy."

Timon choked and sat down quickly. The Archons turned toward Daphne. Timotheus smiled at her.

"You, Daphne, were present when this happened. Can you throw any light on how this fire started? It has been urged that Hippocrates of Cos set the fire because he alone was in the manuscript house just before the fire was discovered. We hesitate to believe such a thing, since we have known this distinguished Greek and loved him well, as boy and man. It is said that he might have been jealous of the fame of your father Euryphon. It has been said, too, that he might have been disappointed when your father refused to give him his daughter to marry.

"If you have facts to present, let us hear them."

"What I have to say," she said, "has to do with Buto. He was in the manuscript house after Hippocrates left and before the fire."

The Archons turned and talked among themselves, while Daphne stood waiting, her eyes shining, her face flushed. A tall young man, the youngest of the Archons, watching Daphne, muttered to his neighbor, "A wood nymph, or better, Artemis, Apollo's sister — poised for the chase."

When all was quiet she began to speak again.

"I have asked the gatekeeper to be present," she said. "He will tell you, if you care to ask him, that Buto's work as gymnast in the rubbing room was finished in the morning. He left as usual, but he returned to the rubbing room, which is next to the manuscript house, before Hippocrates arrived and he stayed there after Hippocrates left."

She looked at the gateman. He nodded and said, "That is all true."

"He will also tell you that Olympias, wife of Timon, entered the gate shortly after Hippocrates departed."

Again the man nodded.

"He may leave us now unless you wish to question him."

Timotheus motioned the man to go.

"My father's servant Xanthias," she continued, "was standing with me before Ctesiarchus' house when that brave young man Cleomedes arrived. What Timon has just told you was true. But let Xanthias describe it for you."

"Speak, Xanthias," Timotheus said. "Report exactly what you saw and heard."

Xanthias straightened up and held his head as high as his creaking spine permitted.

"Daphne tried to enter the burning house," he said. "Cleomedes arrived just then and stopped her. He had evidently been running, for he was sweating and wore only a kilt. Buto came from somewhere. His face and hands were covered with soot. Buto tried to hold Cleomedes back from entering the house. Finally Cleomedes knocked him down."

"Tell them what Buto said," Daphne interjected.

"He said, 'Too dangerous. I've been in there. I tried to stop the fire from spreading to the house . . . I'm your —'" He looked quickly at Daphne, then continued: "'I say you cannot go.'"

"Tell them too," Daphne said with stiff lips, "what Buto said when he got up off the ground after Cleomedes had dropped Ctesias down to us from the burning building."

"I heard him call, 'Cleomedes! Cleomedes! I'm coming to help you. Wait for me, my son.'"

"Thank you, Xanthias," Daphne said.

Timon had turned white. He half rose from his seat and spoke to Timotheus.

"Buto was my son's boxing instructor. His use of the word 'son' had no other meaning than that."

"Of course," Timotheus replied. "That was no more than a form of speech during great stress."

Timotheus dismissed Xanthias and made a sign to Daphne that she should continue.

"Here is my evidence," she said. She looked down at Ctesias, who had been listening to every word, his eyes round with childish wonder and with the effort to understand.

"This is Ctesias, the son of Ctesiarchus. He was saved from the fire by Timon's son." She smiled at Timon as though to thank him and reassure him. Then she added, "Your son was a hero, Timon. None who saw him will ever forget what he did."

Timon would have responded to this, but he could not.

"Yesterday afternoon," Daphne continued, "while Hippocrates was reading in the manuscript house, Ctesias visited him twice. Once the gatekeeper saw Hippocrates holding the door open as he will tell you, while Ctesias ran out and across the enclosure.

"When Ctesias woke up this morning he told me that he had remained in the manuscript house after Hippocrates left to catch the boat for Cos. He saw Buto pour oil on the floor and then crawl out a little window. He saw him toss a flaming torch back and set the oil in flames. Perhaps he will tell you all this himself, if you question him."

Again there was an excited hum of talk by the Archons among themselves, until Timotheus called for silence.

"Come over here, Ctesias," he said.

Ctesias took a few steps forward. Then he hesitated. He looked back at Daphne and beckoned to her. She came to him and he took her hand and held it with both his hands as he looked slowly all around the formidable circle of staring faces. When he came to Euryphon, he smiled with delighted recognition and said *"Chaire."* Then he saw that all the faces were smiling at him and he was reassured.

"Tell me, Ctesias," Timotheus said, "all about your visits with Hippocrates."

The boy did not answer.

Daphne stooped. "Did you see Hippocrates yesterday?"

Ctesias nodded. "Two times," he said.

"Tell them about it."

"Oh! The first time, I felt his muscle. His great-great-grandfather was Heracles. Did you know that? Then he asked me to take a piece of papyrus to you, Daphne. He wrote something on it first."

Daphne blushed and the Archons smiled again.

"After I gave it to you, you wrote something and gave me a little roll of papyrus to take back to him, but . . ."

Daphne interrupted him. "That doesn't really matter. Just talk to them and tell them what happened in the manuscript house."

"Yes, but Daphne," the boy persisted, "I just remembered now that I never gave him the piece of papyrus you told me to take to him."

The boy looked down and opened the purse that swung at his belt. He pulled out a tiny flattened scroll.

"I forgot."

Daphne reached quickly and took it from him. But Timotheus stepped forward and held out his hand for it. Daphne looked at him while her blush deepened. Finally she handed him the papyrus, but she did so slowly, realizing that she could do nothing else and wishing that she could run away and hide.

Timotheus held the scroll in his hand.

"This must be read by me," he said, "or by your father. Which shall it be?"

"Don't read it at all," the youngest of the Archons called out. "Let us hear from the boy, that's enough."

Daphne tossed her head. "You have my permission to read it. Timotheus."

He broke the seal and read and handed it back to her smiling. Then he turned to the Archons.

"This scroll had written on it only one word. It is one of the two most meaningful words a woman can write."

Then he added to Daphne, "At the age of six, boys tell the truth and all the truth."

There was a general laugh. When it was over, Ctesias said gravely, "I'm almost seven." Then he turned to Daphne again.

"The reason I forgot was that I remembered I had to do something for my mother and so I didn't go right back to Hippocrates. I went home to see my mother and she asked me to ask Hippocrates to come and see her and find out why her legs won't move, and I told her that he would make them move all right, but I wanted to ask him to tell me a story first about Heracles and so she said, 'Just one story.' "

He looked at Timotheus and smiled, adding, "I like stories."

"Go on," Timotheus said. "You're telling this story. I have a little boy your age. He likes stories too."

"Well, I went to Hippocrates again through the little door from my house. He asked me if Daphne had told me to tell him anything and I said no but my mother had. Then he told me three stories. Do you want to hear them?"

"Not now," Timotheus said.

Daphne interposed. "Perhaps I can explain. Ctesias' mother had an increasing weakness of the legs until recently, when she could not move them at all. My father could explain this to you."

Euryphon shook his head, and Daphne continued.

"She told me she hoped to have the opportunity of asking Hippocrates to see her. Apparently Ctesias, in the absence of his father, took Hippocrates to see his mother, and then he and Hippocrates went back into the manuscript house. Now, Ctesias, you tell them what happened there."

"I had left my turtle," he said, "in a big box in the manuscript house. I told Hippocrates he could help me feed him. But he said he had to hurry. He lives on Cos, you know. He was going back home. So he went out the big door and locked it."

"What did you do then?" Daphne said. "Go on."

"I sat down on the floor beside the box and began to feed the turtle. Then I heard something. Buto was there. You know Buto — he

has a big, big face. Anna says he looks like a toad. He poured something black and shiny on the floor. Then he turned an amphora upside down and left it running. It made a funny sound, and lots of
oil ran out."

Euryphon stood up suddenly.

"May I question the boy?" he asked.

Timotheus nodded.

"Didn't Buto speak to you?"

Ctesias shook his head. "No."

"Where were you?"

"I was sitting on the floor in the — behind the scrolls."

"You were in the alcove?"

"Yes, the alcove."

"Why didn't you ask Buto what he was doing?"

"I wanted to."

"Why didn't you?"

"I asked him some questions in the morning. He was very cross.
He doesn't like little boys. He said so."

Euryphon sat down suddenly.

"It's quite possible," he observed, "that Buto would not have seen
him, placed where he was." He nodded his head slowly. "I think,
Timotheus, that we are listening to the truth."

"Go on," Timotheus said.

"Well, after that, Buto climbed out through the hole in the wall
and his feet waved up and down. I think it was pretty hard to get
out."

"Then what happened next?"

"Buto put his head back through the hole. Then he reached in
with a big torch in his hand. He threw it on the floor. Then everything was fire. There was lots of smoke. I ran out and went upstairs
to my mother and I told her."

At this point the youngest Archon interrupted.

"Ctesias, was anyone helping Buto?"

"I think someone talked to him but I could not see her."

"That is enough," Timotheus said suddenly. "I shall not call for a

casting of ballots. I assume that we are agreed that Buto is guilty."
He paused for a moment and every Archon said, "Yes." He glanced
at Euryphon, who nodded slowly. "Yes . . . yes."

"Final judgment," Timotheus continued, "must be postponed until
Buto can be brought before the Council of Cos. This investigation
is over."

He turned to Timon.

"Thank you, Timon. We have been honored by your presence.
When you bring this matter before the Council of Cos, I will be present there if you wish it."

Timotheus turned to the youngest Archon, who was waiting to
speak to him.

"Why," the young man said, "did you block questions about
Buto's accomplice? He certainly had one."

Timotheus made a gesture of impatience and spoke so others could
not hear.

"I saw where the evidence was leading us as well as you did. But I
had to block the inquiry, at least for now. We must not make the
problem too difficult for Timon to face. When you see a viper in the
basket, it is better to keep the cover on until you know what to do
with it. I'm sorry for Timon."

The young Archon nodded. "And I am sorry for Hippocrates."

"Yes," Timotheus agreed, "I'm sorry for Hippocrates too, but we
have done as much as we could to clear his good name. We cannot
silence people's tongues until the trial takes place in Cos. Buto can
only be finally convicted there."

Timotheus called to Daphne:

"Take Ctesias back to your house. You will care for him, I hope,
until Ctesiarchus returns."

She took the boy by the hand and would have started off, but
Ctesias refused. Standing his ground, he looked about at the Archons.

"Has anyone seen my mother?"

There was a sudden silence.

"The turtle got out of the fire all alone. Xanthias found him this
morning. The fire only changed his color a little."

His lip trembled. "I want my mother."

"Come on, Ctesias," Daphne murmured, and she took him in her arms. He was sobbing now and looking at the Archons over her shoulder.

"I want my mother. Please — look for her."

So it was that the burning of the medical manuscripts of the great School of Medicine in Cnidus — the burning of the world's first medical library — became an event that was recorded in subsequent history and reported falsely. The people of Cnidus continued to repeat the initial falsehood. They told how Hippocrates of Cos, Euryphon's famous rival, had set the fire. Some said the cause was rivalry among physicians. Some smiled and said it was all because of a woman.

And the ships that sailed away each day from the port of Cnidus spread that news from port to port till every barber in greater Hellas had a version all his own to tell. And men spoke too of the brave deeds of a new hero in Greece — Cleomedes, son of Timon of Cos.

And later, when the case was finally settled and the truth was told in Cos, another wave of news went out across the sea, as when a pebble is dropped in a still pool. But the second wave could never quite overtake the first.

CHAPTER TWENTY-FOUR

Apollo's Grove

~~~~~~

Two DAYS AFTER the meeting of the Archons in Cnidus, Pindar brought news to his master in Halasarna. "Rumor has it now," he said, "that Buto set the fire! Timon arrived in Cos yesterday morning and orders were issued at once that Buto should be brought before the Council of Cos. But he broke away from those who came for him, and they are still hunting for him in Apollo's grove."

Hippocrates nodded, but said nothing. "I have just come from Timon's villa," Pindar went on. "Olympias is in a strange state. Timon asked me to help, but I can do nothing with her and I'm afraid for Penelope's safety. Timon begs you to come to see her at once, and his swift mules are waiting at the gate to take you there."

Hippocrates felt a sudden wave of resentment, but after a pause, he said, "Very well. I will go with you, although this is the last woman I would care to see as a patient. But I shall return here to Halasarna afterward and stay until the affair of the fire in Cnidus is completely settled."

When the two physicians reached the villa, Timon came to meet them on the terrace.

"You have come to a house of gloom, Hippocrates," he said. "Cleomedes is dead, Olympias is in a fearful state, and even Penelope is in danger. Buto, the villain who brought all this sorrow on us, has escaped and no one can find him. There is a rumor that he was seen

near one of the villages at the edge of the forest this morning. I have
ordered the men in my household to arm themselves."

Penelope had appeared as they talked, and Hippocrates smiled as
he watched her coming toward them. She was dressed in a tight
Spartan chiton, which was split down one side so that the curves of
thigh and calf could hardly be ignored, even by a preoccupied young
man like Pindar. Instead of the long black braids that she had worn
a month ago, her hair was coiled at the back of her head and held in
place by a snood scattered over with tiny jewels. But there was something more; she seemed to have a mysterious consciousness of her
own charm that was, in itself, altogether charming.

"I'm very glad you have come," she said to Hippocrates. "My father
needs your help. So do we all, my mother especially. I tried to talk
with her this morning, but —"

She shook her head and glanced at her father. "I know you two
would rather talk alone for a little while. I'll go for a walk, and perhaps Pindar would like to come with me."

"Don't go far into that wood," her father warned, "not until after
Buto is caught."

As the young couple walked away, the voice of a nightingale
echoed through the aisles of cypress trees and Penelope called back:
"There is Philomela singing for us now!"

Timon shuddered. "I used to love that song," he said. "I called it
Apollo's forest flute. Now the song gives me a feeling of dread."

"I'm glad to see Penelope looking so well," Hippocrates said, hoping to change the direction of his thoughts.

Timon's face lit up. "She has changed, hasn't she? She is my only
comfort now. But I'm afraid for her, unless you can do something
about her mother. . . . Yesterday morning, when I arrived, I found
Olympias sitting silent in her room, with curtains drawn across the
door. She would not eat. She would not speak.

"Last night I woke from a sound sleep, hearing her call my name.
There she stood beside my bed and would not speak another word.
But she let me take her in my arms and she clung to me. Finally, I led
her back to her room. Her slave was asleep there still. You see,

Olympias and I sleep in separate rooms usually, and I let her have the *thalamus*.

"After that, the house was quiet, and at last I fell asleep again. But in the gray of the dawn I woke — this time I heard my daughter screaming. I rushed into the court and up the stairs to her room. I found her alone there, still sobbing. When I could quiet her, she told me that something had wakened her, and she had seen in her doorway in the dim light the silhouette of her mother. She lay quiet and watched. At last Olympias moved toward her across the room and raised her arm. She held a long knife in her hand. Then it was that Penelope screamed and her mother vanished.

"I found Olympias cowering in her own room, but I could not find the knife and she would not speak. It must have been my own knife, which is very long and very sharp. I could not find the key to the wine room that opens off the *thalamus* — she may have hidden the knife there.

"This morning I sent for Pindar, but Olympias will not talk to anyone. The servants are silent; of course they are frightened. Penelope is, as you see, restored, but she is deeply troubled, and grieving for her brother. I myself — but perhaps I have told you enough. I beg you to examine Olympias and tell me what can be done for her."

Timon clapped his hands and Olympias' slave appeared. She led Hippocrates through the villa door into the front court and around the altar of Zeus to the door of Olympias' room.

"Hippocrates has come!" the servant called. They waited. Hippocrates looked at the slave. Probably a Scythian woman, he thought, magnificent body and slow wit. He noticed that her eye was bruised.

"Did your mistress strike you?" he asked in a low voice.

"Yes," she said, showing her white teeth in a sudden smile. "I tried to comfort her."

She called again. "Hippocrates is here!" Then she whispered, "It is just the way it was on the morning of Penelope's medical consultation. I stood at the door then and told her you were here, but she would not answer." The slave pulled the partly closed curtain back and set the door screen to one side.

Olympias was standing before her long bronze mirror, her back to the door. Hippocrates could see her dark eyes watching him in the mirror. He motioned to the servant to leave. Then he put the screen back across the doorway, which shut them off from the court but left the room flooded with light from the sky above.

He turned to her then, but said nothing — he knew he would learn more about her thinking if she took the initiative. So he waited, watching this strange woman's stubborn back. She had been his worst enemy. Could he examine her dispassionately? He knew he must try. She was his patient now.

He considered the medical problem this woman presented. She had begun by making him her confidant when she came to see him that first morning in his *iatreion*. But she had only opened a part of her mind to him. Her thinking was never straight. In some ways she was quite illogical, in others very clever. She was brazen and at the same time frightened; charming, but with it all, hateful and dangerous. Her wrong thinking had brought unhappiness and tragedy to those about her and to herself.

What could he do for her? He could not treat her body. Was there a pathway to her mind by which he could treat some disease of thinking? Had he any access to a spirit within her? If there was such a pathway, could the gods then speak to us along it and we to the gods? Thargelia's dying question came back to him, "And when there is no body at all — what then — will God love me?" Could the gods have changed Olympias in her lifetime if she had opened her thinking to them? And could any physician hope to do this now?

He turned a critical eye on her. This naturally fastidious woman was glancing at him from time to time over her shoulder. Her hair was disheveled and she was wearing a clean chiton over a soiled one. The outer one was made of transparent silken tissue, the kind that Coan women had begun to weave from imported silk. He could see a large black mark on the chiton beneath — it might, he thought, have been made by a dirty hand. The outer one showed no wrinkles. She must have pulled it on recently, perhaps just before his entrance.

He glanced about for further information. Beyond the mirror, which was in the middle of the room, was her bed against the wall.

Blankets and other things were heaped on it in surprising disarray. In the wall at the foot of her bed was a closed door, probably the wine cupboard. There were dirty marks on the door. As he looked at this, Olympias whirled about and faced him.

"Cleomedes is dead," she said. "Burned! . . . And I go on thinking . . . thinking."

Her eyes stared and there were deep dark circles under them. Her face was gray and blank like a mask, as though the conflict of thoughts and emotions within produced nothing that could show itself on the surface in meaningful expression.

"Dead," she said again in the same flat voice. She looked down at herself. The under chiton was torn, and one breast was quite bare, except for the outer filmy chiton. She made no move to cover herself. Instead, she raised her eyes to his and a cruel smile came to her lips.

"Men say you set that fire, Hippocrates." She started to laugh, but stopped and put her hand to her head as though the laugh had made a headache worse.

Then, at last, Hippocrates spoke. "You know, Olympias, that you have just repeated the lie you coined yourself. You know who set that fire. The Archons of Cnidus have met in council. They know too that Buto lit the fire. But you know, and I know, more — that you told Buto what to do."

Her pupils grew wide and dark.

"So," she said. "You know — but do the gods know? That is what I still must learn. Did the gods see the lighting of the fire that killed my son? Tell me, do they know who it was that lit Buto's torch?"

"I suppose they do," Hippocrates said. "If they are gods, they must know all."

"Then the voices that I hear today," she said suddenly, as though in despair, "the voices are theirs! And I must obey what I hear them say. I told Timon there were no gods, but I was wrong. They talk to me, and none can flee their vengeance.

"I heard them say that someone was to die. I thought they meant Penelope . . . not me. Timon loves Penelope. He loves me too — he loves me still. I went to him in the night, and he loves me still. It must be me the voices mean! Their vengeance — ah — my mind goes round and round . . ."

She wrung her hands. Then, in a whisper: "But what if I should help the gods to vent their wrath on Buto? What then? Would they forgive my sin?"

Hippocrates was silent. She came nearer and her eyes stared at him.

"Does Timon know that his wife did this?" she asked at last. "Does Timon know who Buto was and what he did? It's Timon I love . . . "

An expression of incredulity crossed Hippocrates' face.

"Oh, yes," she said. "There are many ways a woman may love a man, but you would hardly understand. I didn't know how much I loved, but now I do. And what did I do to him and my poor Cleomedes?"

She looked at Hippocrates fiercely. "Does he know? Does Timon know?"

Hippocrates hesitated, then he said, "No — Timon does not seem to know."

"Hippocrates!" she exclaimed. Her face was changing now. It had begun to register purpose and plan again.

"Hippocrates," she repeated, "will you keep my secret now and after I am gone? You cannot come between the gods and me, but you can do something else. You are a physician — will you keep my secret? Will you protect Timon, keep him from knowing what I have done? Promise me, Hippocrates."

He knew he could not lie to her, and behind those pleading, staring eyes he saw the real woman taking shape. She was a tigress that had snarled and fought and had lost the fight. But she was a woman too, a woman so sad she could not weep.

At last he answered, "Yes."

She had no word of thanks for him, no thought except for herself and hers. She only nodded her head.

"The gods know all, and I must pay," she said. "But Timon will not know, not now, and Cleomedes died a hero's death and men will praise my boy. And none will know who his father was, nor guess it was I who lit that fire."

She turned to her mirror and began to comb her hair. Hippocrates left the room and crossed the court. He found Timon outside on the terrace, scanning the cypress grove. He was holding a javelin in his hand, resting the butt on the stone of the terrace.

"I have a feeling," he said, seeing a look of surprise in Hippocrates' face, "that we may have to deal with Buto. He's just stupid enough to come back here. I used to throw the javelin quite well when I was a boy in the games. If the opportunity should present itself now," he said, squaring his stocky shoulders, "I could kill, I think, at quite a distance. I never liked Buto from the beginning."

Hippocrates waited for what might come next.

"Did you ever hear," Timon asked, "the story of Cleomedes, the Olympic boxer who killed his opponent in cold blood?"

"Yes," Hippocrates answered. "Why do you ask?"

"No reason, except that Buto reminds me of him just a little. I only saw that boxer once. Olympias and he grew up on the same island, you know — they were cousins."

He raised the javelin above his head and balanced it thoughtfully. Then he put it down again.

"Tell me about my wife's condition," he said.

Hippocrates shook his head gravely. "She says she has been hearing voices. I know that is generally considered a sign of madness, but I am not convinced yet. I would recommend a diet of barley gruel for her at frequent intervals. Otherwise, we can only wait. You would do well to send Penelope away every night and let her return each morning. That might be better for both of them."

Timon nodded. "Cleomedes dead, Olympias mad, Penelope in danger! Hippocrates, I fear there is something behind all this misfortune, something sinister."

He swung about and pointed. "There it is — in that forest of towering trees. We are cursed . . . A man does foolish things sometimes for the woman he loves. Strange about my wife; she was always afraid of something. She said it was the trees on the terrace that made her so. I cut them down."

They heard a sighing sound far above them. It was only the wind in the treetops, but it rose like a voice and fell again. Then all was silence except for the brook that gushed from the ground in the garden below, and rushed and chuckled away toward the sea.

Finally Timon spoke again. "I am a man of action, Hippocrates, I have a plan. The priest of Apollo and a priest of Asclepius will be here tomorrow. I want you here. I will explain it then. I will send a messenger to you to let you know exactly when I want you to come."

Hippocrates flushed. He looked at Timon for a moment. Then he walked away, saying, "I must be starting for Halasarna."

Timon sensed his sudden resentment and hurried after him. "Wait, Hippocrates! You will come, won't you?"

Hippocrates stopped at the top of the terrace steps. "Why should I?"

Timon caught up with him. "I expect to pay you. I'll pay you well for all your visits here. I'll give you —"

"Stop," Hippocrates interrupted sternly. "Of course you will pay me, exactly what is due for my services to the sick, no more and no less. But the physician's responsibility is to the sick, not to the person who promises to pay for his time. This is a difference between medicine and trade. Many do not seem to understand it.

"Because you are this woman's husband, you may call me to care for her disease. For the same reason, it is your right to send me away and to call another physician. That is your right whether you eventually pay or not. Until you decide to send me away, however, I shall do what I believe to be best and come when I choose. You cannot buy the right to command.

"I will serve Olympias," he continued, as Timon stood speechless, "not you. I will serve the woman who is sick and who needs such help as I can give, even though I owe her no debt of gratitude — far, far from it!"

He smiled bitterly.

"Forgive me," Timon said. "I did not mean to speak to you as if you were a slave or an oarsman on my trireme. We all of us need your help because you are a wise physician and you understand disease. It's not only Olympias; Penelope is in danger. It's this family that needs you — what's left of it."

Timon turned and walked haltingly to a bench, suddenly seeming very sad and small. He sat there with his head in his hands. Hippocrates returned and sat beside him.

"You must be proud of Cleomedes," he said quietly.

Timon raised his head. "Yes," he replied. "I cannot stop grieving for him, but I'm glad he could die a hero. He would have saved the wife of Ctesiarchus too, if there had only been more time. Cleomedes always reminded me of my father. You could see a strong resemblance even when he was a boy."

There was pride in the little Archon's face now, and Hippocrates thought of Olympias' question, "Does Timon know?" There were so many things that Timon did not know, or was it that he refused to recognize them? This is the man, Hippocrates thought, that the tigress loves, the man she has so long shielded from knowing the truth about herself.

"What Cleomedes did," he said aloud, "is far more to be praised than the winning of many boxing crowns. Danger brings out greatness in a hero's heart. When risks are small, then little men may also win. Cleomedes knew how great the risks were, and his glory will not vanish soon."

Timon smiled proudly and quoted Solon's words: " 'Call no man happy until he dies.' "

Hippocrates nodded. "The gloomiest skies of life may change to glory at sunset. In spite of all the sadness of his loss, Timon, you must find some quality of gladness in your mourning."

They were silent a moment. Then Hippocrates asked abruptly: "Is the back door of the villa kept locked? — The one that opens to the stables?"

Timon looked at him quickly. "I thought of that this morning and ordered it locked." Then his face brightened.

"If you can spare the time, Hippocrates, I might explain to you right now the plan I mentioned. Let us walk up and down while I talk. You see, when Olympias and I were married, I bought this part of the cypress grove and I paid for it and I built this villa here. And yet, it seems, it was never mine. The grove is sacred to Apollo, and I know now that I must give it back. Man's time on earth is short. When he works against the will of the gods, all his efforts come to nothing."

They heard laughter now coming from the direction of the cypress grove.

"That sounds like Penelope," Hippocrates said.

"It probably is. I can't keep her out of that gloomy wood. There she is with Pindar — he seems to be a conscientious young physician."

"Father!" Penelope called. "May I speak to you?" She came running alone from the wood, and stood before them radiant. With her came the faint scent of perfume — lotus, Hippocrates thought.

"Father, I want to speak to you on a most important matter. It seems quite proper to do this before Hippocrates because he is Pindar's master and that is nearly the same as being his father, isn't it?"

"Couldn't you bring this up later, Penelope?" Timon asked. "At the moment we are discussing a very grave problem. It is important to you and to all of us."

"I know, Father. Your problems are always grave and always important. But this is my first important problem, my very first, and it's very important and very grave. Pindar is coming now to talk with you seriously. I asked him to do this. He didn't tell me just what he was going to say."

She laughed and put her arms about her father and her cheek against his.

"Pindar is very shy," she said. "You'll help him to say what he ought to say, won't you? And then when he has said it — you will answer yes, won't you?"

Her father apparently had not listened to what she said. "Penelope, why do you talk to me about Pindar? It is your future I am considering. I want to get you away before something happens to you."

"But I want it to happen!" she cried. "If it would only happen, then I'll go away with you anywhere. He would go too and live with us, wouldn't he?"

She started back toward the wood, and Pindar emerged. Hippocrates turned and looked out toward the sea to hide a smile.

"I've drawn up a plan of action," Timon was saying. "I feel there is no time to lose."

But Pindar was approaching them now. He looked at the stocky little Archon with speechless embarrassment. At last, standing before him, he stammered, "I have land — I have land in Boetia, but very little money —"

"Well," Timon replied impatiently, "I have land and money both. But there is a curse on my family, and I am about to lose a great deal of land and some money too. Don't go away now, Pindar. What I have to say to Hippocrates may interest you.

"I am a man of action, as you know, Hippocrates. I offered sacrifices in the temple of Apollo this morning. But this is not enough, I know. I must do something more."

"Yes," Hippocrates said, glancing across at Pindar with a smile of understanding. "I often tell the young asclepiads that when they are treating the sick, prayer is good, but while calling on the gods, don't forget to take care of the patient."

Timon nodded and then continued, speaking with great dignity as though he were addressing a meeting of the Council.

"You may not know this, Hippocrates, but there is on the island of Cos at the moment a messenger who has come from the priest of the great temple of Asclepius in Epidaurus. He came to find a favorable site to build a temple. He chose Cos because of the medical fame that you and your father Heracleides have brought to our island. Your name, that brought Empedocles here, has brought him.

"I have talked with him and with the priest of Apollo today. We are agreed that I shall give this villa and all the land about it, together with the waters of Vorina Fountain running through it, to Apollo Cyparissius, to whom this forest is sacred. Then the priest will rent it out to Asclepius the God of Healing. This is the present arrangement at Triopion. The *temenos* of the shrine of

Asclepius there pays rent to the Triopian Apollo, since that area too belongs to Apollo."

Timon was striding back and forth in his excitement.

"So, you see," he continued, "an *asclepeion*, a shrine dedicated to Asclepius, a lovely temple, will soon be built right here on this terrace where you and Pindar and I are standing now. Thus do I hope to lift the curse that rests, I know, on me. Thus I hope to protect my family."

"Timon!" Hippocrates exclaimed. "What a man you are! And what a gesture to the gods!"

Timon smiled. "It will be a large gift, a big sacrifice. But Cleomedes is dead, and Olympias and Penelope are in danger. What can I do better with my wealth? The priests agree that this will please Apollo and perhaps lift the curse. I've paid too little attention to the gods during my busy life as shipowner and Archon. But I know that there must be gods, somewhere. I've worked continuously for the good of the Greeks of Cos. If giving my wealth to this great project will free me from the curse and bring beauty to our island, I'll give it gladly."

Hippocrates was so amazed by this project that he too forgot Pindar, who stood shifting from one foot to the other, and Penelope, waiting at the edge of the wood.

"I do not myself believe," Hippocrates said thoughtfully, turning toward the balustrade, "that either gods or devils send disease and madness to men. To believe this would lead to giving up medicine as an art. For that same reason we cannot leave healing to the god Asclepius or any other god. And yet, physician and temple should not be at odds, since both aim to give men health in body and mind.

"Apollo is the god of physicians," he continued after a moment's pause. "We asclepiads like to think of Asclepius more as Homer first described him, the blameless physician of Tricca who trained his sons and sent them to fight against Troy. We have been loyal to this memory and have practiced the art he taught his sons. But since the Greeks have chosen to make this physician their god of healing, so be it."

Even Pindar, impressed with the greatness of the Archon's proposal, was willing to put aside his own concerns for the moment. "An *asclepeion* here," he exclaimed, "like that at Epidaurus? What a wonderful scheme!"

Hippocrates looked at him and came back to the present with a start. "Timon," he said. "Pindar has something to say to you, something very important."

"Yes!" Pindar blurted. "I should explain that when I referred to the fact that I had some land in Boetia but very little money, I was concerned with your daughter Penelope."

"Exactly!" Timon exclaimed. "Exactly. She is in danger and I want to act before Apollo's curse can bring harm to her again, but I don't think we need your land."

"But I mean," Pindar persisted — "I mean I want to marry her."

"Marry her!" Timon exclaimed. "Is that what you meant? To marry her? Then that must be what Penelope tried to tell me with all her talk!"

He looked questioningly at Hippocrates. "I suppose she could do worse than to marry this young man?"

"Pindar," Hippocrates said, smiling, "is the finest young asclepiad I know. He comes of a good family in Thebes. I love him well. Furthermore, as Euryphon pointed out to us at our first consultation, marriage would be excellent for Penelope."

"Well, well! I remember now that she did ask me to say yes to you about something, so I probably shall. I think I shall still have enough ships and money for both of us."

He turned to Hippocrates. "You were right. This is important. If this is Penelope's wish, Pindar, I will give her to you and Hippocrates can stand in place of your father. . . . Yes," he mused, "this is important. I wish I could talk to Olympias now."

He shook his head and then continued. "Perhaps you, Pindar, with Penelope, will give us two the immortality that we might hope for."

The three men stood silent for a moment, drawing their cloaks about them. The sun was setting, and they could feel a cold current of air coming down the mountainside through the dark aisles of the cypress grove. Suddenly they were aware of the evening chorus of the nightingales, as though a door had opened into another world. . . .

Then a shrill cry startled them: "Master!" Olympias' Scythian maid was running toward them from the villa. "Master! Master!" she screamed. "Buto! He's in the mistress's room, oh, oh! — lying on her bed — and the long knife is through his body! Blood is running all across the floor!"

In the stunned silence that followed they heard a voice, a frightened voice far above them. They looked up and saw, to their horror, high on the villa's parapet, the figure of a woman. It was Olympias, swaying back and forth against the blue sky with nothing to steady her.

"Timon!" she cried. "Timon, I'm afraid!"

Hippocrates saw, in a flash, that she was dressed now in her best — he saw the scarlet robe, the bracelets, the long black curls.

"Don't do it, don't jump!" Penelope screamed, running from the wood. "Wait for me, Mother! I'm coming!"

Penelope ran across the terrace and into the house. Olympias swayed and seemed to close her eyes. Then she toppled, toppled forward, her arms at her side. And so she fell, her mantle fluttering — down, down, down. There was a cracking thud on the terrace stone, then all was still.

Hippocrates ran and knelt beside her, bending down to look and touch and listen. Then he covered the heap with the crimson robe, and lifted his head.

"Apollo!" he cried. "She's dead!"

CHAPTER TWENTY-FIVE

The Torch

〰〰〰〰〰〰〰〰〰〰〰〰〰〰〰〰〰〰〰〰〰〰〰〰〰

It was noon next day before Hippocrates arrived in Halasarna again. He talked with Phaenarete, examined her hip, showed the neighbor woman how to massage the limb, and discussed the diet for her. Finally he made his way to the *oecus* and sat down to give himself up to a consideration of his own life, his own future. It seemed to him clear enough that Daphne, who had not troubled to reply to the message he sent her by Ctesias, did not love him. His reputation here among his people would be, perhaps irretrievably, damaged by these false accusations. Without a good reputation, practice of medicine was unthinkable. Perhaps after all he might have done better to become the court physician in Macedonia. It would be easier to forget there.

Lost in gloomy thoughts, he did not hear the outer door of the house open nor the patter of small feet crossing the court, so he was startled when a child's voice said, "May I come in?" A little boy stood silhouetted in the doorway.

Believing that it was the son of the neighbor woman, he said, "Your mother has gone home."

"No," the child replied. "My mother is dead. Daphne and I would like to come to live with you. Will you take us?"

"Ctesias!" Hippocrates shouted. "Ctesias!" He sat up, rigid, waiting. "What was that you said, Ctesias? Say what you said over again."

"My mother is dead," the boy continued soberly. "I'm going to live with Daphne. My father told her I could — he can't take care of me now. He hasn't any house."

Ctesias came and leaned against Hippocrates' knee and looked up at him.

"Will you teach me to be an asclepiad like my father and you? Will you? We want you to take us to your house. Will you let Daphne be your wife? She would be a good wife — please."

Hippocrates could not speak. He pulled Ctesias to his lap and held him close.

"Did Daphne come with you?" he asked at last. "Where is she?"

"We came in our own boat," Ctesias said, "Daphne and me and the turtle. We left the turtle in the boat. She thought it would be best that way."

"But where is Daphne now?" Hippocrates asked again, putting the boy down. "Tell me."

"She wouldn't come in with me. I knocked on the door with the stone she gave me. But she stayed down at the gate beside the well. I'll go and call her — Hippocrates? — Where are you going? — Hippocrates!"

But the man had vanished, and Ctesias heard nothing more except the booming sound of the great door closing. Then he saw the kind face of the gatekeeper's wife, who came in carrying a tray with bread and honey and milk.

As Hippocrates raced across the court and through the door, his mind raced too. Daphne must love him in spite of everything. "Will you let Daphne be your wife?" Let her! Could it really be a message from Daphne? Or was it the boy's idea? Either way . . . how wonderful!

Down by the well, Daphne had found the waiting hard to bear. Her heart had begun to pound when Ctesias knocked and the great door creaked. But when Hippocrates did not come, she thought of all the dreadful things that might have happened. Perhaps after all he did not care!

Her hand was cold on the well's wet brim, and deep within,

the water dripped — dripping away the time. She looked down the well. In the crannies there were pallid ferns and farther down a mirror of light that broke into running ripples each time a drop of water struck. She counted the drops to measure the time, and the time seemed long, so long. He had loved her once; did he love her still?

But listen — the door was creaking again. She heard his voice calling her name. . . . Suddenly weak, she leaned against the well. He stopped before her, searching her face, and it seemed to her that all the love he had never spoken was glowing in his eyes.

"Oh, Daphne! Did Ctesias really speak for you?"

"Hippocrates," she whispered as he took her in his arms, "I thought you would never, never come."

Their lips met in a moment of thrilling discovery. Then she hid her face against his shoulder and clung to him, while he exclaimed:

"Thanks be to Apollo!"

She pulled away from him.

"You might give thanks to Ctesias too, and to his turtle. It was while he was trying to feed that turtle in the manuscript house that he watched Buto set the fire. He did not tell us about it until the next morning."

"And did you believe that night that I had set the fire?"

"Oh no, no! I told my father you couldn't. I told him I loved you and I would always love you no matter what you did."

Hippocrates laughed exultantly. "Did you believe the stories about Thargelia?"

"Well no, not really. Thargelia herself told me the truth. Poor Thargelia!"

"She told you!" he exclaimed.

"Yes, after you left us that morning in such a hurry."

Daphne smiled at him and shook her head.

"Perhaps, if I am to succeed where Thargelia failed, I shall have to call on Aphrodite — I know what I'll do! I'll call to her to come to my aid, as Sappho did."

Her gay laugh rang out suddenly. "Take care, Hippocrates. I hear her coming now driving her:

'sparrows fleet and fair
with whir of wings above the swarthy earth
through middle air . . .
Who is to be persuaded of thy passion [Daphne]
Name thine enemy.' "

He laughed and said, "I hear her too:

'Hippocrates is the enemy's name.
No need to draw the bow again.
Her arrow quivers in his heart!
And brings him such delightful pain.' "

Her eyes sparkled. "I never thought to hear an asclepiad rise to verse, even medical verse. Asclepius must be blushing for you now, to hear his favorite son so far forget himself — and the art! But once you surprised me even more. That was when you wrestled with Cleomedes. How magnificent you were! And how frightened I was! I made you a wreath of laurel then, but you put it aside; I kissed you and you walked away."

She had broken some twigs from the tree above her head and she began to make a wreath of olive leaves. "If you refuse this prize, you are refusing me and Ctesias too. He is going to live with us, you know."

When she had crowned him with the wreath, Hippocrates spoke with mock gravity: "Your agent Ctesias tells me that you would make a good wife, though I don't know how he can prove it. It is, however, a provable hypothesis and I would be glad to put it to the test. But meantime, he told me nothing about the marriage contract or the plans."

She laughed again. "My father and your mother have arranged all that. He is going to Macedonia in your place. I hope you agree —"

He interrupted her with a question: "When are we going to be married?"

"Tomorrow . . ."

After that there was no more talk — at least none that anyone could have heard. It may be that Aphrodite lingered on, as he held

Daphne in his arms, to listen to their whispering and to smile as only Aphrodite can.

Eventually they mounted the path together and paused outside the house.

"How is Phaenarete?" she asked.

He shook his head gravely. "Her hip is healing and the position of the bones is good. But she is near the end of life. The gatekeeper's wife tells me there is a time to die."

They entered the house, and crossing the court, they stood in the *thalamus* beside Phaenarete's bed. She seemed to be asleep, but when Daphne spoke, she opened her eyes and smiled at her, showing no surprise at all.

"You did want to come, didn't you?"

"Yes."

"I thought so." Phaenarete sighed. Then she turned her eyes to Hippocrates and murmured: "She'll do. I'm glad you went to fetch her."

She looked at Daphne again and all the kindly wrinkles in her thin old face formed themselves into a smile of affection.

"I'm happy now," she said. "I'm glad I could wait. You'll be happy, Daphne, too. Life with a physician is mostly hard work. But it's happy work if you can teach him how to live. Physicians may understand others, but not themselves. It takes a good wife to do that."

Daphne slipped an arm under Phaenarete's shoulders. She rearranged her pillow deftly with the other hand. Then she picked up a comb and ran it through her wavy white hair, admiring it as she did so, and whispering things which Hippocrates could not hear.

The two women looked up at him smiling, and Phaenarete said, "He's done the best he could without a wife, this grandson of mine. Be patient with him. Remember he's only a man. Now run along, both of you."

Outside in the court they found little Ctesias waiting for them. He looked at Daphne with a meaningful glance.

"Did you ask Hippocrates — you know?"

"Oh yes!" she said. "Ctesias and I want to know if you will take the turtle into your family as well as us."

"Will you?" Ctesias asked anxiously. "He doesn't eat very much."

"Yes, I'll take the turtle and all who come along with him."

"Do you know," Daphne said, "what Ctesias found in his wallet the morning after the fire? Along with worms and a many-legged thing for the turtle? A flattened roll of papyrus! He produced it at the Archons' investigation and the Chief Archon broke the seal. Inside there was only one word. It was 'Yes.'"

Hippocrates struck the palm of his hand on his knee. "I should have guessed it, of course. Oh, if I had only known that, I never would have —"

Daphne had held up her hand to stop him.

"I'm sorry," Ctesias said, a suspicion of tears in his eyes. "I forgot."

Hippocrates squatted down beside him. "Never mind," he said. "You have brought Daphne to me today and that makes up for everything. I hope your father will leave you with us for a long, long time. I'd like to start your training as an asclepiad."

The boys swallowed. Then he said after a pause, "Do you know what the gatekeeper's wife said to me? She said that when I get to be a man I shall be a famous asclepiad like you and Euryphon. She said she had a feeling that the King of Persia would send for me to come to his court."

"That well might be," Hippocrates said. "But now, if there is room for me in that boat you brought from Meropis, we had better all sail back together — after we have had something to eat and said good-by to Phaenarete."

It was very early next morning when Sosander came to his brother's house and knocked. Praxithea opened the door and put her finger to her lips. "They are all still asleep," she whispered and stepped outside, closing the door.

They arrived quite late last night. Hippocrates carried Ctesias all the way from the harbor in his arms. I don't think the boy woke up at all."

"Euryphon came in late last night too," Sosander replied, "and Timotheus with him, aboard the Macedonian trireme. It has anchored in the harbor to wait till the wedding is over. I've seen them already. There is to be a meeting of the Coan Council which they will attend. Then Euryphon and I must go to Apollo's temple to make the wedding sacrifice there for the two families."

"Be sure," his mother said, "that the priest gives back the best cuts from the animals after the offering. That's what makes a good marriage, good meat and a good cake at the feast."

"Well," Sosander laughed, "there are other things too — the wine, the lovely bride, the bridegroom, the singing of the epithalamion. There is the bridegroom's mother too — she is most important! But remember, you must do all the cooking in the ovens outside the house. Euryphon has asked that the hearth should be cold at the time of the wedding."

Praxithea turned and opened the door. She beckoned to her son and they walked quietly across the court to the door of the *thalamus*. She pulled the curtains back and they stepped in. The room had a wonderful sweet smell. The walls were white and spotless. Daphne's wedding chest, made of polished Triopian oak with shining handles and locks, was against one wall unopened. The marriage couch was covered with a cream-colored spread; in the pattern of the weaving was the staff of Asclepius with the serpent of healing.

"I made it all," she said, "the cover, the warm blanket and the soft sheets, all woven here and all new, all for Hippocrates and his bride when he should have one. It only remains to cover the bed with flowers before they enter tonight."

She glanced at her elder son and pointed to an elegant oval mirror on the table. "Do you know what that is?"

"It's a very valuable mirror," Sosander replied. "Corinthian work almost certainly, with those admiring male figures done in bronze."

"Thargelia's mirror," she said. "Daphne brought it."

Sosander looked at it in surprise. "My brother may have some trouble in understanding this bride of his."

"He doesn't need to understand her," Praxithea said. "She will understand him, and that's enough. He only needs to love her."

They left the room, and she sighed as she closed the curtain. "Thirty years I have slept there — we remember so much, we women who were once in the current of life with its joys, its births, the growing up, and the dying! The stream of life runs through us for a time, and then at last, we step aside and watch the stream flow on through others. Your father was so young, so gay, when we were married, he and I. But I see him still today, in my two sons."

Sosander smiled. "You are both of you alive in us."

Some time after Sosander's departure Daphne came down the stair to find Hippocrates and his mother talking in the court. Daphne's eyes were shining, and a delicate aura of jasmine scent came with her.

Praxithea kissed her and turned to her son. "This is no time to talk," she said. "I'm busy, and you two must take your baths and get ready without my help. Here on the floor of the court you see these two sheepskins full of water. They were filled from the sacred Vorina spring. Dear old Podalirius brought them last night for your wedding baths. It is a long tradition that the water for your bathing today must be fetched by a relative."

She turned to Daphne and said, "Podalirius is Hippocrates' cousin. No one on the island of Cos who hopes for the blessing of Apollo is married without bathing in water straight from the spring above Apollo's cypress grove."

"I've bathed already," Hippocrates said. "This is nonsense."

"But you will bathe again, my son," Praxithea replied with quiet authority. "Podalirius walked all the way out to the spring last night after he had finished caring for the patients. When he arrived here, leading a mule with these skins over its back, he looked tired. But he stood very straight and made his little speech just the same.

"He gave to both of you his own blessing and he wished you happiness. Then he laughed, which is rare for Podalirius. He said he looked forward to playing with your children."

"Is he a bachelor?" Daphne asked.

"Yes, and he is nearly twice the age of my son. But here he comes now."

Podalirius, boyish pleasure on his face, was crossing the court. He looked at Daphne with undisguised curiosity.

"*Chaire*," he said to her, and then again, "*Chaire*." He turned to Hippocrates with a shy smile. "I am glad that good fortune has come to you — and such beauty! But it has just occurred to me that you will be marrying in the waning phase of the moon. It might be better to postpone the wedding until the moon is waxing. That, it has always been said, encourages the conception of children, and they are so important."

"Thank you, Podalirius," Hippocrates replied patiently. "Thank you also for the water from Apollo's spring which we are just about to use. You were good to bring it. But I am afraid we will have to go on with the wedding regardless of the moon, because Euryphon leaves this evening for Macedonia."

Praxithea accompanied Podalirius to the door and told him how much all the family depended on him. He smiled and felt himself a part of something new and exciting as he hurried away to take care of the morning's work.

Hippocrates turned to Daphne. "There you have it again," he said, "belief in the unknowable and the unprovable. A physician believes that because a woman's womb times its action to twenty-eight days, as does the moon, we must consider the moon before we wed."

Daphne blushed and started to turn away, but Hippocrates carried on, intent upon his argument.

"My mother half believes that water direct from Vorina's rill will bring us greater fortune. And even you — you feared the cat that crossed our path and welcomed the woman who spat in her breast to ward off evil. It's as bad as the belief that a god or a devil lurks behind every disease and disability. All nonsense!

"Nevertheless, you and I had better get on with our baths. I'll carry your sheepskin into the bath room first and put it on the shelf. You have only to open and close this buckle on the hind leg and your bath will flow out at your will. I hope Apollo's blessing will soak in through your lovely skin."

After bath and breakfast, Hippocrates walked beneath the trees within the asclepiad enclosure. This, he thought, was a strange day, his wedding day. He had asked Daphne to go for a walk with him, but she was too busy. He should be busy about something, it seemed — everyone else was. He heard Bobo barking and realized that both gates had swung open. Sosander was crossing the square, and with him was the father of the woman Hippocrates was to marry. He went to meet them.

"Alas, Euryphon," Hippocrates said. "I am sorry about the fire, and the death of Ctesiarchus' wife, and the loss of your treasure of medical scrolls."

"Thank you, Hippocrates." Euryphon straightened up and looked at him without a smile. "Much has happened since our consultation at the bedside of Thargelia. I regret more than I can say that you should have been accused falsely in regard to her and in regard to the setting of the fire. We understand now who started these slanders, and why."

His expression softened then. "Medicine has its problems, but they are as nothing compared with the difficulty of diagnosis in the affairs of women. Well, Daphne is happy now and I am happy for her."

Hippocrates smiled. "I am happy too. But let me say that I want to give back to you the medical scrolls you gave me. They will start you again on a new collection of manuscripts."

"No, I do not want them back. I gave them to you and I want you to keep them now as the dowry that comes to you with my daughter. Unfortunately, it is all the dowry I can give. You, Hippocrates, have in your possession the only copies of the Cnidian Sentences in existence, the only copy of my own writings, and also my only daughter. My reputation and all the things I loved that were left to me are in your hands. But here comes Daphne now."

As Euryphon went to greet Daphne, Hippocrates realized with astonishment that people were coming toward him from all directions and more were crowding in through the gate. The Archons of Cos came first, and the townspeople pouring in after them. Timotheus was there, First Citizen of Cnidus, and even Timon, First Citizen of Cos. Tragedy had left its mark on him; he was pale and there were dark circles under his eyes, but he stood as straight and as proud as ever. It was Timon who held up his hand for silence.

Hippocrates realized then that his disciples had gathered in a body close behind him, while Sosander and Podalirius and Pindar stood beside him. It gave him the warm comfort that can only come from loyal friends.

"Hippocrates," Timon began in a loud voice. "I speak first for the Council of Cos. We regret that you have been accused falsely. We proclaim in public that Buto, who died two days ago in my house, was guilty of setting fire to the buildings of the asclepiads of Cnidus. He was guilty too of the death of those who lost their lives in that fire.

"Furthermore, I speak for all of the people of Cos when I tell you that we are proud of the fame you have brought to this island. It will be a source of pride to Coans always that you were born here and that you remained here to practice and teach when the world beckoned to you."

He paused, making an effort to control his emotion. "Finally, in my own sorrow, I thank you for the friendship and the kindness that you, a great physician, have shown my son and my wife who are gone. Thank you too for your kindness to me and to my daughter, kindness that no money, I know, can ever repay."

"Timotheus," he added as he turned away, "will speak for the Council of Cnidus." The crowd made way for him in respectful silence, and Timon walked out. At the gate Penelope joined him and they disappeared.

Then Timotheus spoke: "The Archons of Cnidus also found Buto guilty of this crime. I know very well that a wound to reputation is sometimes slow to heal, but I shall carry this news, this cure for slander, back to Cnidus. The Dorians of the great Pentapolis take pride in their asclepiads. Today the ancient school of medical teaching in Cnidus is united with the younger school of Cos by a new understanding and in a happy marriage. Euryphon and Hippocrates have faced the ordeal of great loss and great injustice as good Greeks should. Hail to the asclepiads!"

A great shout went up then, and as the people came crowding around them, Hippocrates turned to Sosander and saw tears in his brother's eyes. And Pindar said to his master: "Your disciples are happy with you. We will never forget your example, nor your dream of adding science to medicine, nor the oath."

Later in the day Daphne found Hippocrates sitting alone in his consulting room.

"What are you thinking about here all alone?" she asked.

"There seems to be nothing for a man to do on his wedding day; I've been wondering what happiness really is."

"Are you not happy, Hippocrates?"

"Yes, completely! That's why I'm trying to analyze it. Yesterday the most charming woman in all Greece pledged herself to me, and to-day my reputation is returned to me so I can practice medicine again. The false accusations to which Olympias gave birth are dead. They were buried this morning officially, though I suspect that rumors of scandal will continue to walk about the earth for many a day, like spirits of the dead."

"I've been thinking too," she said, "remembering — realizing how wonderful life is. I've been thinking that we should share our thoughts as much as we can. I was afraid of marrying a man who had few thoughts. Now that I have the opposite, I suppose I must face my fate! Tell me what happiness is."

He smiled and shook his head. "I see clearly what it is not. It is not the sum of many pleasures. It is not a body delight such as that which comes to me when I touch you, or even look in your eyes, or when I eat a well-cooked fish or drink my favorite wine."

"Hippocrates!" she cried. "How dare you compare me to a fish or your favorite wine! — Well, go on."

"Those things are pleasures," he continued, "and I wouldn't like to be without them. They may contribute to happiness and yet they are quite different from it. I would not be happy even with you, lovely as you are, if I were not also content, content that I could take care of you and practice the art of medicine and strive for the truth that lies beyond. Contentment is a prerequisite to it, while happiness is a recurring sense of exhilaration, something added to life as it is lived. It is an awareness, a reward perhaps, that comes to a man who is working toward God's purposes established for him in nature." He shook his head, dissatisfied.

"I suppose," she said, "that you would not be Hippocrates if you did not try to analyze even this. But we have happiness now. Why not just be grateful for it without trying to test its weight, or measure its breadth and length, or give it another name? — But come now. They are waiting for you and me."

As they entered the house, the sun was dropping toward the west, but its rays still slanted into the court flickering through the branches of the palm tree. The wedding guests were wearing their best cloaks with an air of excitement. Podalirius hurried off to find Ctesias. Then Sosander clapped his hands to call them all together.

"Pindar," he announced, "has written verses for an epithalamion. We will sing it for the bride and groom at the proper time, later tonight but, as Euryphon will be on his way to Macedonia by then, I have asked him to read them to you now."

Pindar, who was the only person present not connected with one family or the other, read his verses, using the sonorous tones of an actor on the stage of a Greek theater. When he had finished, Sosander produced a quince and held it high for all to see. Then he danced, as Dionysus might have danced with a bunch of grapes. He lumbered about, slapping his feet on the pavement stones, and took a ludicrous pose before Daphne, while shouts of laughter echoed from the court. People passing along the shore heard it and smiled at one another, and carried away the news that the marriage of Hippocrates had begun.

"This quince may be sour" — Sosander laughed as he gave it to her — "but it's good for brides. It keeps them from speaking for a very long time, and that is what every husband wants. Wives should eat one quince at every meal. That's my prescription for them."

He glanced at his own wife with a wicked smile, and went on.

"It makes women fruitful too, they say. I nibbled a piece from this quince today." He made a dreadful face at Ctesias, whose childish laugh rang out above the others.

"You've talked quite enough!" Sosander's wife exclaimed.

"Perhaps I have," Sosander replied. His manner changed abruptly. He nodded at Praxithea, who had been laughing with the others. She took her place now beside Hippocrates. Daphne stood beside her father and Ctesias came to her on the other side. Sosander raised his hand then, and old Xanthias entered with a flaming oil lamp in his hand. The old servant turned to give Daphne a smile, then he carried the flame to the end of the court. In the room that opened beyond him there were cooking implements on the walls and a hearth on which fresh kindling was piled. Spring flowers were banked on either side.

In the silence, Daphne listened to the roar of the surf outside on the Coan shore. She looked about her, realizing what this meant — to be the mistress here. She glanced at her father, aware of the loneliness in his heart. He moved a little closer to her, while Ctesias gripped her hand more tightly. She looked across at Sosander and his mother and at Hippocrates towering above them, so strong, so alive. They exchanged glances.

Sosander had begun to speak now.

"Hippocrates and Daphne: This morning in the temple of Apollo your nuptial sacrifice was burned upon the altar of the god. We have done our part, Euryphon for his daughter and I for my brother. We removed the gall bladder from the animal before the burning, and prayed that bitterness may never come between my brother and his bride. It is my hope that tonight when we sing the epithalamion and when Hymen comes to you to take the veil from the bride, the god will bless your union."

Silence followed while Praxithea adjusted the new cloak her son had given her and tears stole down her cheeks. Then Euryphon cleared his throat, and walking to the end of the court, took the lamp from the old servant.

"Xanthias lit this lamp," he said, "at our hearth in Cnidus; he kept it alight during the journey to Cos, and here it is — Cnidian fire."

He stooped and laid the flame to the kindling on the hearth. Then he stepped back, with the lamp still in his hand, and straightened up, his face impassive as always. The little flame grew and the fire began to burn.

Presently he spoke again quietly. "I have lit the hearth for you,

Daphne, doing this in place of your mother. You are the wife of Hippocrates now. The fire from our house burns in your house. I have given your mother's veil to Praxithea, and she will put it on you. I cannot wait to watch you go to the *thalamus*, but I give you your mother's blessing and mine."

He looked at her and was silent for a moment while his lips quivered. Then he continued.

"You are the wife of a teacher of medicine. You will not be rich, but I have no doubt you will be happy. Perhaps, when I return from the court of Perdiccas, I may bring you something more for a dowry. And — who knows? — you may have a child or children then to show me, and I may go on to Cnidus and take up my teaching again.

"Now that my part in this ceremony is over and you are joined in marriage, there is another act that I would like to carry out. Life is handed on from generation to generation. Life has meaning because of this continuity. Medicine is the same, its skills and knowledge must be handed on. The fire of this lamp symbolizes the continuity of the art of medicine too."

He motioned to Xanthias, who brought him an unlit torch. He lit it with the lamp and handed the lamp back to Xanthias, who extinguished it. Then, holding the flaming torch, Euryphon looked directly at Hippocrates and gave him one of his rare smiles.

"This torch has another meaning for you, Hippocrates. Think of this as the fire of our art, the art that came to us from the days of old when Asclepius was a physician. You have studied medicine in its light under your father here, and for a time with us in Cnidus. You have learned what the asclepiads of Caria could teach. The torch is your to use."

He crossed the court and set it in a torch holder.

"You, Hippocrates, are not like other men, content to teach the learning of the past. You have dreamed of a science of nature and life. You have set a new goal before physicians. Don't be discouraged that the light of our knowledge is so feeble, the darkness of the unknown so vast. Keep this torch lit. Hand it on, a torch for all time."

After the wedding feast, which had followed the ceremony, the wine was poured and Pindar brought his lyre and sang Homer's hymn to Apollo:

> " 'Fetch me my lyre, fetch me my curving bowl
> And, taught by these, shall know
> All men, through me, the unfaltering will of Zeus! . . .
>
> " 'Then slide your song back upon ancient days
> And men whose very name forgotten is,
> And women who have lived and gone their ways:
> And make them live again . . .' "

When Pindar had finished, Euryphon looked about at the company — at Daphne in her mother's wedding veil and at Hippocrates in his bridegroom's cloak of white. She sat on the foot of his couch, looking at him, and her veil framed the delicate face, the straight line of forehead and nose, the smiling lips, the curving throat.

"All this will be live in my memory," Euryphon said, "when I am far away. But before I go, I would like to hear another song, a song that Pindar's uncle wrote. It begins: 'Man's life is a day. What is he?' "

The nephew smiled and took his lyre and sang:

> " 'Man's life is a day. What is he?
> What is he not? A shadow in a dream
> Is man: But when God sheds his brightness,
> Then light is on the earth
> And life is honey sweet.' "

So the feast came to an end, and Daphne removed her wedding veil and Hippocrates his white cloak and they walked out on the beach to catch a last glimpse of Euryphon. Soon the trireme came coasting swiftly out of the harbor and along the water passage to the sea. The oars dipped and swung in time to the coxwain's song: "Op-o-op! Op-o-op!" As the great ship swung around and headed north, they could see Euryphon, small and alone on the afterdeck. They waved till he disappeared beyond the point of land.

Then they turned and walked along the shore. Across the water, the mountains of Caria glowed in the light of the setting sun in shades of blue and reddish brown, and snow shone white on the peaks. They walked in silence while Daphne's thoughts hovered over the lonely figure on the afterdeck of the departing trireme.

Hippocrates looked at the drooping limbs of a tamarisk tree at the water's edge. The needles were still green and small and fuzzy, and the red bark showed through the swaying curtains of green, as it always did in the spring.

"Still spring!" he said. "It seemed like winter on this island after you sailed away from Halasarna. Now it is spring again. What strange power is there in you to change my world for me? I never believed in magic before. But now I do. This is the magic of life.

"When I met you at Timon's villa, you were promised to another man. I met you on the stair. First I saw your foot and then your face, a young woman you seemed to me, no more no less — probably intelligent, in spite of the fact that you dropped your scarf and I had to run down the steps after it. But as I left the villa that morning, you walked with me across the terrace. You looked into my eyes and laughed. Something must have happened then, for I returned along that highroad a changed man, not knowing why nor how. I was alive to the sounds and sights and smells of spring. The pebbles scattering under my foot made singing sounds. And now it is worse. Your power has grown so great that when I come near you, something takes me by the throat, I can no longer think."

They were facing each other and he saw a blush sweep over her face and neck. She turned her head away.

"Look," she said. "Here comes Ctesias."

The boy was running toward them along the beach and they could see that he was sobbing as he ran. When he reached her, Daphne knelt and took him in her arms.

"I thought you went away on the ship!" he sobbed, and buried his face in her robe. "I was all alone — please don't leave me — I wish my mother could come back."

Daphne held the boy while her own tears fell and mingled with his. After a time she looked up at Hippocrates.

"It's only five days, after all, since he lost — only five days since the fire."

Then she sang a little song to him from Aesop, about the tortoise and the hare and how it comes about that "steady plodding wins the race."

When Ctesias was quiet, she said:

"Some day soon a nice *pedagogos* will come to our house and take you to school each day and bring you back home, and you will learn to read with other boys. And then, when you are older, you will be an asclepiad, and you can help Hippocrates with his torch."

Ctesias struggled to his feet with his eyes on Hippocrates. She tried to wipe his grimy face, but he pulled away from her.

"Could I carry the torch?"

"Yes," Hippocrates said, smiling. "Yes, I think you might do it very well."

"What is the torch for?"

"The torch?" Hippocrates answered. "That was just a little story of Euryphon's."

"No," Daphne interrupted. "Tell us both, in words he and I can understand, what it is you hope to do in medicine. I want to hear it too. If Ctesias doesn't quite understand, I'll try to explain it to him later on."

Hippocrates hesitated. "I should be able to tell you that — You see, truth is all written out for us in nature. It is there, to be discovered, in the nature of men and women, the nature of all things. It is written in the nature of disease. I want my disciples to learn to observe, to watch the working of nature and of disease with me, and so come to understand. That is science, natural science. What we learn that way will be the truth.

"But it is so slow, this reading of nature, and the sick can't wait for us. To try one way of treatment against another is full of danger for them. Physicians have usually taken the easy road with no guide but the guess of the past. They shrug away all hope of discovery by saying, 'The gods have done this, the evil spirits have done that.' That leads them along the road to idleness. There are no tasks, no problems there."

"Don't you understand, Daphne?" Ctesias said. "Hippocates wants to go with Aretê on the rough road for the strong."

Daphne smiled and nodded, but Hippocrates looked at the boy with astonishment.

"Do you remember that story so well, the story I told you in the manuscript house?"

Ctesias nodded gravely. "That is the road that Heracles took. We will certainly need a torch on that road."

"Yes, we will," Hippocrates replied.

He looked away across the water and was silent, not seeing the light on Caria's coast. When he spoke again, Daphne thought it was as though he were addressing other physicians, far away in place and time perhaps:

"Life is short, the art so long, opportunity so fugitive. Experience is deceptive and judgment difficult.

"Human needs compel us to decide and to act. But if we go on with critical mind, knowledge will grow from error as well as from success. And so, little by little, truth will emerge and wisdom will come to those who practice the art."

Acknowledgments

~~~~~~

THE AUTHOR expresses his sincere thanks to men and institutions in various parts of the world who have helped him to produce this book. First to be mentioned are my colleagues at McGill University and the Montreal Neurological Institute who so generously made it possible for me to be away from active medical responsibilities at intervals during the past six years. The book was written entirely in those vacation intervals.

I owe a further debt of gratitude to many scholars for personal advice and consultation on the archaeology and history of the fifth century B.C.: the late Henry Sigerist, distinguished medical historian of Switzerland, Johns Hopkins and Yale; G. Pugliese Carratelli of Pisa and Florence, presently engaged in the study of the inscriptions from the Cos *asclepeion* (Herzog collection); Luciano Laurenzi of Rome, who directed the Italian archaeological explorations of Cos; A. Suheyl Unver, Director of the Institute of Medical History of the University of Istanbul; George M. Bean, Professor of Classics of the University of Istanbul; and J. M. Cook of Bristol University, former Director of the British School of Archaeology at Athens.

Professor Bean and Professor Cook helped Mrs. Penfield and me to plan our second visit to the Cnidian (Datca) Peninsula. Thanks to their guidance and their recent work, we were able to explore in 1956 the sites of Cnidus and Triopion in the time of Hippocrates. We are indebted also to the Turkish Government, who so generously provided transportation and hospitality during that difficult time of exploration. We are especially thankful to the Kaymakam (Namik Sesgin) of Marmoris for his courtesy and the Kaymakam (Ekincioglu) of Datca and his wife for hospitality in their home while we were in this little-frequented part of Turkey.

On the island of Cos, we are indebted to Governor George Mihalopoulos and to the Coan archaeologist Miltiades Nicolaedes for help in explorations of Cos, and to citizens of the island for hospitality and guidance, especially Mrs. Marie Economidy and Christos Laomtis.

Thanks to the Director, Dr. Robert Oppenheimer, I was a temporary member of the Faculty of Historical Studies of the Institute for Advanced Study in Princeton during the spring terms of 1958 and 1959. Living at the Institute, it was possible to write the final drafts of this book in a stimulating atmosphere, temporarily removed from the demands of an active neurosurgical practice. The classical scholars and archaeologists of the Institute for Advanced Study gave me much needed help and guidance, particularly B. D. Merritt (in Athens and in Princeton), H. T. Wade-Gery and Mrs. Wade-Gery (in Princeton), and Homer Thompson (in Athens).

Most important of all, Mr. Arthur Thornhill, Jr., Executive Vice-President of the publishing house of Little, Brown and Company, has helped me with constructive editorial criticism and patient reconsideration of the manuscript during the years in which this novel was growing up. In all this he was assisted to very good purpose by George Hall of that publishing house.

Finally, my affectionate gratitude goes to Wilder Penfield, Jr., for his thoughtful criticism of the first and second drafts, and my thanks to Katherine Swartz Penfield, who suggested to me the name of this book, *The Torch*.

Notes

~~~~~~

THE SOURCES for any historical novel laid in the fifth century before Christ are apt to be derived at the outset from literary and historical study and from archaeological exploration. In these Notes the reader will find the names of some of the scholars from whom I have borrowed material to set the stage for this book. My own planned reading on the life and times of Hippocrates began in the London Library in 1954 and continued in the library of the American School of Classical Studies in Athens, the Firestone Library of Princeton University, the Library of the Institute for Advanced Study at Princeton, and the Redpath Library of McGill University.

There is often a lag between the historical record and new findings — a gap that a student with a special problem must fill in for himself. Travel and research have gradually brought to me a wealth of material — bits of history, old knowledge reinterpreted in the light of recent archaeology — which, added to the productive scholarship of many minds in many fields to be found in books and journals, has helped to re-create the past.

Mrs. Penfield and I spent the autumn of 1954 in Greece, but the gap between the history and the archaeology was too great for us to bridge. So, after further study, we returned, and spent the spring of 1956 in Greece and Turkey. Finally the inconsistencies were largely resolved. We learned to know Cos and Cnidus and the site of the

Temple of Triopian Apollo as Hippocrates must have known them, and we grew to know the people of the islands and the local legends.

There are of course many sources for the writing of any book which cannot be listed in a bibliography. Among such sources which are particularly relevant to this book are the years I spent as an undergraduate majoring in philosophy at Princeton University, and even the time devoted there to college wrestling and football, and the time that followed as football coach. But more than anything else, my own experience in medical practice and medical teaching has helped me in this task.

Under the chapter headings which follow, notes are set down that may be of interest in amplifying the background of the text. The Reader's Guide which follows the Notes section is for the reader's convenience in locating material in the notes touching on any one subject. Terms set in italic type in the text of the notes are the terms which are listed in the Reader's Guide.

I. CONSULTATION

(a) In this chapter and elsewhere through the book the writings of Hippocrates have, of course, been a guide to the medical thought of the times. The *Hippocratic Writings,* sometimes called *Corpus Hippocraticum,* are considered by many to be a collection or a library rather than the writing of any one man. There is a splendid translation in French by Emile Littré (10 volumes, Paris, 1839-1861). There is also an excellent translation into English by a scholarly country practitioner of medicine, Dr. Francis Adams of Banchory, Scotland (The Genuine Works of Hippocrates, Sydenham Society, London, 1849). The English translation on which I have drawn most heavily is that of W. H. S. Jones assisted by E. T. Withington. This includes the Greek text and presents constructive discussions of the material throughout.[1]

[1] Jones, W. H. S. *Hippocrates.* 1952-1958. Cambridge, Mass.: Harvard University Press. London: Heinemann. The Loeb Classical Library.

(b) *Hippocrates in history*. Charles Singer, a distinguished medical historian, wrote after detailed discussion of Hippocratic writings[2]:

"We may now turn to the Hippocratic Corpus as a whole . . . it is certain that we have no criteria whatever to determine whether or no a particular work be from the pen of the Father of Medicine . . . yet among the great gifts of this collection to our time and to all time are two which stand out above all others, the picture of a man, and the picture of a method.

"The man is Hippocrates himself. Of the actual details of his life we know next to nothing. — He had many pupils, among whom were his two sons, Thessalus and Dracon, — his son-in-law, Polybus — But though this glimpse is very dim and distant, yet we cannot exaggerate the influence on the course of medicine and the value for physicians of all time of the traditional picture that was early formed of him and that may indeed well be drawn again from the works bearing his name. In beauty and dignity that figure is beyond praise. Perhaps gaining in stateliness what he loses in clearness, Hippocrates will ever remain the type of the *perfect physician*. Learned, observant, humane, with a profound reverence for the claims of his patients, but an overmastering desire that his experience shall benefit others, orderly and calm, disturbed only by anxiety to record his knowledge for the use of his brother physicians and for the relief of suffering, grave, thoughtful and reticent, pure of mind and master of his passions, this is no overdrawn picture of the *Father of Medicine* as he appeared to his contemporaries and successors. It is a figure of character and virtue which has had an ethical value to medical men of all ages comparable only to the influence exerted on their followers by the founders of the great religions."

The great medical historian Henry Sigerist,[3] after discussing at some length the *Hippocratic Writings* which were first collected as a Corpus in the tenth century and have been re-edited, translated

[2] Singer, C. 1921. Chapter on Medicine in *The Legacy of Greece*. Ed. Livingstone, R. W. London: Oxford University Press. P. 211.

[3] Sigerist, H. 1934. Notes and Comments on Hippocrates. *Bull. Hist. Med.* 2:190-214.

and discussed continuously ever since, exclaimed with some impatience:

"God only knows when the Corpus will produce its Hippocrates."
Illusions, he pointed out, may be destroyed by historical analysis, but
— "the ideal will remain untouched. . . . It is a great thing that the
medical profession has in Hippocrates a living hero, a hero that it can
worship and follow."

(c) *Hippocrates' appearance* as described in this chapter and elsewhere is derived in part by inference from what is known of his
character. But there are many representations to be seen of him
throughout the world, which vary from complete fantasy to possible
authenticity. There is even in Istanbul a fanciful miniature of him
in fine colors. He is dressed in a turban and rides on the neck of a
"fabled bird" on his way to the place of learning, the "fabulous
mountain." [4]

There are many statues, said to be of Hippocrates, in various cities
of the world from the British Museum in London to the Archaeological Museum of Cos. Edelstein[5] made a scholarly study of the *busts
of Hippocrates* and concluded that the head (No. 1036) in the Villa
Albani, Rome, was the most likely to be authentic, since it was
clearly the work of a sculptor of the fifth century B.C. and was clearly
a portrait study. It resembles, he states, certain coins that bear Hippocrates' likeness.

Another "bust of Hippocrates" which is said to resemble the coins
has been discovered more recently in Ostia, Italy, by Giovanni Be-
catti.[6] But certainly there is no resemblance between the two por-
traits.

As I have visualized the man, the bust in the Villa Albani could

---

[4] Unver, A. Hippocrate et sa grande place dans la mythologie Turque.
Archiv. Balkaniques de Méd., Chirurg., et leurs spécialités. Year 1, No. 1,
1939.
[5] Edelstein, L. Hippokrates von Kos. *Paulys Real-Encyclopädie der Classi-
schen Altertumswissenschaft.* Suppl. Bd. VI. Stuttgart, 1935.
[6] Musella, M. Una grande scoperta archeologica: l'identificazione di Ip-
pocrate. *Progressi di Terapia.* N. 1, 1948.

quite well be that of the true Hippocrates done at about sixty years of age. I made the following note in my diary after we eventually gained permission[7] to see this bust in September 1954: "Beautifully shaped head, bald, high forehead, well-shaped ears, straight nose — a smile on his lips that reminds me of the statue of Hughlings Jackson at Queen Square, London. Thoughtful, not vain.

A physician of Athens, Skévos Zervos, had the figure of Hippocrates sculptured in marble in 1936 according to his own conception ("mon inspiration personnelle"). A copy of it may be seen at the University of Athens or in the Academy of Medicine, Paris.[8]

His Hippocrates is young, athletic, intelligent — a good deal like the excellent statue in the museum of Cos which is catalogued "Hippocrates." This latter portrait was unearthed by Luciano Laurenzi while excavating the theater at Cos Meropis. It seemed to have been hidden under the amphitheater seats, but Laurenzi himself discovered no proof that it was in fact a bust of Hippocrates.

Each reader will no doubt visualize the man for himself, as I have done.

(d) *Euryphon* was the most distinguished leader of the asclepiads of Cnidus. Although somewhat older than Hippocrates, history reports that he was called to the court of Macedonia to care for King Perdiccas either alone or perhaps with Hippocrates. There is no historical reference to a daughter by the name of *Daphne* nor any suggestion that Euryphon was father-in-law to Hippocrates. For Hippocrates' father Heracleides, his mother *Praxithea* and his grandmother *Phaenarete* there is historical evidence. They lived on the island of Cos. His two sons and one son-in-law, all physicians, are all referred to in later history. But there is as yet no reference to his wife nor any

[7] Unfortunately, this statue of Hippocrates is part of the private collection of the Principe Torlonia in Rome. Although listed for public inspection, admission is granted only with the greatest reluctance, in our case after three days of begging!

[8] Zervos, S. Le portrait d'Hippocrate. *Procès-Verbaux de la Société Médicale*, 1950, pp. 196-226. Pictures of a number of other Hippocratic busts are in this paper as well.

certain knowledge of whose daughter she was. Hippocrates' brother *Sosander* and the other members of the asclepiad school of Cos are fictitious as well as *Timon* and *Olympias* and their children.

I saw the young woman I have described as *Daphne* one afternoon in a crowded street of Athens, and realized that I had found at last the perfect Grecian profile, the delicate beauty and grace that so delighted the sculptors of classical times. It was beauty that would have arrested the attention of a preoccupied physician in any age!

(e) The *asclepiads* of the fifth century B.C. were Greek physicians who formed a large professional family or guild. They claimed descent from *Asclepius the man,* the twelfth-century physician who had lived in Thessaly. But along with their own sons they admitted as apprentices or disciples worthy young men who could not claim this descent. In time they all went out as asclepiads (practicing physicians). The *asclepiads* are not to be confused with the priests of Asclepius.[9] Asclepiads are first referred to by Theopompus as practicing medicine in Caria (Asia Minor) at a place called *Syrna*.

(f) *Asclepiad training.* In the so-called "golden age of Pericles" there were two great centers for asclepiad teaching and the practice of medicine, *Cnidus* and *Cos*. Pericles came to power in Athens in 460 B.C., the year Hippocrates was born. There is a general discussion of *Greek medicine* in Brock's introduction.[10]

A quotation from Protagoras, written by Plato, throws much light on the asclepiads in general and *Hippocrates* in particular.

Plato describes how *Socrates* was wakened before dawn one morning by an impetuous disciple of his who also bore the name of Hippocrates. He begged Socrates to take him to a new teacher lately arrived in Athens. The teacher was Protagoras, a sophist. Socrates rose and, as they walked up and down in the morning twilight, he said to the young man:

9 Withington, E. T. 1921. *Studies in the History and Method of Science.* Vol. II. Ed. Singer, Charles. London: Oxford University Press. Pp. 192-205.
10 Brock, A. 1929. *Greek Medicine.* Ed. Barker, Ernest. London: Dent. The Library of Greek Thought.

"Take a similar case. If you had conceived the idea of going to your namesake Hippocrates of Cos, of the house of the Asclepiads, and paying him a sum of money as a fee for your tuition, and if you were to be asked what Hippocrates was, that you meant to pay him this money, what would you answer?

— I should say, he replied, a physician.

— And what would you expect to become?

— A physician, he answered.

— Again, if you had taken it into your head to go to Polyclitus of Argos or our Athenian Phidias and pay them a fee for your tuition, and you were to be asked, what Polyclitus and Phidias were, that you intended to pay them this money, what should you reply?

— Statuaries [sculptors], of course.

— And what would you expect to become yourself?

— A statuary, to be sure. . . .

— And what do you expect to become yourself, that you go to Protagoras?

At this he blushed. By this time there was just a glimpse of day, so that I could see his face. Why, he said, if this be at all like the two former cases, it is clear that I must become a sophist." [11]

(g) *Machaon* and *Podalirius*. Euryphon refers in this chapter to the two sons of Asclepius. In the Iliad, Homer wrote that Asclepius, the "blameless" physician of Thessaly, had two sons, Machaon and Podalirius, who served Agamemnon at the siege of Troy as leaders and as "cunning leeches." When Machaon was "smitten on the right shoulder with a three-barbed arrow" he was hurried out of battle and back to the ships:

> For a leech is of the worth of many other men
> For the cutting out of arrows and the spreading of
>   soothing simples.

[11] *Socratic Discourses, Plato and Xenophon.* 1910. Everyman's Library No. 457. London: Dent. New York: Dutton.

Henry Sigerist points out that surgeons have claimed Machaon as the father of surgery, leaving Podalirius to the physicians. There was no good evidence of such early separation of skills among physicians, but the wounded and sick were nursed then as now by women. Indeed, it was "Nestor's slave, Hecamede, who washed the blood from Machaon's wound." [12]

(h) *Cos* and *Cnidus*. For a discussion of the genealogy of Hippocrates and a historian's admirable analysis of the information available to him in regard to Cos and Cnidus, see Sudhoff,[13] also Paton and Hicks.[14]

Unfortunately, there is much information of which Sudhoff was ignorant, some of it being quite recent. His seemingly authoritative pronouncements led me in 1954 to search for the haunts of Hippocrates at the west end of the island of Cos, where the ancient city of Astypalaea was located, although this was contrary to the local Coan tradition that Hippocrates taught his pupils under the plane tree at the other end of the island. It also led me to explore the site of Cnidus at the tip of the Cnidian Peninsula, a city not built there until after the death of Hippocrates. Further study led to more rewarding travels in 1956.[15]

A great and urgent archaeological opportunity waits in the Cnidian Peninsula. Excavations, when carried out at ancient Cnidus and especially at the proposed site of the temple of Triopian Apollo, are

[12] Sigerist, H. 1951. *A History of Medicine.* New York: Oxford University Press. This is a magnificent study of medicine throughout the ages.

[13] Sudhoff, Karl. Sketches on Cos and Cnidos. *Ann. Med. Hist.* 1930, 2-13-19.

Sudhoff, Karl. 1945. *Kos und Knidos.* Munich: Verlag der Munchener Drucke.

[14] Paton, W., and Hicks, E. 1891. *Inscriptions of Cos.* London: Oxford University Press.

[15] Penfield, W. The Aegean Cradle of Medicine. *Trans. and Studies of the College of Physicians of Philadelphia.* 4 ser., Vol. 24, No. 1, June, 1956.

Penfield, W. The Asclepiad Physicians of Cnidus and Cos with a Note on the Probable Site of the Triopion Temple of Apollo. *Proceedings American Philosophical Society.* Vol. 101, No. 5, October, 1957.

sure to throw important light on the history of the great cities of the Doric East and the history of medicine.

(i) I have discovered no sure evidence of the form of government in Cos at the time of Hippocrates. It is assumed to be similar to that in Athens, where the chief magistrates were *archons* and the form of government was democratic. B. D. Merritt, in a personal communication, states that he considers it likely that the chief magistrate in the government of Cos at this time would have been an archon elected annually by a popular council.

2. THE MANTLE OF HERACLEIDES

(a) *Theocritus.* The highroad along which Hippocrates walked from the Archon's villa, on the edge of the famous forest of cypress trees, to the city of Cos Meropis may well have followed the course of the road that one can walk today. Theocritus, the Greek bucolic poet who has been considered the founder of pastoral poetry, lived much of his life on the island of Cos. In his charming poem "Harvest Home," [1] he must have been describing this road as he found it two centuries after Hippocrates. He described how great Chalcon:

> Planted one stalwart knee against the rock,
> And lo, beneath his foot Burine's rill
> Brake forth, and at its side poplar and elm
> Shewed aisles of pleasant shadow, greenly roofed
> By tufted trees. Scarce midway were we now . . .
> "And whither ploddest thou thy weary way
> Beneath the noontide sun, Simichidas?
> For now the lizard sleeps upon the wall,
> The crested lark folds now his wandering wing.
> Dost speed, a bidden guest, to some reveller's board,
> Or townward to the treading of the grape?
> For lo! recoiling from thy hurrying feet
> The pavement stones ring out right merrily."

[1] *Idylls of Theocritus.* Translation by Calverly, C. S. 1913. London: Bell.

"*Burine's rill*," the water of *Vorina fountain*, rises from a magnificent spring high on the mountainside. It supplied the fountains of the temple of Asclepius built in the cypress grove after Hippocrates left the island, and it furnishes the city of Cos today with its splendid supply of water.

3. OLYMPIAS

(a) The story of the Olympic boxer *Cleomedes* of Astypalaea is told by Volonakis,[1] and by Pausanius.[2]

(b) There is no historical or archaeological evidence for the *asclepiad enclosure* described here in Cos and again in Cnidus. But there is good evidence for the *palaestra* and the *gymnasium*.

[1] Volonakis, M. 1922. *The Island of Roses and Her Eleven Sisters*. London: Macmillan.
[2] Pausanius VI, 9, 6-8 and Plutarch's Romul. 28, Proepar. Evang. V. 24.

4. APHRODITE AND ARTEMIS

(a) The cypress grove on the slope of the mountain is called *Apollo's grove* in this story. At the time of Hippocrates there was a temple to Apollo in the grove. Five centuries later this famous forest figured in history. After the murder of Julius Caesar, when Marc Antony and Octavius were preparing for their struggle for supremacy, Antony needed new ships for his navy. Consequently he commissioned P. Turullius, one of the original conspirators against Caesar, to build large new ships. Turullius did this on the island of Cos, and cut down the magnificent cypresses from the sacred grove of Apollo for the purpose. The dire consequences of this so-called desecration are recounted by Ralph Major in his interesting monograph.[1]

[1] Major, R. Hippocrates and the Isle of Cos. *Bulletin of the Society of Medical History*, Chicago, June, 1946.

5. THE SACRED DISEASE

(a) There is a Mediterranean plane tree on the island of Cos which all Coan citizens insist shaded Hippocrates when he taught there. It is forty-five feet around the trunk at its base and about fifteen feet tall. The enormous trunk is completely hollow. A dozen men might well stand inside it. But the shell of the trunk is strong. Two very large branches are supported by marble columns and braced with poles, evidence of loving care on the part of Greek and Turk alike. There is much life in it, and from its roots are growing new trees with sturdy trunks. *Hippocrates' tree* has become a shrine to which tourists flock from all the world.[1]

This tree is situated a stone's throw from the shore of the sea and a stone's throw from the walls of a crusader's fortress built during the Middle Ages on the island that protected and formed the harbor of Cos Meropis. The tree today is much as it was when pictured in an etching by Choiseul-Gouffier, who visited Cos in 1776.

W. H. S. Jones pointed out that Hermocrates mentioned a plane tree as a landmark on the island of Cos in the fourth century B.C.

"Alexander the Great," Jones continues, "must have stood beneath this tree, and Paul of Tarsus, to name but two of the host of historical persons who have passed that way. There is no reason to doubt that it [the present *Hippocratic plane tree* of Cos] is more than 2500 years old.

"Sir George Birdwood said as much, in a letter to The Times of August 16, 1906, where he gives a long list of ancient trees, many of them older than this."[2]

During the four centuries that Cos was occupied by the Turks, the tree was guarded as the teaching place of Hippocrates and a mosque was built before it. Exactly how old the tree is, no one can prove. I have examined a plane tree in a public square on the neigh-

---

[1] In 1956 I had the amusing experience of seeing a large group of German tourists, just landed from a ship, sitting under the tree as asclepiads had sat before them, while their guide lectured to them with great authority.

[2] Jones, W. H. S. (See Note 1, Chapter 1.) Vol. 4. P. lix.

boring island of Rhodes that is authenticated at four hundred years of age. It seems no more than a lusty sapling as compared with the venerable tree at Cos.

(b) *Coan legends*. Certain it is that for twenty-four hundred years Hippocrates has been the chief source of pride of the people of Cos. In 554 A.D. (nine hundred years after the birth of Hippocrates) a dreadful earthquake came to Cos. The Greek poet and historian Agathias visited the island and wrote of Cos Meropis that "nothing remained of the glory of the town except the fame of the asclepiads and the pride in Hippocrates." (Ralph Major; see note to Chapter 4.)

(c) In the discussion of *epilepsy* (the divine disease, the *sacred disease*, the falling sickness) in this chapter, the thought and scattered quotations are drawn directly from the Hippocratic writings. In some paragraphs, the text of the translation is used without alteration as indicated by second quotation marks. The book entitled "Sacred Disease" (in Volume II, pp. 127-185, of Jones's translation; see notes to Chapter 1) was evidently prepared as a lecture. The conception of brain function presented in this chapter comes entirely from those writings, a conception not to be equaled for more than two thousand years. Certainly this was the writing of one of the greatest geniuses in medical history.

Some of the features of epileptic attacks which Hippocrates describes in this chapter do not come from Hippocratic writings, but they represent what he must have seen many times.

6. RELUCTANT NYMPH

(a) The *Athenian tablet* which bore the tribute list referred to by Timon in this chapter was discovered in the present city of Cos (ancient city of Cos Meropis) in 1933, when an earthquake shook down a house in which this tablet had been used as a building stone.

It has been described by Segre[1] and by Merritt, Wade-Gery and McGregor.[2]

(b) *Cnidian scrolls.* In this chapter Euryphon gives Hippocrates two scrolls. One of them contained Euryphon's own contribution to the diseases of women. Scholars have concluded that the book on this subject, which has been preserved for posterity in the writings in the *Corpus Hippocraticum*, must have been written by Euryphon.[3]

The other scroll, called *Cnidian Sentences*, has been lost. We know of it through the writings of later authors, especially Soranus and Galen.

[1] Mario Segre, *Clara Rhodos* IX, 1938, 147-178.
[2] Merritt, B., Wade-Gery, H., and McGregor, M. 1939. *The Athenian Tribute Lists.* 2 vols. Cambridge: Harvard University Press.
[3] Jones, W. H. S. (See Note 1, Chapter 1.) Vol. 2. P. xvi.

7. EMPEDOCLES THE MAGNIFICENT

(a) *Empedocles.* Most of the writings of this remarkable man have been lost. His views, however, have long been a subject of interest to philosophers and theologicans[1] as well as biologists.

An excellent discussion of the contrasts in the thinking of Empedocles and Hippocrates may be found in the writings of W. H. S. Jones.[2]

Empedocles' view of the relationship of *heart and thought* is expressed in the following translation of one of his poems by William Ellery Leonard [3]:

> *In the blood-streams, back-leaping into it,*
> *The heart is nourished, where prevails the power*

[1] Burnet, J. 1939. Empedocles of Akragas. *Early Greek Philosophy.* London: Black. Chapter V.
Jaeger, W. 1947. *The Theology of the Early Greek Philosophers.* Gifford Lectures, 1936. London: Oxford University Press. Chapter VIII.
[2] Jones, W. H. S. Philosophy and Medicine in Ancient Greece. Supplement to the *Bulletin of the History of Medicine,* No. 8, Johns Hopkins, Baltimore, 1946.
[3] Leonard, W. The Fragments of Empedocles. *The Monist,* Chicago, XVII, 1907, pp. 451-474.

That men call thought; for lo, the blood that stirs
About the heart is man's controlling thought.

This may be contrasted with the views of Hippocrates expressed in Chapter 5.

(b) *Temple sleep* is described by Empedocles as he experienced it at Epidaurus. Curiously enough, the best description of this practice that has come down to us may be found in Plutus, a rowdy comedy by Aristophanes. This psychotherapeutic technique was used for centuries in many temples of Asclepius.

8. INVITATION

The quotation from Sappho in this chapter is given in the translation by Sir William Marris.[1]

[1] *The Oxford Book of Greek Verse in Translation.* 1938. Ed. Higham, T., and Bowra, C. London: Oxford University Press.

9. FLIGHT OF THE NYMPH

Pelea is now called old Pyli, or Paleo Pylle, to distinguish it from the modern village of Pylle. There are a few herdsmens' cottages on the site of the ancient city high on the northern slope of Mount Oromedon. Few cities in the world could have had a more magnificent outlook. Few could have been such impregnable strongholds. The climb today from the village of Amaniu along the bank of the tumbling brook up to this ruined city is steep and long, but the view is magnificent, and the bells of goats and sheep still higher on the mountainside make a chorus one is not likely to forget.

10. HALASARNA

(a) *Halasarna,* now a village of about a thousand people, is called *Cardamena* today. Remains of the ancient theater on the side of a hill are still visible.

(b) *Thimari,* as described here, is plentiful on the island of Cos. Excellent tea is still made from the dried leaves.

(c) The technique of treatment for *fractured hip* is taken from the Hippocratic writings. Hippocrates was criticized by a physician of the Cnidian School (Ctesias) for his radical attempts to set this bone.

(d) The lines from Alcaeus are from C. M. Bowra's translation.

11. A CROWN DENIED

The poems by Sappho in this chapter are from the translations of D. G. Rossetti ("Like the sweet apple") and Sir Maurice Bowra ("In loveliness the dew").

Hesiod's poem is from the poet's Works and Days, as translated by Jack Lindsay.

12. LOVE IN STRANGE CLOTHING

The description of the signs of approaching death in this chapter is quoted from the writings of Hippocrates. Teachers of medicine to-day commonly speak of the *facies hippocratica,* referring to this description of the facial appearance that may precede death.

13. EMPEDOCLES AND THE GODS

(a) *Empedocles on Medicine.* The scroll given to Hippocrates by Empedocles might well have contained his contributions to medicine. This is suggested by the following evidence:

Scholars who have studied the collected writings in the *Corpus Hippocraticum* consider that one section, containing an excellent discussion of the heart, could have been written by Empedocles himself. In addition to a good anatomical description, it contains the expression of views characteristic of the thinking of Empedocles and contrary to the opinions of Hippocrates.[1] Empedocles might well have given it to him.

Jones considers that the Hippocratic writing on epilepsy, "The Sacred Disease" (see Chapter 5), may be considered a part of a polemic against Empedocles and the Sicilian School of Medicine.[2]

(b) The book entitled "Ancient Medicine" in the *Hippocratic Writings* may be considered a defense of *natural science* and *medicine* against the unprovable hypotheses of the philosophers and against blind belief in the supernatural as a cause of disease. Jones (see notes to Chapter 1) points out that the word *hypothesis* appears first in the Hippocratic writings. The word was used then to mean an unverifiable assumption or postulate.

(c) Empedocles died about the time of the action of this story. There are varying legendary versions of how he died. Matthew Arnold's well-known dramatic poem[3] *Empedocles on Etna* is a description of his supposed climb up that mountain to his death.

(d) The quotations in this chapter are from the following translations:

Aeschylus ("Behold what I") is given as translated by J. S. Blackie.[4]

Aeschylus ("Oh, Death the Healer") was translated by Plumptre.[5]

Quotations from the Bible are taken from the King James translation.

(e) *Greek religion* must be considered through the eyes of the Greeks themselves in that particular period. This is done brilliantly

[1] Singer, C. (See Note 2, Chapter 1.)
[2] Jones, W. H. S. (See Note 2, Chapter 7.)
[3] *The Poems of Matthew Arnold.* 1909. London: Oxford University Press.
[4] *Aeschylus.* Ed. Blackie, J. S. 1906. Everyman's Library. London: Dent.
[5] See Fragment 250 (Aeschylus). *Bartlett's Familiar Quotations.* 13th ed. 1951. Boston: Little, Brown.

in the writings of Gilbert Murray.[6] No adequate reference could be given to the many sources from which insight can be gained into *Greek philosophy* as it was in the latter part of the fifth century B.C. The writings of Jaeger and of Burnet and Jones referred to in the notes on Chapter 7 have to do with philosophy in relation to religion and medicine and the writings of Empedocles.

Understanding of *Greek thought* in general, also *Greek history* and the *Greek way of life*, calls for wide reading. I must admit my own debt to H. F. D. Kitto,[7] to C. E. Robinson,[8] to C. M. Bowra[9] and to Edith Hamilton,[10] and to the collection of writings edited by Livingstone.[11]

The writings of Plato (which may be found in numerous translations for those who, like myself, are not able to appreciate them fully in the original) present the *thinking of Socrates*, who was eight years older than Hippocrates and who could hardly have failed to influence him. Those who desire an anthology of *Greek literature* will enjoy the book by James and Janet Todd,[12] as I have.

[6] Murray, G. 1925. *Five Stages of Greek Religion*. New York: Columbia University Press.

[7] Kitto, H. 1951. *The Greeks*. A Pelican Book. London: Penguin.

[8] Robinson, C. 1930. *Hellas: A Short History of Ancient Greece*. Boston: Beacon.

[9] Bowra, C. 1957. *The Greek Experience*. Cleveland: World.

[10] Hamilton, E. 1930. *The Greek Way*. New York: Norton.

[11] Livingstone, R., Ed. 1921. *The Legacy of Greece*. London: Oxford University Press.

[12] Todd, J. and J., eds. 1955. *Voices from the Past: A Classical Anthology for the Modern Reader*. London: Phoenix.

14. FESTIVAL OF APOLLO

(a) The location of *Cnidus* and of *Triopion* on the Cnidian Peninsula in the time of Hippocrates has long been a subject of archaeological and historical debate. Much new evidence has been brought forward recently by G. E. Bean and J. M. Cook.[1] Their in-

[1] Bean, G., and Cook, J. The Cnidia. *Annual of the British School at Athens* 47:171, 1952. Also The Carian Coast III, *Annual of the British School at Athens* 52:58.

terpretation of the writings of Herodotus, verified by their own analysis of the fragments of surface pottery on the peninsula, has seemed to settle these questions.

Mrs. Penfield and I can substantiate their conclusions to this extent. We found the site (proposed by Bean and Cook) of the temple of Triopian Apollo, above the Bay of Camara, to be very rich in sherds of ancient pottery. The same was true of the proposed site of ancient Cnidus at Datca. Although no more than amateurs in such matters, we were the first interested visitors to these sites after the publication of the Bean and Cook findings. Some of the sherds which we gathered from the ground in both places clearly date from the fifth century B.C., and before, in the opinion of various experts to whom we have shown them.

Our own observations made during that visit were communicated to the American Philosophical Society.[2]

(b) The story of the great boxer of Rhodes, *Diagoras*, and his daughter *Pherenice*, who trained her son *Peisirrodus* to be a champion boxer, is told engagingly by Volonakis.[3]

(c) *Herodotus*. Much of the material in his oration may be found in his monumental history.[4]

(d) *Aretê*, to which the Chief Judge refers, is a word which the Greeks used to describe the surpassing excellence which might be shown in contests of skill, of strength and of thought. It was a special kind of virtue. As Kitto expressed it in his excellent book,[5] "It was aretê that the games were designed to test — the aretê of the whole man, not merely a specialized skill."

2 Penfield, W. (See Note 15, Chapter 1.)
3 Volonakis, M. (See Note 1, Chapter 3.)
4 *Herodotus*. Translated by Godley, A. D. 1938. Loeb Classical Library.
5 Kitto, H. (See Note 7, Chapter 13.)

15. THE GAMES OF THE DORIC PENTAPOLIS

Our understanding of *athletics* in classical times has been greatly extended by the contributions of E. Norman Gardiner, to whom the author is much indebted.[1] During the writing of this book we visited many of the sites of Greek games. This was of some assistance in the writing of this and the previous chapter. Especially helpful were the ruins of Olympia, Delphi, Pergamum, Priene, and Epidaurus. The *gymnasium* described in this chapter is patterned largely from the remains of the gymnasium at Pergamum.

[1] Gardiner, E. 1930. *Athletics of the Ancient World.* London: Oxford University Press.

16. THARGELIA

(a) A glimpse of the teaching center at Cnidus is given in this chapter, but no effort is made in this book to present the origins of ancient *Cnidian medicine*. There is a recent study of this subject in the book by Stever and Saunders.[1]

(b) The quotation from Sophocles ("A wise gamester") is from a fragment of his; see Unknown Dramas.[2]

[1] Stever, R., and Saunders, J. 1959. *Ancient Egyptian and Cnidian Medicine.* Berkeley: University of California Press.
[2] In Bartlett (see Note 5, Chapter 13). P. 16.

18. CTESIAS

(a) The key which Hippocrates used to open the door of the manuscript house would have been a bronze rod of considerable length bearing on one end a pair of flat hooks that turned away from each other. He passed the hook end through a vertical slot in the heavy door. Then, turning the key, he pulled back so as to catch the hooks in the locking pins inside. Then he pressed down on the key handle, thus disengaging the locking pins and raising them from the bolt inside. After that, the bolt could be slid back by pulling on an unlocking thong that came through a small hole and hung outside the door.

(b) In connection with Hippocrates' discussion of veins, it may be pointed out that Aristotle, writing some years later, stated that Hippocrates' son-in-law, the asclepiad physician Polybus, carried out a valuable research study on the veins.

(c) The cause of erysipelas in the first woman was the streptococcus. When it was transferred to the opened uterus of Thargelia on the hands of Euryphon, this bacterium caused her fever and the secondary clotting of blood in the veins of her leg. A fragment of that clot broke off and was carried by the blood stream to the lung as a pulmonary embolus producing almost instantaneous death.

Hippocrates, in his attempted analysis, could make the first step toward understanding this chain of events. He could conclude that something might be transferred from patient to patient, something that caused fever. This line of thought may well have led him to forbid his disciples to carry out abortion, as described in Chapter 20.

Hippocrates could hardly guess that microscopes would be invented to discover the world of bacteria, of which the streptococcus was only one type. However, he might well have suggested later to the young asclepiad who was to marry his daughter that he should study the veins of man.

19. PURKAIA!

(a) About five hundred years after the time of Hippocrates, Soranus of Ephesus wrote a biography of him. "He left his own country," Soranus wrote, "for *burning the library* in Cnidus, if we may believe a malicious writer, Andreas, in his book of the Origin of Physick." Andreas' book has been lost completely. The reference to a medical library in this bit of scandal is the first evidence that there was at least one library of scrolls as early as that.

Pliny, writing a century earlier, gave another version of this malicious rumor by making the statement that it was the habit of those cured in the temple of Asclepius of Cos to write on the walls of the temple the remedies that had brought them relief, so that others might profit. Then he speaks of Hippocrates, whom he describes elsewhere as the "Prince of Medicine," as follows: "Hippocrates, they say, copied these inscriptions and after having (this at least according to our own Varron) burned the temple, he instituted the medicine called clinical. After that the profession became more and more lucrative." [1]

This calumny is preposterous in the light of modern knowledge. It seems clearly established that the temple of Asclepius was built about 350 B.C., one hundred and ten years after the birth of Hippocrates! [2] It is likely that it was built because of the fame Hippocrates had brought to the island.

The case reports on the walls of this temple of Asclepius on Cos, like those at Epidaurus, were stories of miraculous cures with happy endings, stories that would help a physician not at all. The case reports in the Hippocratic writings, on the other hand, most often concern patients whose illness ended in death, as described in Chapter 21. Hippocrates recorded them obviously in the hope of bringing about a better outcome in subsequent cases.

[1] Littré, Emile. 1883. *Histoire Naturelle de Pline.* Vol. II, Book XXIX. *The Historie of the World.* Commonly called, the Naturall Historie of C. Plinius Secundus. Translated into English by Philemon Holland. Two ptomes. London. Printed by Adam Islip 1601.
[2] Edelstein, L. and E. 1945. *Asclepius: A Collection and Interpretation of the Testimonies.* Baltimore: Johns Hopkins.

20. PHYSICIAN'S OATH

(a) The *Oath of Hippocrates* is given here as translated from the Greek by Jones.[1] The paragraphing has been added. One paragraph is omitted which read as follows:

"I will not use the knife, not even, verily, on sufferers from stone, but I will give place to such as are craftsmen therein." This is clearly

[1] Jones, W. H. S. (See Note 1, Chapter 1.) Vol. I. Pp. 298-301.

an insertion made by someone who copied it long after the time of Hippocrates.

I have presented in earlier chapters reasonable medical and social experience which might quite well have led Hippocrates to write this oath just as it has come down to us (with the omission of this reference to operation for stone in the bladder). The prohibition against poison may seem at first unnecessary, but every experienced physician who knows the meaning of compassion must have helped sufferers from incurable pain and distress out of this world by every means short of poison. The need of a clearly stated rule of conduct in this regard must have been obvious always. The rules of conduct in the oath were clearly intended for physicians who visited the sick in their homes and who made case notes such as those described in Chapter 21.

Ludwig Edelstein[2] makes the suggestion that the whole oath may have originated with the Pythagoreans, although he admits that it was added to the Hippocratic writings and came to bear the name of Hippocrates. If his suggestion is true, then the indenture actually used by Hippocrates must have been removed from the writings. He certainly had one, as shown by the remarks of Socrates in the quotation from Plato's Protagoras — See note (f) to Chapter 1.

Edelstein's arguments are based on a considerable knowledge of Pythagorean philosophy. Unfortunately, no similar body of historical information is available for the *Asclepiad School* of Cnidus and Cos. Hippocrates could quite well have borrowed from their thinking, but he is more likely, in my opinion, to have considered the medical evidence first when composing the "oath" and the "indenture."

Edelstein points out that the Pythagoreans forbade *abortion* on religious and political grounds. On the other hand, as I have visualized medical practice in those days, the prohibition of abortion contained in the *Hippocratic Oath* might quite well have depended upon medical experience alone as presented in this chapter and in the death of Thargelia.

[2] Edelstein, L. The Hippocratic Oath. *Bull. Hist. Med.*, Supp. No. 1, 1943, Johns Hopkins, Baltimore.

Before bacteriology became a science in the nineteenth century, physicians not infrequently transferred virulent bacteria unwittingly from other patients with active infection to the uterus of a woman in labor or to the instruments used to carry out abortion. This produced what was called "childbed fever," as first elucidated by Oliver Wendell Holmes[3] in Boston (1843) and independently by Ignaz Semmelweiss, a Hungarian working in a Viennese hospital.

(b) The legend of *"Hippocratic abortion."* Professor Skévos Zervos of Athens, who was born on one of the Dodecanese Islands, gave me the following information. Midwives on the island of Cos today tell young women who want an abortion to use the "method of Hippocrates"! This method, it appears, is to "jump from a height or to bump their buttocks up and down on something hard"!

[3] Holmes, who was also a poet, was Professor of Anatomy at Harvard University. The brilliant research on the cause of childbed fever was carried out when he was a young man.

21. HIPPOCRATIC TEACHING

(a) The advice which is given to medical students in this chapter is a paraphrase, and sometimes a quotation, of the best teaching to be found in the Hippocratic writings. The case reports of patients are copied exactly from those writings, as translated by W. H. S. Jones.[1] No better evidence of the high level of *medical practice* can be found than these case notes.

(b) *Hippocratic Writings.* The author may well be criticized for quoting directly. Since the books in this body of writings are not signed, how can anyone tell whether Hippocrates wrote the words himself or whether the writing in question came from another associated physician?

These objections are, of course, strictly valid. I have assumed, however, that Hippocrates was the real leader of thought in the Coan

[1] Jones, W. H. S. (See Note 1, Chapter 1.)

group and the central body of thought in these writings coincided with his thinking. As judged by the critical medical standards of any century, these case notes were made by a very superior clinical observer. They constitute the best evidence of the presence of one very great physician.

(c) *Hippocratic teaching.* It is true that none of the books or lectures in these writings is signed and that some must have originated in other schools of medicine, such, for example, as the manuscript thought to have come from Empedocles. The same is true of the manuscript that reflects the thinking of Euryphon. They do not correspond with the writings that bring forward a central body of thought. Whether Hippocrates wrote the latter or whether he inspired his disciples to write them is of little importance.

One thing is clear enough: Hippocrates of Cos was the outstanding physician of his time and school. The oath, the precepts and the writings have been considered his throughout the ages. If, for example, the book on the Sacred Disease was written by an interloper, a man not even taught by him, then there was in that period a physician of equal or greater stature than Hippocrates. Strange that Socrates, Plato and Aristotle, who refer to Hippocrates with such respect, should be ignorant of this other man!

There are some judgments which a physician is qualified to make, even in the presence of philologists or classicists. The Hippocratic case histories constitute evidence of greatness that is just as clear as the insistence on a science of nature as opposed to explanation by unproved hypothesis or past authority.

24. APOLLO'S GROVE

(a) As mentioned in the source notes on Chapter 19, the *Asclepeion of Cos*, or the *temple of Asclepius*, was built after the time of the action of the story, probably even eighty years later. It was built on the terrace where I have described *Timon's villa*, and the water from the *Vorina fountain* was used in the temple. The asclepeion was excavated in 1902-1904 under the direction of Rudolf

Herzog, who finally published his study,[1] although incompletely.

Ralph Major has given a most interesting review of the history and archeology of this asclepeion, with photographs of the site as it appears today and reproductions of the pictured restorations of Herzog.[2] He also gives the history of the sacred cypress grove and much else of general interest.

(b) In this chapter Hippocrates states the attitude of *asclepiads* toward Asclepius — man and god.

Asclepius the man lived in Tricca, Thessaly, about the twelfth century B.C. Our knowledge of him comes to us from Homer's Iliad, written in the ninth century B.C. to describe the great war between the Greeks and the Trojans which had taken place three hundred years earlier. Homer referred to Asclepius as the "blameless physician" and the father of two physicians, *Machaon* and *Podalirius*, who fought on the side of the Greeks. But some time between the ninth century B.C., when Homer wrote, and the fifth century B.C., when Hippocrates was born, the Greeks had transformed Asclepius into a god.

Asclepius the God, or *Aesculapius*, as the Romans came to call him, was the god of healing and of medicine. The Greek storytellers seem to have created him as they elaborated their whole remarkable mythology. They gave him a birth story more appropriate to a god. According to this second version, he was born at Epidaurus, on the hills of Argolis in Peloponnesus, and was the son of the nymph Coronis and the god Apollo. The myth-makers even went on to give him divine daughters, Hygeia and Panacea, and a son, Iaso. He was said to have been trained in medicine by the centaur Chiron, who also taught medicine to Achilles.

In his temple or *asclepeion*, Asclepius appeared in marble as a kindly, bearded man holding a staff about which the snake of healing coiled. This serpent-staff is now the emblem of the medical pro-

[1] Herzog, R. 1932. *Kos, Ergebnisse der Deutschen Ausgrabungen und Forschungen.* Berlin: Keller. The inscriptions from this excavation are being further studied by Professor P. Carratelli in Florence.

[2] Major, R. (See Note 1, Chapter 4.)

fession throughout the world. There were many temples for the worship of Asclepius, but the most famous in the time of Hippocrates
were those at Epidaurus and at Tricca.

Like the shrines of the Christian era which followed, these temples
served the Greeks very well as places of faith healing. Some of them
also became fashionable resorts, like the spas of modern times. At the
magnificent Asclepion of Epidaurus, men and women were well
housed and well entertained and treated to baths, massage and minor
surgery.

25. THE TORCH

(a) The gatekeeper's wife indulges in prophesy. History tells us
that the private physician to King Artaxerxes in the Persian court
was *Ctesias of Cnidus.* There is no certain knowledge that he studied
under Hippocrates, but thirty-one years after the time of this story,
Ctesias accompanied that king to the battle of Cunaxa (401 B.C.)
against the king's brother, Cyrus the Younger. He is said to have
cured the breast wound which Artaxerxes received from the hand of
Cyrus.

Ctesias wrote a scholarly history of the Persian wars in thirty-two
volumes. His sources were Persian, but he wrote in Ionic Greek, as
Herodotus did and also Hippocrates and Euryphon. The historical
works of Ctesias have been lost — we know of them today only
through the writings of others. Xenophon, who was also at the battle
of Cunaxa fighting on the side of Cyrus, and who led the Greek
mercenaries back home after the death of Cyrus, was one of those
who read Ctesias' history and quoted from it.

According to *Galen,* Ctesias also wrote on medicine but there is
no further record of it. He is said to have returned to his home in
Cnidus three years after Cunaxa.

(b) A useful study of Greek *home life* and of marriage customs is
to be found in Blümner.[1] For *Greek dress* and ornaments, I received

---

[1] Blümner, H. 1893. *The Home Life of the Ancient Greeks.* Translated by
Zimmern, A. London: Cassell.

help from Abrahams[2] and from Lady Evans,[3] but for the most part I was guided by pottery paintings and sculpture. Large brooches such as that described as worn by Praxithea were much in favor among the Dorian women of the East, who looked on them as the badge of the independence and self-reliance of Aegean women.

Greek life is described exhaustively by T. G. Tucker,[4] and the *manners and morals* of the Greeks are discussed against a vivid background of history by Will Durant.[5]

(c) Homer's Hymn to Apollo is given as translated by Sir Arthur Quiller-Couch. Pindar's Pythian Ode (VIII) is given as translated by H. T. Wade-Gery and Sir Maurice Bowra, with slight alteration in the third and fourth lines.[6]

(d) The lines that begin the last paragraph of the book — *"Life is short,* the Art so long, opportunity so fugitive. Experience is deceptive and judgment difficult" — constitute the first aphorism in the Book of *Aphorisms, Hippocratic Writings.* The translation used here, with slight changes, is that of a physician, Elisha Bartlett, who wrote a charming but little-known study.[7]

[2] Abrahams, E. 1908. *Greek Dress.* London: Murray.

[3] Evans, M. 1893. *Greek Dress.* London: Macmillan.

[4] Tucker, T. G. 1916. *Life in Ancient Athens.* London: Macmillan.

[5] Durant, W. 1939. *The Life of Greece.* New York: Simon and Schuster.

[6] Both of the foregoing translations may be found in Todd, J. and J. (see Note 12, Chapter 13).

[7] Bartlett, E. 1852. *A Discourse on the Times, Character and Writings of Hippocrates.* New York: Bailiere. See Elisha Bartlett, a Rhode Island Philosopher in Osler, W. 1909. *An Alabama Student.* London: Oxford University Press.

Reader's Guide to the Notes

The Notes are on pages 341-367. Numbers in this guide refer to chapters in the Notes; the letter identifies the note within the chapter. For example, to find the first entry (Abortion), see note (a) in Chapter 20.

~~~~~~